WHAT YOU DON'T KNOW

With a lovely husband, two gorgeous children, and a job in the real world, some would think that Helen Collins has it all. So when plain, bald Graham Parks walks into her office, ready to be cross-questioned about his book, Helen isn't expecting to fall for him. He's the exact opposite of her good-looking husband Alex, who woos women daily in his role as a TV character. But after fifteen years together, Helen wonders what it would be like to sleep with someone else. What begins as harmless flirtation quickly develops into something far more threatening, pulling Helen to the edge of something that may just turn her world upside down. It's exciting, alluring, all-consuming. But is it worth the risk?

LIZZIE ENFIELD

WHAT YOU DON'T KNOW

Complete and Unabridged

CHARNWOOD
Leicester

First published in Great Britain in 2011 by
Headline Review
an imprint of
Headline Publishing Group, London

First Charnwood Edition
published 2011
by arrangement with
Headline Publishing Group
An Hachette UK Company, London

The moral right of the author has been asserted

British Library CIP Data

Enfield, Lizzie.
    What you don't know.
    1. Adultery- -Fiction. 2. Wives- -Psychology- -Fiction.
    3. Chick lit. 4. Large type books.
    I. Title
    823.9'2–dc23

    ISBN 978–1–4448–0973–2

Published by
F. A. Thorpe (Publishing)
Anstey, Leicestershire

Set by Words & Graphics Ltd.
Anstey, Leicestershire
Printed and bound in Great Britain by
T. J. International Ltd., Padstow, Cornwall

This book is printed on acid-free paper

For Mick
(now you will have to read it)

1

She wondered what it would be like to sleep with him.

By imagining herself going to bed with Graham Parks, Helen had not singled him out for special attention. She considered briefly what it might be like to sleep with quite a few of the people she encountered, not always because she wanted to, in fact often quite the opposite.

Sometimes she'd be sitting facing someone on the tube, some great hulk of a man with his legs wide apart, using far more than his fair share of personal space and constantly wheezing or coughing, and she'd find herself wondering if he coughed and wheezed while having sex. She would picture him afterwards, spreading himself across the bed, with total disregard for whoever he shared it with, his arms and legs flung wide, forcing his poor partner to curl up near a pillow and try to sleep in only one eighth of the bed space.

She was particularly fascinated by the Polish builders who'd helped extend their kitchen. They'd often appeared to be arguing, raising their voices and spitting out guttural-sounding words. But if she'd asked them what they were discussing, they would smile and say in their gentle, sing-song English voices things like 'I ask if he likes to go clubbing tonight.'

There was something in the accent that always

made them sound cross. If she asked if they'd like a cup of tea, one would invariably shout to another, who'd reply with a guttural outburst that would then be translated to her as 'Yes please, thank you very much, that would be very nice.'

What, Helen wondered, did 'You are the most gorgeous, unbelievable woman and I want to cherish every inch of you' sound like when uttered in the heat of the moment between the sheets in a Polish bedsit?

In cases like these, she was never more than a detached observer, but every now and then someone would come under her radar who would make her wonder what it might actually be like to sleep with them. Graham Parks had, within moments of their first meeting, transformed himself from the unflattering image on his book's dust jacket to one such person.

Helen put her curiosity down to fifteen years of sleeping with the same person. It seemed only natural that if you went to bed with the same man night after night, you would wonder what different would be like.

'Have you read the book?' Graham Parks brought her back to the here and now, catching her unprepared.

'I haven't finished it.' Helen decided to be truthful. 'I was only assigned the job this morning, so I didn't have much time.'

'I'm not sure that any of the journalists I've met today have actually read it.' The author didn't seem perturbed by this. 'You're the only one who has actually admitted it, though.'

'Sorry,' said Helen.

'It's okay.' He smiled. 'I've never read any of your articles.'

Helen laughed and put down her cup of tea, looking around to see if the publisher's PR, Claire, had witnessed this exchange. She seemed to have disappeared.

'But you don't have to write anything about me,' she said, adding, 'Do you mind if I move and sit next to you? Then I can get the recorder a bit nearer.'

'Shall I hold it?' Graham asked, in a way that suggested he was used to being interviewed, aware that his world would be picked up better if the microphone on the tiny digital recorder were directed towards his mouth.

'Yes please, as long as you don't rattle it,' Helen said, half rising from her perch, thinking that if he was holding the machine then she didn't actually need to be on the same couch.

Graham Parks had the sort of physique that when he was younger would have been described as 'being built like a brick shithouse'. Helen had never quite understood the terminology, which was usually deemed complimentary, though quite why someone should find satisfaction in being described like a toilet block she could not think. She would have said he was built like a gladiator, or a matador, constructed from an impenetrable mass of muscle, which as he got older and less active had gradually turned to flab. Or perhaps it hadn't. It was hard to tell beneath the shirt and sweater that he was wearing. Perhaps the girth was still all muscle.

There was something powerful about him. He appeared physically strong. She imagined he could break up a fight simply by standing up. She hadn't encountered anyone with such physical presence for a long time. He was the opposite of her husband Alex, who'd been scrawny as a young man but had graduated to lean as he got older.

'Tell me about the book.' Helen sat up straight and tried to focus on the job in hand. 'It's been described as a Nick Hornbyesque *Bridget Jones* for men.'

'I know.' Graham Parks sighed, implying he didn't like the tag any more than he liked the photo of himself on the dust jacket. 'And I've been described as a literary James Blunt.'

'I hadn't heard that one.' Helen rather liked James Blunt. She knew it wasn't cool to admit to this, especially in the offices of the *Sunday Review*, where everyone professed their hatred for 'that posh singer with the wishy-washy sappy lyrics', but along with all the millions who had bought his album, she enjoyed his music. She also quite fancied him and had wondered what it would be like to sleep with him. 'I suppose that's because you used to be a soldier,' she said. 'Do you mind the comparisons?'

'I quite like being compared to Nick Hornby,' Graham confessed. 'I'm not so sure about James Blunt.'

'I like James Blunt.' Helen decided to confess herself. 'He seems quite happy with who he is.' She decided not to say out loud that it was a quality she found very attractive in a man, along

4

with the newly discovered ones of baldness, bulk and grey-blue eyes.

'Well, I'm not very like him then.' A momentary look of sadness passed across Graham Parks' face.

Helen felt a sudden rush of compassion for him. She wanted to reach out and put her hand over his and tell him that she liked him, as far as she could tell, but that would have been unprofessional. No, it would have been ridiculous. She was here to ask him about his book. Yet she felt strangely connected with him. She wanted to know about him, and not just so that she could write the piece.

'Is that because you care what the critics say?' She tried to phrase her next questions carefully. 'Or because you're not happy with yourself?'

'A bit of both, I think.' Graham considered what she'd asked. 'I haven't had any reviews yet, so I'm not sure how I'll react when everyone says the book is terrible. I'm steeling myself for negative stuff — and stockpiling antidepressants. And I'm not particularly happy about myself,' he continued. 'When you read the book, if you read it, you'll realise I'm a little disturbed.'

Helen leant back against the sofa again. She felt unusually comfortable with him. She could be at home on the sofa with Alex, in the comfortable silence that comes from knowing someone so well that you don't have to talk to them. She felt like just sitting for a bit. Why did he make her feel like this? He was fat and bald, just like the photo on the dust jacket, but with a raw, understated appeal too.

'Is the book autobiographical, then?' she asked.

'Not really.' Graham leant back as well. His arm just touched hers, but he didn't adjust his position and neither did she. 'The Ed character is fictitious, but there's quite a lot of me in him. I suppose he's an amalgam of various friends, but his emotions are quite often mine.'

'So how is he like you?' Helen now wished she had had time to read the book.

'Sad, single, screwed up, trying to sort out his life at an age when it really should be sorted.' Graham was writing her piece for her. She wondered if he realised.

'There's my headline.' She sat up and drained the rest of her tea, aware that a door had opened somewhere behind them.

'Five more minutes,' said Claire in a stage whisper, making it seem as if she was not actually interrupting.

'Have you got enough?' asked Graham.

'Almost,' Helen replied, aware that she still did not have a clear picture of what he had been doing since leaving the army.

'If you need to know more, we could always continue the conversation somewhere else,' he said. 'I'm hungry and I wouldn't mind grabbing a bite to eat before going home.'

Claire looked alarmed at his suggestion. 'I'm sure we could have the room for another half an hour or so,' she suggested.

'To be honest, I could do with a change of scene.' Graham was not going to be swayed. 'As long as Helen doesn't mind?'

'I don't mind at all,' she said. Now they were presenting a united front.

'Will you call me when you're done?' Claire was addressing Graham now, unsure if her duties as his chaperone for the day were over or if she needed to hang around out of sight until they'd finished.

'I'll give you a call in the morning,' Graham said, adding, 'Thanks for organising everything today. Hopefully it will shift a few copies of the book.'

2

At the restaurant, Helen wondered if there was any significance in the fact that she was having a meal with another man on the day her husband had finally agreed to have a vasectomy. Having decided to put an end to the possibility of bearing any more of Alex's children, was she subconsciously seeking out someone who could successfully impregnate her?

Studying Graham's face again as he looked at the menu, she couldn't imagine for a moment that he had had the snip. He seemed too masculine. Did that mean that by having put pressure on Alex to end his fertility, she was somehow emasculating her own husband?

'What do you fancy?' Graham was looking over the top of his menu. His gaze was a bit too intense. Helen felt herself blushing. She wondered if he could tell she had not been concentrating on what to order but instead wondering if all his bits were still intact.

'Ummm . . . ' She scanned the menu. 'I think I'll have the chicken with baby vegetables.'

Almost as soon as she'd said it, she regretted this. Not because she didn't like chicken with baby vegetables; it was just that eating infantile carrots, peas and sweetcorn seemed somehow inappropriate, given the way her mind was preoccupied with the not having of any more babies.

'Or maybe . . . ' She looked at the menu again.

'Something else?' Graham raised his eyebrows as he spoke, and she noticed for the first time that there was a small scar in the middle of one brow, which made it appear to split in two.

She wanted to know how he'd got the scar, but she didn't know him well enough to ask. After all, she'd only met this man half an hour ago. She had a husband and two children waiting for her at home. Yet here she was, sitting opposite him in a dimly lit restaurant, wanting to know all about him.

'No, chicken and baby vegetables it is.' She tried to sound decisive, businesslike, like the journalist who had just interviewed him and agreed to get a bite to eat in the hope of finding out a bit more about him. It was not unprofessional, this having a meal with an interviewee. She could even legitimise it by putting it on expenses.

'How about you?' she asked, vocalising her intent to make things appear entirely normal. 'I can put it all on expenses, so . . . '

She trailed off, which, she realised, made her sound not entirely convincing. But then she was not here because she needed to be here. She was here because she wanted to be here. It was only a meal, but it felt disloyal to Alex, especially today.

★　★　★

Helen had gradually, over the past eight years, been wearing Alex down into submitting to the knife. Initially, after Joe was born, although she

9

didn't want any more children, she couldn't quite reconcile herself to the idea of not having any more either. So when the doctor asked what they were doing for contraception, she told him she didn't want to go back on the pill, muttered something about condoms and left it at that.

A lot of her friends had been more proactive, bringing vasectomy information leaflets home from the hospital with their babies, even though doctors advised them to wait a while, hedging around the fact that if their newborn for some reason did not survive the early years, they might want to reconsider their no-more-children position.

After Joe was born, Helen had had periods when she really wanted another child, but money had been tight, Alex, an actor, had been away and as their daughter Emma had got older and easier, the thought of returning to mountains of nappies and sleepless nights had grown less appealing.

Alex had initially come out with a thousand reasons why he should not have the operation, ranging from 'It might hurt' to the more fatalistic 'What if you are all killed in a car crash and I want to have more children with someone else?' Moreover, he reasoned, wrongly, Helen would be infertile in a few years' time anyway.

'Surely you won't be able to have children after you're forty?' he'd said, ignoring the fact that a lot of her friends had only started having them once they hit forty.

'Look at Cherie Blair,' she had countered. 'She

had Leo at forty-six and then a miscarriage after that.'

'The Blairs are Catholics, though,' argued Alex, as if was Cherie's faith rather than her fertility that had caused her pregnancies.

'And being a Catholic probably prevented Tony from having the snip,' she'd retorted.

'I wonder,' mused Alex, enjoying this new line of thought. 'Don't you think world leaders need fully functioning tackle to maintain their global status? I wonder if George Bush has had his tubes tied? Or Fidel Castro, a man whose name suggests he may have undergone a more radical surgery?'

And so he had shied away from the issue, returning to it a few months later when Helen had reconsidered her position and was again not sure if 'no more children' meant 'no more children *ever*'.

'I've decided to have a vasectomy,' he had announced in the same breath as telling her he had decided to leave his theatrical agent and sign up with a woman who had been making overtures towards him for a while. She wondered if the two things were related.

Helen was rather frightened by all these new decisions. It was not in her nature to be decisive. If you asked her if she wanted tea or coffee, she found herself in a quandary, even though she didn't actually like coffee. She also hated her computer, which was forever questioning the small decisions she had managed to make on her own.

'Are you sure you want to shut down now?' it

11

would ask her, implying she'd only been working for a couple of hours and would surely be shirking if she stopped so soon.

'Do you want to save this document?' it enquired when she tried to close her work, as if it thought it wasn't really worth saving and causing her to question whether she actually wanted to keep it or not.

If she found decisions like that difficult, the question of whether to decide once and for all if you were never going to have any more children was almost impossible.

'What made you decide that?' she asked Alex, feeling and sounding suddenly panicky.

'I thought you wanted me to,' he countered, confused that his munificent gesture was not provoking the appropriate reaction.

'I do,' said Helen. 'At least, I did. It's just that it seems so final.'

'That's the general idea,' said Alex. 'Unless you have decided that you *do* want another child.'

'I don't,' said Helen firmly.

'Well then . . .'

There followed a conversation in which it emerged that the main driving force behind Alex's decision was that he thought they would make love more often if he had the operation. Helen had told him once that there was always a slight nagging worry in the back of her mind that she might get pregnant and that this made her hold something back. So Alex, thinking it would lead to no-holds-barred, multifaceted, every-day-of-the-week sex had decided the snip was a price worth paying.

This had made Helen weigh up her options again. Which was going to be the most tiring — another baby, or sex on demand? At that point in their married lives, she would probably have gone for another baby, reasoning that it might be the more tiring but probably the more rewarding option.

The subject had been dropped for a couple of years, until Helen brought it up again, unsettled by the news that a friend of hers in her mid-forties was expecting another, unplanned child. The word 'expecting' when applied to babies seemed to her an oxymoron. Getting pregnant was often the last thing anyone expected, especially when, like Beth, they had had a coil fitted in order to prevent it. Unluckily for her, she was the one per cent left over from the ninety-nine per cent effective statistic. Helen and Alex's own roulette of reliance on withdrawal, Helen not being fertile at certain times of the month and using condoms when Alex could be bothered to go to the bathroom and get one seemed increasingly risky.

'You certainly pick your moment,' Alex had said when she broached the subject as he lay in the bath one morning.

'Would you rather I'd called you to discuss it while you were on set?' Helen replied, wondering if there was ever a right time to suggest your reluctant partner render himself voluntarily infertile.

'Is it really necessary?' Alex asked, sitting up in

the bath and hiding his expression behind a mountain of shaving foam.

'I thought we went through this last time,' she retorted. 'You thinking that I ought to be infertile by now and me having to disappoint you by saying I could be conceiving children until I'm fifty, for all we know.'

But this time, Alex had another line of defence ready.

'No, I meant, do we actually have sex often enough to make it necessary?'

'What do you mean?' said Helen, wondering how the discussion had moved so quickly from the minor operation to what for Alex was always the more major matter of her libido. 'How often is often enough?'

'I don't know,' said Alex. 'More than seven times a year.'

'We shag more than seven times a year!' protested Helen. Honestly, what was the point of making a conscious effort to ensure they had regular sex if Alex didn't even notice? That was the trouble with being with the same person for so long. While sometimes they did still have what Alex insisted on referring to as 'nights of torrid passion', more often it was simply a case of going through a well-rehearsed routine. Not that the well-rehearsed routine wasn't good, but possibly (obviously in Alex's case) it wasn't that memorable.

'I know we do,' he replied, scraping the shaving foam from one side of his face. 'I'm just saying that enough would have to be more than seven times a year.'

'Then we have sex enough!' Helen was winning ground again.

'I'm not saying that a few more than seven times is enough, just that less than seven would definitely not be. Sixty sounds like a good figure to me. At least once a week and then a few more for birthdays and Christmas and coming home really drunk.'

He was laughing now, but was probably still serious. She didn't know. It had been an issue when the children were young. Her libido had more or less disappeared beneath a wave of tiredness and the fact that she was already having an extremely satisfying physical relation- ship with another man, even if that other man was her nine-month-old son.

Alex's figure of seven was probably plucked from that time. It hadn't been enough for him, and his frustration had manifested itself in his obsessive-compulsive behaviour (repetitively checking the sell-by dates of the unused condoms in the bathroom cabinet) and resulted in him spending longer periods at work. Helen wondered, when she had the energy to think, if he was getting it elsewhere. There were a number of women on the set who, apparently, constantly told him he had a nice arse or looked much younger than his actual age, and there were plenty of opportunities on tour and on overnight shoots. But if he did take advantage elsewhere, he never let on and he always came back to her.

Helen reckoned that, on average, these days they did it around twice a month, which, if any

15

of her friends were telling the truth about their own sex lives, was pretty good going. She imagined Graham Parks would be horrified to hear this. He had never been married. That much she knew.

'I think you'd have to take away a few potential shags for you being away, or cross with me for failing to unload the dishwasher, or because you were distracted by the attentions of the make-up artist,' said Helen.

It was like justifying the cost of a new dress by dividing it by the number of times you were likely to wear it. If the dress cost two hundred pounds and you only wore it once, then it had cost two hundred quid, but if you wore it four times, it had only really cost fifty, and twenty times made it a bargain at a tenner.

So, Alex reasoned, if you had sex fewer than seven times a year, a vasectomy was an emotionally costly procedure; around twenty-four times it would probably be worth it in the long term; but over fifty-two and it was (literally) a snip.

Saying 'Do you fancy boosting the annual statistics?' had been his idea of foreplay since they'd had this conversation, and his methodical mind had obviously been logging the bedroom activity in a mental register, because on the phone that morning, as she'd been about to leave for work, he'd announced that he'd decided to go ahead and have the snip and would see the doctor later in the week and put himself on the waiting list for the operation.

It was a milestone in their relationship; the

end of an era but perhaps the start of something new. Helen should have said something to show him she appreciated the sacrifice he was making. She could have offered to find a babysitter and take him out to dinner, something they would be able to do more often as Emma and Joe got older. Instead she'd phoned him, told him she'd be late home and directed him to the freezer for sustenance.

⋆　⋆　⋆

'Do you think you'll have any more children?' Graham asked as Helen shovelled the last of the miniature sweetcorn into her mouth.

'No, I don't think so,' Helen replied, considering for the first time that one unforeseen consequence of Alex's operation would be to make it far more risky for her to sleep with anyone else.

3

Alex had swept Helen off her feet when he met her. It was the weekend, and she'd been going for a swim at one of the open-air ponds on Hampstead Heath. As she had stepped out to cross the road that led to the Heath, she was vaguely aware of a man on a bicycle speeding around the corner.

The next thing she knew, she was sitting at the bottom of some wide steps leading to one of the vast double-fronted houses that lined the road. There appeared to be a cat sleeping in a large flowerpot next to her. The cat looked warm, stretched out in the sun, and she felt warm too. She realised that her heat came from a heavy black wool jacket wrapped around her, which was odd, because she'd set out only in a T-shirt and skirt, her swimming costume already on underneath her clothes.

The jacket must have belonged to the man she was leaning against. His arm was wrapped round her and he was muttering, 'Hurry up, hurry up!' She wondered who he wanted to hurry. Perhaps it was her. Was he waiting for her to wake up? She had no idea who he was or why they were there together. She looked at him and saw a man slightly older than herself, with a worried expression on his face. He seemed reassuringly familiar, though she wasn't sure why. His face registered that she had woken up.

'Are you okay?' She realised he had been worried about her.

'I'm not sure,' she replied. She felt okay. She couldn't recall how she came to be here, but now that she was, she felt curiously comfortable, sitting on the steps of a north London mansion being held by a man who seemed just right for holding her.

It must be his coat, she decided. It smelt nice, warm and musky. Was this his house, too?

The door at the top of the steps opened and an elderly man came out, carrying a tray. Maybe he owned the house.

'The ambulance is on its way,' the older man said, bending down with arthritic difficulty and setting the tray down next to them. There were two tall glasses of water, and a couple of smaller ones with an inch of orangey-brown liquid in the bottom.

Helen wondered about the ambulance. Was it for the old man's wife? Had she fallen down the stairs and broken her hip? Or was it something worse? Were they sitting out here waiting to lead the ambulance crew up the stairs to wherever his wife was? Really he should be inside with her, not out here serving drinks.

'I think she's coming round,' the man who was holding her was saying.

She wondered if he was her boyfriend. It seemed likely from the way he was holding her. She seemed to fit comfortably against him. Her head was resting on his chest, lulled by the rise and fall of his breathing. She could hear his heart beating rather fast. Did it always beat like that?

The arm that encircled her was lean and muscular, with a light covering of sandy hair; the wrist was ensconced in a thick leather watch strap holding in place an old watch, not unlike the one her dad wore.

Helen found forearms rather appealing. She suspected that this stemmed from working in an office where the men still wore shirts and jackets. Very little of their bodies was ever exposed. They spent most of the day safely wrapped up in the unofficial uniform of the cub reporter. Only the editor, having taken the morning meeting, would remove his jacket and loosen his tie. But when the cubs came back from a story and sat down at their desks ready to write it up, they would sling their jackets over the back of their chairs, unbutton their cuffs and roll up their sleeves. She liked this revealing of forearms, found the rolling of sleeves more alluring than the unbuttoning of a shirt, and thought the quiet flexing of muscles between the wrist and the elbow strangely seductive.

'Can you hear me, Helen?' the man was saying. He knew her name, so she must know him. She looked at him properly, but still couldn't quite place him. He had sandy hair, which had been cut short but had grown out and stuck out around his head. His face was slightly irregular, narrow, with one deep blue eye larger than the other and a gently lopsided mouth. He didn't immediately appear good-looking, but he was.

'Helen, can you hear me?' he said again. He had a nice voice, soft but clear, with a slight trace

20

of an accent she could not place. She wanted him to say something else so that she could listen to him for longer.

The old man was talking to her now as well.

'Do you want a glass of water?' he was saying. 'Or some brandy? You've had a shock.'

So that was what the orangey liquid was. The old man had a nice face as well, kind, concerned. Perhaps he was her boyfriend's dad.

'I'm not sure she should drink,' her boyfriend was saying. 'Perhaps we should wait for the ambulance to arrive.'

Helen looked down the street and recognised it as the one that led up to the Heath. She remembered crossing it on her way to the Ladies' Pond. She'd been going swimming. She felt underneath her T-shirt: she still had her swimming costume on. Her bag was on the step next to the mystery man.

'What happened?' she asked. 'And who are you?'

She was interrupted by the arrival of an ambulance. The old man went over to greet it.

'There's been a slight accident,' he was saying.

'Are you okay?' A paramedic had appeared and was talking to her now. 'Can you tell me your name?'

'Helen,' she said.

'Helen Collins,' said the man. How did he know that?

'I need to see if she can remember it herself,' the paramedic told him. 'Can you tell me your name and where you live?'

'Helen Collins, 66 Battersea Park Road,' she

told them. The man with his arm round her was nodding, as if he knew this was right. 'I can't remember who he is, though.'

'That's okay.' He was smiling at her, pleased that she was talking. 'You've never met me before.'

'Oh . . . ' Helen was confused.

'You were knocked over.' The paramedic seemed to know what had happened, even though he'd only just arrived. How come everyone knew so much about her? 'You were out for a bit. We need to check you over, make sure you're okay. Do you think you can stand up?'

Helen didn't see why not, although she liked being held by the man who obviously wasn't her boyfriend as they'd only just met. She sat up straight and removed his arm. Her own right arm ached a bit, but apart from that she felt fine. She stood up.

'Can you walk to the ambulance?' the paramedic asked.

It was easy. She got inside and they asked her a few more questions, looked at her arm, shone lights in her eyes and declared that she appeared okay.

'You need to go home and rest for a bit,' the paramedic told her. 'We'll take you in the ambulance. We're not really supposed to, but we have to go past on our way back to the station.'

'Can I come with her?' asked the man who was not her boyfriend.

'Afraid not,' said the paramedic. 'Will there be someone there to look after you?'

'Richard will be there,' Helen told them.

'Is he your boyfriend?' She realised it was no longer the paramedic asking the questions but the young man that she didn't know.

'He's my flatmate,' she answered. 'He doesn't usually get up until midday.'

'We might need to wake him up, then.' The paramedic was closing the doors of the ambulance, leaving the young man and the older one standing on the edge of the street. 'You'll need someone to keep an eye on you for a while.'

'Thanks for looking after me,' Helen said to them both as the doors clicked shut.

'He knocked you flying with his bike,' the paramedic told her, as the ambulance moved away from the kerb and into the middle of the road.

It was only when they reached her flat and Richard didn't answer the door that Helen realised she'd left her bag with her keys in on the steps of the house.

'Which room does he sleep in?' asked the paramedic, looking at the front of the building.

Helen pointed to the room on the second floor to the left of the front door. The curtains were still firmly drawn.

'Let's wake him up, then,' he said, diving back inside the ambulance and switching on the siren and flashing lights.

It worked. A few moments later, a bleary-eyed Richard appeared at the window, wondering what was going on. The paramedics waved, and noticing Helen with them, Richard retreated and came to answer the door.

Once inside, she felt incredibly tired.

'That's normal,' said the paramedic, talking to Richard now. 'She's had a slight concussion. If she sleeps, wake her up every couple of hours to make sure she's still okay, and if she develops any other symptoms, she needs to go to the doctor.'

'Okay, fine,' replied Richard, slowly registering what was going on.

Helen lay on the couch and closed her eyes.

⋆ ⋆ ⋆

'Helen, wake up!' Richard was following his instructions. She didn't think she'd been asleep a couple of hours, but the sun, which normally shone straight through the living room windows, making it almost unbearably bright in summer, appeared to have moved around the block. She closed her eyes again, not yet wanting to take in the familiar surroundings.

'Alex is here to see you,' Richard was saying.

'Who's Alex?' asked Helen. Her eyes were still closed, but she could sense Richard hovering close by. There was a scent of flowers in the room. Usually it had the lingering air of cigarettes, even though Richard opened the windows and flicked his ash on to the pavement below when he smoked.

'I am,' someone said in a soft voice. 'I've brought you some flowers, to say sorry, and your bag, which you left behind. How are you feeling?'

'Sleepy,' Helen said, sitting up and taking Alex in properly for the first time. He didn't seem to know quite what to do. He was standing in the middle of the living room holding a huge bunch of lilies.

'Did you think I might be dead?' she asked, nodding towards the flowers.

'I thought you might be able to smell them, even if you were too woozy to see them,' he laughed. 'Although this morning when I knocked you over, I was worried that you might have been. Where shall I put them?'

'Give them to Richard,' she said.

Richard took the flowers and disappeared into the kitchen, where clattering indicated that last night's washing-up was still spread over the work surfaces, hampering his search for something to put them in.

'How did you know where I lived?' Helen wondered if he'd remembered the address she'd given the ambulance driver.

'I went through your bag, I'm afraid . . . ' He held it out to her.

Helen felt light-headed. She wondered if this was an after-effect of the mild concussion, or whether it had been brought about by seeing Alex again. He was nice-looking, she thought, as he sat down next to her on the sofa, resting his hands on his knees so that the muscles in his forearms tautened slightly. Gorgeous, in fact.

'I'm glad you did,' she said, thinking that if he

had not, she would have lost her valuables and might not have seen Alex again. Then she remembered that she was wearing her swimming costume and that her underwear was in the bag with her purse and keys.

4

Helen hadn't been expecting to interview Graham Parks when she went to work that morning. She'd spent the last few days preparing to quiz American literary heavyweight Buddy Jackson about *his* new book.

It was a big interview and it would appear on the front page of the Review section. She'd been delighted that the editor had asked her to do it. It proved that, although she only worked part time and didn't even have her own desk any more, she was still valued and trusted enough to be assigned this particular scoop.

'Buddy Jackson this morning,' she said to Shana, editor of the Review section of the *Sunday Review*.

She had intended it to be a statement that demonstrated she was ready to take him on and wow the readers with her witty but analytical profile, but it came out as a question. Shana, like her computer, always made her question everything.

'Change of plan,' Shana replied, confident as always that her decisions were the right ones. 'Someone from Books is going to do the piece. Apparently they've interviewed him before.'

Case dismissed.

Helen knew that arguing that she had spent every spare minute of the past week wading through the massive tome of weighty prose that was American literary heavyweight Buddy Jackson's latest book would be fruitless.

'Something else has come in,' Shana said. 'There's a book on the desk over there. Can you take a look at that and try to set up an interview with the author?'

'All right?' asked Vincent, moments later. Vincent was a freelancer who came into the office every week to write his opinion piece. He was sitting at the desk assigned to people who weren't there all the time, which included Helen.

'Fine,' she replied. 'Shana says there's a book here that she wants me to take a look at.'

'Here you go.' Vincent passed the book with an apologetic shrug, which implied he had over-heard her exchange with Shana. 'Lover Boy brought it in. Apparently the author's a friend of his.' He watched her expectantly, waiting to see how she would react to the snippet of information.

Lover Boy was the name Helen's colleagues used when talking to her about the paper's chief foreign correspondent, Jim Keeble. Jim was tall, good-looking and fearless, and had been known to pull stunts such as carrying gunshot victims in Bosnia to safety as a sniper continued to fire on a crowded marketplace, ensuring that he was often part of the story he was reporting on.

He was the sort of journalist that the male paperback reviewers privately wished they could be and the female fashion hacks wished they could sleep with. He was secretly admired by everyone, and a little bit of that admiration had rubbed off on to Helen when she had revealed that she had, briefly, been out with him when they'd worked together on the *Hastings Gazette*.

That had been over twenty years ago. It had been a brief relationship, partly because Jim was working his way through the entire female staff and partly because not long after he arrived at the paper he had managed to wangle himself a trip to write a travel piece about Kuwait, arrived as Saddam began amassing troops on the border, filed copy to every paper in the UK bar the *Gazette* and come home having secured himself a job on the *Guardian* foreign desk.

When he arrived at the *Sunday Review*, the editor had held a big meeting to introduce their new chief foreign correspondent. Helen had not expected Jim to take much notice of her. But in a crowded conference room filled with people waiting for him to make a speech about how pleased he was to have got the job, he had picked her out, telling the assembled crew that he was delighted to be working for the *Review* and 'to be reunited with the gorgeous Helen Collins, who I have not seen for several years but who has hardly changed at all!'

In the days following the meeting, Helen felt briefly transformed from unnoticeable part-time working mother who wrote unremarked-upon features, to someone her peers now found slightly intriguing. They had gossiped when Jim Keeble strode into the Review section office and insisted she have dinner with him, and looked at her with renewed admiration when he casually touched her in a way that suggested they were more intimate than they actually were.

They had lost interest when he was dispatched to the Sudan, but nevertheless continued to refer to him as Lover Boy in Helen's presence.

'Is he in the country, then?' Helen asked, forgetting for the moment that she was still annoyed at having the Buddy Jackson interview snatched from under her nose.

'The mighty Jim Keeble?' asked Vincent, knowing full well that that was who she was referring to. 'Apparently he dropped into the office this morning, bearing the book you have in your hands but probably looking for you!'

Vincent sat back in his chair, delighted to have been the imparter of this particular piece of news.

Helen looked at the book she was holding tightly with both hands, in order to prevent herself from subconsciously touching her hair at the mention of Lover Boy's name. She perched on the edge of the desk and pulled the accompanying publisher's press release from within the pages.

*　*　*

Graham Parks could not meet her until five p.m., which threw Helen's carefully orchestrated childcare into disarray. She was supposed to leave work at five in time to pick Emma and Joe up from the child-minder. Instead she'd be holed up in the offices of a publishing house.

Alex was still in Manchester, recording this week's episode of *Muddy Water*, a sitcom about a shopping centre overlooking a river somewhere in the north of England. Its location was unspecified, but the centre was a cross between Bluewater in Kent and the Metro Centre in Newcastle. The show was broadcast on BBC3 on a Saturday and repeated on Wednesdays. For an hour you could watch men, women and children with a variety of accents congregating inside the glass and steel structure of the Water's Edge shopping centre.

Alex played Kev, the Liverpudlian security manager, who came to work in order to pay the mortgage but harboured dreams of being the next John Lennon, secretly composing on a mini electronic keyboard in the booth from which he managed security.

Alex would be travelling home by train, and was not usually back until seven. Helen had wanted to get home before him, to sort out the mess that the house became when he was away and get the children fed and bathed and ready for bed so that, having not seen Alex for a few days, she would be able to relax when he did arrive home.

Graham Parks had unwittingly messed up this plan.

'I wish I could wriggle out of this,' Helen muttered to herself, as she dialled Katie Ryan's number. Katie, introduced to her by Emma as 'my friend Hannah's mum', was now almost by default one of Helen's closest friends.

'Hello!' Katie always answered with such a voluble cheeriness that it made Helen feel she had been waiting to talk to her. 'How's the wonderful world of work?'

31

Katie was one of the few people she knew who did not work but had a very strong sense of identity. If anyone asked her what she did, she replied, 'Fuck all!' with such conviction that they instantly wanted to know more. In contrast, Helen felt that although she could do without the hassle of work, she'd be at a complete loss to answer the question of what she did instead.

'It's seriously shit,' she replied. 'The powers that be have decided that someone with better credentials should interview the author whose book I spent all week reading, and I've been fobbed off with someone else.'

'Anyone I've ever heard of?' Katie was always interested in Helen's work.

'Someone no one has ever heard of,' Helen told her. 'A man called Graham Parks.'

'No, never heard of him,' Katie laughed. 'What is there to know about him?'

'Very little, according to the press release that came with the book. Although there is enough going on in his life that he can't meet me until five this evening, which means I need a favour.'

'Do you want me to pick up Emma and Joe for you?' Katie could always be relied upon to offer without having been asked.

'Would you mind?' Helen hoped she wouldn't, as she had no Plan B. 'I know it's very late notice, but I can't get out of this interview and Alex won't be home until seven. I'll call him and ask him to pick them up from your house on his way back from the station.'

'I'll bring them home when he's back,' Katie told her. 'I've got to drop something off in your area anyway, and Phil's home already, so it will give me an excuse to make him do bedtime and I can get out of the house.'

'Are you sure you don't mind?' Helen didn't like to have to keep asking Katie to help her out with childcare when she was working, especially as she rarely returned the favour.

'Absolutely not,' Katie assured her. 'Hannah will be delighted to have Emma to play with for a while, I get to leave the house during the witching hour and I can say hello to your handsome husband while I'm at it.'

'Well, if you're absolutely sure . . . ' Helen almost wished that Katie had not been so ready to oblige. Perhaps then she could have got out of this particular interview.

'I am,' Katie replied. 'I'll call Alex and arrange when to bring them back. Have fun with the mystery man.'

5

'He tried to kill me and then he looked at my underwear,' Helen told Graham Parks, in response to his question about how she had met her husband.

It was a well-rehearsed line and it annoyed Alex every time she used it, which wasn't very often any more. They'd been married nearly ten years and most of their friends and acquaintances knew the story of the accident, the ambulance, the forgotten bag containing her underwear and the jokes about how he'd immediately dived into her knickers and put his hand under her bra.

Helen felt conspicuous sitting in a darkened corner of the restaurant, Graham Parks sitting opposite, blocking her view of the other diners, so she could not be sure if she was being watched by someone from work: one of the subs grabbing a quick bite to eat before catching the train from Charing Cross, or one of the theatre critics eating before a press show, knowing they would have to return to work and file copy and this might be the last chance they got.

Not that she was actually doing anything wrong. Her interview with Graham had been in the early evening; he hadn't eaten for a while. It had seemed natural to carry on talking elsewhere.

Graham had found a bistro pub around the

corner from the publisher's offices.

'How does this look?' he asked.

It had seemed a good choice to Helen. She knew that he wanted to eat, but she wasn't sure if she was included in his plan. This was the type of establishment where she could get a drink and he could have a light meal without their intentions seeming mismatched.

Once they were seated, the conversation they were supposed to continue changed direction.

Helen felt vulnerable to Graham's line of questioning: 'Where did you grow up?' 'Why did you go into journalism?' 'Are you happy in London?' Her defence against it was to start talking about Alex, as if she were not responsible for any of the life decisions she had taken but had happily handed them over to her husband.

'Alex likes living in London,' she confided. 'He likes to be close to auditions, and when he's recording the hours are long so it's better if he can get home quickly.'

This was better. She felt safer for having steered the conversation towards her husband, Alex Mills, an actor, previously out of work quite a lot but now with a big part in a weekly sitcom.

'I think I've seen it once or twice,' Graham said, when she told him about *Muddy Water*. 'Is he the good-looking one?'

'I think so,' Helen replied, smiling to herself, not at the thought of her husband being generally considered good-looking, but because now, sitting in a restaurant having something to eat with an interviewee and telling him about her husband, she no longer felt in danger. She hadn't thought through what she might actually be in danger from; she had just felt unsettled. She should have refused to carry on their conversation, told Graham she had enough information for the piece she would be writing and gone straight home. But she hadn't.

'Is Alex the love of your life?' he was asking now, taking them back into uncharted territory. The question was too direct. She wasn't sure how to answer it. Was Alex the love of her life? She had certainly thought so when they'd first met and his string of solicitous calls and visits to her flat had eventually turned into a relationship.

Helen had been in her mid-twenties then, recently returned to London after her spell on the *Hastings Gazette* to work on the *North London Reporter*. Alex had had a small part in a play at the Hampstead Theatre. Neither of their careers was established, but they were both going somewhere. Falling in love seemed to accelerate that process. With Helen in the background, Alex's stage presence increased and he was given a bigger role in a touring production. Being loved by Alex made Helen more confident, more willing to take risks; within months of having met him, she was promoted to chief features writer and some time later was poached by the *Sunday Review*.

Getting married and having children was further manifestation of how right they were for each other. Alex made everyone cry at their wedding when he told them how he had to pinch himself every morning when he woke up and found Helen lying there beside him. When

Emma was born, he cried and told Helen she was the most amazing person in the world, while Helen looked at their perfect, beautiful baby and saw her as proof of how perfect she and Alex were for each other.

Inevitably their relationship had settled into a less heady groove. She still loved Alex, still fancied him, admired him at work and was amazed at the way he was with the children, but the sense of being made for each other was no longer there. Their lives seemed somehow less interdependent. They were bound together by marriage, mortgage, children and a shared history. They were happy, but they no longer seemed to need each other in the way they had when they first met.

So instead of telling this man whom she had only met three quarters of an hour earlier that yes, Alex was the love of her life, she came out with another reply.

'I'll have to tell you on my deathbed,' she laughed, pretending to make light of it, but knowing that had she been asked by someone this time yesterday evening, she'd have been more positive. Now, sitting opposite Graham Parks, she couldn't bring herself to say with absolute confidence that her husband of ten years was the love of her life.

'You don't sound sure,' Graham said. Or did he ask? She didn't quite catch the intonation. Was he just underlining her own previous statement, or did he want to know if she was open to invitation, if she thought that the love of her life was still out there, as yet undiscovered?

'The love of *my* life was Katherine Fitzsi-mons,' he told her. 'We started primary school on the same day together. I was terrified, crying and holding on to my mother, begging her not to leave me, but Katherine was calm and kind and ready to face the other children. She took my hand and said she'd look after me and I suddenly felt all right, as if I could do it. I went in with her, without even saying goodbye to Mum, and it was okay.'

'What became of Katherine Fitzsimons?' Helen asked. She'd read a piece in the paper recently about people who were reunited with their childhood sweethearts and fell in love with them all over again. Some had been married for years but still found the legacy of their first love impossible to leave behind.

'She held my hand nearly every day until the second year,' Graham told her, 'then the family went to live in Ireland. I think her mother was Irish. I never saw her again. I was heartbroken at first, really lost without her.'

'Joe has a friend like that.' Helen thought of her five-year-old son, happier at the prospect of starting school than she had been at letting him go. It had felt like the end of an era to her. For the first five years of his life she had been the centre of his world, but on his first day at school Anna Evans had caught his eye and he'd let go of Helen's hand as they waited outside the entrance to the classroom and gone to sit with her on a wooden train.

They'd been more or less inseparable ever since. When Emma tried to tease him by saying

38

that he loved Anna, he simply replied, 'Yes, I do.' And he did. He might be only five years old, and if Anna left and went to Ireland tomorrow he would eventually get over it, but that didn't take away from the fact that he loved her. His world was much richer for the fact that she was in it.

'Sometimes I catch them sitting on the sofa together, watching *The Simpsons*, and I can imagine them side by side on a couch in an old people's home, watching old movies from the beginning of this century, still together. Perhaps she is the love of his life.'

'Who was your first boyfriend?' Graham asked.

'Billy Russell.' She thought back to the reception class of the primary school in the village where she grew up. 'He was very naughty, always getting in trouble, always talking, never able to sit still; he probably had undiagnosed attention deficit disorder or something. I was very good, never got in trouble, always working, never talking. We were a classic case of opposites attracting. He was my five-year-old wild side!'

'What happened to him?' Graham asked.

'I don't know.' Helen was surprised she could even remember Billy's name. She hadn't really thought about him for at least thirty years. He definitely wasn't a contender for love of her life.

'Nobody can ever really touch your first love,' Graham said. 'It becomes the benchmark against which all future relationships are compared.'

'Perhaps.' Helen pondered what he'd said. 'But I'm not sure that I believe there is only one person out there who is absolutely right for you.'

'No?'

'No. Think how awful it would be if you never met them. There are probably lots of people who could be the love of your life, if you allow them to be. It depends where you are and what you want at the time you happen to be with a particular person.' Helen believed this.

'So before Alex tried to kill you, and somehow turned attempted murder to marriage,' Graham continued, 'if I'd asked you who the love of your life was, who would it have been?'

'Probably a guy called Miles,' she considered. 'A Kiwi; I met him backpacking when I was eighteen. He came to live over here for a couple of years and we carried on seeing each other.'

'Don't tell me he left you for another woman?' Graham turned the statement into a question.

'No, he left me for another country,' she said. 'His work visa had run out and he had to go back to New Zealand. He wanted me to go with him but it seemed too big a thing at the time.'

Helen thought about Miles more often than she remembered Billy Russell. She often wondered what would have happened if he'd been English. Would they still be together? Or if he'd stayed here a little longer, would their lives have become inextricably bound together and would she have agreed to go with him?

'He sounds like a possible contender for love of your life,' said Graham, as if reading her private thoughts.

'Why?' Helen hadn't actually said very much about Miles.

'You never really had a chance to get tired of

him,' Graham mused. 'He left before the honeymoon period was up, before he morphed from the man you couldn't live without to the one who irritated you by leaving his dirty socks on the floor.'

Helen smiled privately to herself, thinking that Alex, who was by default the love of her life, never left his dirty socks on the floor but filed them away in the laundry basket more or less before he'd even worn them. He was the one who got irritated with her for leaving a trail of once-worn clothes around their bedroom.

She wondered how Alex would respond to Graham's line of questioning, if he would say that Helen was the love of his life. Would he claim that as soon as he saw her he knew he was going to have to run her over with his bicycle so he had an excuse to steal her bag and bring it back to her?

Was she the love of his life or just someone he'd met at a time when all his friends were gradually doing what he called 'falling by the wayside'. Had she been 'the one', or had it simply been time for him to fall?

6

Alex did not talk to Helen when she got home, rather later than anticipated. The silent treatment was not because he was cross with her, not that she knew of anyway, but because there was an important football match on the television and saying more than 'How was your day?' would have distracted him from managing his team from his position on the sidelines (or rather the sofa).

Alex's ability to focus on television sport to the exclusion of everything else was one of the things that annoyed Helen about him. He hadn't seen her for three days and yet whatever it was he was watching was more important than finding out how she had been during that time. Graham Parks, she noted, had not been anxious to get home to see whatever the unmissable match of the day happened to be.

She screwed her eyes up to make out the names of the teams at the top of the TV screen. TUR 0 — SWI 0. She couldn't imagine who either team could be; not Liverpool or Manchester United or one of the Premier League teams, who, if playing, required absolute silence in their living room, silence broken only by Alex's screams of 'That was offside' or 'Get in there.'

When Alex was enjoying his divine right to watch football, Helen loathed him. Taking up his position on the sofa with the remote in one hand and a beer in the other, he morphed from a kind, considerate, interesting newish man to a rude, inconsiderate, loutish unreconstructed bore. If anyone so much as dared to traverse his eyeline, he'd shout at them to get out of the way. If they weren't sure whether he was shouting at them or one of the players and ventured to speak to him, he'd bite their head off. If Helen made any attempt at physical contact, such as kissing him because she'd just come home from work, he'd brush her off so violently it could almost be classed as assault.

When she was nearly nine months pregnant with Joe, the World Cup had been in progress. Alex had turned down a touring production of *A Midsummer Night's Dream* in order to be at home when the baby came, or so he claimed. Helen suspected he had actually turned it down in order to coach teams from across the globe via the screen in the corner of the living room. She had thought that with Alex at home she'd have the chance to slow down and get some rest before the new baby burst into their lives. In her head she pictured him taking Emma to the park after lunch, while she went upstairs to sleep, emerging refreshed and serene to find the two of them making something from an old cereal packet, having first helped each other to get supper in the oven.

In reality, she found herself coping with a fractious Emma, who resented being yelled at every time her Baby Annabell went anywhere near the television screen, and facing more or less permanent exclusion from the living room, unless she promised to breathe quietly and not say anything stupid.

On one occasion she joined Alex to watch England attempting to qualify for the next round. When the game reached the penalty stage, she became interested. Two hours of chasing a ball around she had no time for, but the dramatic tension of the penalty shootout was like watching gangsters playing Russian roulette. Each player suddenly became a character, the future of the competition at their feet, the burden of responsibility displayed in their sweating brows, the disappointment written in their grown men's tears.

When she remarked to Alex that she loved the shootouts, he accused her of displaying her total lack of regard for the beautiful game by actually relishing seeing the outcome reduced to chance rather than unfolding on the pitch.

Seating her heavily pregnant self on the opposite end of the couch to Alex, she took a sharp intake of breath when Michael Owen kicked the ball the wrong way, putting England a goal down. She was by this time genuinely fearful of what might happen, afraid that the next player would do the same, eliminating England altogether. But Alex, who was screaming at the set, believed she was deliberately sabotaging his enjoyment of the game.

'Stop pretending to have contractions while I'm watching the football!' he yelled, so loudly that she momentarily thought he was still giving advice to the players.

'I'm not pretending to have contractions,' she yelled back, to this suddenly hated father of her soon-to-be-born child. 'I was holding my breath so that I didn't put Gareth Southgate off getting the ball in the back of the net.'

'You always do this,' Alex counter-attacked. 'Come in at the last minute and try to ruin the game for me.'

'In case you hadn't noticed,' Helen was livid now, 'I am due to give birth to your child, and I wanted to sit down in my living room for ten minutes after running round the park with your other child all afternoon, which does not seem unreasonable.'

'That's it. It's all over,' screamed Alex. It took Helen a moment to realise that he wasn't initiating divorce proceedings, but gradually turning back into the gentle, softly spoken, considerate man who would be with her, holding her hand and mopping her brow, when the tiny footballer inside her belly emerged from the tunnel.

Normal Alex appeared not to remember the accusations of pretend contractions and his aggressive dismissal of her presence. It was as if the football fanatic who possessed him for the duration of matches was nothing to do with him, but a Dr Jekyll alter ego who receded back into his subconscious once the final whistle had blown.

'What have you two been up to?' he asked, narrowing the gap between them on the sofa and resting his remote-wielding hand on her football-shaped stomach.

'What would happen if I went into labour during a match?' Helen asked.

'Well, it wouldn't be that quick, would it?' Alex said. 'I mean, you wouldn't be likely to need to go to hospital right there and then, would you?' The implication was that she could labour away quietly somewhere until the match was finished, and then he might drive her to hospital.

This was why Helen hated Alex when there was football on the television. She suspected he hated her when she failed to unload the dishwasher as soon as it had finished, and when she sulked quietly and told him there was nothing wrong when there clearly was something bothering her. She also hated him when whatever he was doing was more important than whatever she had arranged to do, causing her to rearrange her plans.

That was inevitably part of the for-better-or-for-worse deal, and the rest of the time she mostly loved him.

This evening, however, even though he was glued to TUR 0 — SWI 0, she found she did not hate him. In fact, she felt protective towards him, because he didn't know that she had briefly felt connected with another man.

If he hadn't been busy handing out advice to the SWI players on defence formation, she would have given him a bigger than average hug, and if she hadn't been fearful of blocking his view of the goal, she would have kissed him in a way that was more than cursory. Because even though if she did either of these things he was likely to push her away and mutter something about her being selfish, she loved him.

'Yes!' Alex had risen involuntarily from the sofa, thrown up into the air by the magnetic power of a ball going into the back of a net. On screen, hundreds of other people, who were actually within spitting distance of the goal, also rose from their seats.

'Hello,' he said, allowing her on to his imaginary bench for a few seconds while the players regrouped. 'You're back.'

'Yes,' she said. She wouldn't have his attention for long. 'I had to interview a man called Graham Parks, over dinner.'

She knew he wasn't really listening to her. But she thought it best to tell him where she had been. She loved him now even as he was turning away from her back to the flickering 32-inch screen, because she feared that if she allowed herself, she could also love Graham Parks.

7

The door of Emma's room had a new sign, evidence that earlier in the day she had obviously had an argument with Joe and decided to forbid him entrance to her bedroom.

No Jo-Jo ALOUD, it read.

Emma often dealt with arguments like this, and it seemed to Helen to be quite a mature way for an eight year old to tackle childish frustrations. Her bedroom signs were the infant equivalent of writing an email to whoever was giving you grief, but deleting rather than sending it.

Often when Joe was torturing her, mentally or physically, rather than hitting him back or telling him he was an even stupider durbrain, she would leave the room, announcing her intention to make a sign, then barricade her door, take pens and paper from the shelf and set about creating a work of art through which she could express her feelings towards her little brother.

Concentrating on the details, she would often forget why it was she was angry with Joe and, having tacked her masterpiece to the bedroom door, would then invite him in to arrange Sylvanian creatures around a miniature picnic table or teach him how to draw elephants.

What Emma lacked in spelling ability she made up for in artistic talent.

Helen paused to examine the new sign before

48

going to check on her sleeping daughter. In the centre of the paper was a large black and white draught board; an exact sixty-four squares had been drawn, thirty-two of them filled in in black. On the board, counters showed the latter stages of play. There were five black pieces surrounding one white king. White was clearly going to lose, and the white player was a small boy with floppy blond hair, a good likeness of Joe. His face was contorted with anger, and his arm was stretched out across the board. Opposite him sat a girl with long pigtails and big blue eyes, Emma's self-portrait. The picture captured the moment before Joe would dash all the pieces from the board, effectively ending the game before his older sister could win it.

It was a frequent scenario in their house. Joe loved playing games, but couldn't bear to lose them. Rather than admit defeat, he would spoil the game at the last minute. Furious, Emma would declare herself the winner anyway, which usually resulted in Joe hurling pieces of the game at her. The bruise on her cheek left after a game of bowls went the wrong way for Joe was still visible, even though the game had been played ten weeks previously.

Despite the meticulous attention she had paid to all the details, right down to the three aeroplanes on Joe's T-shirt and the hole in the knee of his trousers, Emma had not shrunk from defacing her picture with a large black cross, semi-obliterating the image of her brother. Lest anyone was in any doubt about the wording on the sign, she had made it clear that Joe was barred.

Helen smiled to herself, smiling also at the fact that Emma had pretty much forgotten that her little brother was actually called Joe.

When he was born, both she and Alex had liked the name Joe, but worried that it was too brief for a smiley baby and that, wanting to baby-talk him with something a bit longer, they would end up calling him Joey. So they'd called him Joseph but immediately shortened it to Joe. Then, finding that that was not enough, Jo-Jo. The name had stuck. Joe himself thought it cute; he revelled in being the smallest member of the family — the blond-haired, blue-eyed boy who got all the smiles and hair-ruffles from passers-by.

He was also blissfully unaware that the name was slightly ridiculous.

'Muuum,' he'd once shouted while watching television, greatly excited that one of the presenters had introduced herself as Jo-Jo. 'Jo-Jo is a girl's name as well as a boy's name.'

'Yes,' she'd replied, not quite able to bring herself to tell him that really it was a girl's name, if it was even a name at all, rather than just a repetition of one.

She had only come across one other male Jo-Jo, in the rather sad story of a nineteenth-century Russian wolf man who was so covered in hair that he was exhibited around the world. Originally called Joseph, he was given the name 'Jo-Jo the wolf man' while on tour in Liverpool, and the name had stuck.

Helen crept into her daughter's bedroom. Emma was asleep, her hair, curling from a day in plaits, spread across her face, tickling her every time she breathed in and out, causing her to screw up her face in minor irritation. Helen sat on the edge of the bed and smoothed the hair away from her face.

Emma woke up. She didn't ever seem to go though the stage in between being asleep and being wide awake. While Joe would rub his eyes and close them again and take several moments to reach even a semi-comatose state, Emma would be fast asleep one minute and awake and totally compos mentis the next.

'Hello,' she smiled. 'Today at school we read a story about a clown who made everyone laugh but was actually really unhappy. What did you do, Mummy?'

'I met a man who wrote a book to entertain everyone, but who is also quite unhappy.' Helen summarised her impression of Graham Parks, gleaned from her interview and his subsequent revelations in the pub. When she had quizzed him on the record about the missing ten years of his life, he'd talked vaguely about military debriefings, various undemanding jobs and then starting to write. His answers hadn't seemed entirely satisfactory. He appeared to be being honest with her, but she felt he was holding something back.

Emma was asleep again; her moment of consciousness had been brief. Helen wondered if she would remember that she'd been in during the night and spoken to her, or whether by

51

morning their exchange would have been wrapped back up with sleep.

Joe was in the room on the other side of the bathroom. He'd kicked his duvet on to the floor and was lying sideways across the bed, his hand down the front of his pyjamas, oblivious to anything and utterly adorable.

Before Joe was born, Helen hadn't really wanted a boy. They'd seemed too noisy, boisterous, emotional and inarticulate at an early age. When people had asked her if she was hoping for a boy, she had muttered something about not minding what sex the baby was, but secretly she had hoped for another girl. Everyone had told her that mothers and sons had a special relationship, and she could see that her friends adored their mini-men, but she wasn't sure that she would.

Then Joe arrived and she'd backtracked in an instant. He was the most gorgeous, delightful, handsome male ever and she loved all the things she had feared she wouldn't like: the broadness of his back and muscular buttocks; his slow, faltering attempts at speech; his obsession with anything with wheels on. If she had thought boys only became boys because of the way they were raised, Joe made her realise she was wrong. He was male right from the moment he was born, and she loved him for it.

She loved Alex more too. Traits that she had once found irritating in her partner, she now saw as part of his membership of the male sex. His inability to hear what she was saying, or even recognise that she was saying anything at all, she saw repeated in Joe, who, intent on moving a car across the carpet, would be totally oblivious to her calling him for lunch. Alex's habit of watching television apparently unaware that his hand was down the front of his trousers was shared by his son, who sat glued to CBeebies, one hand holding his comfort blanket over his nose, the other cradling his bits.

Joe stirred slightly, reaching out in his sleep to relocate the blanket, which had strayed from its regular position right over his face. He seemed to have an automatic sensor that enabled him to find and reposition it, snuffling contentedly when it was in place.

He had had a friend at nursery who possessed an almost identical comfort blanket. The two boys used to compare size and markings and then, as Joe explained to Helen, 'We go into the corner of the room, put them over our noses and sniff!' He'd inhaled loudly to demonstrate, with the vigour of a cocaine user, and she had visions of the pair as teenagers, shuffling off behind the bike sheds to inhale substances more dangerous than comfort blankets.

She listened to his breathing now. It was steady and even. Joe was asthmatic, and at the first signs of a cold it would become heavier and more laboured.

As she bent towards him, automatically Joe put his hand up and ran it over the back of her head, tactile and loving even in sleep. She tried to imagine what her life would have been like without Alex, Emma and Joe and everything that came with them, but found it impossible.

She kissed Joe's head, taking a deep breath and inhaling the smell of his hair as she did so. Happiness was breathing in the aroma of her children's heads. Even when their hair was filthy and nit-ridden, there was something indescribable about that smell.

'Good night, Jo-Jo,' she said.

8

Alex was shouting 'Unbelievable!' at the telly when she came back downstairs, although the game appeared to be over. A replay of the action showed the beyond-credible incident to be a winning goal scored in the last three seconds of play.

Helen preferred it when Joe was watching football too. He was far more inclusive than Alex, shouting at her to come in from the kitchen so he could describe a moment of footballing brilliance to her.

'I hate the black team!' he'd told her at the weekend, after a lengthy description of how the team in question had scored after a penalty had been awarded in their favour. Looking at the screen, she'd seen a team of Fijian players celebrating and wondered where this racist streak in her son had come from and why her husband was doing nothing to correct him.

'Why does he hate the black players?' she'd asked Alex, who'd laughed and said that Joe was referring to their shirts, not their skin; he always favoured the red of Alex's preferred team, Liverpool, over any other colour. Her mother had a similar system for her once-yearly bet on the Grand National, studying the sports pages of the paper for an aesthetic colour combination before putting a tenner on to win.

'It's probably as good a system as any,' her dad

would comment, proving himself right when, with inexplicable regularity, the jockey with the green and blue hooped jumper or the pink and green starred hat was first to push their horse past the finishing line.

Helen decided that the action replay meant it would be a few more minutes before Alex was ready to talk to her, so she headed for the kitchen to make them both a cup of tea. While waiting for the kettle to boil, she texted Katie.

'Thanks for helping out with kids. Just back and all safely tucked up. Neanderthal man watching football and not talking. Did he speak to you?'

'No worries.' Katie's reply came back as she looked for more tea bags. 'Kids lovely and caveman charming as ever. How was mystery man? Are you free on Friday? Shall we meet up?'

Having located a fresh supply of tea bags, Helen threw two into the bottom of a couple of large cups and began pouring hot water on to them. She could hear Alex muttering things that indicated the football was over.

'Sounds good,' she replied to her friend's text. 'Mystery man was mysterious . . . Caveman appears to be turning back into Prince Charming. Speak soon X X X'

★   ★   ★

'Two goals scored in the last three minutes,' said Alex, as Alan Hansen and Alan Shearer began a post-match discussion with Gary Lineker from behind a desk somewhere in Europe.

'How are you?' he asked, remembering that he was back in the living room and no longer commentating from the sidelines. He stood up and embraced her, adding, 'What kept you at work?'

'The interview with Buddy Jackson was cancelled,' she told him, wondering whether he had been listening that morning when she'd reminded him she had a big feature lined up. 'Or rather reassigned to someone more suited to interviewing literary heavyweights. At the last minute they sent me to talk to a new author called Graham Parks.'

'Any good?' asked Alex.

Helen thought he was probably referring to the book rather than the time she'd spent with the author.

'I didn't get a chance to read it,' she replied, taking her copy of *Excuse Me, I'm Lost* out of her bag and putting it on the table in front of the sofa. 'How was *Muddy Water?*' she asked.

'Good.' Alex was giving the book the once-over, reading the blurb on the back, glancing inside the back cover.

'Looks interesting,' he said. 'Although if I were the publisher, I'd have left his photo out if I wanted to shift copies.'

'They always have an author photo on a hardback.' Helen decided to keep to herself the fact that in person Graham Parks was quietly attractive and unnervingly sexy. 'It's not exactly the usual *Sunday Review* fodder, but he's a friend of Jim Keeble.' She thought that bringing Jim into the conversation might throw Alex off the scent of Graham Parks, not that he seemed to have sniffed out anything of interest in him.

Alex looked up from the book. He usually referred to her brief relationship with the dashing war reporter in much the same way her colleagues did, but Helen wondered if he was secretly jealous.

'Is Lover Boy back from Iraq, then?' he asked.

'Afghanistan, actually,' Helen corrected. 'Apparently he met this Graham Parks in Iraq, though, during the first Gulf War.'

'Isn't that where he was headed when you two split up?' Alex was flicking though the pages of the book absent-mindedly.

Helen had been upset but secretly relieved when Jim Keeble had left the *Hastings Gazette* and gone on to greater things. She had loved being with him but always felt he was too good-looking and too adventurous for her. She had feared it was only a matter of time before he stopped coming back to her seafront flat after late shifts and began visiting someone else's. His moving on to another paper and another country had made his leaving easier, and they had remained friends, or at least friendly whenever they saw each other.

'Apparently he brought the book into the office this morning,' Helen made it clear that she hadn't actually seen him, 'and charmed Shana into giving it coverage.'

Alex had put the book down on the table and was sipping the cup of tea she'd brought.

'Anyway,' Helen continued, 'sorry it made me late. I had been hoping to get home sooner and have a chance to talk to you about the big decision.'

'What big decision?' Alex looked genuinely puzzled.

'The S.N.I.P.,' Helen said, spelling it out. Their discussions about it had been so many and varied over the last few years that she could no longer bring herself to say the word out loud.

'Oh, that,' Alex replied, as if she was simply reminding him he'd agreed to go to Sainsbury's on his day off. 'Yes. I phoned the doctor today and I'm going to see him on Friday. Apparently I have to have a chat with him before they put me on a waiting list.'

'And you're absolutely sure about it?' asked Helen.

'Yes. It's what you want, isn't it?' Alex looked at her for confirmation. 'And I don't want any more children, so it seems logical to go ahead.'

'It just seemed to come rather out of the blue,' Helen said, feeling unsure about the decision now that it appeared to have been made.

'It did not come out of the blue.' Alex was laughing as he said this, and moved closer to Helen on the sofa, putting his arm around her. 'We've been talking about it for years.'

He kissed her on the cheek. It was a kiss that said, 'Now you're being daft. Stop it.'

'We seem to have got used to discussing it but nothing actually happening.' Helen tried to make light of it too. It was the right decision, but that didn't stop her feeling a sense of loss. 'I think it will be better for us.' She looked directly at Alex as she said this, and he moved forward and kissed her again on the lips, less dismissively this time, letting her know that he knew what she meant by this.

'I don't want any more children,' she said, leaning back and taking her husband's hand. 'But I still feel upset that we won't have any more. Does that make sense?'

'Absolutely.' Alex squeezed her hand. 'I feel the same way. We could go on having children for ever, and I'm sure they'd all be absolutely gorgeous like Emma and Joe, but we have to stop sometime, and we haven't had one for a while . . . '

'You're right,' Helen concurred. 'And I really don't think I could face going back to nappies and sleepless nights. It's just the thought of never having another tiny newborn that saddens me.'

'We'll get a rabbit,' said Alex, patting her hand.

'Really?' Helen was surprised. Emma and Joe had been on at them for ages about getting a pet of some sort, but Alex had always been resistant. Too much work, too smelly/hairy/noisy, nowhere for it to go were just some of the objections to the children's carefully prepared speeches about why they should get a dog/guinea pig/ rabbit/cat/ parrot/hamster.

'It might not be happy being locked up all the time and we'd have to find someone to look after it every time we went away,' had been his reason for batting away Emma's recent plea to buy one of the baby rabbits they had seen at a local children's farm a few weekends ago.

'I didn't think you liked rabbits.' Helen wondered if Alex was being serious.

'I do like them,' he answered slowly, as if he hadn't really been serious when he first mentioned a rabbit but was now giving it some consideration. 'I used to have one when I was a child.'

'Did you?' Helen thought she knew everything there was to know about her husband, but every now and then he would surprise her. Of course she realised that you could never really know everything about a person and that there would always be parts of them that remained closed, but a thing like having a rabbit when they were young was hardly a secret.

'Yes.' Alex nodded. 'I got him for my sixth birthday, a little black rabbit called Benjy.'

'Oh, how sweet.' Helen liked the sound of that. 'What happened to him?'

'He died,' said Alex, matter-of-factly. 'But he'd lived for about six years, so I'd lost interest in him by then.'

'You heartless beast.' Helen gave him a small shove.

'Emma and Joe will be the same.' Alex shrugged. 'You'll see. If we get a rabbit they'll love it for a while but it'll be you that ends up having to do all the work.'

'But you are prepared to have one?' Helen asked. She knew that she would probably have to do most of the work anyway and that she could perfectly well go and get the children a rabbit herself, without Alex being particularly happy about it. She'd known this when they'd had previous pet conversations and seen the baby rabbits at the farm, but it seemed that having one would be easier if Alex was on board.

'Yes,' Alex said, straightening his back as if he was about to get up. 'Because the kids may get bored of it, but I know you won't! More tea?'

9

'How was Katie?' Helen asked, as she followed Alex into the kitchen.

'Good.' Alex began filling the kettle, and Helen leafed through a pile of mail on the table. 'She looked really well, in fact.'

'She always looks really well,' said Helen, opening the phone bill.

'Yes, I know.' Alex made no secret of the fact that he found Katie Ryan totally gorgeous. Everyone did. She was. If Katie had brought the children home while Alex had been watching the football, he would probably have switched it off and offered her a glass of wine, even in the middle of a penalty shootout.

Whenever Katie was around, Alex moved the charm up an extra gear. Helen didn't mind. She herself quite fancied Katie's husband Philip, and it seemed harmless, flirting with a friend's husband. She would never in a million years dream of doing anything that would hurt Katie, so Philip was safely off limits to her. It was quite obvious that Alex thought Katie was utterly lovely but that that was as far as things went. It was the women who Helen didn't know, who weren't married, who appeared to her to pose more of a risk.

'So what happened in the great shopping centre up north?' She asked, getting the milk out of the fridge.

Keeping track of the comings and goings in *Muddy Water* was the least she could do in exchange for having more or less compelled Alex to take the part of Kev.

He'd been uncertain whether to audition for the role when his new agent, Nikki, had suggested it. But Nikki was persuasive, and when he was offered the part of the security manager, Helen found that she was too. It was a regular job, three or four days a week, week in week out, with a break during the summer. As far as actors were concerned, that was about as good as it got.

Apart from the odd small part in various network dramas, Alex hadn't done much TV work before, nor had he wanted to. He maintained, with the self-obsession of a true thespian, that treading the boards was more demanding than television, and reasoned that if he started playing drug addicts in *The Bill* on a regular basis, he would never be offered film work. The latter, he thought, was only ever likely to come his way if he toured *Hamlet* with the Royal Shakespeare Company or appeared in new plays in out-of-the-way venues that never transfered to the West End. This meant that he was either away, or at home lapsing into despair that he might never work again, while Helen was breadwinning at the *Sunday Review*.

When Emma was born, Helen began working part time, and money was tight. So when Alex left his agent and signed up with the glamorous, go-getting Nikki, Helen found herself agreeing that he should be trying to do more television and would be perfect for the new BBC sitcom that was currently being cast.

She realised that by taking the part of Kev, Alex had mentally said goodbye to any hopes of film work and to the life touring with a community of actors that he had loved. He told her when he accepted the job that he couldn't keep on as he had been for ever, but she knew he'd done it for her, and for Joe and Emma, shouldering the responsibility of family life even though it meant forgetting his dream.

His new role suited her. He travelled to Manchester for a few days each week, sometimes staying over if the week's storyline involved a lot of Kev. He was never away for more than a couple of days, though, and as Helen usually tried to work one of her three days at home, they only needed minimal childcare.

Gone were the days of readjustment to each other. Previously, when Alex had been away for a long time, she would fall thankfully on to him when he came home, while he was mentally still circling the airport, not quite ready emotionally to land.

Alex seemed happy enough. He enjoyed the times when people recognised him, sometimes as Kev 'off that programme' and sometimes merely as someone who looked vaguely familiar but they weren't quite sure why.

He was stirring the tea now, slowly, his back towards her.

'I think I probably told you . . . ' he began, focusing his attention entirely on the job in hand.

Helen knew this meant he definitely hadn't

told her. Whenever he had anything difficult or awkward to discuss with her, he prefaced his sentences with 'I think I've already mentioned this', or 'I'm sure I've already told you, but', and then finished them with bombshells he definitely had not already told her.

'What might you have told me?' she asked, her tone slightly aggressive, commanding him to get on with it.

'I'm not sure if I mentioned it or not.' Alex was still prevaricating. The tea had definitely had enough stirring. 'I thought it was just talk before and would probably never happen, but Venetia Taylor has joined the cast.'

'You definitely never mentioned that.' Helen would certainly have taken note, even if it was only a possibility and more than likely that nothing would ever come of it. Venetia Taylor would certainly raise the profile of *Muddy Water*. She was bound to attract more viewers, prolonging its life, keeping Alex in regular work for a few more years yet.

Venetia Taylor had been acting since she was six weeks old, when she had appeared in a baby bath commercial. Even then she'd been stunningly beautiful; not just scrumptious and pretty and endearing like most babies, but beautiful, her arresting blue eyes gazing out of a perfect oval face surrounded by a halo of blond hair. Baby Venetia had an unnerving air of wisdom. As she splashed in her tub of bubbles, she looked as if she knew exactly why she was here and exactly where she was going.

Now in her forties, she looked much as she

66

had done when she appeared in that bath on television. Trying to work out which adult had been which baby was usually pretty much guesswork, but Venetia had looked like herself from the moment she first engaged with the public consciousness.

And this she had continued to do for the rest of her life, taking on the roles of a variety of waifs and strays in Dickens adaptations as a child, before a risqué role as a teenager who set out to seduce her mother's boyfriend confirmed her as a serious film actress. She'd continued to make regular appearances on both the big and small screen as well as, latterly, in the tabloids, after her marriage to and subsequent divorce from Dave Horton, centre half for a Premier League football team.

The newspapers told of wild excesses in Venetia and Dave's private life, of how Venetia was dropped from a major feature film because of these excesses and of how about a year ago, Helen remembered, ecstasy tablets were mistaken for Smarties at their son Flynn's second birthday party. This latter revelation had turned Venetia seemingly overnight from hot property to risky investment. The tabloids had lost interest when she divorced Dave, went into rehab and moved with Flynn to a stone cottage in the Peak District, though she was still occasionally snapped wheeling her son in a buggy, dressed in jeans and a T-shirt, without make-up, but looking beautiful nevertheless.

'Apparently she wants to start working again,' Alex was saying. 'But she wants it to fit around her son so that she doesn't have to leave him for days on end with a nanny.'

'And what part,' asked Helen, 'is the still utterly gorgeous Venetia Taylor going to play?'

'I haven't seen the scripts yet,' Alex answered, turning with a cup of tea in either hand and motioning with his head towards the living room.

Helen sat down at the table in the kitchen. She wanted to hear more about Venetia Taylor, and she knew that if they went into the living room, Alex would inevitably switch the news on and only give her half-answers.

'But they've created a part for her?' she persisted.

'Yes,' Alex said. 'It's still a bit sketchy, but I'm told her character is recently divorced and suddenly needs to work, so she applies for a job in security.'

'Not that far from real life, then?' Helen mused, wondering why Alex had not mentioned her joining the cast before.

'Art mirroring life,' he agreed.

'And if she's in security, Venetia Taylor will be working under you, will she?' she continued, knowing that Alex would love being able to tell their friends that he'd had Venetia Taylor under him, and worrying slightly that he would probably also like that to be true.

10

Helen wondered, as she cleaned her teeth, if Alex had thought about Venetia Taylor at all before, during or after they'd had sex the previous night.

He was still asleep when she got up and jumped in the shower, hoping to be out and dressed before anyone else woke up. But he had woken shortly afterwards and wandered blearily into the bathroom, where he had a piss, then undid the towel she'd been wrapped in and gave her a big naked embrace.

'Morning, number one shag,' he said, which was all very nice except that she'd just heard a big thud in Joe's room, which indicated that he was awake, had leapt from his bed and at any moment would come bursting in, asking if it was morning and if she would play air slammer with him.

'Not now, darling,' she would tell him, which was also what she told Alex, extracting herself from his embrace, retrieving the towel and rinsing her toothbrush under the cold tap.

'And who is your number two shag?' she asked, putting her toothbrush in the holder and taking her clothes from the hook on the back of the door.

'Mrs Hazel, I suppose,' Alex answered, referring to Joe's class teacher, whom he (Alex, not Joe) referred to as the Dominatrix, for no reason other than that she had been known to wear high-heeled boots and according to Joe was very strict. She was also quite young and very pretty, and for some reason a lot of the fathers of the children in her class made a concerted effort to take their offspring to school in the mornings, whereas fathers of children whose teachers were older and less alluring generally seemed to have more important things to do.

'I'm sure you're very high in her imaginary shag rankings too,' Helen laughed, pulling her T-shirt over her head as the door swung open, revealing Joe, blanket clutched to his chest, wide-eyed and questioning.

'What is an imaginary shablanky?' he asked, unconsciously winding the end of his blanket round and round his index finger.

Alex took his dressing gown from the back of the bathroom door and knelt down to fill a vital gap in his son's knowledge.

'An imaginary shablanky is what grown-ups have instead of a rag like this,' he told him. 'They don't actually have one, because they're too old, so when they go to bed, they think of something warm and cuddly, which smells lovely, and they think about cuddling up with it and then they can go to sleep.'

This, thought Helen, was a pretty good definition of both what she had said and what Joe had heard. But having asked the question, Joe no longer seemed interested in the answer.

'Can you play air slammer with me, Mum?' he asked.

'Not now, darling,' she said, for a second time.

'I'll play with you when I've made a cup of

tea.' Alex was heading off downstairs to put the kettle on. 'I'm taking you to school this morning, Jo-Jo. Mummy's going to work,' she could hear him saying as he reached the bottom of the stairs.

Left alone with her thoughts again, Helen went back to wondering if he fancied Venetia Taylor and whether she had entered their bedroom via the recesses of Alex's mind (or even the forefront, for that matter).

Venetia could pass herself off as ten years younger than she actually was. So could Alex. He was forty-six, a few years older than Helen, but most people thought they were the same age. Youthful looks were an asset in his profession, extending the range of parts he could play. His age was something he liked to mention on an almost daily basis, beginning sentences with statements such as 'I was talking to Karen about the World Cup final in '66 . . . '

Helen always knew exactly where these opening statements would lead. There were variations in the anecdotes that followed them, but the conversation always went along the lines of 'Surely you don't remember the World Cup in 1966?'

'Yes, I do. I watched it in the living room with my parents. I was wearing my England strip at the time.'

'But you must have only been a baby.'

'No, I'm forty-six, actually!'

'Never!' General disbelief all round, and murmurs of how good he looked for his age.

Helen wondered if it was because Alex was an

actor that he needed this reassurance that he still looked good, or if it was just because he was a man. He did look younger than he was, though, she had to admit. If you scrutinised his face, there were plenty of telltale lines, and the fact that he kept accusing her of shrinking his trousers in the wash showed that he was spreading a bit, but he still had a full head of sandy hair, and a slim, almost boyish figure.

'That's because I keep you young,' Helen would tell him, when he'd come to the inevitable conclusion of his conversation about the World Cup final.

She wondered who or what kept Venetia Taylor from ageing.

Helen thought the actress must be around the same age as her, but she looked early thirties at most, even though she'd partied her way through the last two decades. She must have amazing genes, and plenty of alimony with which to pamper away the years, Helen surmised.

Where would Venetia feature in Alex's imaginary shag rankings?

Helen wondered why she felt jealous and slightly mistrustful of an actress who, by all tabloid accounts, had suffered an unhappy marriage breakdown and was just beginning to rebuild her life, and whom her husband had yet to meet. She also wondered if Venetia joining the cast of *Muddy Water* had spurred Alex's decision to have a vasectomy. She remembered how when she'd been sitting with Graham Parks in the restaurant the night before, she had suddenly realised that if Alex had the snip, it

72

would make it more risky for her to sleep with anyone else. Had it occurred to Alex that there would be one less thing for him to worry about if he decided to stray?

It was the 'I think I probably told you . . . ' statement that had made her suspect that Alex harboured secret fantasies about Venetia Taylor. If he'd had absolutely nothing to hide, he would have just come straight out and told her: 'We had some exciting news today. Venetia Taylor is joining the cast.'

Who wouldn't be excited by the news? There would have been something very wrong with Alex if he hadn't been delighted, if not a little nervous, about appearing alongside one of the country's leading sex symbols, and there would be something slightly wrong with Helen if she didn't feel a slight nervousness about the amount of time Alex would be spending with Venetia, away from home.

Not that Helen didn't trust Alex absolutely. She was as certain as it was possible to be that he loved her and was loyal to her. But she had absolutely no idea how faithful to her he was in his head. No matter how well you knew a person, you could never tell what they were thinking. Even if you asked them, how were you to know if they were telling the truth? And would you want to know anyway?

If she'd asked Alex what he was thinking about while they made love, and he'd told her he was imagining fucking Venetia in the dressing room, it would only have upset and worried her and made her feel insecure. She knew that sometimes

Alex must be fantasising about someone else, as she did, if not during lovemaking then before or after. You could be faithful to someone for fifteen years in practice, but in your head it was impossible.

Helen knew the real reason why she suspected Alex of shagging Venetia Taylor in his head. When they'd gone to bed the night before, she had been hoping he wouldn't fall asleep, exhausted by the day's recording and the train journey back from Manchester. She'd been hoping that he'd want to have sex with her, because she wanted to have sex with someone, having been aroused earlier in the day by Graham Parks.

11

Helen checked her watch as she pushed the down button in the lift at the *Sunday Review*. Four thirty. With luck she could be home by half past five, two hours earlier than usual.

Shana had said something about realising she'd had to work late the night before and not needing to attend a meeting at five o'clock. Helen had jumped at the chance, not even wanting to find out what the meeting was about. Getting home early on Thursday would extend the weekend. She'd have a whole evening with Alex tonight; she'd arranged to meet Katie tomorrow, and this would be followed by a Saturday and Sunday with nothing planned. Luxury.

She checked her watch again. It was 4.31 when the lift stopped to let people in on the seventh floor. She was still studying it, for no other reason than that it gave her something to do instead of looking up and making eye contact with the newly arrived occupants of the lift, when she felt someone wedge themselves into the space beside her.

'Four thirty!' said the presence next to her. 'Time for a quick drink with me before you head off wherever it is you're heading off to?'

This seemed to be more of a command than a question, and it had been uttered by the *Sunday Review's* chief foreign correspondent.

'Hello,' Helen said, looking up at the tanned face of Jim Keeble. 'Shouldn't you be in Helmand Province?'

'Home leave,' pronounced Jim, stooping to kiss her. It was more of a snog really. Jim never bothered with pecks on the cheek. Why would he, when there were always plenty of women willing to kiss him several degrees more passionately? Helen could feel the eyes of the rest of the lift's passengers looking at them with some curiosity, while pretending not to.

'So, how long have you been back?' she stuttered, trying to keep the conversation inane until they reached the ground floor.

'A few weeks now,' Jim told her.

'You must be finding it rather quiet,' she mused.

'Not exactly,' Jim replied as the lift finally reached ground level. 'Where are you off to? Have you got time for a quick drink?'

Helen checked her watch again. Still only just after half past four. She wasn't expected home for a couple of hours, and although she'd planned to surprise Alex and the kids with an early appearance, she could squeeze in half an hour with Jim and still be back in good time.

Nevertheless, she felt slightly guilty about it. She'd been late the night before and missed Emma and Joe's bedtime, and felt she ought to redress the balance tonight. But then again, she was at home for the next four days and she hadn't seen Jim Keeble for a couple of years. Having a quick drink wouldn't do anyone any harm. It would give them a chance to catch up, and she had an ulterior motive for wanting a drink with him too.

'Okay,' she agreed. 'But it'll have to be quick.'

'The Grape Press?' he suggested, referring to a wine bar round the corner from the tower block that housed the *Sunday Review*. 'Or the Crested Canary?'

The Crested Canary was a slightly longer walk but likely to be quieter. It was favoured more by City types and was less likely to fill up with hacks. Contradicting her earlier statement that she'd have to be quick, Helen opted for the Crested Canary.

'So what have you been up to?' Jim asked, as they walked by the river to the pub.

'I met up with an old friend of yours, actually,' Helen told him, her ulterior motive for having a drink with him surfacing sooner than she'd intended.

'Don't tell me,' Jim interrupted. 'Not someone from the *Hastings Gazette*?'

'No,' Helen went on. 'Someone from the battlefield. Graham Parks.'

She said his name quietly, not wanting to give away any emotion.

'Oh yes, Graham Parks.' Jim stopped outside the Crested Canary and held the door for Helen. 'I haven't seen him in a few years, but I know he's written a book.'

'That's right.' Helen paused on the other side of the door, waiting for Jim to come to the bar with her. '*Someone* gave it to Shana, and muggins here had to do a last-minute interview.'

'Guilty.' Jim laughed and put his arm round

77

her. It was just a friendly gesture, though Helen was aware that it made them appear to be a couple when they arrived at the bar.

The barman addressed them as a single entity. 'What are you having?' he asked, pushing a bowl of olives towards them as he spoke.

'Are you still a Sauvignon Blanc girl?' Jim asked, skewering an olive with a cocktail stick.

'I'm not sure that I qualify as a girl any more,' Helen told him. 'But no, I haven't changed my drinking habits in the last fifteen years. A glass of Sauvignon Blanc, please.' She directed the latter request to the barman.

'And a glass of Shiraz,' Jim said. 'I haven't changed my drinking habits either. I just seem to drink more of it. So what's Graham's book like?'

'I haven't read it,' Helen told him. 'You only brought it into the office yesterday morning. I got sent to meet him last night.'

'Sorry.' Jim seemed willing to accept his role in the last-minute interview. 'He's a nice bloke, though. Did you like him?'

'Yes,' Helen replied, keeping to herself the thought 'quite a lot, actually'. Out loud she asked, 'So, apart from upping your alcohol intake, what have you been doing since I saw you last?'

Jim began filling her in on the details of the last few years. He'd spent time reporting in Karachi, Basra, a brief stint in Kabul and latterly Helmand. In between, his wife, Penny, had had another child and they'd acquired a nanny so she could go back to derivatives trading in the city within months of Toby being born.

'How about you?' he asked. 'I gather Alex Mills has become something of a household name. Are you two still together?'

'Yes,' said Helen, finishing her drink and looking at her watch. 'In fact, I really ought to go home now. I was late last night and Alex is up in Manchester half the week, so we don't get that many nights when we're both home.'

'One more drink.' Jim put his hand on her shoulder, urging her to stay put.

'Haven't you got a home to go to?' Helen joked, gathering her bag up in a gesture that signalled she did have a home and wanted to get back to it.

'That's a good question,' Jim replied. 'And one that I can only answer if I have another drink. Join me?'

'Oh go on then.' Helen put her bag down again. 'Another glass of white wine,' she said to the barman. 'And another Shiraz.'

The barman poured two fresh glasses of wine and took the twenty-pound note Helen offered him in return.

'What's happened to your home, then?' She turned back to Jim. 'I can't believe you and the financially astute Penny got a dodgy mortgage deal and are now facing repossession.'

'No.' Jim took a large gulp of wine. 'I still have a home. I'm just not very welcome in it any more.'

12

Katie Ryan hadn't yet become invisible. This was quite an achievement, as all the requirements for invisibility were in place. She was in her late thirties, had two small children, one still trailing around after her for much of the day, and no gainful employment for the time being. Yet people saw her.

As a rule, they didn't see Helen.

Her invisibility had been a gradual process. She wasn't like Harry Potter with his cloak, which he could throw around his shoulders to make himself disappear; she was simply slowly fading. It had started when Emma was born. Attention automatically focused on the baby. Helen would go into shops and find people addressing the bundle in the pram, and realised she was no longer a fully fledged person in her own right, but an arm that steered the pram through south London's congested streets.

At work she found she had changed from a solid presence that occupied a position in the office on a daily basis to a shadowy figure that occasionally flitted in and out but, because it only did so part time, could largely be ignored.

Even people associated with the children appeared unable to see her very clearly.

Last week she'd been in the supermarket with Joe, choosing a cucumber with which he could shoot other shoppers. Joe had been shouting

'Bang, bang!' when Helen had noticed the teacher from the class next door to Joe's browsing in the tomato section. This particular teacher was a man, and therefore highly visible to the armies of mothers stuck at home for much of the day, whose only male company came in the form of five year olds or the occasional knock on the door from the postman.

'Hello,' she had said. 'We're just choosing an AK47.'

He'd looked at her as if she was completely mad, and when the child with him had asked, loudly, who that was, he had replied that he had absolutely no idea.

Helen suspected that if he'd come across Katie trying to select Kalashnikovs from the fruit and vegetable aisle, he'd have known exactly who she was.

As Katie strode across the park towards Helen now, a picnic basket slung over her shoulder and a folded rug tucked under her arm, a group of teenagers momentarily paused in their game of football to give her the once-over. They hadn't seen Helen until their ball hit her in the small of the back, causing them all to screw up their eyes and squint to try and make out what it was that had passed through their field of play without their noticing.

One of the boys had run towards her. 'Sorry,' he'd muttered, scooping up the ball and turning at the same time. Helen wondered whether, if it had turned out that the impact of the ball had caused her spleen to rupture and her picture was splashed across the front of the local newspaper accompanied by a 'Mother dies after being hit by football' headline, any of the boys would recognise her; whether they would put their hands up to their part in this tragedy or if they would already have genuinely forgotten that she existed.

They'd remember Katie, though. They were taking in the details now, as she walked towards Helen. The above-the-knee dress that revealed fantastic legs, the glossy brown hair still unfettered by grey, and the large, dark, smiling eyes.

Having had a momentary gawp, one of the boys kicked the ball, but his friend was still transfixed by Katie and it shot past him and through the makeshift goal composed of two hoodies placed at strategic points on the grass.

'You just scored a goal,' Helen told her as Katie sat down on the rug, stretching out her tanned legs before scanning the near distance to check that her child was still with her.

'Did I?' she asked, happily, as if that was the one thing she had hoped to achieve that day. Perhaps that was what made Katie so visible: she exuded upbeat contentment. She wasn't fussed about getting older, didn't mind having only a two year old for company for much of the day, didn't secretly crave the stimulation of a job while beating herself up about neglecting her children. She just got on with life and enjoyed it.

'What's the gossip, then?' Katie asked. When they had first met and she found Helen worked for the *Sunday Review*, she had expected her to be able to reveal gossip of national interest.

Sometimes Helen could oblige, revealing that the Home Secretary had been seen at a lap-dancing club or that a famous film star was a closet transvestite. More often the gossip was less titillating: a new book about to be published or a film she'd seen the preview of. Today it concerned herself.

'Well . . . ' She waved at Leonard, Katie's two year old, who was toddling towards them carrying a large teddy. 'Venetia Taylor is joining the cast of *Muddy Water*, Alex has decided to have the snip, Jim Keeble has been having an affair and we are going to get a rabbit.' She decided to hold back on telling her friend she was still feeling deeply unnerved by her meeting with Graham Parks.

'Wow.' Katie seemed excited by the prospect of being able to discuss all of this. She moved the teddy, which Leonard had deposited on her lap, on to the rug and ruffled Leonard's hair before he turned and ran off towards the sandpit. 'Are they connected?'

'I'm not sure.' Helen was about to tell her friend that the rabbit was definitely a third-child substitute and that she feared the snip decision might have been brought about by the imminent arrival of Venetia Taylor, but they were interrupted by the strains of 'Don't Worry, Be Happy' emanating from Katie's bag.

She fished her phone out, mouthed, 'I'd better get this' to Helen and answered it.

'Hello, Philip,' she beamed. 'I'm in the park with Helen and Leonard.'

Dr Philip Ship was the love of Katie's life and

possibly the unrequited love of several of his students. He taught poetry at South London University, and since most of the would-be poets were either suicidal or hopeless romantics, he tended to inspire desperation and devotion in equal measures. Katie appeared to take all this in her stride, laughing when the word *Dreamboat* was found scrawled across the door of his office, taking it as an indirect personal compliment when the students dedicated their poems to him and professing publicly that she would rather they found him dreamy than tweedy and staid.

Dreamboat was not just a reference to his name. There was something compelling behind the impression Philip gave of chaotic distraction, a spark beneath his loosely buttoned laidback attire, a passion in his softly spoken syllables. Dr Ship was the sort of person people wanted to sit next to at dinner. He'd listen to what you had to say, make you feel that it was brilliant, throw an observation of his own into the mix that confirmed your theory was insightful and astounding, and laugh as if he liked you. It was easy to see why his students loved him, yet Katie didn't appear to feel threatened by his almost universal quality of attractiveness to members of the opposite sex.

'Okay, see you later.' She was winding up the conversation. 'I love you.'

'That should keep his students at bay,' Helen commented. 'Calls in the middle of the day to a wife who loves him.'

'Yes, I should really have said 'I like you',' joked Katie. 'Or rather, 'I only quite like you when you get back just before the children go to bed, timing it so they have had baths, been read stories and are so sleepy that all they require of you is a quick kiss.' Or 'I find you slightly irritating when, having given them that quick kiss, you pour yourself a glass of wine, sit down to dinner and then take a phone call in which you start discussing the effect of opiates on the poetry of Coleridge instead of talking to me.' But that would take too long to say at the end of every conversation.'

'There must be a way of programming it into your phone,' mused Helen, 'so that you could just say goodbye and then press the right button and the phone would say it all for you.'

'There probably is.' Katie raised her eyebrows in an expression that implied the phone was capable of all sorts of things but she was not. 'But signing off all my conversations with Phil like that probably wouldn't do much to keep the students at bay. Oh God, Leonard is sitting halfway up that tree.'

Leonard had wandered off and somehow clambered up a tree. Katie went to get him down but could not quite reach the branch he had wrapped himself around like an overgrown, podgy caterpillar. Helen heaved herself off the rug, intending to help, but she wasn't needed. The footballing lads were already there. One of them had jumped on to the shoulders of another, and in this giant formation they had been able to scoop the two year old down and hand him back to his beautiful mother.

Katie's body language was flirtatious as she

thanked them. She was smiling and extending her chest just a little as she raised her hand to flick hair away from her eyes. The gesture seemed unconscious, but Helen was sure the lads had noticed. They were in no hurry to get back to their game, stopping instead to wonder with Katie how Leonard had got up there in the first place, disappearing only when Helen heaved into view and said hi.

Perhaps flirting was not exactly what Katie was doing. It was more that she exuded such a sense of wanting to communicate with everyone around her that people found her intoxicating. In many ways it was this that made her the perfect foil to Dreamy Phil. While scores of twenty-something women and quite a lot of twenty-something men fell under his intellectual spell, scores of other men, and a few women as well, were inexplicably drawn to Katie.

'Do you ever worry about Phil's students?' Helen asked, when they were back on their rug, unpacking foil-wrapped sandwiches and Tupperware boxes of grapes.

'I try not to think about it really,' Katie replied, trying to prevent Leonard from heading back up the tree by biting through the cellophane on a packet of chocolate fingers. 'I mean, half the time I like the fact that people find him attractive.' She paused. 'In an abstract way it validates what we have together. I chose a man that a lot of others would like to have chosen, and he chose me.'

'But doesn't it bother you that he gets to say seemingly meaningful things about poetry to groups of people intent on finding meaning, and you just get to tell him that Leonard got stuck up a tree?'

'Sometimes, but none of that is real.' Katie held out the packet of chocolate fingers to Helen, who shook her head. In the last few days since meeting Graham Parks, she hadn't been eating nearly as much chocolate as usual. Katie continued. 'I mean, they don't have to live with him. They don't know the real Phil. If they did, they would probably end their phone conversations with 'I only actually quite like you', although . . . '

'What?'

'Sometimes I wonder if he might overstep the student/teacher boundaries.' Katie bit off the end of a chocolate finger. 'I was waiting for him in his office the other day and found a card from a student thanking him for helping her with her dissertation.'

'And?'

'I don't know. There was just something about the wording that made me wonder if we've got it right.'

'What do you mean?' Helen wanted to hear about Katie's insecurities. She wanted her to worry about Dreamy Phil in the same way she had begun to worry about Alex and Venetia Taylor. It meant she wasn't being paranoid, just normally anxious.

'I wouldn't want to swap roles,' Katie continued. 'But sometimes I wish there was someone to worship me the way Phil's students worship him.'

'Yes.' Helen thought about what her friend had said. She had Graham Parks' mobile phone number and email address folded up inside her wallet. She hadn't contacted him yet and she knew it would be better if she didn't. But she wanted to, desperately. She wasn't quite sure what it was that she wanted from him or what he wanted from her, but she felt she had to see him again.

13

'Is this what kept you at work the other night?' Alex was flicking through a pile of papers left lying around in the garden centre café, while Emma and Joe ran riot through a maze of flowerpots. They were having a break in between buying rabbit accoutrements and heading to a children's farm in Croydon to pick up a small furry something to go with them.

Alex held up the section of the *Sunday Review* he'd been reading and showed Helen the piece she had written about Graham Parks.

'Careful, Joe,' Helen shouted. She watched him knock the corner of a tall terracotta planter as he rushed past in pursuit of his older sister, who appeared to be hiding, not very well, behind a large blue ceramic sphere. 'You might break something.'

Joe turned to face his parents, his face flushed from running but also in anticipation of where they were all going just as soon as they had finished drinking tea and looking at papers.

'Can we go now?' he asked, helping himself to a sachet of sugar and beginning to tear it open.

'Don't do that, Jo-Jo. You've had enough sugar.' Alex had bought the children each a large jam doughnut, which had fuelled their breakneck-speed slalom through the ornamental pot section of the centre. 'We'll go in another ten

89

minutes. The farm doesn't open till lunchtime anyway.'

Neither of the children could believe their luck when Alex had told them they'd decided to get a rabbit, and Emma had remained sceptical about the possibility of it actually happening until Alex had logged on to Freecycle, found an unwanted hutch (previously used by a ferret breeder who had been shut down by the RSPCA, though he spared the children this detail) and brought it home. In almost the same sweep of grand gesture, he'd been on the phone to the children's farm and booked a baby rabbit to be picked up on Sunday morning, and in between all of this he'd somehow managed to fit in a visit to the doctor and booked himself in for a vasectomy.

This week was turning out to be full of surprises. Alex was waving the relevant section of the *Sunday Review* under Helen's nose. Her piece was small and tucked away in a corner, allowing maximum exposure for the feature on Buddy Jackson. She cursed inwardly, but was pleased they had at least run her brief piece. They'd only slotted it into the 'Ones To Watch Out For' section, but it was there. Beside a small picture of the author (it didn't look so bad reduced in size), his life and book were reduced to eight hundred words, written by her.

'Not much to show for a week spent reading his book.' She nodded towards the giant photo of Buddy Jackson. 'And a late-night interview.'

She handed the paper back to Alex, who scanned it briefly and grunted before turning the page. Helen was relieved that he didn't seem the least bit interested. Obviously she was doing a good job at disguising the feelings Graham Parks had stirred in her.

'Ha!' Something had caught Alex's attention on the next page. 'That must be an old photo. He doesn't appear to have aged at all.'

'Who?' Helen had no idea what he was talking about.

Alex flashed the page he was looking at towards her. There, accompanying a picture of a helicopter hovering over mountains in Afghanistan, was a photograph of a youthful-looking Jim Keeble striding through a bombed-out village, wearing a flak jacket. He looked much as he had done a few nights ago in the bar at the Crested Canary, tall, still fit, definitely handsome, even if he appeared a touch arrogant. He knew he was all of the above and seemed to think he was brave and daring to boot.

'It looks fairly recent to me,' she said, before realising that this was not what Alex wanted to hear, for two reasons. Firstly, while he was ageing well, it was important to him and his ego that everyone around him should be growing rapidly older and showing all the signs of it. Secondly, she hadn't told him that she'd not only seen Jim Keeble since he arrived back in the country, but also been for a drink with him.

'Have you seen the George Clooney lookalike recently, then?' Alex picked up on both these things immediately.

'Yes, I bumped into him in the lift when I was coming home the other night.' This was, strictly speaking, true. She had bumped into him in the lift. She was just omitting to tell Alex that they'd then gone for a drink in the Crested Canary.

'And?' Alex was looking at her curiously.

'And what?' Helen met his gaze and tried to look unflustered.

'How was he?' There was something slightly challenging in Alex's tone. 'Apart from still ridiculously handsome.'

Helen noticed the headline that was hovering above the pictures of the helicopter and Jim: *HOW LONG WILL WE BE AT WAR?* She smiled as she read it.

'Why are you smiling?' Alex didn't seem to want an answer to his earlier enquiry about Jim Keeble's health.

'It's just this headline.' She showed it to him. 'When I ran into Jim at work, he told me he and Penny were having a few problems. He used military terminology to describe the state of their relationship. I wonder if the headline is aimed at her?'

'You never mentioned that.' Alex looked slightly put out.

'I forgot. There were more important things on my mind.' She didn't say, 'Like Graham Parks, like your forgetting to tell me that Venetia Taylor had joined the cast of *Muddy Water*, like your decision to have the snip and get a rabbit.' But she thought all of those things.

'So what's up between him and Penny?'

'Apparently he'd been having an affair with a French war reporter he'd met in Basra. Penny found out and is livid.' Helen summed up Jim's marital situation as she understood it from what he'd told her in the pub.

'I'm not surprised.' Alex looked pleased to have found a chink in the handsome war reporter's armour. He didn't ask how she had managed to find out such a lot from a brief encounter in the office lift.

'That Penny is livid or that he's been having an affair?' Helen wondered if either fact was really surprising.

'Both,' Alex said, almost gleefully. 'Penny must be furious, but then Jim Keeble's the sort of person who would have an affair.'

'Is there such a thing?' Helen wondered if some people were more predisposed to having affairs than others or whether they just found themselves in different sets of circumstances. She didn't think Alex was the sort of person to have an affair, but she hadn't thought she was the sort of person to start obsessing over someone she'd met briefly while working, either.

'Where's there a fair?' Emma was tugging at Alex's sleeve. 'Can we go?'

'There isn't a fair anywhere.' Alex laughed. 'So no, we can't go.'

'I meant, can we go now to get Bugsy?' Emma asked. She had made a unilateral decision that this would be what the rabbit was called, despite Joe pleading for it to be called Rabbit.

'Okay, I think we're just about finished, aren't we?' Alex didn't wait for Helen to answer but began picking up a large bag of hay. 'Can you manage the food pellets?'

Helen nodded as she bent down to bring out a packet of condensed grass pellets from under their table. Alex, Emma and Joe were already heading for the exit, leaving her to gather the rest of the newly acquired pet accessories.

She tidied the newspapers before she left, taking a quick look at the beginning of Jim Keeble's article before she closed it. He'd written something about 'opening lines of communication', a phrase she seemed to remember him using about trying to talk to Penny.

She'd been shocked when he told her he'd been having an affair, not least because it had been going on for two years and had started just after their second son was born.

'I was lonely,' he'd told her, as if that excused his behaviour. 'I've been away from home such a lot these last few years. I love Penny and the boys. It didn't mean anything.'

'Two years is a long time for something meaningless to carry on,' Helen had said, instantly taking Penny's side. 'And being away from home is no excuse.'

She meant this. Absence was supposed to make the heart grow fonder, not the loins go looking for another pair of loins. It didn't really say much for Jim that he thought being away from home for long periods of time justified his actions, but like Alex, she wasn't really surprised. Jim had always had a selfish streak and put his needs above those of others.

Helen had given him an edited version of her thoughts as they'd left the pub that evening to go their separate ways, but he'd persisted in trying to rationalise his behaviour.

'Lots of the guys out there are having affairs. You've no idea what it's like. It's not just the fact that you are away but the situation you find yourself in. You need some sort of comfort.' He should really have left it at that, but he asked Helen one final question before heading off in the opposite direction.

'Don't you ever worry about Alex when he's away?'

14

The next morning, Helen decided she would email Graham Parks. She'd been wanting to contact him since they'd met but had been putting it off because she wasn't quite sure if she ought to.

He had handed her his email address, written on the back of an old bus ticket, when they had finally ended their conversation or finished the interview (depending on how Helen was treating the encounter in her head) and said goodbye. She'd nearly emailed him several times but had held back, partly delaying the gratification of the moment, and partly because she didn't want to look too keen.

Alex was going up to Manchester a day earlier than usual, staying over an extra night. The change of plan was something to do with a script meeting occasioned by the addition of Venetia Taylor to the cast. Helen wasn't sure of the exact details or if Venetia would be there. Alex had seemed vague on this point and he appeared slightly distracted now.

'What are you up to today?' he asked, emptying the bowl that was a receptacle for everything that didn't have a place on to the kitchen table. He was evidently looking for something.

'Finishing off a bit of work this morning,' she told him. 'Cleaning out the rabbit hutch.

Hannah's coming home with Emma after school tonight to meet Bugsy. Katie will probably stay for a drink when she comes to pick her up.' She didn't tell him that she was finally going to email Graham Parks — for obvious reasons.

Alex ignored her and went on rummaging through the contents of the bowl. She could probably have said 'Getting in touch with a man I met last week and was instantly and inexplicably attracted to' without him paying much attention.

'Are you looking for something?' she asked.

'I can't find my keys.' Alex was perplexed. He knew he had put them in the bowl, because that was where he put them, religiously, every time he walked through the door, so that he would know where they were every time he walked out of it.

'They might be in my bag.' Helen picked it up off the floor and added its contents to the scattered objects on the table, creating a centrepiece that reminded her of the memory game she had loved as a child, in which a number of objects were placed on a tray, players were given a minute to look at them and then had to recall as many as they could.

She surveyed the table briefly now, as if she were about to play, mentally noting what had come out of her bag and the bowl. Chewing gum, sunglasses, a half-eaten packet of Rolos, lipstick, a packet of fuse wire, a spud gun, half a mouldy potato, diary, mobile phone, her keys and Alex's keys.

'Why were they in your bag?' Alex was annoyed. He'd lost valuable time looking for them and he had a train to catch.

'Sorry.' She assumed an apologetic tone. 'I had to go to the corner shop before breakfast as we'd run out of milk, and I couldn't find mine.'

'I'm not surprised,' muttered Alex. He never expected Helen to be able to find anything, because she never put anything away, or, if she did, not where it was supposed to go.

Pocketing his keys, he carried on with the routine he went through every time he left the house. This involved checking and double-checking he'd got everything he needed. It drove Helen mad that he would say goodbye and ten minutes later still be there, making sure the back door was locked and that he'd put his wallet in his overnight bag and remembered his wash bag.

'Did I pack my toothbrush?' he asked. He wasn't actually asking her, but she decided to answer anyway.

'You probably did, and even if you didn't, I imagine Manchester runs to toothbrushes. So you could always buy one.'

'You sound as if you're trying to get rid of me,' said Alex, locating the toothbrush exactly where he would have expected himself to have put it. 'Bye, darling.' He kissed her and held her briefly. 'Back on Thursday evening. Will you . . . '

'Will I what?' Helen suspected he'd been about to check that she would clear up the mess on the kitchen table, which he had helped create, but thought better of it. She would, but probably not until Thursday, about half an hour before he was due home. Alex away for three nights meant nearly four days of not having to put everything

98

where it was supposed to go the minute it was supposed to go there.

'Nothing.' He kissed her again and headed for the door.

Once she heard it close behind him, Helen switched on the computer in the corner of the living room.

She had another quick look at the piece she had written about Graham Parks. She didn't really like it, because she'd written more or less what Shana had told her to. Shana wanted the story of the soldier turned author who had penned a Bridget Jones for men. This was the persona the publishing company had obviously hoped would emerge when they wrote their press release to accompany the book. No one except Helen seemed interested in the lost years, the sadness behind the humour of the book, or the man he actually was.

She was afraid he'd be disappointed, let down, after giving her so much of his time. So although she was finally allowing herself to type in the email address he'd given her, she was also reluctant to do so.

To: graham.parks@virgin.net
From: helen.collins@ntlworld.com
Subject:

She couldn't think of a subject, so she left it blank.

'Dear Graham,' she began.

Helen knew that 'Hi' was the generally accepted way to begin an email, but she didn't like it. She hadn't quite got to grips with the brevity of the form, and was always surprised when PR companies answered her lengthy and formal interview requests with one-liners such as 'That'll be fine.' She still wrote emails as if she was writing a letter. She sent the equivalent of a short letter to Graham Parks.

It was very good to meet you the other day. Thank you for your time and the extra time you gave me too. I have now read the book and it is utterly brilliant! I'm afraid you were vying for space on the page with Bloody Buddy Jackson, and as you will have seen if you picked up a copy of the *Sunday Review* yesterday, my piece about you was squeezed to almost nothing. Also, I know and you know that you are so much more than a literary James Blunt or a male Bridget Jones, but those are the clichés that appealed to my editor and therefore remained in the piece.

Sorry if it seems the extra time you gave me was wasted. I will tell everyone I come into contact with that you have been undersold and are an amazing and brilliant man, best accessed via your book.

Very best wishes,
Helen x

She put a kiss at the end because he had kissed her when they left the pub, a formal peck planted on her right cheek, an identical kiss, in fact, to the one he had given Claire, the PR, but a warm one nevertheless, which reinforced her feeling that something had passed between them.

She reread the email before sending it. She'd tried to tread a line between being professional and wanting to put something of herself and her feelings towards him into the few words she'd allowed herself to write. She pressed the send button and watched the 'Message sent' confirmation appear on the screen, along with an invitation to add Graham Parks to her contacts. For some reason she declined, preferring to remember his email address, along with those of a select group of friends and work colleagues who were regular recipients of emails from her.

Helen wondered if he would reply. There was no reason why he should, but then again there was no reason why he should have given her his email address either. But he had. Was this purely so she could contact him if she needed any more information for the article? Or was it also so that they could continue their conversation?

She sat staring at the screen, with its 'Graham Parks has not been added to your contacts' announcement, trying to pigeonhole in her own mind the feelings Graham had stirred inside her. She was not quite able to categorise them. He wasn't good-looking in any conventional sense, but she was definitely attracted to him. He was slightly on edge, and yet she felt entirely comfortable with him. She loved her husband and children more than anything and wouldn't do anything to jeopardise their family, but she desperately wanted to hear from Graham Parks again.

She'd been sitting for so long that her

computer put itself to bed. When she woke it up again with a tap of the keyboard, there was a message-received icon flashing. She went straight to her inbox. There was just one new message, no subject, but the sender was Graham Parks.

Dear Helen ☺,

I'm glad you emailed because I had no address for you and didn't want to appear too stalkerish by phoning the *Sunday Review* and asking for it. However, I did do a bit of cyber-stalking and spent the weekend reading some of your articles (and you read the book — so that makes us even). I love the way you write. You analyse everything with a lightness of touch that made me want to read or go and see everything you have written about. I am sure there are many authors, actors and others out there who have reason to be grateful to you. I include myself among them. The word count may have been low, but you managed to perfectly encapsulate the spirit of the book and paint an intriguing picture of me, which, were I not already overfamiliar with the book, would make me want to read it. Not everyone was so kind. Moreover, even if the piece had been dropped entirely, I would not consider any of the time I spent with you wasted. It's a cliché (I can't seem to get away from them), but it was a pleasure to meet you.

Graham x

15

It was apparent from the way Alex was orchestrating breakfast that his mind was elsewhere. Helen had thought he seemed distracted when he came back from Manchester the previous evening; now, as he dolloped honey on to a piece of toast that wasn't actually on a plate, she knew that something was wrong.

He was usually so pernickety, and breakfast was no exception. It bothered him if the children started eating toast without first removing their cereal bowls from the table. He was visibly distressed if a pudding fork found its way into the cutlery compartment intended for dinner forks, and he was perpetually annoyed with Helen for failing to monitor the sell-by dates on food in the fridge.

He hated the way she ate toast more or less straight from the toaster, pausing only to butter it in mid-air before munching it while moving round the kitchen. He had a complex ritual of transferrals: from toaster to plate, from plate to toast rack (a Christmas present from Helen's mother, who, despite thinking that Alex should have a proper job, admired his attention to domestic detail), then from toast rack to individual plates to be buttered and spread. Sometimes Helen thought Alex ought to have been a Buddhist monk, since he seemed to prefer the ritual of preparation to the actual eating of food. Warming the teapot was his personal form of meditation, which got his days off to a good start.

But here he was spooning honey on to toast that had somehow got itself on the work surface and looked as if it might be transferred straight to his mouth without a plate so much as getting a look in.

'Are you okay?' Helen asked, trying to sound concerned rather than critical. Alex usually regarded any enquiries from her regarding his health or state of mind as a precursor to criticism, her way of opening a debate on issues such as why he appeared offhand, why he'd forgotten that it was Joe's school play on Friday or why he hadn't thought to pick up anything for dinner on the way home. As in 'Is there anything bothering you, because you have forgotten to do what I asked you to while I was at work?'

'Fine,' he said, taking a bite of the errant toast.

She left it at that and took the opportunity to make some for herself so that she could eat it straight off the side with impunity — a rare treat.

Helen had learned to live with Alex's slight obsessive-compulsive streak, checking her natural tendency towards chaos and recognising that his orderliness was an asset to a house whose occupants were constantly searching for something. Unlike her, Alex instantly knew what the state of play was with Joe's PE kit. He could recall exactly where in the laundry cycle his football shirt was likely to be, and if it was still in the machine, he knew that his spare shirt was washed and dried though still in a pile of clothes yet to be put away.

Initially Helen had been rather fearful of Alex's preoccupation with order, scared that she was failing him with her total disregard for it, troubled by the annoyance he showed when she failed to meet his standards. But now she recognised that having a place for everything and everything in its place was Alex's way of dealing with the chaos of life. There were infinite numbers of variables over which he had no control: offers of work or the lack of them, the probability of terrorists striking London again, Joe's asthma, and whatever it was that had started to bother him while he was away this week.

The world outside their four walls was full of uncertainties, but here at home, the semblance of order he could create was reassuring.

Sometimes Helen revelled in the deliberate destruction of Alex's pristine existence. On one occasion he suffered a complete sense of humour failure after she had written a piece about cyberchondria, the self-diagnosis of various illnesses via the internet. As an example, she had cited her husband, who could barely log on without discovering that the slightly bad back he'd complained of was the first symptom of MS. Of course, she'd exaggerated her account for the sake of the piece, which was light in tone, but Alex was petulant, slamming the newspaper down on the table, calling her childish and exploitative and leaving for work without saying goodbye.

She was so annoyed by his disproportionate reaction that she struck where she knew it would hurt, deliberately sabotaging the alphabetical ordering of his CD collection in a way that was carefully calculated to cause maximum annoyance. She could have gone for the straightforward total jumble, but that would have been too easily identifiable and felt too reckless. Instead she moved albums to locations that, she would later argue, were more appropriate, but which she knew Alex would find toe-curlingly unbearable. So, KC and the Sunshine Band (why it was there in the first place she had no idea), carefully filed under K, she switched to S; Graham Parker and the Rumour was moved from P to R and Radiohead (and this was stretching the point) from R to H.

Alex was mystified when it gradually dawned on him that everything was not in its place but not entirely out of place either. Initially he blamed Emma, who, a week or so previously, had staged an impromptu disco in the living room with two of her friends. They'd drawn the curtains and put the lights out, created strobe effects with a selection of torches and taken turns DJ-ing with the CD player. Helen, now slightly scared of how Alex might react if he found Bob Marley and the Wailers filed under W, wondered whether she should let a couple of eight-year-old disco queens take the blame. Eventually she confessed, subjecting herself to further accusations of childishness.

Alex had been angered not so much by the wanton destruction of the order he had so meticulously created, but because by attacking his weak spot she had abused his trust. Not many people realised that he had this slightly obsessive streak. To the outside world he appeared cool and laid back, his easy manner disguising his inner insecurities. Helen was one of the few privy to his anxieties, and by exploiting them she was aiming below the belt.

When Helen first met Alex, she had simply thought his immaculate flat was the result of a day spent cleaning and tidying in an effort to impress her. When he invited her there for dinner a week or so after trying to kill her, she didn't believe his assertion that he'd spent the day cycling out to Epping Forest (he would later tell her that only a vast amount of physical exertion could quell his pre-match nerves), but imagined that somewhere out the back there would be a mountain of bin bags, containing the detritus he had spent hours obliterating. When a year into their relationship the flat remained spotless, even on the occasions when she surprised him by dropping by unannounced, she realised that the sparkling surfaces in the bathroom were not for her benefit.

So when Alex put the honey pot back in the drawer that he had insisted was for herbs and spices, she knew there must be something bothering him. That particular jar lived in the cupboard above the toaster, with its family of jams and sandwich spread — a place he had earmarked specifically after taking time off work for that purpose when their new kitchen was installed several years ago. Although he rarely cooked, it was he who thought the knives should live in the drawer on the other side of the room from the cooker, and though this was impractical, Helen didn't have the energy to argue or upset his way of doing things.

'Is anything bothering you?' she asked again, wondering if the extra day away had occasioned some incident that was preventing him from settling back into life at home.

'No, everything's fine.' He put his arm around her and kissed her forehead. 'How about you?' He was looking at her closely. 'Are you okay?'

'Why wouldn't I be?' Helen herself was not good at replying to genuinely asked questions or receiving compliments. She tended to pull a face if anyone made the error of telling her she looked nice, or glance over her shoulder expecting someone else to be the recipient of the remark.

She wondered if he'd noticed that her mind was elsewhere. Was his distraction simply a mirror image of her own?

Alex stiffened at the brusqueness of her reply.

'I was only asking,' he said, removing his arm from her shoulders.

16

'Graham Parks has invited me for a meal,' Helen told Alex as he was wiping down the surfaces in the kitchen. 'Is it okay if I go?'

'Mmmm,' said Alex, polishing the granite surface with a microfibre cloth that he said stopped it from looking smeared, though it seemed to Helen that it just meant you had to wipe the surfaces twice. She preferred not at all.

'Mmmm' was not quite the response she had anticipated. She wondered if he had heard her or if as far as he was concerned she was mute, as well as sometimes invisible.

'I'm thinking of taking up pole dancing,' she said, in order to test her vocal cords.

'Really?' Alex stopped mid-stroke. 'How extraordinary. I thought they were all twenty-something Poles.'

'They are not necessarily Polish,' she informed. 'They are called pole dancers because they dance around poles.'

'And tend to be Polish,' asserted Alex.

Helen wondered when he had become an expert on the country of provenance of UK pole dancers. Did he go to those sorts of clubs with the crew after they wrapped on the set of *Muddy Water*? She would have liked to ask but she was still trying to use her Get Out of Jail card so that she could have dinner with Graham Parks.

'What do you think of the idea?' she

continued, as Alex poured bleach into the sink.

'Go ahead if you want to,' he replied. 'Apparently it's very good exercise.'

'How is having dinner good exercise?' she queried. 'Do you need to pour the whole bottle down the drain?' she added.

'I thought we were talking about pole dancing.' Alex replaced the childproof top on the bleach, checking that he had secured it properly by trying to twist it open again.

'I think I'm probably too old for pole dancing.' Helen paused, giving Alex space in which to deny this, or protest that he didn't want all and sundry watching his wife cavorting in her underwear, or at least say something that proved he could actually hear her. He didn't say anything, so she continued.

'I was telling you that Graham Parks, the author I interviewed last week, wants to have dinner with me.' Surely being told a virtual stranger wanted to take your wife out to dinner would provoke a slight reaction?

'You already said.' Alex busied himself with the cupboard under the sink. 'And I said that was fine.'

'Did you?' Helen thought he should at least have asked *why* Graham Parks wanted to have dinner with her. She was going to tell him anyway, but it would have seemed more natural if it were him plugging her for information, rather than her trying to force-feed it to him. 'I heard you say mmmm, but I wasn't sure if you were humming while you worked or actually talking to me.' She paused to allow Alex in on

110

the conversation, but he failed to grab the opportunity so she continued, 'Anyway, apparently he really liked the thing I wrote about him, and he wants to use it and possibly get me to write a bit more for his website.'

'You'd imagine he'd be able to do that himself. He is a writer, after all.' Alex was hanging his rubber gloves on the specially designated hook by the sink. Helen wondered if the twenty-somethings on the set of *Muddy Water* would find him attractive if they knew about his obsessive streak.

'Well, I suppose he writes fiction. He said he liked the way I 'analyse everything with a lightness of touch' and wondered if I'd help him.' Helen was still delighted by what Graham had said about her writing. 'So . . . do you mind if I meet up with him one day after work?'

'Fine by me.' Alex really didn't appear to be bothered at all. 'Do you know when?'

'No,' said Helen. 'I said I'd need to check with you — to see if you, or we, had anything on. I wasn't sure whether to go or not.'

'Why not?' Alex was surveying his blitz of the worktop with satisfaction. 'If he becomes the next Andy McNab, having written his website won't do you any harm, will it?'

'I suppose not.'

Helen had mixed feelings about the exchange. On the one hand she did desperately want to see Graham Parks again, and the prospect of dinner with him dangled before her like a summer holiday at the beginning of February. But the other half of her wanted Alex to consider the possibility that this man might actually be interested in his wife for more than her crisp, concise copy skills. The thought appeared not to have entered his head.

Another thought apparently had.

'Will Jim Keeble be there?' he asked, picking at a stubborn bit of what looked like jam, which appeared to have welded itself to the work surface.

'No, why would he?' Helen was momentarily confused.

'Well, you said they were friends and that Jim put you on to this Graham whatshisname in the first place.' Alex's cool was a bit ruffled. 'I just thought you might be having a happy three-some.'

'No,' Helen reassured him. 'I am pretty sure that Jim Keeble is not invited.'

It was funny, she thought, that her bumping into her glamorous ex had thrown Alex entirely off the scent. It would never have occurred to him that she might be remotely attracted to anyone who was not cast in more or less the same mould as himself. A few years back, one of her colleagues, who was in the process of separating from his wife, had transferred his affections to Helen. Knowing that he was on the rebound, lonely and likely to go back to his wife when his midlife crisis was over (he did), she had been flattered but had not paid much notice to his attentions.

Others had. A well-intentioned colleague had sat her down in the canteen one lunchtime and asked if she realised that Christopher Bailey was falling for her. Helen had replied that she didn't think he was actually falling for her, just falling away from his wife and not quite sure which way to land. Another colleague, who'd had one too many at the office party, asked Alex if he knew that Christopher Bailey had the hots for his wife. Helen had overheard Alex responding with an apparent non sequitur, 'Isn't he supposed to be very brilliant and tipped for the top?' — as if this precluded him from taking Helen at all seriously.

'He will if he doesn't fuck it all up,' replied the colleague, making it clear that it might not only be Christopher Bailey's career but Alex's wife that got fucked in the process.

'Not with that beard,' she heard Alex saying, definitely. 'Helen doesn't like beards.'

Why, she wondered now, had he thought that? He'd never actually asked her if she liked beards or not. In the same way he had never stopped to consider whether Graham Parks might think his wife was brilliant, witty, compassionate and beautiful, or whether she found him empathetic, horny and handsome.

He just presumed that since both men appeared to be going places and Helen was not, and since neither was an exact physical replica of himself, there was no possibility of any attraction either way.

'You know there's a studio recording of *Muddy Water* next Friday?' Alex asked now. 'Will you come and watch?'

His question interrupted her wondering how she would phrase her acceptance of Graham Parks' invitation to dinner.

'I'd like it if you were there,' he added. 'Everyone would like to see you too.'

'Yes, I'd enjoy that,' said Helen, and she meant it.

When she'd first met Alex, he'd been appearing in the play in Hampstead. After she'd recovered from the shock of coming off her bike and being taken home by ambulance, he'd asked if she would come and see him in it. If she hadn't already fallen for him, she would have done after seeing him on stage. He appeared to grow in stature and confidence, and everyone around him seemed to look up to him and respect him.

She liked seeing him like that. Watching members of the audience clocking him and trying to catch his attention after the show, and then looking disappointed when he scanned the room, obviously seeking someone, until his eyes landed on her and he came over and kissed her.

Sometimes, in the day-to-day drudgery of home life, she lost sight of that Alex, in the same way that he viewed her as the mother of his children and the person who did most of the shopping. Watching him do what he did best, being himself while pretending to be someone else entirely, and seeing him brush aside the adulation of fans and colleagues in return for a little from her was a reminder of one of the reasons why she loved him.

'I'd really enjoy that,' she reiterated, thinking she would use the same line in response to Graham Parks.

17

Helen wondered who Katie was talking to as she queued to buy them both teas at the café in the local park. It was unusually sunny for the time of year and they'd decided to take the children out after school and make the most of it. The light was beautiful, and leaning against the café railing with a backdrop of trees, Katie and the stranger looked like the beautiful people in an advert for something. Helen tried to think what the advert was for, but couldn't remember. It was one of those ads that were always appearing on the television. It featured two beautiful people, laughing and moving quickly in a variety of situations — the subtext being that if you bought whatever it was that was being advertised, you too could be beautiful and happy and always rushing from one exciting thing to another.

Adverts were usually wasted on Helen. She often remembered the scenario played out on screen but never what product it related to. She could recall countless times when she'd said, 'There's a great ad for something' and been about to comment on the amusing or interesting thing in the ad when Alex had interjected with 'What is it for?' She'd then say she couldn't remember and try to get on with the story, but he would spoil it by saying that if she didn't know what it was for then it wasn't a good ad.

Katie looked as if she could be selling any one

of a number of things as she approached the bench by the play area where Helen was sitting, a cup of tea in each hand and a plate with a piece of cake balanced like a roof between the two of them.

'Thanks,' Helen said, accepting the proffered polystyrene cup and moving her bag off the bench so Katie could sit down. 'Who was the bloke you were talking to?'

'Cary Sullivan.' Katie sat down. 'His son started going to Leonard's playgroup a few months ago.'

'That's an unusual name.' Helen clicked the plastic top off her cup. 'I don't think I've ever met a real live Cary before.'

'Apparently his mother named him after Cary Grant.' Katie glanced back towards the café, but Cary appeared to have been served and had gone from the terrace. 'She was Irish and a huge movie fan and she thought if she named him after a film star he would have a wonderful life.'

'Well, he's certainly good-looking,' Helen said. 'Does he have a wonderful life?'

'No, rather tragic.' Katie looked around to make sure Cary was not in earshot. 'His wife died of breast cancer when Connor was only a year old. Apparently she discovered a lump when she was pregnant, so they couldn't do anything about it until the baby was born, and by that time it had begun spreading.'

'God, that's awful.' Helen was silent for a moment. 'I can't imagine what that must be like. So Cary has to bring him up on his own?'

'Yes.' Katie was attempting to get the cake out

of its wrapper. 'He's really good with Connor. I wish Philip was like that with Hannah and Leonard.'

'So he's handsome, tragic and good with small children,' Helen mused. 'He must cause quite a stir at the playgroup.'

'Well, let's just say,' Katie offered her a piece of cake, 'that there are plenty of mothers willing to help out in whatever way they can. Connor is forever being invited on play dates, and I suspect most of the kids whose houses he goes to don't even like him.'

They both laughed, knowing that in the world of young children, men were a rarity. Despite equal opportunities at work and notions of equality at home, it was still women who did most of the childcare, including collecting their offspring from school. Men, when they did put in an appearance, almost immediately took on a godlike status. Cary was actually genuinely good-looking, not just because he was the only man in the playground. Helen could well imagine there were many mothers keen to invite him and Connor round for a bit of lunch or a cup of tea.

'So, has Connor been to play with Leonard?' Helen asked, giving Katie a conspiratorial look.

'He has, come to mention it.' Katie laughed. 'They get on very well, actually.'

'Oh, do they now?' Helen raised an eyebrow.

'Yes, they do,' Katie replied firmly. 'Talking of men, I forgot to ask how the interview with the mystery man turned out last week.'

'It was okay.' Helen smiled to herself as she

117

thought of Graham Parks. 'He was interesting, and . . . '

'What?' Katie looked quizzical.

'I don't know,' Helen replied. 'There was just something about him. I really liked him, actually.'

'What, like *like* liked?' Katie sounded like Emma, who could barely say a sentence without uttering the word 'like' several times.

'No, not exactly. I can't quite explain. I just felt very at home with him.' Helen decided that that was enough on the subject of Graham Parks. 'Anyway, talking of men we like like, how is Dreamy Phil?'

'Oh, you know.' Katie scanned the playground to locate Leonard, who appeared to be happily eating sand in the sandpit. 'Busy at work. He seems to be spending a lot of his time holed up with one particular PhD student. Maria Romano.'

'She sounds glamorous.' Helen waved at Emma, who was standing at the top of the slide with Hannah, Katie's daughter.

'Yes, doesn't she?' There was a certain bitterness to Katie's tone.

'You're not jealous, are you?' Helen asked.

'No, not really. It's just that sometimes I think he finds his students more interesting than me. When they're bright and young and exotic-sounding, it's not always easy to ignore the fact that he doesn't get home until after nine because they've been discussing poetry in his office.'

'I know what you mean.' Helen gave Emma and Hannah the thumbs-up as they flew down the slide together. 'It probably sounds ridiculous, but I don't really like the idea of Alex spending half the week away from home in the company of Venetia Taylor.'

'But you trust him, don't you?' Katie asked.

'Yes, of course I do. You have to, don't you?' Helen paused, but her friend didn't answer. 'I mean, Alex is away such a lot that I've got no choice. That doesn't mean I'm not slightly jealous at the idea of him sitting in a bar somewhere in Manchester after a recording, flirting gently with Venetia Taylor.'

'Mind if I join you?' Cary had appeared out of nowhere and was eyeing the empty space on the bench beside Katie.

'Of course not, sit down.' Katie took her paper plate off the seat. 'This is Helen. Helen, this is Cary. Helen has just got a new rabbit.'

'Really? How wonderful.' Cary spoke with the sort of soft Irish lilt that made everything sound like poetry. 'Would that be a baby rabbit?'

'Yes,' Helen confirmed. 'Eight weeks old. He's very sweet, but I'm a bit worried that my son Joe is allergic to him.'

'Why would that be?' Cary asked.

'He's asthmatic,' Helen told him. 'And I don't think rabbit fur helps. He seems to start wheezing whenever he's been playing with him.'

'It's a third-child substitute.' Katie appeared to have no qualms about sharing the details of Helen's life with a near stranger. 'For Helen, anyway. Her husband has decided to have the snip. They won't be having any more children, so they've got a rabbit instead.'

'Perhaps I should do that,' Cary replied.

'What, have the snip or get a rabbit?' Helen knew this wasn't really an appropriate question to ask someone you'd only just been introduced to, but she was getting back at Katie for announcing to the world, it seemed, that Alex was having a vasectomy.

'Well, I don't really have much need for a vasectomy,' Cary said, instantly making Helen feel bad. 'Or much prospect of having another child, so a rabbit could be a good playmate for this little one.'

Connor had toddled over as he spoke and was wiping his nose on the knee of Cary's jeans.

'Oh, I'm sorry.' Helen realised she'd put her foot in it already. 'I know . . . I mean, Katie told me about your wife. I'm sorry . . . '

'It's all right.' Cary smiled at her. 'You don't have to apologise. Anyway, a rabbit is probably a good substitute for a baby, but it's too small to fill in for a wife.'

'Perhaps you should get a dog,' Katie suggested. She obviously knew Cary well enough to joke around the subject of his dead wife.

'Ahh, dogs. Friendly creatures, but not too maternal. Perhaps a chicken would be better.' He ruffled Connor's hair as he spoke. 'Anyway, time I was getting this little one home for his tea. Nice to meet you, Helen.' He stood up and took her hand in a gesture that was not quite a shake but more of a brief friendly hold.

'I'll be seeing you later in the week.' This comment he addressed to Katie, bending down to kiss her on both cheeks as he spoke. He picked up a rucksack with a toy panda attached to one of the straps, took Connor's hand and began leading him towards a buggy left near the gate of the park.

'He seems very nice,' Helen said, glancing at his departing back.

'Yes.' Katie too was watching him as he walked away. 'He is.'

18

Everything was conspiring against Helen having dinner with Graham Parks that evening.

Joe had managed to delete the email with the name of the restaurant where they'd agreed to meet, along with everything else in her inbox and the article she'd more or less finished writing on why exercising makes you fat. (Half-hearted jog round the park or a few gentle laps of local pool make you hungry. You eat Mars bar, thinking you have done some exercise so it won't matter. Mars bar has far more calories than you actually used, plus the swim tired you, so you slump at desk for rest of day and would have been better off not bothering.) It was almost as if he knew there was a danger in his mother meeting someone after work to discuss a 'potential website'.

Quite how he had managed to wipe so much material from her computer, however, not to mention signing himself on to a site for over-eighteens that allowed him to play virtual knife crime games, was beyond her.

Helen was concerned that Joe was addicted to computer games. He demanded, 'Can I go on the computer?' almost as soon as he woke up, began twitching at the prospect of getting his daily fix when they rounded the corner into their street after school, and suffered an aggressive and grumpy comedown when she told him it was time to stop.

'He'll end up with attention deficit disorder and more ASBOs than A levels,' she would say, trying to enlist Alex's support in getting Joe to do something else. 'Or repetitive strain injury.'

'Good practice for when he's a teenager,' Alex would reply, laughing at his own repetitive strain injury joke. 'Anyway, all boys like computers.'

Alex was less worried than Helen. He regarded Joe's ability to navigate his way around the internet as an asset and his obsession with all things with buttons and a screen as entirely natural. Helen, on the other hand, was a Luddite who had maintained for several years that she did not need an internet connection before it dawned on her that she actually couldn't live without it.

She wondered if her fears that playing 'Virtual Motorway Pileup' would turn Joe into a hooded heroin-addicted joyrider were well founded, or if computer games were simply the punk music of the next generation. Her own mother had been pretty convinced that listening to C90 recordings of the Sex Pistols or the Clash with her bedroom door closed would lead Helen inevitably to prostitution. She had been wrong.

Helen had entertained the possibility that she might be wrong too. Joe was probably gaining valuable life skills, at an early age, which would turn him into some kind of technical wizard who'd make a fortune in his twenties and would be able to retire before he'd reached thirty. Perhaps he would throw a few thousands her way while he was at it.

He didn't, however, show great promise in this

future career when Helen asked him if he knew what had happened to the entire contents of her inbox.

'I think I just closed it,' he said absent-mindedly, having graduated from the computer screen to the television screen, where he was busy absorbing every detail of a new type of bread 'containing all the goodness of organic wholemeal but with all the elasticity of sliced white'. 'Can we get some of that bread, Mum?'

'Maybe,' Helen answered, realising that Joe had moved everything that had been in her inbox to the drafts folder and the 'exercise makes you fat' piece to the waste bin.

She was now able to retrieve her message from Graham and the address of the restaurant where she had arranged to meet him at 6.30, straight after work. Any later would have made it seem more of a date than a meeting in which she would give her opinions on his proposed website.

'Will you be back at the normal time?' Alex shouted from the kitchen. 'I'm going for a drink with Marcus tonight. Have you had breakfast?'

'No,' Helen shouted back, involuntarily. She wasn't sure if she was saying no to the breakfast question or the statement about Alex having a drink with Marcus.

She had told him she was going out straight after work and would need him to babysit. He had not told her that he had planned to have a drink with his old friend from drama school, who was now writing sitcoms for US TV and was in London for the week as part of a team trying to sell them to the UK.

'But I told you, I'm supposed to be meeting Graham Parks after work tonight.' She realised as she said this that she sounded slightly panic-stricken, as if anything that might get in the way of this meeting was a potential disaster. She hoped that by repeating it more calmly she would not alarm Alex.

'I'm supposed to be meeting Graham Parks, the author I interviewed the other day,' she qualified. 'And his agent.'

The latter was a lie, but it made the meeting sound more businesslike and less cancellable. She justified it to herself on the grounds that whenever they had a diary clash, it was always Alex who won out. Whatever his prior engagement was, it was always more important than hers.

His solution to the problem was invariably 'We can get a babysitter', which translated roughly as 'You can organise a babysitter' or, failing that, 'You could cancel your engagement.' For some reason, his meetings with friends or attendance at screenings of new films were always more pressing than whatever she might have planned. He also managed to pass off most social engagements as work-related, thus legitimising his priority pass: 'James is now casting director for a big ad agency', 'Callum is planning to write another movie with a character that I might be suitable for' and 'I need to hobnob with the producer' had all been used; or sometimes simply, 'I haven't been out with my friends for ages; you see yours all the time.' No amount of explaining on her part that talking to the parents of children who happened to be in Emma's swimming class while sipping coffee from polystyrene cups at the poolside did not count as socialising would make him give in, and if she could not find a babysitter, it was usually Helen who cancelled her plans.

'But Marcus is only here for a few days.' Alex had by now wandered into the living room, causing Helen hurriedly to close the window of her inbox. 'You never know, he might want to cast me in one of his shows, and he'll want to talk to me about Fiona.'

Fiona was Marcus's wife, possibly now his ex-wife. About a year ago, she had thrown him out after discovering he'd been having an affair with a script supervisor. Marcus had at first insisted it meant nothing but was simply an on-location fling, but then, finding himself with nowhere to live, he'd moved in with the other woman, insisting all the while that he still loved Fiona and wanted to return home. It hadn't seemed to occur to him that shacking up with the script supervisor wasn't an act that was likely to increase the possibility of this.

'Then why don't you ask Moira if she can babysit?' Helen wrong-footed him before he could suggest the same to her.

'Which one is Moira?' Alex tried to wriggle out of organising anything by displaying total ignorance on the subject of the various teenagers who often came to look after his children.

'The one who lives next door, who you were chatting to over the garden wall only last night,' Helen admonished. Why was it Alex could

126

remember the names of all the producers, agents and casting directors he ever came into contact with at work but not those of anyone vaguely connected with home or childcare?

'Which side?' Alex may well have exchanged a few words with one of the neighbours while bringing in the washing, but he didn't recall them.

'That side,' said Helen, nodding towards the wall. She closed the computer and picked up her bag before kissing Joe and Emma and heading for the door.

'I am going to work now,' she told Alex, although it was obvious that what she actually meant was 'You sort it!'

'Okay.' Alex was momentarily floored. He kissed her goodbye. 'I'll call you at work,' he said, as Helen closed the door behind her.

She replied to the space on the other side of the front door that if he rang her to say he hadn't managed to sort a babysitter but couldn't contact Marcus to cancel and could she come home, then she would kill him.

The space outside the front door happened to be occupied by the postman, who was just rounding the corner of the hedge in the front garden and making his way down the path.

'Who are you planning on killing?' he asked, as if murder were the most natural thing in the world.

'I haven't quite decided,' Helen told him.

'Oh well, have a nice day,' he responded, jumping over the wall that wasn't really a wall, more of a demarcation line, between their house and the babysitter's.

'I'll do my best,' she said, although he didn't appear to be listening.

* * *

Helen phoned Katie as she left the office at lunchtime to pick up a sandwich. The fact that Alex had not yet called to tell her he'd sorted out a babysitter suggested he had not, and she wondered if her friend might be able to fill in.

'It's the woman who's always asking you for favours,' she said when Katie picked up the phone.

'Hello,' Katie replied. 'Can you hang on a minute? I was just going out and Leonard is already on the pavement.'

Helen listened to what appeared to be the sound of Katie negotiating the buggy through the front door and down the steps on to the street, and strapping Leonard into it.

'Sorry.' She came back on the line. 'We're just going swimming. How can I help you?'

'No, I'm sorry,' Helen said. 'I always seem to be asking you to help me out. I've got a late meeting tonight and my fuckwit husband said he would babysit but promptly forgot and has arranged to do something else. If he can't find anyone, I don't suppose you could pop round for a couple of hours?'

'Sorry, Helen.' Katie sounded slightly breathless as she pushed the buggy along the street. 'I'm not quite sure what time I'll be back this evening.'

'Oh.' Helen knew it wasn't fair to assume her friend would have nothing planned; it was just she usually hadn't. She might have expected her to say that Philip was stuck at a faculty meeting and so she couldn't get out, or that one of the children was ill and she didn't want to leave them, but it was unusual for her to be doing something herself. 'Anything nice planned?'

'Well, just kids' stuff really,' Katie replied. 'We're going swimming now with Cary and Connor and then when I've picked Hannah up we're all having supper with them at their place.'

'Oh!' Given what Katie had told her about Connor and his play dates, Helen could not help a hint of suggestiveness creeping into her voice.

'Sorry, Helen, got to go now.' Katie cut the conversation short. 'Our bus is coming. I need to fold up the buggy.'

19

Helen flicked her phone straight on to voicemail when she saw Alex's number come up. It would be harder for him to wriggle out of not having managed to find a babysitter if he couldn't actually speak directly to her. She'd reached the sandwich shop near the office when it rang and was deliberating over the merits of ham versus tuna when it bleeped to indicate a message had been left.

It was a text. Ha! He hadn't got the courage even to tell her voice-mail that he had messed up on the arrangements and wanted her home.

She decided to have tuna and took it to the counter to pay, succumbing to the charm of the Italian on the till, who asked if she wanted some chocolate biscuit cake to go with it. Helen looked at the slabs of cake and was about to say yes but then changed her mind. It wasn't going to make much difference, but if she was going to have dinner with Graham tonight, she didn't want to draw attention to her midriff.

It didn't usually bother her, the extra layer of fat that seemed to be accumulating around her stomach. She regarded it simply as something you had to accept in exchange for having children and growing older. She was in reasonable shape for her age and regarded a few extra pounds as nature's answer to Botox. They helped fill out some of the cavities developing in her face while at the same time giving Alex something extra to squeeze.

'I think you look better than ever,' he would say to her if she bemoaned the extra flesh. Today she wondered if he really meant it or if he'd preferred her when she was more lithe.

Settling herself on a bench in a nearby square, she unwrapped her sandwich and opened her message.

'Moira not free,' it read.

Helen knew it. He hadn't managed to get a babysitter and would expect her to come home.

'But Zoe will sit. I won't be late. Have a good evening. Alex xx'

Oh well, she'd been wrong. He *had* managed to find a babysitter, though not one she had ever heard of. Who was Zoe? she wondered. Where had he found her at such late notice? Did the children know her? Would they like her?

She decided to call Alex back.

'Hi, darling.' He picked the phone up almost immediately. 'You got my message?'

'Yes, I did. But who is Zoe?'

'She lives about four doors down. A friend of Moira's, apparently. I went round to ask Moira but she had a dance class or something and suggested Zoe. She sounds nice.'

'So you haven't met her?' Helen didn't really think that sounding nice made you a suitable person to leave in charge of two young children who had never met you before.

'No, but I spoke to her on the phone. I'm sure she'll be fine.'

Helen wasn't so sure. Joe had an antipathy to

strangers, especially strange babysitters. Until recently, the only way they could actually leave him with a sitter was by pretending that everything was normal and putting him to bed, then pretending to put Emma to bed too and only when he was asleep allowing her to creep back down again in order to play games with the babysitter. They'd leave strict instructions that if Joe woke for any reason, the sitter was not to tell him they were out, merely that they were busy working and that she would put him back to bed. Usually Joe was so sleepy as he made his way to the toilet or to get a glass of water that he would accept this without a fuss.

Suddenly Helen felt uneasy about the whole thing. She didn't like the thought of leaving the children with someone she'd never met. What if they hated Zoe? What if Joe's asthma flared up and she didn't know how to administer his inhaler? What if she spent the whole evening on the phone to her boyfriend and didn't hear Joe crying from the top of the stairs? Worse still, what if Joe fell down the stairs? And she, their mother, wouldn't be there, because she was out pretending to have a work meeting with a man she'd only met once but wanted to see again.

Her children were the most important things in her life, and so was Alex.

'I'm not so sure,' Helen told him. 'Perhaps I should just cancel this meeting and come home.'

'But it's been arranged for over a week, hasn't it?' Alex queried. 'If you're really worried, I could always cancel the meeting with Marcus.'

'No,' Helen insisted. 'Don't do that. I know

it's important that you see him.'

'But your work is important too, I know that,' Alex replied, surprising her, because she suspected he didn't really believe that.

'This isn't really important,' she insisted.

She suddenly felt very uneasy about going to any lengths to have dinner with Graham Parks. If she cancelled now because they didn't have a babysitter, she could relax and never see him again.

'Listen,' Alex was saying, 'I really want you to go. It might be useful if you ever decide to go freelance.'

Helen was always talking about working freelance but didn't have the nerve to take the plunge. Previously Alex's work had been too sporadic to risk it. Now that he had the closest thing there was to a steady job in the acting profession, she could theoretically afford to try it, but she felt she was too old and would be outstripped by a new generation of writers who knew all about blogs and online journalism and various other areas that were more or less a mystery to her.

'I'm not sure.' She was waiting for him to say he would cancel the babysitter and expect her home at the normal time. But he didn't.

'I'll tell you what.' Alex was being unusually considerate, though to be fair, it wasn't actually unusual. He was generally a considerate man. 'I'll get Zoe to come round an hour before I need to leave, and if she is a cocaine-snorting, multi-pierced child-eater, I'll cancel.'

Helen laughed and wished she and Alex went

out more often than they did.

'Okay,' she replied. 'I'll try to keep it short so that I'm not back too late. Don't forget to feed the rabbit before you go out.'

'How could I forget our lovely third child?' he joked. 'Have a good evening, then. Love you!'

'I love you too,' she said, even though he had already put the phone down and could no longer hear her.

20

Helen's phone bleeped into action as she emerged from the tube, alerting her to a missed call and a voicemail message. She saw the call was from Alex, and wondered if the babysitter had turned out to be psychotic and she was being recalled from her dinner date. The voicemail was also from Alex, but it was Joe's voice she heard talking, excitedly telling her he had a big part in his class assembly as a hedgehog.

Helen could not quite see how a hedgehog could command centre stage, but then Alex cut in explaining that it was indeed a big role: the assembly was about sharing, and Joe and another hedgehog would spend much of it fighting over who got the greatest share of the hedge.

Helen laughed and put her phone away, but the voices of Alex and Joe were still clear in her head when she spotted Graham Parks waiting outside the restaurant. Her stomach made an involuntary flip.

She wondered why he hadn't gone in already and found a table at which she could have joined him. Now they'd have to walk in together, as if they were a couple. Or was she being overly self-conscious? She went out to lunch often enough with male work colleagues and never thought twice about walking into a restaurant with them. But that was lunch and this was dinner. The hour and the gathering darkness made it all seem more intimate.

Graham was looking up the street. He looked different in a way she could not quite put her finger on: definitely attractive, slightly smarter, more closely shaven, as if he'd made an effort. She'd made an effort too, working out something to wear that wouldn't be out of place in the office but wouldn't look too businesslike in the evening, washing her hair even though she planned to go swimming the following morning and would usually have left it until then, and reapplying lipstick on the tube, even though she harboured doubts about the wisdom of coming at all.

He hadn't seen her yet. She could always turn around now, head for the nearest underground and call him when she was several stops away. She could use the babysitter as an excuse, apologise for letting him down at the last minute and suggest rearranging, thinking he probably wouldn't bother after a no-show.

It was too late. He'd seen her and was walking towards her, smiling. He stretched his hand out towards her, and Helen was about to take it and shake it before she realised he was using it to gather her into a clumsy embrace, kissing her right cheek as he did so.

'I'm glad you came,' he said, as if he knew that she'd spent the day wondering whether she should. 'Shall we go in?' His blue-grey eyes smiled right into hers and she momentarily lost the power of speech, recovering it only when they were safely on the other side of the restaurant's revolving doors.

'Dinner with you twice in two weeks,' she said, trailing off as she wished she hadn't. There didn't seem to be an appropriate end to that sentence. 'People will start talking' was all that came to mind, and she wasn't about to say that out loud.

Graham raised his eyebrows a fraction. Helen couldn't interpret the look. Did it mean 'That was a stupid thing to say. Why on earth did you say that?' or 'Yes, I know and I'm hoping we might be able to make it four times in four weeks'? Or did it mean 'Well, once we've discussed you helping me out with my website, we won't need to meet again, not for a while at any rate'?

She tried again, thinking it didn't really matter what she said, as long as she said something.

'Do you come here often?' she heard herself saying, and then realised that actually it was better to say nothing at all than to say the first thing that came into your head.

'Not very often.' Graham Parks was laughing, and Helen started laughing too. The tension was dispersed until he put his hand lightly on her shoulder to guide her towards the table that was reserved in his name.

It was only a brief moment of contact and the lightest of touches, but she felt the warmth of his hand penetrate right through her jacket and make its way down to the pit of her stomach.

Shit, she thought. What the fuck am I doing here?

'It must be a very popular restaurant if you

need to reserve a table at six thirty,' she said, fighting the impulse to put her hand up and touch his.

'I'm not sure that I did need to.' Graham was holding her chair out, waiting for her to sit down. It was an unusual gesture, old-fashioned and gentlemanly, and Helen liked it, but she also wished he would get himself over to the other side of the table, putting a relatively safe distance of at least two feet between them.

The table was tucked away slightly from the main body of the restaurant, round a corner behind the bar, so other diners couldn't see them.

'I realise I'm taking up your time, when you probably want to be getting home to your family,' Graham said, picking up the menu. 'Do you have time for a starter? I won't be offended if you need to get something quick.'

This was her chance to keep it businesslike, to say she didn't have a lot of time for him, today or on any other day, but she didn't take it.

'No, I'm not in a great hurry. Alex is babysitting and the children will be asleep in the next hour anyway, so I don't need to rush back.' She realised as she told the lie that she was trying to give the impression that she hadn't had to go to any great lengths to fit him into her schedule, when the opposite was true.

She hoped the potentially cocaine-snorting babysitter did not pass out, forcing Emma to call an ambulance and then her mother, exposing the lie and making Graham realise that she had attached enough importance to their meeting to

138

warrant getting a babysitter.

'What do you fancy then?' Graham asked.

'I'm not sure yet.' Helen glanced at the menu, and realised to her horror that there were about twenty-five different choices of starters and even more for mains. Her favourite restaurants were ones that had set menus, with a choice of two dishes for each course, or better still, no choice at all. With twenty-five possible starters to choose from, the likelihood of opting for the one that was not as nice as the other twenty-four was high.

'The lamb parcels look good,' she said. 'But so does the stuffed aubergine.'

This was torture. Then she saw light at the end of the tunnel in the form of a meze dish, containing a little bit of everything.

'Oh, actually I think I'll have the meze,' she said, at the same time realising this had a minimum-of-two-people directive attached to it. 'Except that's for two.'

'I'll have that as well, then.' Graham looked over to where the waiter was standing.

'Are you sure?' Helen panicked. She didn't want to force him to eat the meze just because she couldn't make her mind up. 'I'm sure there are plenty of other things I'd like. I don't want you to have to have it just because I am.'

'No, I'd like it.' Graham was adamant and the waiter was flourishing the pages of his notebook.

'Okay then.'

They ordered the shared meal and a bottle of white wine. Helen suspected Graham might have preferred red but once again he deferred to her choice.

'So, how's the book going down?' she asked as the waiter retreated.

'Well, there was a great piece about it in the *Sunday Review* written by a very sympathetic journalist, but apart from that, it's only had the briefest of mentions in the local free paper, which everyone puts straight into their recycling.' Graham's forearms were resting on the table, his palms upturned in a gesture of openness.

'But what about all those interviews you did?' Helen realised she was twisting her own hands nervously around each other and hastily moved them under the table so that the most obvious sign of her nervousness was concealed.

'Rather a lot of those were for columns such as 'My First Teacher' and 'My Travels', and there was even one journalist who quizzed me endlessly about my health regime. I think Claire must have set that one up by mistake, but she says it's all good publicity.'

Was it Helen's imagination, or had his hands moved closer to her side of the table?

She looked down at her own hands, which were beginning to look more and more like her mother's. They seemed to have aged faster than any other part of her.

'And the website?' she asked, as the waiter returned and clattered cutlery and wine glasses, pouring a half-inch for Graham to taste before filling both their glasses. 'Tell me about that.'

'Well, at the moment there is no website.' Graham raised his glass slightly.

'Cheers,' he said. 'Thank you for coming, Helen.'

They clinked glasses and momentarily made eye contact. Helen looked down quickly, wondering if she was blushing, while Graham continued.

'Claire tells me that all authors have their own websites and the publisher will help me set something up, but I need to come up with stuff that people will want to read about me.'

Helen was familiar with the format. 'Surely that's something you can do yourself?' she queried, leaning back to allow the waiter to rearrange the table to make room for their food.

The meze was served on one large plate from which they both had to fork their individual mouthfuls. It seemed suddenly very intimate, eating from the same plate. It felt like sharing a toothbrush, something you only did with someone very close.

'Have you had any ideas about it?' Helen asked, advancing her fork to spear a stuffed vine leaf, then realising, as their forks clashed, that Graham was going for it too.

They both paused, forks hovering in mid-air, before Graham moved his back slightly, saying, 'Go ahead.'

Helen took the vine leaf and began chewing, while Graham started to outline some of his website ideas.

'It sounds as if you don't really need me.' She finished her mouthful and looked up to find that he was looking at her intently.

She directed her attention to the plate in

between them and scooped up a clump of cous-cous, brushing Graham's hand as she did.

This time it was her turn to look at him, and this time she did not glance away when he held her gaze.

'I probably could do it without you,' he said. 'But I'd rather do it with you.'

'I'm not sure how much time I could give you,' Helen told him, focusing her attention on the food again, trying to avoid fork contact, which was unnerving her deeply.

As if sensing her discomfort, Graham put his fork down and sat back.

'I know you've already got a job,' he said.

Helen speared a lump of grilled halloumi cheese and stuffed it into her mouth, giving herself a few moments before she had to speak again.

'And a husband and two children,' she reminded him, although she didn't think she really needed to. 'That doesn't leave a lot of time for . . . '

'Working on websites?' Graham interjected, as she trailed off. It was a question rather than a statement.

'Anything much really,' she said.

Now it was Graham's turn to look uncomfortable.

'I know you've got a pretty full life, Helen.' He took a large swig of wine before continuing. 'I don't want to put pressure on you if you don't want to do it, but . . . '

Helen looked up at him as he carried on speaking.

'Perhaps if I think about it a bit more, work out exactly what I want, and you had a bit of time to think about it too, then maybe we could meet again?'

Helen had already drained the contents of her glass, and she thought if she attempted to refill it she might knock the bottle over. Instead, needing to do something with her hands, she picked up her paper napkin and began nervously shredding it.

'That sounds good,' she said. 'I do probably need a bit of time to think about it.' She wondered what exactly it was she was supposed to be thinking about. Was it still the website, or something else?

She stopped shredding the napkin and put her hand on the table, and Graham reached across and covered it. Not for long, but with intent.

'No pressure,' he said, removing his hand as the waiter arrived and asked if they'd finished. 'It would be good to see you again, even if you think you haven't got the time for any extra work.'

He filled her glass up for her and she gratefully drank from it.

'I'll definitely give it some thought,' she said, considering exactly what the implications of seeing Graham again might be.

'Thank you,' Graham said softly. 'I know your situation, and I appreciate you don't have a lot of spare time.'

In a reflex action, Helen looked at her watch.

'Do you have to go soon?' Graham asked. 'Or can you stay and have dessert?'

Again Helen realised she had an opportunity to pull back from whatever it was she was getting herself into, an opportunity she ought to take. But she didn't.

'I'll stay,' she said.

21

Alex was asleep on the sofa when Helen got home, a half-drunk cup of tea still in his hand, its stone-cold contents dripping slowly on to his stomach as it tipped with every breath he took. The house was quiet. Emma and Joe were asleep. The dishwasher was unloaded, the back door was bolted and the kitchen lights were off. Alex was obviously ready to go to bed but was waiting for her. After all the years they had spent together, he still never went to bed until he knew she was safely home.

She sat down next to him on the sofa and took the cup of tea from his hand, setting it down on the table and lifting his shirt away from his stomach slightly so that the patch where the tea had soaked through was out of contact with his skin.

Alex stirred slightly, and Helen wondered, if she hadn't come home, at what point during the night he would have woken, realised she wasn't there and raised the alarm. He opened his eyes slightly and appeared to register her presence, though she wasn't sure if he was actually awake or not.

'Are you undressing me?' He smiled, registering her hand tugging at his shirt. He took it in his, placing it back on his stomach.

'No,' said Helen. 'I was getting you dressed again. We've just had sex on the sofa and now you have to go to work.'

Alex looked slightly panicked, and Helen wondered if it was because he thought he had to go to work, or because he'd had sex with his wife and couldn't remember it.

He looked at his watch and recalled exactly where he was and why, and registered that Helen was now home and he could, if he wished, go to bed.

Right now he didn't wish!

Helen looked dishevelled and beautiful. She'd probably walked back from the station, even though he'd told her to get a taxi. Her cheeks were flushed from the cold but her hands were warm. She must have been wearing gloves and walking fast.

He pulled her toward him and kissed her.

'That was a great shag,' he said, 'but I'm knackered now and need to go to bed.'

'I'll be up in a minute.' Helen released his hand. She didn't want to go to bed yet. She never could go straight to sleep after coming in. No matter how late it was, she always needed a period of readjustment from being out to being home. Tonight she needed extra time to sort out her thoughts, in the hope that they wouldn't keep her awake half the night.

Alex shifted as if he was about to get up but had had second thoughts.

'How was your meeting?' he asked.

'Okay.' Helen was non-committal. What else could she be? 'I'm not sure anything will come out of it, though. He was a bit vague about the website.'

'Was the agent equally vague?' Alex had not forgotten what she'd told him.

'Neither of them seems to have given it a lot of thought,' Helen said. 'But I got a good meal out of them anyway.'

In the past week she had probably told more lies to Alex than she had in the past year. If she hadn't told him that Graham's agent would be at the meeting, what would she have said about the evening that she had just had? Certainly not that she found Graham Parks unnervingly attractive, or that they had shared a meal, or that, while they had talked about his website, there appeared to be another unspoken conversation unfolding between them and another agenda being discussed.

She had allowed Graham to walk her to the nearest tube station. She had walked closer to him than was necessary and had kissed him on the lips; only briefly, but their lips touched for slightly longer than they should have done.

She'd texted him as soon as the train pulled out of the station: 'Thank you for a lovely evening. Hope to meet again soon.'

'I hope so too,' came his reply, almost instantly. 'Thank you too. Goodbye for now.'

'Goodbye,' she texted, feeling rather sad as she did, but putting her phone to the bottom of her bag to resist the temptation to say anything more.

It beeped almost immediately.

'Don't walk home. Make sure you take a taxi.' She was momentarily confused by this, until she realised it was from Alex. She had known he

147

would be waiting up for her, concerned about her getting home safely.

'Do you think he'll follow it up?' Alex was asking her now. 'Or is it up to you?'

'I'm not sure,' Helen said. 'I don't really know if I've got time for it anyway. I told him as much.'

'Time for bed,' Alex said, standing up. Helen couldn't see how he'd reacted to what she'd said, though he appeared unperturbed. 'Don't forget to put the light off,' he said, before going upstairs.

Helen made herself a cup of tea and drank it before heading up herself. She looked in on Emma as she passed her room. Her daughter was fast asleep but was sucking her thumb so loudly, Helen was surprised she didn't wake herself up. Joe also appeared to be asleep, but opened his eyes when she bent over to kiss him and threw his arms around her, saying, 'I love you, marvellous Mummy,' before falling straight back to sleep.

Alex's doze on the sofa seemed to have revived him, because by the time she got into bed, expecting to find him breathing deeply, his arm flung across her side of the bed so that she had to lift it and lay it down by his side in order to get in, he was in fact awake, propped up on the pillows and waiting for her.

She climbed into bed. It was cold in the bedroom. She shivered, and in response, Alex curled himself around her back, draping his arm over her stomach and stroking it in a manner that could have been foreplay but was

148

more likely to be habit.

She pressed herself closer to him and could feel him hardening against her.

'How was Marcus?' she asked.

'Good, actually.' Alex rolled away from her so he was lying on his back.

Helen turned to face him, propping herself up slightly on one elbow. 'Really? Has it all turned out happily ever after with the script supervisor, then?'

'No, he's back with Fiona,' Alex told her. 'They agreed to give it another go and he says they're getting on better than ever.'

'Really?' Helen was surprised by this news. She couldn't imagine after the hurt that Marcus had inflicted on her that Fiona would willingly have taken him back.

Fiona and Marcus had met in America, drawn to each other by the fact that they were both ex-pats. They'd seemed well suited even though they were very different. Marcus was an extrovert, striking-looking, and the sort of person people gravitated towards at parties. Helen had always attributed his success in the States as much to this as to his writing skills. People would want to work with him even if he wasn't that good at his job, though given how well he had done, he probably was. If Marcus was a butterfly, Fiona was more of moth. She was quieter, less sociable and more serious, attractive once you got to know her rather than instantly. She worked as a graphic designer, creating images for one of the big film studios.

They'd been introduced at a party and

discovered they had mutual friends. Alex was one of them. He knew Marcus from acting school and Fiona had once gone out with one of his school friends.

'He only moved back home quite recently,' Alex told her. 'Apparently the script supervisor wanted him to settle down and maybe have children, and he realised that wasn't what he wanted. So he moved out and began talking properly with Fiona.'

'She must really love him to take him back after all of that,' Helen mused, wondering if she would be able to even begin to forgive Alex if he had an affair like that.

'For better or for worse, I suppose,' said Alex, putting his arm around her and drawing her to him.

'In a funny sort of way,' Helen said, putting her head on Alex's chest, 'I sort of envy people who have been through something really awful like that.'

'What do you mean?' Alex was kissing her neck and not really listening. She pulled away slightly.

'It's like you said.' She looked at him. 'You say 'for better or for worse' when you get married, but until you have had the worse, how do you know if you really will stay with someone?'

'So you want something awful to happen to see if our relationship pulls through?' Alex asked.

'No, of course I don't want anything awful to happen,' she said, moving closer to him again. 'I just wonder if it makes people stronger as a couple, having decided to stay together despite something having happened.'

'You know what your problem is?' said Alex.

'What?' Helen switched the light off.

'Your problem is that you don't have a problem,' he said.

Not yet, thought Helen, wondering whether, if either she or Alex had an affair, they would manage to put it behind them and get on with their lives without lasting repercussions.

How would she cope if she found out Alex had been playing away whilst on location? How would he feel if he'd been a fly on the wall in the restaurant this evening?

Alex pulled her towards him and kissed her. Helen wanted to reclaim some of the ground she felt she had lost by agreeing to have dinner with Graham Parks. She wanted to be reassured that although Marcus had cheated on Fiona, Alex would not do the same to her.

She sat up and took off the T-shirt she wore in bed.

22

They were woken by a howling sound moving slowly down the corridor towards their bedroom. Helen heard it first, or at least reacted to it first. Alex had got the knack of ignoring distressed children down to a fine art. He could wait just long enough to ensure that Helen got out of bed and dealt with whatever it was before he needed to.

He would never sleep through the crisis entirely, but he would inevitably sleep through it a staged fraction longer than Helen, knowing that if he sat up, as if he was about to spring into action, just as she was already out of bed and nearing their bedroom door, she would probably reassure him that it was only a bed-wetting incident or a nightmare and that she had it under control. He could then murmur something sympathetic from the safety of the duvet and go back to sleep.

Sex and high emotions the previous evening had induced a deeper than usual sleep in Helen this morning, and she was slow to react to the crescendo of sobs. When she realised they were not simply a soundtrack to the dream she'd been having, her autopilot kicked in and she began extracting herself from Alex's arm and the duvet, both of which held her firmly in their grasp. In her guilt-induced dream the sobs were her own, occasioned by Alex telling her he was leaving.

'Where are you going?' he was asking now, as if they'd been dreaming in tandem and the ghosts of marital discord were haunting him too.

'Emma's crying.' Helen briefly touched his face, wanting to re-establish contact, wanting also, she realised as she felt the slight stubble on his cheek, to sleep with him again, and wondering if he would be suspicious if she initiated sex twice in twelve hours.

It was light on the landing and Emma was fully dressed, suggesting she had not woken her parents in the middle of the night but simply roused them from a Saturday-morning lie-in.

Her face was red and streaked with tears and her chest was convulsing with the effort of trying to find the words that would explain why she was so upset.

'Shh, shh.' Helen knelt down and held her, stroking her hair to calm her before she asked what the matter was.

'The tooth fairy didn't come.' Emma's sobs began again as she opened her mouth to reveal a new gap, fresh blood still visible in the centre, where yesterday morning there had been a tooth hanging by its last threads.

Helen hadn't known it had come out. She inwardly cursed Alex for probably having known but not having thought to do anything about it.

'When did it come out, darling?' Helen was aware that Alex had now joined them on the landing.

'Fuck,' she heard him muttering, confirming her earlier suspicions.

'Yesterday, when we were having supper.'

153

Emma was still mildly hysterical. 'Daddy made chicken drumsticks and I thought I'd swallowed a bit of bone but then Jo-Jo realised my tooth wasn't there and Daddy said I must've swallowed it.'

'We wrote a note to the fairies to explain.' Alex had joined the huddle outside the bathroom. 'I told her they might leave her something anyway.'

Helen caught his eye and raised her shoulders in a movement that she hoped implied 'What bloody good is it writing a note and raising her expectations if you don't follow it up with action?'

'I'll just go to the loo and then I'll help you have a look.' Helen dived into the bathroom, where the trousers Alex had been wearing the previous evening were folded and hung over the back of a chair. She searched the pockets for loose change and found a two-pound coin, around which she made a tight fist before re-emerging and heading for her daughter's room.

Emma lifted her pillow, scattering half a dozen soft toys across the bed and revealing a sheet devoid of fairy money.

'Have you looked on the floor, in case it fell out?' Helen asked, bending down and surreptitiously rolling the coin under the bed.

'There is something under the bed.' Emma sounded vaguely hopeful. 'Yes, there is! It's a two-pound coin! They brought me two pounds even though they didn't get a tooth. Can we go to the market this morning so I can spend it? I

154

want to buy a present for Bugsy. Can I watch telly now?'

Helen was surprised that Emma still believed in fairies. When she herself was that age she'd simply presented her teeth straight to her parents, who had immediately stumped up the money. She supposed it was because she had older brothers and sisters that her childhood had been stripped of magic. The older ones had soon seen to it that she knew exactly who put presents in her stocking and replaced teeth with cash, not to mention the mechanics of sex.

Emma was still blissfully ignorant of such facts, although she had had the where-do-babies-come-from chat with Helen. Helen hadn't realised that in doing so she had unwittingly painted Alex as an aggressor who 'did that thing' to her. For weeks afterwards, Emma had eyed him suspiciously, as if she no longer quite trusted him, knowing exactly what he was capable of.

'I would have made it clear that you were gagging for it,' Alex said, when they were having lunch with friends who'd noticed a certain frostiness between him and his daughter and asked the reason.

'I was not gagging for it,' Helen had spluttered into her soup. 'I was just up for it, on an equal basis, as it were . . . ' She trailed off and took another spoonful of soup, aware that the male half of the couple they were having lunch with was giving her a look of what could best be described as renewed admiration.

'If you're still gagging for it after however many years it is that you've been married . . . ' he

155

started saying before his own daughter burst in from the garden asking if they could have something to drink.

'Lemonade or Coke or something, please.' She was breathless as well as thirsty. 'What does gagging for it mean?'

Alex had been secretly pleased that he'd managed to let slip in front of friends that his wife was still up for it, seeing this as testimony to his own irresistibility.

Helen, though, had felt she was letting the side down in front of Sarah, who had confessed earlier that she and Donald had not had sex for at least nine months. Sarah and Donald had been together for longer than Helen and Alex, and Helen wondered if this was how monogamy played itself out, with the mutual loss of interest in your sole partner.

Alex, however, was still interested.

'Yes, you can go and watch TV for half an hour,' he told Emma. Joe emerged from his own room, where he'd been quietly Lego tank-fighting until someone came to tell him it was morning. 'Then I shall make us all pancakes for breakfast and we can go to the market.'

Joe and Emma disappeared down the stairs arguing the merits of CBBC versus CBeebies.

'Half an hour?' Alex raised his eyebrows questioningly and gestured towards the bed-room.

Helen raised hers back, wondering who had synchronised their libidos. 'I'll just put the TV on and make sure they are settled.'

She followed the children downstairs, opened

the curtains in the sitting room and switched on the television. The bag she had taken with her the previous evening was still on the floor, and it beeped to alert her to a text message.

She took out her phone and opened the inbox. 'Did you get home safely? Gx' it read.

Helen resisted the temptation to text back immediately, and instead deleted the message.

'Daddy and I are going to have a bit more sleep,' she told Emma and Joe before going back to her bedroom, locking the door behind her and sliding into bed.

'I've never had sex with a tooth fairy before,' Alex said, pulling her towards him. 'Sorry, I forgot all about the tooth.'

Helen didn't reply, partly because now wasn't the moment to decide who was ultimately responsible for the failure of the tooth fairy to put in an appearance during the night, and partly because she was feeling the full weight of parental responsibility in a way she had not done for a long time.

She knew that in the great scheme of things it didn't really matter if the tooth fairy forgot to visit. She could, as she had this morning, stage the discovery of money that had somehow been lost, or remind the children that the tooth fairy had a day off on Friday, or even come clean about the whole incisors-under-the-pillow cha-rade. They would emerge from any of the scenarios without being too emotionally dam-aged.

She also knew that loving her family involved much more than performing the multitude of daily tasks that included being the tooth fairy. It meant putting them above everything else, above her own needs and desires. It meant she had to pull back from whatever it was that seemed to be pulling her off course.

Alex was shifting himself on top of her, pulling her physically back from the mental space where she was hovering. For the moment at least.

23

'Joe, get off the computer now.' Alex was in a bad mood. He'd already got cross with Helen and Emma; now it was Joe's turn.

'We need to go soon. And you're not supposed to be on it anyway.'

When Helen had asked if there was anything wrong, he had pleaded tiredness. Helen had bitten back the urge to point out that she was the one who actually had the right to be tired.

Joe had woken several times in the night. The first time it was a nightmare; the second he was convinced he was having an asthma attack and demanded to be given his inhaler, even though his breathing appeared perfectly normal. The third time, he'd wet the bed. Helen had got up on each occasion, reassuring, calming him and changing sheets.

Alex appeared blissfully unaware that her sleep had been disturbed, and seemed to find it unreasonable that when Joe wandered into their room at five a.m. saying he could not find his blanket, Helen asked him to get up and look for it.

It should have been her that was ahead in the 'I've had less sleep than you have' stakes, but Alex appeared to think that he was suffering more.

Possibly it was because he didn't really want to have lunch with Katie and Philip today. The date had been in the diary for weeks, he liked Philip and Katie, the kids were looking forward to it and the weather was beautiful, but Alex maintained he was really tired from the week and it was not how he would choose to spend the day.

'I said he could go on Club Penguin for half an hour.' Helen intervened on Joe's behalf. 'He's tired and I thought it best if he did something quiet before we go.'

'We're all tired,' Alex growled. 'Let's not get into an argument about it. What time are we supposed to be there, anyway?'

'One-ish.' Helen bit back the temptation to point out that she was not the one trying to start an argument.

'And how long will it go on?' Alex was doing his best to provoke some sort of reaction from his wife.

'I don't know.' Helen tried to stay calm. 'We'll probably stay till five or six, not much later. The kids have school tomorrow.'

'And I've got a hefty script to read through before I go to Manchester,' Alex replied. 'I could have done with a day off today.'

'It is a day off,' Helen retorted. 'And we're spending it with friends. Can't you just stop thinking about work and enjoy it?'

She realised as soon as she had said this that it was unlikely to improve Alex's mood. Fortunately Joe interrupted before they were able to up the level of bickering.

'I've stopped now, Dad.' His tone was appeasing. 'And there's a new message for you, Mum.'

'Good boy.' Helen ruffled his hair and went to look at her inbox, half hoping the message would be from Graham.

★   ★   ★

'Come in, come in, come in, come in!' Katie welcomed each of them individually. 'You've arrived just in time. I need to get the barbecue going, but Philip is ensconced in his study, on the phone to one of his PhD students.'

She ushered them into the back garden, where the children disappeared into a makeshift den that Hannah had prepared earlier.

'What do you want to drink?' Katie asked Alex, who had risen to the barbecue challenge and was already piling charcoal into the triangular prism shape he always insisted was essential to get the fire going.

'I'd love a beer, please.' His mood seemed to have lightened since he'd been in Katie's presence.

'I'll help,' said Helen, following her friend through the patio doors into the house.

'You've cheered him up,' she said when they were out of earshot. 'He's been in a foul mood all morning.'

'So has Philip,' Katie said in a hushed voice, although Philip was still nowhere to be seen. 'Says he's got work to do. It's a Sunday, for Christ's sake.'

On cue, Philip emerged from his study.

'Hello,' he said, kissing Helen. He nodded towards the study door. 'Sorry about that. A

161

dissertation crisis for one of my students.'

'Are they allowed to call you on a Sunday?' Helen asked, in order to show solidarity with her friend. But Philip was already heading towards the flames Alex had managed to conjure up and didn't hear her.

'He called her,' Katie said, her voice hissing in unison with the bottle of beer she had just taken the top off.

Helen raised her eyebrows and took the beer out to the garden, where she could hear Alex telling Philip about the latest addition to their family.

'I suppose rabbits are easier than babies?' Philip asked.

'He's pissed off,' Katie said quietly to Helen, 'because Leonard woke several times during the night.'

'So did Jo-Jo,' Helen sympathised.

'I'm sure we could all kill for a night's uninterrupted sleep.' Philip had caught the drift of their conversation.

'Alex is lucky,' Helen said. 'He gets to stay in hotel rooms half the week, with no one to disturb him.'

'They're not always quiet.' Alex wasn't going to admit that he did enjoy the luxury of nights in a bed alone, with no one coming in complaining of nightmares and no one turning over and taking the duvet with them.

'Well at least you don't have to put up with Joe kicking you all night.' Helen thought back to a recent occasion, when Joe's breathing had appeared erratic and she'd let him sleep in the empty space left by Alex, only to find that his breathing was fine but he appeared to have bad dreams all night and kicked her continuously.

'But you jump at the opportunity to have him in our bed!' Alex teased. 'Cheers, everyone.'

'Cheers.' They clinked beer bottles. Helen said nothing in reply to Alex's comment, which was essentially true. 'So, is it just us, or is anyone else coming?' Alex asked Katie.

'No, it's just us,' she said, prodding the barbecue coals with a skewer.

'Katie did invite her new boyfriend,' Philip said, putting his arm around her as if to show them that he was not serious, but looking round for a reaction. 'He couldn't come, though.'

'Who's that, then?' Alex asked, looking rather anxious as his perfect prism of charcoal was destroyed by Katie's slightly agitated prodding.

'Some stay-at-home dad she met through Leonard.' Philip's tone was jocular, but Helen wondered if this masked a level of concern.

'That's not fair,' Katie interjected. 'He used to run a successful internet marketing company but he gave it up to look after his son because his wife died of cancer.'

'Oh, the lovely Cary,' Helen found herself saying, and when Katie glowered at her, she wished she hadn't.

'You've met him, then?' Philip asked.

'Yes, I've met him in the park,' Helen said. 'He seems nice, and it must be very hard to bring up a child on your own after losing your wife. I gather a lot of the other mothers try to help him out a bit.'

She hoped this last remark would make up for the way she'd first reacted to mention of Cary.

'Helen's old boyfriend is just back from Afghanistan,' Alex said, apropos of nothing, or possibly apropos of Philip describing Cary as Katie's new boyfriend.

'Who's that?' Katie asked, unwrapping a packet of sausages. 'Or do you mean Jim Keeble? Helen told me they'd had a drink the other night.'

'That's the one,' said Alex, taking the sausages from her and beginning to arrange them over the smouldering coals. If it occurred to him that Helen hadn't told him she'd been for a drink with Jim Keeble, he didn't say anything, commenting instead on the state of the barbecue. 'Damn! What's that saying about pouring oil on troubled waters? There should be one about adding sausages to barbecues. The fat is making this thing flare up.'

Katie said something about taking the sausages off again, while Helen wondered if there were any particular troubled waters Alex was referring to.

24

Helen knew it was ridiculous to feel massively disappointed that there were no emails for her. At least, none from Graham Parks. There were a couple of work-related messages — a query from a sub and a possible date for an interview with a violinist — and one from Jim Keeble asking if she was free for lunch or a drink later in the week. But that was all.

Her reaction was out of all proportion. She felt very down. This was ridiculous, she told herself. She was behaving like a love-struck teenager, desperate for a text from some spotty adolescent she had hardly spoken to but had convinced herself she was in love with because he had looked at her once in a maths lesson.

She'd bought Graham a card at the Saturday market, ostensibly to thank him for dinner, which he'd ended up paying for, but in reality because she wanted to maintain contact.

She replied to the two work emails, then sent another to Jim Keeble that she hoped was light and friendly in tone.

Hi Jim,
    Lovely though it was to see you the other day, not sure I'll be able to squeeze you in in the near future. Would love to tell you I have a diary packed full of glamorous occasions, but in fact it is simply packed with parents'

meetings and trips to the vet — oh, and I am going away to visit Alex on location in Manchester, a rare treat with a hotel thrown in. Hope things are settling down at home. No doubt will run into you in the canteen if you remain in the country.

Helen x

She left her computer on and went to make a cup of tea, her third of the day. Helen was a self-confessed tea addict. She had Alex to blame for that. As her gran would have said, he made 'a lovely cup of tea'. He did it with the same fastidious attention to detail he applied to everything else. There was no casual slinging of a bag into the bottom of a cup, sloshing in some water and milk and giving it a big stir before chucking the bag in the bin. Alex would carefully put just the right amount of milk into the cup before adding a tea bag, and then slowly pour just-boiled water from the kettle on to the bag, agitating it all the while with a teaspoon so that the flavour was released slowly.

The resulting cup of tea took on a deep golden colour and tasted better than anything else Helen had drunk. She now consumed an average of nine or ten pints a day, and sometimes worried what unseen damage this addiction was doing to her.

Mindful of the fact that making her third pint of the day was distracting her from getting down to work and likely to be unnerving her liver, she opted for decaf before returning to the living room, where her computer was set up in an alcove. Before children it had seemed tucked away, but now it was pretty much in the middle of everything. Certainly it was far too much on view to check private emails.

Her inbox was not showing any new messages. She took a swig of tea. It didn't taste the same, decaf; didn't have any real bite, didn't get her brain going if she had a piece to write and was struggling to find the words.

On this occasion, though, it did alert her brain to the fact that she never checked her junk email and that there was just a slight possibility that there might be something from him lurking amongst the offers of Viagra and penis enlargement.

Bingo! An email from Graham Parks, subject 'Your fucking awful handwriting'. No wonder it had been sent straight to the junk folder.

The computer, used by all the family, had a strict system of parental controls. Helen had thought the fact that it was in the living room was control enough, until Joe stumbled across a porn site after Googling images of Virgin aeroplanes.

Now, with new controls in place, emails containing anything slightly suspect went straight to the junk bin, including those with the word 'fucking' in the title — not that there were many of them.

Helen trawled through the rest of the junk box to see if there was anything else that should by rights have gone to her inbox. A friend who worked in local government had told her that a lot of emails sent to Scunthorpe council went astray because of the fourletter word contained in the city's name.

Helen's junk was mostly offers of loans or requests from people called Kofi or Murat to send them money to help prop up small nation states that without her help would surely collapse. But there was also one from her niece, whose email contained the word 'spunk'. She opened this, to be told that she had a message on her Facebook wall. Getting that would involve having to go through a whole new electronic process just to find a picture of said niece clubbing in Bristol on a Friday night. She marked the spunky email address as safe, closed it, took a sip of tea and decided that now was the time for the delayed gratification of reading the mail from Graham Parks.

'Hello ☺,' it began. He always used the smiley-face logo that, until he began emailing her, she had thought was some sort of punctuation error.

> Thank you for your card. It was a beautiful card but you have fucking awful handwriting! Who'd have imagined that someone so quietly beautiful on the outside could be wrestling with such demons on the inside? I've never had such a lovely letter that so resembled hate mail before . . .

Helen smiled. The email had that effect on her. She read the paragraph again, straining to see the subtext beneath the words. From where she was sitting, the subtext was probably good. He'd liked the card, had admitted for the first time that he actually found her attractive (she'd been wondering if the attraction was mental and not physical at all) and yet had managed, by mocking her scrawl, to keep them where they were at — a part-time journalist and an interviewee with an unacknowledged mutual attraction they were not (at least she was not) at liberty to do anything about.

It was true Helen did have uncharacteristically terrible writing. She had once had it analysed by a forensic graphologist for a feature about handwriting. The graphologist had been enjoying his fifteen minutes of fame after helping police with a high-profile rape and murder case and her editor had decided they should do something with him. This turned out to be asking a handful of journalists, Helen included, to submit samples of their handwriting for analysis and persuading the graphologist, much against his professional instincts, to match the culprits with their scrawls. He had said that Helen's sample showed signs of arsonist tendencies and had assigned it to the wild, bearded man from the post room who had also been drawn into the exercise.

She read on.

I hope when you have had time to think that we will be able to meet again. I hope I am not speaking out of turn when I say there seemed to be a connection between us. I feel

I have taken something from you that is positive and that our random meeting will have a good effect on both our lives. Enjoy your week.

Graham x

25

The copy of *Ruby* magazine that Helen bought to read on the train to Manchester had a small snippet about Graham Parks' book.

> Forty-something Ed is fairly new to the world of 'proper' work.
> Having travelled and bummed during his twenties and thirties, he has finally settled into teaching. But when he is caught taking cocaine in the pupils' toilets, he is forced to exchange his job for rehab.
> Ed is a man haunted by his past, a past that has led him to ruin his present. *Excuse Me, I'm Lost* is the story of a man struggling to lay his past to rest and get on with his future.

Helen wondered how much of Graham there was in Ed. Both were in their early forties and still single, and she sensed that despite his easy manner and almost serene demeanour, there were demons that prevented Graham from getting on with his life.

She didn't think the mention in the magazine gave *Ruby* readers a real taste of the book, but it did give her an excuse to contact the author.

'*Ruby* magazine cites you as an October 'must read',' she texted. 'Now hundreds of middle-aged women will find themselves compelled to buy your book.'

She sent the message and returned to the magazine, wondering as she flicked over the month's 'must see' films whether her mother would manage to find the way to Joe's classroom. The school was confusing in its layout, and although her mum had come with her to pick the children up on a number of occasions, navigating the maze of alleys and stairwells to the door where she would find Joe was difficult.

Helen's mother had agreed to bring the children home from school and spend the night at their house so that Helen could be a part of the audience at the live recording of *Muddy Water*. She didn't like to ask her mother to babysit too often, as she knew she found it exhausting. The children also found it an effort trying to be good for Granny, which had the side effect of making them particularly obnoxious when Helen came home. But she felt she had to publicly support Alex, plus she was curious to meet Venetia Taylor, who, since joining the cast of *Muddy Water*, had made such a big impression on her husband.

The scriptwriters were moving towards Kev and Patsy, Alex and Venetia's characters, having some sort of fling, so Alex was spending more time with her than with anyone else. But Helen couldn't help wondering if there were other reasons why he found himself compelled to bring her name up time and again.

It didn't take Graham long to reply to her message.

'Hundreds of middle-aged women is a slightly daunting prospect,' he texted. 'I suppose I should think of *Ruby* readers not as one mass entity but as lots of individuals, some as young and lovely as you.'

'Ha ha,' she texted back. 'I'm almost the same age as you, lovely boy!' This was an epithet she often used for Joe, but in the course of her emailing and texting Graham Parks, she had begun to extend it to him.

In an earlier conversation she had told Graham how Joe had burst into tears when the parents of an older and bigger friend had passed on a pair of nearly new trainers. At first she had thought that Joe had inherited his father's slight obsessive-compulsiveness and that the idea of second-hand shoes appalled him, but as the sobs subsided it became clear that he was simply on the lookout for his friend.

'But that means Max will have to go to school without shoes,' he'd sniffed, only stopping once she had reassured him that Max had other shoes.

'He sounds like a lovely boy,' Graham had written, adding that he himself used to worry that Santa lived in abject poverty because he gave away everything he had.

'I bet you were a lovely boy too,' she'd said, realising as she wrote it that Graham Parks had certain childlike qualities still. He reminded her of a lost boy, and she wondered if her attraction to him wasn't partly wanting to rescue him.

She told herself sternly that she had a rabbit as

a third-child substitute and that she should stop texting fully grown men and concentrate on the men who were in her life already.

'Why are you reading *Ruby* magazine at 3 in the afternoon?' Graham texted. Helen decided not to tell him she was on the train to Manchester to see Alex.

'That's what urban housewives do when they're not putting up new curtains or shagging the postman,' she replied.

Modern communications made it so easy to take innocent flirting a step further. If you met someone and liked them, there was no need for clandestine phone calls or sending letters marked 'Private' to workplace addresses; you could simply email and text in the knowledge that it was likely to remain between the two of you.

Unless of course you were particularly unlucky, or stupid, like one of Alex's former colleagues, who'd texted his lover thanking her for a wonderful evening and promising to find the time to do it again soon but sent it by mistake to his wife. For a while their marriage had looked as if it might be over, but they'd got through it and appeared to be living happily ever after again.

Helen wondered whether, if she had met Graham in a pre-electronic age, she would have kept in touch. If she had had to pick up the phone and call him or write an actual letter, would she have bothered? Taking such steps seemed more dangerous than merely texting or emailing. She wasn't sure she'd have taken the risk.

Yet now she *was* taking a risk, keeping in touch when she knew he wanted more than she was willing to give, e-flirting, thinking it harmless, knowing deep down that it was more dangerous than she was willing to admit.

26

The receptionist at the Manchester television studios was very young and very beautiful, probably an aspiring actress or television executive, thought Helen. All jobs were a foot in the door these days.

'Hi, I'm here to see the recording of *Muddy Water*,' she told the girl, who had looked up but not yet taken her in. 'I'm Alex Mills' wife. Could you let him know I'm here?'

The receptionist looked at her properly for the first time, registering surprise. This was an increasingly common occurrence since Alex had begun to be seen regularly on television. When he was Alex the jobbing actor, largely supported by his journalist wife, Helen had fitted whatever idea people held about what she might be like. Probably they didn't actually have an idea and so just accepted her as she was. But now that he was Alex the weekly soap star, he had increased in stature and Helen appeared to have diminished as a direct consequence.

Projecting yourself into people's living rooms via their television screens appeared to give you increased presence, greater curiosity value and made you more attractive and desirable.

Helen felt she no longer appeared to fit the perceived image of what a television actor's wife might be like. People seemed to expect someone younger, more beautiful and certainly more polished than she was. When she and Alex had first met, they'd seemed an equal match. Although Alex was older, the precarious nature of his work meant he lacked the status of an older man, and physically they were on a par — both reasonably attractive, neither extremely beautiful nor handsome.

According to physiologists, people chose partners on a level of equal attractiveness and often with similar physical characteristics too. Helen had noticed that this appeared to be true when she was expecting Emma and went to antenatal classes. Dark-haired, dark-eyed women were mostly sporting dark-haired, dark-eyed men, while fairer mothers had fairer partners.

Finding a partner on an equal attractiveness level was the unwritten rule, but obviously there were exceptions. Wealth and fame could override what you lacked in looks; even a steady income or being recognisable from the television.

This was why Alex appeared to have suddenly shot up in the attractiveness ratings and she felt herself lagging behind. Perhaps it was this that had caused her to be drawn to Graham Parks, she pondered. While Alex's attractiveness levels were rising, was she subconsciously seeking refuge in someone who, like herself, was showing obvious signs of ageing? Or was it just because by seeing something in her, Graham allowed her to value herself as a person in her own right, not just a mother less needed than she had been, a career woman whose career had plateaued, and a wife who no longer matched up to her husband?

'Okaaay,' said the receptionist, drawing out the

vowel sound in slight disbelief, as if she needed the extra time to take in this fact. 'I'll call through to the studio and let them know you are here.'

'Thank you,' said Helen, noting the 'let them' rather than 'let him'. While Alex was here, he was public property. Someone close to him would be told that she was here, and they might pass on this information to Alex, depending on whether they thought he needed to know or not.

'Hi, Chloe, it's Vanessa Hargreaves.' She said this with an air of knowing that she would one day be someone, not deigning to add that she was calling from reception, expecting whoever she was talking to to know who she was. 'I've got Alex's wife in reception. She's come to watch the recording but wanted to let him know she's here.'

There was a slight pause while Vanessa listened to what was being said.

'Is he expecting you?' she asked Helen.

'Yes!' Helen almost shouted it. She was tempted to take out her mobile and call Alex direct, but his phone would probably be switched off and the move to show who was in control of whether she was allowed to see Alex or not might backfire.

'Someone will come down in a few minutes.' Vanessa motioned her head towards the sofas arranged in a semicircle by the window.

Helen did as she was obviously meant to and sat down, wondering if the someone who would come down might be Alex.

'Hi, Helen!' She looked up and saw Chloe,

178

Muddy Water's production assistant, striding towards the sofa, smiling and welcoming. She had met Chloe only once before, but she'd talked to her on the phone on a number of occasions, when Alex's mobile had been switched off and she'd needed to contact him.

'How lovely to see you again.' Chloe embraced her as if they were old friends, kissing her on both cheeks and making her feel welcome, even though Helen suspected she embraced total strangers in much the same way. 'Alex told us you were coming. Everyone's really looking forward to seeing you again.'

'That's nice.' Helen let herself be guided towards the lifts.

'Alex is in make-up at the moment.' Chloe explained her presence. 'I'll take you up there so you can see him before the recording starts.'

'Alex in make-up still takes some getting used to,' Helen joked as the lift doors opened and they stepped inside.

'Didn't you realise you'd married a closet transvestite?' Chloe pressed the button for the fourth floor.

'I had my suspicions,' Helen replied, 'but I thought I could live with it.'

They walked along the corridor to a room at the end where she found her husband sitting in an Eames-style chair, his hair scraped back in a hairband while a make-up artist expertly applied foundation. It was a slightly off-putting sight, and she wished the Vanessas of this world could see him like this, or for that matter at home, watching football with his hand down the front of his trousers. That was more the real Alex than the good-looking but rough-around-the-edges security manager he projected on screen.

'Hello, I like that shade of lipstick,' she said, kissing him, although he was caked in make-up and it felt odd. 'Do you know what it is?'

'I think it's called Just Kissed, isn't it, Agathe?' Alex inclined his head towards the make-up artist, who took him literally and picked up the tube of berry-coloured face paint and examined the label.

'No,' she said, 'it's called Demi Rose.'

Helen stayed a few moments before she allowed Chloe to lead her to her seat in the studio.

As they left the make-up room they passed Venetia Taylor heading in the opposite direction. She smiled in acknowledgment of Helen, though ignorant of who she was, before going into make-up herself.

'Hey!' It was a greeting full of warmth and excitement, and it was Alex who delivered it. Helen wanted to stop and listen in on the rest of their exchange, but Chloe was shepherding her back towards the lifts.

Once in the studio, she was seated next to a fifty-ish man. He appeared to be on his own, and perhaps because she was too, he decided he would talk to her.

'Bit of a coup, the programme getting Venetia Taylor,' he said with no introduction. 'I've always liked her. Looking forward to seeing her today. How about you?'

Helen wasn't entirely sure what he was

180

referring to. Did he wonder if she too had a long-held affection for Venetia or merely if she was looking forward to seeing the show?

'Ummm, my husband Alex plays Kev,' she said, deciding this was an apposite reply.

'Lucky him.' Her companion for the duration of the recording gave her a knowing look. 'Way things are going, he'll probably end up in bed with Venetia before the month is up.'

The floor manager asked for quiet. Helen sat back thankfully in her seat as the lights dimmed around the audience.

*　*　*

Helen felt a sharp pang of anger when she saw Alex standing with his arm around Venetia. He was bending towards her, saying something and rubbing her shoulder in a manner that suggested affection or, to give him the benefit of the doubt, reassurance.

It was Chloe who had sought Helen out amongst the audience and led her to the green room, where they were having a small aftershow party.

'Alex is great, isn't he?' she enthused. 'I know you see the show on the television, but when you're watching him live, you get a better understanding of what he does. He's a great actor, obviously, but he also brings out the best in all the others. We think he's a bit of a star.'

Helen had to agree. Seeing Alex performing live in front of the cameras did give him an extra dimension. He appeared confident in his role and the other actors seemed to take their lead from him. He had been patient when people fluffed their lines, causing an umpteenth retake, considerate towards an extra playing a shoplifter with no lines, praising the way she'd stuffed a jumper under her jacket and including her in the general cast banter, and endlessly good-humoured when things went wrong and the stage had to be reset and lights redirected.

She could see he was an asset to *Muddy Water,* not only for his acting skills but also for his team-playing ability. She was proud of him, but also jealous that in the studio there was a general attitude of shared ownership towards him and she was only a minor stakeholder.

Now she found him striking a proprietorial pose with Venetia. She reminded herself that it was not unusual for Alex to have his arm around somebody. He was, as she frequently teased him, 'a luvvy'. His luvviness extended to 'doing' the room by kissing everyone goodbye when they left a party together, leaving her standing by the door having thought a general wave would suffice.

Once when Emma had been a baby they'd broken down and were waiting by the side of a roundabout for the AA to arrive. A traffic policeman on a motorbike had drawn up alongside and asked if they were all right. As Alex told him they'd called the AA and were waiting for 'a very nice man!' to arrive, he'd unconsciously put his hand on the policeman's shoulder, running it down towards his elbow while thanking him for stopping.

'I can't believe you got all touchy-feely with a traffic policeman!' Helen had laughed, after the officer had roared off on his bike. 'Honestly, I thought you might be arrested for indecent assault. You should have seen the look on his face.'

So Alex, surrounding himself with theatrical types who were by their nature tactile, was often to be found in closer contact with other people than might initially appear appropriate. Helen knew this but still found herself feeling put out by his proximity to Venetia.

'There's Alex over there, in the corner.' Chloe appeared unperturbed by the scene that greeted them. 'By the way,' she added, 'I read a piece in the paper that you wrote about Graham Parks. He used to go to school with my older brother. They're still friends. Jack tried to help him when he had his breakdown.'

Alex had momentarily moved in closer to Venetia and kissed her on the cheek. It appeared to be an exit kiss, as he was now turning, scanning the room, searching for Helen. He smiled when he saw her, making his way through the crowded room and kissing her publicly in front of everyone.

'Thank you for coming.' He kissed her again, putting his arm around her and turning back to the room. 'Come and meet some of the others.'

She went with him because that was what she wanted, to be there with Alex as his wife, but she was also tempted to stay with Chloe a while longer and find out more about Graham Parks.

27

The hotel where Alex and the rest of the cast stayed was a former warehouse. The interior acknowledged none of its past as a centre for weaving and spinning but had been refurbished in a style that Helen joked was mock-Tudor meets Gothic horror. The wood panelling in the reception and the heavily carved staircase complete with grotesque gargoyles were at odds with the minimalist style of the bedrooms, which were all marbled ensuites and Egyptian cotton duvet covers.

'Nice room.' Helen looked around, noticing Alex's clothes folded neatly and put away in the wardrobe that segued neatly into the bottom of the L shape caused by the intrusion of the bathroom.

Alex must be a chambermaid's dream, she thought to herself. Not because he appeared better-looking than he actually was due to being on the telly, but because she was almost certain he made his own bed every morning before leaving for the studios, hung the towels neatly on the heated rail and tidied away any personal possessions that threatened to spoil the general look of the room. She imagined the mystified hotel staff opening the door, all Marigolded up and ready for the morning blitz, and then closing it again, telling their supervisor that the room had already been done. The supervisor would check the schedule and assure the skivvy that it had not. The skivvy would reopen the door to display the spotless surfaces and perfect hospital corners on the bed, and they would both scratch their heads, wondering who had upset their methodical way of working through the rooms.

'It's fairly bog-standard,' Alex replied to her comment. He stayed in hotels often enough to find them homogenous and devoid of charm, whereas although Helen still went on the odd press trip courtesy of the *Sunday Review*, she did not do so often enough to be inured to the delights of free toiletries and the possibility of room service.

She put her small holdall beside Alex's larger one, not wishing to disrupt the oasis of calm he was able to create in her absence, and sat on the bed.

Alex sat next to her, put his arm around her shoulder, slid his hand down the front of her shirt and began playing with her breast but in such an absent-minded fashion she was not sure if he was even aware he was doing it.

'So . . . ' he said, a favourite preamble to sex. 'Are you glad you came?'

She thought about telling him she hadn't come yet and it would take more than a quick fumble inside her shirt to achieve that, but decided to avoid the subject of sex, as she wasn't really in the mood.

'Of course,' she replied. 'It was great to see you live on the set, and nice to meet the rest of the cast too.'

'They all really liked you.' Alex stood up, took

off his jacket, hung it round the back of a chair and pulled his shirt over his head.

'I didn't really get the chance to talk to Venetia, though.' She wanted Alex to reveal something of how he felt towards Venetia. 'She seemed a bit frosty.'

'Frosty? Venetia?' Alex was folding his shirt now. 'No, she's lovely. I don't know what gave you that idea.'

'To you, maybe,' Helen continued. 'She hardly said a word to me.'

'Well, it was her first live recording,' Alex said in her defence. 'And there were a lot of people there that she doesn't know very well. It was probably hard for her to talk to everyone.'

'You seem very fond of her.' Helen couldn't help herself. 'Am I right to feel jealous?'

'Ha!' Alex snorted. 'Why would you be jealous of Venetia?'

'Well, you know.' She didn't really know why herself. 'She's a very beautiful woman and you spend half the week up here with her, and she's exciting and a great actress.'

'And you,' said Alex, coming over and kissing her, 'are a very beautiful woman and I spend more than half the week with you, and you're a great mother and exciting and I'm going to go to the bathroom and then we should go to bed.'

He closed the door behind him, and she sat and listened to him peeing and brushing his teeth in anticipation of a night of guaranteed uninterrupted sex with his wife.

★ ★ ★

Alex was quick in the bathroom, but Helen took her time, carefully inspecting the rows of complimentary bath milks, wondering what to use and what to take home as presents for Emma and Joe. As she'd suspected before, Joe was already beginning to show signs of his father's obsessive-compulsive streak, treasuring amongst his very best possessions a medal won at a summer sports school, a stone that he insisted was a dinosaur egg, and a very common football collector's card, which he'd swapped for quite a rare one with a friend who'd insisted it was a good deal. Also, a miniature tin containing a slab of shoe polish and a tiny sponge that Alex had brought back from a previous stay in the same hotel.

She put the sewing kit in her wash bag, knowing Emma would find a good use for the miniature skeins of coloured threads, but decided against taking the disposable razor. She began running herself a bath, delaying the moment when she would have to go to bed with Alex.

It was late now. After the party in the studio green room, they'd moved on, in the way that only middle-aged people move on, to the hotel bar — still officially out, but only a staircase or a lift away from bed. They'd carried on drinking and debriefing until after two a.m., when the staff began making it clear that they had clubs to go on to and needed to close the bar.

Helen had tried to talk to Venetia, but found her habit of beginning every sentence with 'I've already told Alex this . . . ' extremely irritating, and had slowly ceded territory and allowed her to monopolise Alex, which was what she clearly wanted to do.

Helen had been tired and would have preferred to miss the more-drinks-in-the-bar part of the evening, but Alex was in his element and wanted to prolong the atmosphere of self-congratulation a while longer. She had wondered if it would give her the opportunity to quiz Chloe about Graham Parks, and while Alex and Venetia were laughing together about something that had happened earlier in the week that was so hysterically funny that only the two of them could see the joke, she made her move, accompanying Chloe on a trip to the bar and splitting the next round with her.

The drink bought in that round had probably been the one too many that now left Helen longing to go straight to sleep.

'How are you doing in there?' Alex called from the bedroom.

'I'm just making the most of the superior brand of bubble bath,' she said, raising her voice over the sound of the running water. 'And hoping you might fall asleep.' She said this more quietly, so that Alex wouldn't hear and for the moment wouldn't know that even though they had a nice hotel room, had plied each other with drink for much of the evening and had no children to get up to first thing in the morning, she didn't want to have sex with him.

That was, she mused, one of the down sides of female emancipation. You could have sex with pretty much whoever you chose to, you could ask for what you wanted and expect to have an orgasm every time, but all of that made it harder to come up with a good reason for *not* having sex, especially with your husband. At least in the days when women had to lie back and think of England, they could have 'headaches', 'neuralgia', 'women's troubles' and various other euphemisms, which all boiled down to not really being in the mood. These days you had to spell out the fact that you didn't want sex, and that left your waiting-for-it-in-the-bedroom partner wondering why not.

That Alex would be in the mood was more or less guaranteed. His endorphins were still doing mini-marathons after the high of performing in front of a live audience, and he had been buoyed up by waves of adulation from the audience and his touchy-feely 'you were great, Alex' session in the green room and the bar. All of this, plus his cosiness with Venetia, was bound to be making him feel irresistible to womankind as a whole and the woman in the bathroom in particular. Except that the woman in the bathroom was feeling vulnerable and adrift, battered by the co-star's put-downs and unsettled by what Chloe had told her about Graham Parks.

Helen had tried to be casual at the bar, bringing Graham's name up in the same breath as asking if Chloe wanted any crisps.

'Eritrean Fair Trade Sea Salt, Mongolian Goat's Cheese or Myrrh and Tarragon Spice?' she asked, raising an eyebrow at the overpriced upmarket crisps. 'By the way, did you say your brother was an old friend of Graham Parks?'

189

'I thought myrrh was a precious metal.' Chloe appeared to be ignoring the casual remark about Graham Parks.

'No, it's a spice. I'll get a packet of each.' Helen tried to bring the crisps avenue of conversation to a close, leaving only the Graham one open. She placed her order and turned back to Chloe.

'So . . . what were we talking about?'

'Graham Parks?' Chloe's tone was slightly questioning, as if she was suspicious of Helen having brought him up in the conversation.

'Oh yes. You said something about your brother knowing him.' She wanted to remind Chloe that it was she who had raised the subject first, back in the green room.

'They went to school together,' Chloe said. 'A boarding school in Sussex. Jack, my brother, absolutely hated it. He was swotty and academic and not at all sporty and used to cry himself to sleep at night. So he got bullied, but Graham, who was clever and sporty and popular, took him under his wing.'

'Poor Jack.' Helen couldn't imagine being parted from Joe for weeks at a time. She wondered how parents coped with the separation, knowing their child was miserable. 'Was Graham able to bring him round to the delights of boarding school life?'

'Not really.' Chloe was organising the drinks into formations that would allow the two of them to carry them back to the others. 'Even though he was popular and sporty, Graham hated boarding school too, more than Jack by the end.

190

That's why everyone was so surprised when he joined the army. Voluntarily signing up to spend years taking orders in another institution seemed like madness.'

Helen asked the barman for a tray, delaying the moment when they would rejoin the others and this conversation would finish or merge with more talk of *Muddy Water*.

She glanced back to where the cast were seated around a table. Venetia was sitting opposite Alex and leaning across the table, as if to hear more clearly what he was saying. As she did so she knocked a glass slightly and it threatened to fall over, but Alex put out his hand and saved it. Then he briefly covered Venetia's hand, as if to say 'okay, accident averted'.

Helen noted that Venetia was even more beautiful in the flesh. She had expected her to be more ordinary off-screen, but found that while the actress looked tired and her skin, without the set makeup, was not flawless, she had a certain something that Helen could only think of as star quality.

Chloe was still talking.

'Jack tried to talk him out of it, told him he'd make a great lawyer or accountant, but he wanted to be a helicopter pilot and thought that was the only way.' She paused and began piling up the packets of crisps. 'I guess he told you some of this in your interview?'

'No, he was somewhat reticent about his past.' Helen hoped this would not prevent Chloe from being indiscreet. 'And I obviously hadn't done my research very well.'

'Well, maybe he wanted to keep it quiet, though it's not really a secret. In the end, I guess Jack was right. Graham went ahead and joined the army, and he liked the flying part but not the active service. He found some of the stuff he had to deal with very hard and eventually had a breakdown and was retired on grounds of ill health.'

There was something in the way Chloe had stressed the last two words that suggested there was a bit more to it, but as they headed back to rejoin the others, Helen changed the subject. She still wanted to know more, but she wanted to protect Graham Parks from being the subject of late-night speculation amongst strangers. She knew that now he had begun attracting attention on account of his book, his past would slowly begin to emerge into the public arena, but for the moment she wanted to shield him from being talked about by the likes of Venetia Taylor.

'What does your brother do?' she asked Chloe.

'He's a beekeeper!'

Helen wasn't sure if Chloe was joking, but found she was not when, now within earshot, Alex picked up the thread of their conversation.

'I must have told you about Chloe's beekeeping brother,' he said, although she knew he never had. 'Born to a long line of doctors and lawyers but wanted to be a beekeeper since he was four years old and read a picture book about how bees make honey.'

The others laughed. Alex was once again the centre of attention, and as Helen sipped her wine, she tried to work out what it was she now felt for Graham Parks, as new facets of his character began to reveal themselves to her. Her rational self felt relieved that Graham was flawed and came with a set of problems and a history of mental illness that she imagined would be hard to deal with. It was hard enough dealing with Alex's ego, his slight obsessive-compulsiveness, worries about his mother, who was developing dementia, and the multitude of problems that accompanied Emma and Joe. She didn't need another set of problems. She didn't need the burden of Graham Parks.

Her rational self now knew she should stop procrastinating in the hotel bathroom and get into bed with her husband.

Alex was not yet asleep.

'Are you okay?' he asked, when she failed to respond to the set of manoeuvres that signalled he wanted to have sex.

'Actually, I'm feeling a bit sick,' she elaborated. Really she just felt tired and as if she'd had a bit too much to drink.

'Have you got your period?' Alex wasn't going to let her off at the first hurdle.

'No. It's due, though,' she told him, which was true.

'You know my vasectomy's booked for a couple of weeks' time?'

'Yes.' Helen felt that Alex was introducing this not as a piece of information but as a tool for coercion. He was obviously too new and reconstructed a male to make her have sex against her wishes, but he wasn't above using a bit of mental pressure to get what he wanted.

She knew that he was worried that a vasectomy might change things; having agreed to have one, he felt like making the most of having everything in working order while it still was.

By bringing the subject up now, he'd made her feel bad about trying to go straight to sleep.

That was one of the things about being married, Helen mused. If one of you wanted sex and the other didn't, sometimes it was just better to have it. That way you didn't end up in a situation where you hadn't had it for months and it became an issue. There were enough recriminations in a marriage without adding withholding sex to a list of grievances. She switched off the light and turned towards her husband.

28

When Helen woke the following morning, there was a space in the bed next to her and a sound of gentle tapping coming from somewhere across the room. Alex was sitting at the desk, his laptop open and switched on.

'Isn't it a bit early for online gaming?' she asked, knowing full well that he would be ego-surfing, in search of reviews of *Muddy Water*.

A few journalists had been invited by the publicists to watch the show, in the hope that seeing it live would prompt them to flag it up on the television pages. It was too early for any of the papers to have put anything in, but the up-all-night geeks who worked for websites might have added their thoughts to their sites.

'There's a great review on switchiton.com.' Alex ignored her attempt at a joke and read an extract to her. ''Alex Mills is fantastic as Kev, the centre security manager who has not entirely abandoned his hopes of becoming a rock god, while the addition to the cast of real-life ex-rock goddess Venetia Taylor seems likely to produce some on-screen intrigue. Taylor is a little too glamorous for the set, but her performance is polished . . . ' It's great, isn't it?' Alex's question was more of a statement. 'I'm glad you came and saw it.'

'Me too.' Helen had mixed feelings about the

whole trip. She was glad to have seen Alex live in action and pleased to have had some time away from the children, but she knew she had only been afforded a brief glimpse of his other life, away from her and home and the family.

When Alex was in Manchester, he was no longer her husband or Emma and Joe's dad, he was Alex Mills, glamorous member of the cast of *Muddy Water,* potential love interest of new arrival Venetia Taylor. She envied him this freedom, especially as she was never very far away from being Helen, wife of Alex and mother to his two children. Even at work, she was the person who didn't actually have a desk and was always rushing to and from childcare commitments.

'Come back to bed for a bit,' she said, hoping to prolong for a while the time when they were simply Helen and Alex, married and the most important people in each other's lives.

'We have to check out by ten thirty,' Alex said, looking at his watch. It was already past nine. 'I'd better jump in the shower.'

He kissed her in a perfunctory manner, already mentally up and away, and headed towards the bathroom.

'Why don't we go out for breakfast somewhere,' he asked as he picked a towel from a pile of white fluff, 'before we head home?'

'Okay.' Helen got up and opened the curtains. It would be nice to have breakfast out somewhere, just the two of them. They used to do that a lot, when they first met. It was part of the ritual of courtship — meeting somewhere in the evening, going back to her place or his, having sex a lot and then, hungry, going out for breakfast. It was like a post-coital cigarette. Neither of them smoked, so instead they ate in companionable silence, leafing through newspapers, seeing the news with the rose-tinted view of people who were newly in love.

These days, breakfast was always fraught. Helen mostly ate on her feet, running from fridge to table to toaster, interspersing clearing away cereal bowls with packing school bags. Alex, when he was there, was an irritating presence, wiping crumbs up before anyone had finished, trying to appear helpful by asking the children if they had everything they needed without actually having any idea what it was they did need.

It would be nice to have a leisurely breakfast, just the two of them. But first she would check her emails, just in case Emma wanted to tell her about her time with Granny, or someone from work needed to get hold of her with a question about copy due to run on Sunday, or just in case anyone else had emailed her — about anything.

Dear Helen,
It was good to hear from you yesterday and I have now bought my very own copy of *Ruby* magazine. I felt slightly conspicuous asking for it in my local newsagent (they had a copy in the window but not on the stand so had to get it out for me). I felt like telling them it was for my imaginary wife (obviously I would not have told them she

197

was imaginary). Then I realised I was being oversensitive and that the pimply youth behind the counter didn't really care what I was buying as long I was quick and left him to stare into space in peace. Thanks for alerting me to my mention in *Ruby*. I enjoyed being a must-read and now I am enjoying the article on where flirtation ends and infidelity begins. Did you read it? Interesting. I'm saving 'How to lose pounds and ingratiate yourself with people' until after I have been to dinner with old friends this evening.

How are you? It's a beautiful day. No doubt you will be enjoying the sunshine with your children.

Graham xox☺

Helen looked towards the bathroom. The door was closed and she could hear the shower still running. This gave her a few minutes. She wondered why Graham had pointed up the piece about flirtation and infidelity. Was he trying to tell or ask her something? She thought she knew which.

She had read the article after texting him on the train and found it particularly pertinent. She could have written it herself. In the past couple of weeks she had asked herself many of the questions it raised. Where does infidelity begin? Is secret texting harmless flirtation or electronic cheating? Is a kiss with someone who is not your partner disloyal, or does only full-blown sex constitute betrayal? Can you ever be having sex with someone else but still consider yourself faithful to your partner? The feature included various case studies from within the faithfulness spectrum. There was a couple who'd been married twenty years. Both had slept with numerous other people but believed they were faithful to each other within the parameters of their open relationship. At the other end of the scale was a couple who'd sought marriage guidance after the man's Second Life character began having secret assignations with another Second Life character. In his real, actual life he had never so much as looked at another woman, but his real, actual wife saw his virtual flirtation as an indicator that he wanted to look around, and their marriage was nearly destroyed because of it.

Where, Helen wondered, did she fit into all of this? By emailing Graham Parks while Alex was in the shower, was she being disloyal? By flirting with Venetia Taylor, was Alex stating his intention to deceive? Was flirting with other people the glue that held marriages together or the tool that began to prise open the cracks?

Hi Graham,

I'm glad a magazine aimed at middle-aged women has found an eager new audience. Don't miss 'Staying in is the new going out — how to have a great night in'. I could have written that — have been honing my staying-in skills for years and now have falling asleep in front of the telly down to a fine art. Am actually in Manchester now — went to see recording of Alex's show last night and had to make small talk to glamorous cast members who were not remotely interested in me. One of them knows you! Will be hiding from the sun in a train carriage for the next few hours. My mother will be in the park with the mini basking sharks, who she is kindly minding while we stayed over in Gothic horror modernist boutique hotel.

Enjoy your weekend.

Helen xxx

She felt reluctant to tell Graham that she had spent a night away from home, in a hotel, with her husband. She had almost not mentioned this in her email, but felt as if she had to confess, as if she had to underline her married status with a 'here I am staying in a hotel without my children and with my husband, which you might imagine could only lead to one thing' statement. She pressed the send button and logged out as Alex came out of the bathroom.

He was wrapped in the white excesses of a hotel bathrobe, and as she passed him to enter the vacant bathroom, he moved to kiss her. He smelt of an unfamiliar hotel shower gel mixed with the familiar smell of himself. He was flirting with her now, as he stroked her hair and asked hadn't she better put some clothes on.

'Off,' she retorted, pulling her bed T-shirt over her head and throwing it onto the bed as she edged backwards towards the shower.

She could feel Alex's eyes on her as she pulled back the shower curtain and switched the taps on. She turned round and smiled at him before closing the door, wondering if she would be comfortable with anyone other than Alex watching her naked. She couldn't imagine it. Her body was all right for its age, but it wasn't what it once had been. Alex was the one person who knew and appreciated it for what it was, for what it had been through, for what it had done with him over the last few years. The thought of someone else looking at her in the way Alex had just done seemed unimaginable, more unimaginable than the thought of having sex with someone else.

Somehow, the older you were, the more intimate the fact of just being naked became. It was easier to expose your body when it was young and taut and suntanned, but you seemed to reveal more when it was older, stretchmarked and sagging.

As Helen stepped into the shower, she wondered when the last time was that she had actually walked the length of a room completely naked in front of Alex. It didn't happen often any more. They would go to bed in various bits of night apparel, which they might take off to have sex beneath the covers, but they would invariably be half dressed again by the time they actually got out of bed, shy in front of the children, or perhaps in front of each other.

Alex was obviously surprised and pleased by her momentary act of playful nakedness, because he opened the bathroom door and got into the shower with her.

This was not something they had done for a

long, long time. It seemed to vindicate whatever it was Helen was doing with Graham Parks. Even if the flirting was not so innocent, Alex was the beneficiary. She knew that he loved her, as she loved him, but perhaps it took the interest of someone outside the marriage to remind her.

29

'Granny couldn't light the oven, so we didn't have any dinner.' Joe seemed more excited at being able to deliver this major piece of news than he was by the fact that his parents were home.

'So you haven't eaten anything all weekend?' Helen, hugging Joe, could easily believe that her mother, who had not taken to modern technology (ovens, cashpoint machines, computers, televisions), might not have been able to light the oven, but she thought it unlikely that this would have prevented her giving the children anything to eat.

'No dinner,' Joe reiterated, pushing Helen away, cross with her for going away for a night and then questioning his account of what had happened in her absence.

'Mum, Dad!' Emma launched herself down the stairs and somehow reached the bottom without breaking her neck. She suctioned herself on to her prodigal parents. 'We went to the park and a bird pooed on my hair and I had to wash it.'

'And she cried,' Joe added.

'Well you cried when Granny couldn't light the oven, cry baby.'

'You're a cry baby.'

Alex winced; the all-consuming welcome when he came home seemed to get less consuming every time.

Helen was glad to be back, though, glad to be the centre of attention, glad to be the voice of authority that would tell them to stop arguing.

'Hello!' Her mother was hovering on the edge of this family group, waiting her turn to be greeted and accepting of the fact that her daughter had a long time ago stopped being excited at the prospect of seeing her.

'Hello, Mum,' Helen said, disentangling herself from Joe and moving to hug and kiss her mother. 'How have they been?'

It scared Helen, the prospect of one day being like her mother, her children grown up with children of their own who loved her but found her amusing and slightly irritating because of foibles like not being able to light the oven. Her mother seemed happy, but Helen was aware that nobody appreciated her as much as they ought, or if they did, they didn't show it.

Helen's mother and father were still together. They'd celebrated their fortieth wedding anniversary a few years ago, and although there were times when Helen had sensed that the level of general bickering that went on in their household had escalated slightly, or that the atmosphere was positively strained, they never let on publicly, and now appeared to be waltzing into the sunset together.

Helen herself had found relations with her mother difficult when she was in her twenties, taking every 'How's Alex?' And 'so-and-so has just had her first grandchild' as a personal criticism of her lifestyle. But almost as soon as Emma was born, she realised just how much her mother must have loved her, and just how much she had done and continued to do for her.

She'd felt instantly guilty for the excuses she'd made for not visiting her parents regularly and the countless times she'd bristled with irritation when they'd asked her questions in vain attempts at conversation. Gazing at her newborn baby looking back at her with total trust and hearing her cry when she left the room made her wonder how she would bear the time when this baby would rather spend the weekend with friends than visit her and would leave the answer-phone on rather than talk.

Perhaps it was this not being needed quite as much by your children that led women to have affairs. Suddenly they found themselves relegated to outsiders in the workplace and to someone who cooked and cleaned at home, making it all too easy to fall for anyone who could still see the remaining vestiges of themselves.

'How was the recording?' her mother was asking.

'Good,' said Helen. 'Very good. Alex was great. It was nice to see him at work. Everyone obviously thinks a lot of him.'

'Shall I make some coffee, Bridget?' Alex asked her.

'Well, I don't want to get in the way, now that you're back,' her mother replied. It was typically selfless behaviour: she had spent the weekend babysitting for them, but now that they were home, she was aware that they wouldn't want her hanging around for too long.

'Don't be silly, Mum,' Helen admonished. 'Let's go into the kitchen and sit down.'

'Oh well, if you're sure,' her mother replied. 'But I won't stay long. I'm sure you've got things to do. Though you could show me how the oven works, so that I know for next time.'

While Helen made coffee, Alex demonstrated the 'idiot-proof' oven-lighting system. He was joking, but Helen thought he was being unnecessarily rude, or perhaps unusually insensitive.

'I read something about your show in the paper the other day.' Her mother ignored the jibe and made polite conversation with Alex. 'It seems to be getting a lot of attention these days.'

'That's since Venetia Taylor joined the cast.' Alex had his head level with the open oven door. 'There, you see. It's all lit now.'

'Oh yes, how silly of me.' Her mother had learned her lesson. 'Well, I suppose she's quite pretty, although a bit too made up for my liking, and isn't she married to some footballer?'

'Not any more. He left her, which is why she joined the show. They've got a child and I gather he doesn't give her much money, so she had to start working again. She's a very strong woman.'

Helen was pleased that her mother had pointed out the over-made-upness. Alex would have said Helen was being bitchy if she'd said anything detrimental about Venetia. She was also slightly and probably irrationally angered at the way he'd leapt to her defence when really he could simply have ignored her mother and got on with making the coffee.

'Helen met her at the party after the show,' he went on, making matters worse. 'She's lovely, isn't she, Helen?'

'Well, I didn't really talk to her much.' Helen raised her eyebrows behind Alex's back in an attempt to indicate to her mother that she shared her views, but that Alex was momentarily (she hoped) slightly obsessed with Venetia Taylor.

Emma came into the room and produced a piece of paper from behind her back. 'For you!' It was a picture of a smiling girl.

'Oh, that's lovely,' Helen told her. 'Is that you?'

'No. It's you, silly,' Emma looked cross that her mother had not instantly recognised the subject matter.

'You look very like your mother when she was your age,' Helen's mother told her. 'Her hair used to be just like yours.'

Helen studied her daughter's beautiful shining hair and perfect skin and found it hard to believe that she had ever looked like that. Children were a constant reminder of the ageing process, especially when your own parent was on hand to remind you what you had once been like.

'Not any more,' Helen commented. 'Mine is gradually filling up with grey. I hate getting old.'

'You're not old,' her mother said dismissively. 'Wait till you're my age.'

Helen could not quite bear to project herself so far forward.

'Are you hungry?' she said. 'Shall we have cake or something?'

'We were going to do some baking this

morning,' her mother chipped in. 'Emma and Joe wanted to make scones for when you came home, but I'm afraid that because I couldn't light the 'idiot-proof' oven, we didn't get round to it.'

'Never mind, I think there's some that I bought from Sainsbury's.'

Helen searched in the cupboard and produced a banana and walnut loaf that wasn't yet past its sell-by date.

'Daddy, I want to walk up the stairs on my hands with you holding my feet.' Joe wanted attention. 'Granny said it hurt her back.'

'Okay.' Alex was glad of the excuse to remove himself from his mother-in-law's presence. It wasn't that they didn't get on. They did. Alex liked Helen's parents. He just suspected he did not quite match up to their perfect son-in-law expectations and that they would have preferred an accountant or a lawyer. This wasn't true. They loved Alex and frequently told her how lucky she was to have met him, leaving her feeling that she herself did not match up to their expectations.

'So, how are you?' Helen asked her mother, sitting down at the kitchen table and passing her a slice of cake.

'Oh fine, fine.' Helen's mother never complained, so this was her default answer and not necessarily true. 'Your dad's had a bit of a cold, so he's been in bed for a few days, but he seemed to be over the worst when I left.'

Helen's father's colds were like Alex's — the same cold that the rest of the family had but much worse. Helen, like her mother, rarely took to her bed; Alex, like her father, began popping vitamins at the first sign of a sniffle and diagnosed flu on the third sneeze.

'I'm hoping he'll be fully recovered by next weekend,' her mother went on. 'We're supposed to be going to the Gordons' fiftieth wedding anniversary down in Somerset.'

'Wow, fifty years! That's impressive.' Alex had returned from wheeling Joe up the stairs and was pouring himself a cup of coffee. 'What's their secret?'

'Oh, Jim's no bother,' her mother replied, causing Alex to splutter his coffee as he suppressed a laugh.

⋆ ⋆ ⋆

When Helen's mother had insisted that it was time she got out of their way and left, Alex laughed again, this time more obviously.

'I can't believe your mother attributes a fifty-year marriage to someone being no bother,' he said. 'Is that what you'll say about me when we celebrate our golden wedding anniversary?'

'No,' Helen answered. 'I will say that you were extremely tiresome but I put up with you because I'm very tolerant and you knew how to change washers in dripping taps, which is something that annoys me.'

'How very romantic.' Alex smiled. 'I wonder if we will make it to fifty.'

'Can we play Monopoly?' Emma appeared, Monopoly box in hand, knowing that her parents normally refused on the grounds of time, but that having been away, they owed their children time and might therefore capitulate.

'Okay,' said Alex.

'Can we play the short version?' Helen asked. There was a way of limiting the endlessness of the game by dealing out properties along with cash at the start.

'Are you referring to Monopoly or marriage?' Alex asked.

Helen was momentarily confused by the question, then realised that despite the interruption from Emma, Alex was carrying on the conversation he'd been having with her.

They were throwaway comments, but twice in as many minutes Alex had cast doubt on the longevity of their marriage. Was she being oversensitive, or was something up?

'I want to be the dog,' Joe barked.

30

'What's up, Joe?' asked Katie, watching Helen struggling to fill the kettle with Joe following her around the kitchen, his head buried in the back of her cardigan.

He didn't answer, so Helen spoke for him.

'He's had a haircut,' she whispered to Katie, trying to extract Joe's head from the knitwear. 'I think he looks lovely, but it's quite short and he doesn't like it.'

'I love short hair,' Katie said. 'Can I see, Joe? I bet you look really handsome.'

Tentatively Joe took a peek from behind Helen's back, and as she reached up to take the tea down from the cupboard, he was suddenly unmasked. His hair had grown quite long over the summer and while they all liked it long, half the time he couldn't see. Now that they were back at school, it was likely to become infested with nits, so Helen had taken him to have it cut the day before.

'Wow! Don't you look different!'

It was the wrong thing to say. Joe started to cry, and Helen sat down and scooped him on to her lap.

'I think that's what's bothering him,' she said to a mortified Katie. 'He was quite happy sitting there and having it cut, but when he went to look in the mirror, he barely recognised himself. I think he still looks like the most handsome man in the world, though, don't you?'

'Without a doubt,' said Katie. Then, thinking it best to change the subject, 'Do you know where the girls have gone, Joe? Can you make sure Hannah is not being naughty?'

'I think they're in the garden, Jo-Jo,' said Helen, shifting position so he began to slide off her knee. 'They were going to let Bugsy out of his hutch for a bit. Do you want to go and see?'

Joe walked slowly to the garden door, taking one last look at his mother for reassurance before going outside.

'I suppose it must have been a bit of a shock, seeing someone rather different looking back at him from the mirror,' Katie remarked. 'Sometimes I don't recognise myself and it's a bit scary.'

'Yes, I know what you mean,' Helen answered. 'I've been known to catch sight of myself in the mirror in the lift at work and wonder who that cross-looking middle-aged woman is. Then I realise it's me! But you always look fantastic.'

'Is anything else bothering Joe?' Katie ignored the compliment.

'He seems to have had a bit of a falling-out with Anna,' Helen said quietly, referring to Joe's friend and the love of his life. 'He came back the other day saying she doesn't want to play with him any more because he's a boy. He was desolate.'

'Oh, poor Joe,' Katie sympathised. 'Do you think it's just a phase or the start of the end of a beautiful friendship?'

'I don't know.' Helen put the kettle on. 'I

hoped they'd stay friends for a bit longer, but Alex reckons boys and girls always part company around this age.'

'But they really did seem to love each other,' Katie mused. 'Perhaps it's all practice for falling out of love in later life.'

'I suppose so.' Helen slung tea bags into two cups. 'He's so sad at the moment, but I must admit, I rather like him like this. He's extra cuddly and he keeps telling me I'm the nicest girl in the world, so I'm selfishly rather enjoying being the centre of his attention.'

'I know what you mean,' Katie agreed. 'Hannah and Emma seem so independent these days, and sometimes Hannah can barely disguise her contempt for me, but when something upsets her, she wants to sit on my lap and be loved again and I rather like it.'

'I suppose that's what growing up is all about, isn't it?' Helen put the cups on the table. 'Gradually needing your parents less and less until you don't need them at all. You want your kids to be strong and independent, but at the same time you want to be as important to them as you were when they were born.'

Katie's phone beeped from inside her bag, alerting her to a text message. She pulled it out and looked at the screen and smiled.

Helen hated the way text messages pulled people from the conversation you were having with them and excluded you from whatever was being said. Katie was now replying to the message.

As Helen stirred the tea bags around the cups

213

her thoughts turned to Graham Parks. There was something childlike about him. Beneath the strong exterior there was an intangible vulnerability that made her want to reach out to him and look after him. Alex was singularly self-contained at the moment. He was happy at work and confident in himself, and Helen sometimes wondered if he had any real emotional need of her. He needed her to take control of the children's lives, sort out stuff at home and have sex with him, but they no longer seemed dependent on each other the way they had been in the early days of their relationship.

'Sorry.' Katie brought her thoughts back to the table as she finished texting and began talking again. 'It's funny, isn't it? I used to think, before we had children, that you were only capable of loving a certain amount. I thought that when Hannah was born I wouldn't be able to love Philip any more because I'd have to love the baby, but you find you have more and more to give.'

'I know exactly what you mean.' Helen prised the lid off the biscuit tin and pushed it towards her friend. 'I remember thinking I would never be able to love a baby as much as I loved Alex, and then when Emma was born, I loved her more than anything and I loved Alex more than ever for having made her possible. It was the same with Jo-Jo. I thought he'd never be as wonderful as Emma, and now look at me, I'm totally in love with him.'

'I suppose it's the same with boyfriends.' Katie was looking out of the window, where Hannah and Emma appeared to be terrorising the rabbit by bouncing with him on the trampoline. 'Should they be doing that?'

'What?' Helen glanced at them briefly. 'Oh, I'm sure he'll survive. What were you saying about boyfriends?'

'Well, I was thinking that just because you split up with a person and meet someone new, you don't automatically stop loving them, do you?'

'I don't know.' Helen wondered if Katie suspected there was something going on between herself and Jim Keeble. 'I don't have feelings for Jim Keeble any more, if that's what you mean.'

'You must feel something for him,' Katie said. 'Would you be upset if something happened to him?'

'I'm sort of fond of him still,' Helen admitted. 'But I don't really feel that strongly about him. It's all in the past. It's weird, really. I see him now and he's funny and handsome and flirtatious and all of that, but I can't really imagine ever feeling the way I used to about him. You move on, don't you?'

'Unless your ex-partner has died.' Katie appeared to be studying the contents of the biscuit tin as she said this. 'I wonder if you ever really move on if something like that happens.'

'I take it we are talking handsome widower Cary now?' Helen looked at her friend questioningly. 'How did he slip into our conversation?'

'Oh, I don't know,' Katie replied, shaking her head as if to get Cary out of it and reaching decisively for a chocolate digestive. 'We were talking about Joe's lovers' tiff with Anna.'

Right on cue, Joe appeared in the doorway, cradling the rabbit in his arms.

'Emma says she loves Bugsy more than me,' he said, looking as if he was about to burst into tears.

31

If she hadn't recognised him as soon as she saw him, Helen might have mistaken him for a vagrant. He was wandering along the Embankment, apparently talking to himself, although she realised almost immediately that he was talking on a hands-free phone. That was the trouble with modern technology: talking to yourself was no longer the first sign of madness; it might just be an indicator that you had an iPhone concealed about your person.

Before hands-free devices, if you saw someone walking and talking out loud you would have given them a wide berth in case, in their demented state, they decided to knife or mug you. These days, they were more likely to be mugged themselves for advertising the fact that they had a piece of technological kit.

Because he was talking, Helen didn't call out his name until she had almost drawn level with him. He was so absorbed in his call he nearly walked past without seeing her, but she wasn't about to let that happen.

'Graham.' She diverted his attention from his call, and watched him during the split second in which he brought the world around him back into focus.

'Helen!' His face lit up with a smile that seemed to register the same disproportionate lurch that she had felt when she saw him. 'Hello.'

He enveloped her in an awkward bear hug. She could feel the shape of his phone inside his jacket, and worried that whoever he'd been talking to was still on the other end, waiting for him to reply, wondering what he was doing.

'Don't you need to finish your call?' He looked confused. 'You were talking to yourself when I saw you, but I gave you the benefit of the doubt and presumed you were actually talking to someone else on a mobile.'

'I'm afraid you were right first time.' Graham laughed, opening his jacket and pulling a small device from the inside pocket. 'Dictaphone. I was talking to myself. What are you doing?'

'Skiving.'

It was a work day for Helen. She'd been to review the Beatles exhibition at County Hall, one of those jobs that was impossible to put a time on. As it turned out, it had not taken very long. There was no curator to meet and greet and talk her through each and every exhibit. She'd spent an hour walking past images of the Fab Four and dodging guitars, and with the official guide and a wad of press releases to take back to the office with her, she'd been confident she could take a walk along the Embankment without being missed.

'Seen the Beatles.' She waved the press pack under Graham's nose. 'Now I'm taking the slow route back to work. What are you doing, apart from a good impression of a schizophrenic?'

'Walking and thinking,' he smiled, 'and verbally noting some of my thoughts — in case I ever get down to writing a second book.'

There was a slight pause. This was the point in the conversation when Helen would normally have said something along the lines of 'Well, I'd better be getting back to work then', and Graham would have replied, 'Nice seeing you.' Neither of them wanted that.

It was Graham who moved the encounter on.

'Shall we go on the London Eye?'

Helen realised they were standing in the spot where usually there would be queues for this particular tourist attraction. Today it was quiet. A few people were waiting, but they could buy tickets and be on it in ten minutes. Taking a ride wouldn't delay her so much that questions would be asked.

'Now?' she asked, tentatively.

'Why not?' Graham Parks was not afraid of seizing unexpected moments.

'Okay.' She hoped the reluctance she felt didn't show in her voice. She wanted to take this opportunity to spend a small chunk of her day with him; she would just have preferred it if he'd suggested a coffee in the Festival Hall or somewhere else along the river.

For some reason, she didn't want to tell him that she was afraid of heights and mechanical breakdown and terrorist attacks and was slightly claustrophobic, and that a trip on the London Eye provided scope for the manifestation of all these particular phobias.

She'd been on it once, thinking that the excitement felt by Emma and Joe would be contagious. They had been bursting with it as they stood in the queue for half an hour, and she had desperately tried to allow herself to be infused with some of the overspill, but it hadn't worked. As soon as the doors had closed behind them, she had begun to panic that the motor would malfunction and they would be stuck at the highest point until engineers could be brought off their lunch break to sort out the problem. As their capsule had begun to rise slowly over the Houses of Parliament, her resentment of the extended family sharing it with them had mounted and she had had to concentrate hard to stop herself physically abusing the man who for the duration of the journey leant casually against the sign on the door that read 'DO NOT LEAN AGAINST THIS DOOR'.

She had tried not to show her abject fear, and had concentrated on breathing deeply and responding to the children's delighted squeals with appropriate remarks, but as soon as they'd reached earth again, she had bolted through the doors, eliciting a 'Steady on' from the man who'd leant against the door as she ran for terra firma.

Alex had teased her, and the kids had joined in.

'Mum's afraid of hi-ites!' they'd chanted as they went in search of hot chocolate, and Alex had led them in their mockery instead of protecting her.

She didn't want to tell any of this to Graham Parks. Instead she hoped, unrealistically, that they would not be able to get tickets on the spot or that the Eye would be closing for lunch and they wouldn't have enough time. But rather than yielding any opportune delays, time appeared to be speeding up.

Without her noticing, Graham had managed to purchase two tickets, and after a cursory once-over by security guards they were nearing the front of the almost non-existent queue. There was a brief moment of opportunity when she could have pulled back, made a slight fool of herself in front of the other members of the queue and confessed her fears, but it passed quickly, and before she realised it she was inside the capsule.

She looked around at their travelling companions, who comprised a party of Japanese tourists, complete with multitudinous cameras; an older couple who she guessed were in their late seventies and who were smartly dressed for a day in the capital; and a couple of women in their twenties.

She and Graham sat on the central bench, facing out towards the City. She wondered if facing the other way might lessen her fear, but couldn't think of a reason why it should. She was already beginning to cold-sweat when she became aware of the slight heat from Graham Parks' thigh, which rested lightly against hers. Now the fears were piling up. She still had all the ones associated with the Eye itself, and added to them was a new fear of proximity to Graham Parks. She tried to distract herself by spotting landmarks.

'Tower of London, Tower of London,' the

Japanese exhaled, excited by history on the ground below.

'Isn't that your office?' Graham asked, picking out the towers of Canary Wharf.

'The *Sunday Review* is on the fourteenth floor,' she told him, wondering why this didn't bother her when the height they were at now, which was considerably less, did.

The Japanese were living up to their national stereotype and taking photographs. One of their party asked Graham if he would take a picture of them leaning against the side of the capsule, suspended in mid-air with London below. Graham obliged, and as he returned to their seat was asked, 'Would you like picture of you and friend?'

'No!' It came out more vehemently than Helen had intended. Fear made her voice louder and gave it an edge she wasn't used to.

The Japanese man smiled and retreated, bowing as he stepped back to the safety of numbers, treating her rudeness in a way that was natural to him, with the utmost respect.

'What's the matter?' Graham wasn't angry; he sounded concerned. 'Are you scared someone in Tokyo will find out we've been together?'

He said it quietly and kindly, out of earshot of the others in the capsule, and she could feel the warmth of his breath against her face as he spoke.

'No.' She decided that as trying to relax obviously wasn't working, confession might be the better option. 'I'm scared of *heights*.'

She emphasised the heights over her fear of

their being caught together, and waited for him to begin reasoning, telling her that the level they were at barely constituted a height, or reassuring her with an analysis of the safety measures that had to be adhered to. Or perhaps, like Alex, he would laugh at the ridiculousness of it.

Graham Parks didn't do any of those things. He simply took her hand and held it, stroking the top with his thumb as he calmly pointed out the gardens of Buckingham Palace and the stretch of the Mall, soothing her with words like a doctor about to administer something intravenously to an anxious toddler.

And, like a child herself, she found there was some security to be found in the palm of his hand, as if the very act of hand-holding offered protection against her irrational fears. But it was also charged and highly erotic, and she blushed when the smartly dressed older couple noted their hand-holding and smiled, as if they had been caught having sex in public.

This must have been what it was like for the Victorians and Edwardians, she thought, when the sexually repressed mores of the day lent meaning to the slightest exposure of flesh or the briefest moment of physical contact. Having her hand held by Graham Parks was fairly innocent on the scale of physical encounters, and yet it felt incredibly intimate.

Now, instead of wishing the journey through the sky to be over, she found she began to take in the city beneath them and wanted to prolong these moments. Her fear now was that once they reached the ground, this bubble would burst.

When it did, with the opening of the doors, she was gripped again by momentary panic as they all tried to pile out while the capsule kept up its perpetual motion. Graham let go of her hand and she wondered if she simply imagined that he'd been holding it.

They'd been separated slightly by the Japanese and he was a little ahead of her. He looked round and briefly held her in his gaze before he was forced to concentrate on descending the steps.

The fresh air was not a welcome relief as it had been when she'd re-emerged after her journey with Alex and the kids. This time it engulfed her in a cold blast of possibilities.

'I have to get back to work,' she gasped, wanting to be away from him as fast as possible.

'I'll walk with you to the tube,' Graham was saying, but she needed to get away and had said goodbye and begun walking briskly along the Embankment before he could persist. She wanted to look back and see if he was still there, but was afraid to do so.

32

'Shana's been trying to get hold of you,' Vincent told Helen, before she had even had time to hang up her coat.

'She can't have tried very hard,' she answered, taking her mobile phone from her bag to check for messages and then remembering she had switched it off inside the exhibition and forgotten to turn it on again. 'Oh shit! Yes, she did. Six missed calls. Do you know what she wanted?'

'No idea.' Vincent seemed pleased to have delivered the slightly worrying news that the boss was on her case.

'Is she in her office?' Helen asked. 'I'd best go and see what she wants.'

'Good luck,' Vincent called to her departing back. Did Helen imagine that he was smirking slightly, or was she simply still unsettled after her Eye ride with Graham Parks?

'Ah, Helen. I've been calling you for the past hour or so. Where have you been?' Shana intercepted Helen before she even made it up the corridor to her office.

'I know, I'm sorry,' she mumbled. 'I got held up at the exhibition and I forgot to switch my phone on again. What was it you wanted? Was it important?'

'There are a couple of things,' Shana replied. 'I was just on my way to the coffee bar. Do you want to come and we'll have a chat?'

'Okay.' Helen followed Shana to the lifts outside the Review section's offices. Her mobile phone, now that it was switched on again, bleeped as they waited for the lift. She was going to ignore it, but Shana indicated that she should check her messages.

'It might be important,' she smiled.

Helen opened her inbox and saw one text message. It was from Graham Parks.

'Lovely seeing you today. Sorry you had to rush off xx' It was short and to the point and seemed to imply that he might have taken at face value her comment about having to get back to work.

'Was it?' The lift doors were opening and they stepped out and turned towards the coffee bar.

'Was it what?' Helen wasn't quite sure what Shana was talking about.

'Was the text important?' Shana asked, pouring herself a coffee and holding up a cup as if to say 'Shall I pour you one too?'

'No, just childcare stuff,' Helen said, wishing she hadn't as soon as it was out. If there was one thing Shana did not like hearing about, it was childcare issues. 'I'll have tea, actually,' she added, taking a cup and saucer from the tray and pouring herself a cup from the well-stewed brew in the pot.

They each swiped their electronic key fob, which allowed them five cups of tea or coffee a day courtesy of the owners of the *Sunday Review*. Once staff had had their limit they had to pay themselves. Most of the staff at the paper

226

only functioned if fuelled by regular high doses of caffeine and were on to cash well before Thursday, but Personnel, or whoever was responsible for programming the key fobs, had forgotten to amend Helen's limit when she began working part time, so she was still allowed twenty-five cups a week, despite the fact that she only worked two and a half days and by rights should have been limited to twelve and a half hot drinks.

'So,' Helen began as they eased themselves into the fixed seats, 'what was it you wanted to talk to me about?'

'I can't remember, was it you that interviewed that author who used to be a soldier?' Helen felt herself blushing as Shana went on, 'I can't remember his name.'

'Graham Parks?' Helen said, hoping her boss did not hear the slight falter in her voice. 'I did interview him a while back, when his book came out.'

'Oh good, I thought it was you. Do you still have a contact for him?'

'I might.' Helen found herself feeling for the phone in her pocket as if to reassure herself that her contact with Graham Parks was still intact. 'Why? There wasn't a problem with the piece, was there?'

'Oh no, I don't think so.' Shana probably hadn't even read it. 'There's a new report out about stress in the armed forces, and the editor mentioned reading your piece and wondered if we could get whatshisname to write something about it, or if one of us could interview him or something. We can't get serving soldiers to talk, but he might be a good bet. What do you think?'

'I guess so.' Helen was not sure. She presumed that the gaps in Graham Parks' CV were linked to the breakdown that Chloe had told her about. Graham didn't know that Helen knew, and neither did Shana. Helen suspected Graham wanted it to remain that way.

'Maybe you could give him a call then, to try to fix something up?' Shana went on. 'Apparently News is running a big story on Sunday about this report and they want us to do a behind-the-scenes look at the issue. Could you do that?'

Helen wondered how she could get out of it. She didn't want to call Graham today, having just run away from him. 'I've still got a review to write up, and if it's for this Sunday, it doesn't leave me much time.'

'Just a quick interview, or ask him if can write six hundred words or so himself.' Shana brushed her excuses aside. 'Justin is writing the main piece, so liaise with him, get him to show you a copy of the report. We just need a bit of background colour.'

Shana broke off to greet the paper's editor, who was walking past their table carrying a plate of cake balanced on top of a cup of coffee.

'Hello, John.' Her tone was ingratiating.

'Shana Goldberg,' he boomed. He was a tall man and seemed to take up most of the room with his stature and his voice, which carried. Helen found him rather intimidating, and in her time at the *Sunday Review* had managed to stay out of his way.

'How's it going? We need to meet soon to discuss staffing levels . . . ' He lowered his voice slightly as he took in Helen on the opposite side of the table.

'Have you met Helen Collins?' Shana nodded towards her. 'One of our reviewers.'

'I don't think so.' John Wainwright smiled vaguely in Helen's direction. 'Email me some times when you're free,' he said to Shana, before continuing wherever he was going with the cakes. 'Good to meet you, Sophie.'

'Helen,' mumbled Helen, wondering if staffing levels meant jobs cuts.

'So.' Shana dived back in where they had left off, 'can you give him a call when we get back to the office?'

'Okay.' Helen didn't really see how she could get out of it. 'Was that what you wanted to talk to me about?'

She could still hear the words 'staffing levels' echoing around the coffee bar and began to fear that she'd been brought here, away from the office, to be told that her part-time contributions were no longer needed.

'There's also this press trip that no one wants to go on. I thought you might fancy doing it.'

Helen hadn't been expecting that. Usually press trips were allocated on the basis of seniority, with Shana taking more than her fair share of trips to the Caribbean, the chief writer swanning off to India, and Helen herself never being asked to do anything the least bit exotic.

'It's to Spain, next weekend.' Shana had her interested now, even if she was only being asked because no one else wanted to go. She liked the idea of a couple of days away with other writers from the media. 'There's a new BBC drama that has been filmed in Santander, and the Spanish tourist board are organising a tour of all the locations. Tom's very keen on the drama and thinks we should do a travel feature if we can.'

Tom was the Review section's TV critic. The *Sunday Review* gave television as much weight as the rest of the arts, allocating double-page spreads to issues such as how sitcoms influenced career choice and whether property porn programmes had led to the crash in the housing market.

Shana drained her coffee cup and began to get up. 'Shall we go? I've got the details back in my office, but in principle do I take it you are interested?'

'Yes.' Helen had never been to Santander. 'But I'd need to make sure I have cover at home.'

★ ★ ★

Back at her desk, Helen deliberated what she should do first: call Graham Parks or phone Alex and ask if he minded looking after Emma and Joe while she was visiting the scenes of fictitious Spanish murders. Not that he had any reason to mind. After all, he went away for several days every week, leaving her in sole charge; but nevertheless she felt irrationally guilty about time away from the family on her own.

230

Justin May, who was writing the feature on stress in the armed forces, was two desks away. He'd had a brief chat with her about the direction of his piece and reiterated Shana's request that she do a quick interview with Graham Parks, 'to add some colour to the facts and figures'. He was eyeing her now, in between bouts of typing. She imagined he was willing her to get on and make the call so that he could rest easy knowing that at least eight hundred words of his double-page spread would be filled with something he did not have to write.

'Did you find the contact number for Graham Parks?' he asked.

'I'm just going through my old emails,' Helen didn't want to let him know that she had the number on her phone. In her head she was plotting a charade that involved checking with Graham's publisher or possibly Jim Keeble.

She decided to email Alex about Spain.

'Dearly beloved husband,' she tapped out, wondering if Alex would check his emails while on school-run duty. He usually did, looking for the scripts for the following week's *Muddy Water* and having plot e-discussions with the writers.

Because I am so highly valued at work, I have been asked if I would be willing and able to go on a press trip to Spain. (That is, because no one else wants to go.) It's next weekend. Is that possible? Will you be able to look after the children or do you have any as-yet-to-be-revealed sorties planned? I think I should go, if possible. John Wainwright mentioned reviewing staffing levels to Shana in the canteen today, so need to appear indispensable before I get reviewed myself. What do you think?

Have just been given a late-in-the-day interview to chase, so not sure what time I will get back tonight. Love you lots, Helen xxx

She wondered whether she should tell him it was Graham Parks she was being asked to interview again but decided against it. She wasn't really sure why. After all, it was a genuine interview she was being asked to chase, clearly defined work, but she had been trying to avoid bringing his name up too often in case Alex suspected there was a reason why she kept alluding to him, in the way she suspected there was a reason he kept referring to Venetia Taylor.

Alex clearly had no such misgivings himself. He replied almost immediately.

Hello wife, how lovely to hear from you. I can't see any reason why you should not go next weekend. I am around on Friday but may have to go to Manchester early on Monday for a possible photoshoot with Venetia for some weekly women's magazine! Just waiting to hear from Nikki. So go ahead. Ax

Alex had left his previous agent, Peter, an old-school type who had secured him the audition for *Muddy Water*, because he claimed he did not do enough for his profile. Nikki clearly did. Helen reread the email, wondering if she was imagining the excitement she sensed Alex felt about going to Manchester earlier than planned to have his photograph taken with Venetia Taylor. He seemed positively eager to get shot of his wife for the weekend and then disappear almost as soon as she got back. Or was she imagining that too?

'Any joy?' Justin asked, reminding her that she was supposed to be pursuing Graham Parks.

'Yes, his publisher has just emailed the number,' she lied. 'I'll give him a call now.'

As a delaying tactic, she checked her inbox again. One new message. This time from Jim Keeble.

Hello Gorgeous, just saw you sloping back to the office after what, judging by the time, must have been a long lunch. What, no time to have lunch with me? Am being sent to Chad in a few weeks. It is very dangerous and I wish to see you again before I go.

You won't turn down my last request, will you?

Jimxxx

Helen laughed. She didn't think Jim was being serious, but he never could resist trying to get people around him to fall for his charms, even if he wasn't particularly interested in them. Graham Parks was the opposite, quieter, more diffident, less demanding but equally compelling.

Helen picked up her mobile phone and took a

deep breath, trying to calm herself. After their encounter on the London Eye she felt nervous about calling Graham, and she was also aware that her call was being listened to by both Justin and Vincent, who was now hovering nearby. She concentrated on breathing slowly while she waited for the mobile network to connect and Graham's phone began to ring.

'Hello,' she heard him say.

'Hello,' she replied before realising that she'd reached his voice-mail.

'This is Graham Parks' phone,' his disembodied voice told her. 'I'm sorry but I can't take this call at the moment. Please leave a message and I will get back to you.'

'Hello.' Helen paused before launching into a message that would sound businesslike and professional. 'This is Helen Collins from the *Sunday Review*. I interviewed you a few weeks ago and I wondered if it might be possible to speak to you again.' She wondered whether to tell him exactly what was required of him and give him time to decide whether he wanted to do it, or just to get the message-leaving over with as soon as possible. She decided on the former. 'We're running a big feature about stress in the armed forces and wondered if we might be able to ask you a bit about your own experiences. Anyway, if you could call me back, I'd be very grateful.'

She hung up.

'You forgot to leave the office number.' Justin was on to her as soon as she had put the phone down. 'You'll have to call him back.'

Reluctantly she pressed the call button again. This time he answered immediately.

'Hello, Helen Collins from the *Sunday Review*,' he said, obviously having listened to her message. 'I take it you are back at work, then?'

33

'You're back early.' Alex looked up from his laptop. He had closed it abruptly when Helen walked into the room.

'Am I?' She checked the clock in the kitchen. It was seven p.m. That was the time she usually got home after a day in the office.

'You said you might be late.' Alex was shutting his computer down now. 'You had an interview to chase or something.'

'Oh yes.' Helen put her bag on the floor next to the bin. 'I'm doing it tomorrow morning now.'

'Anything interesting?' Alex asked, getting up from the kitchen table and wandering over to the fridge. 'Glass of wine?'

'Yes please.' She was in desperate need of a drink to steady her nerves. 'Not really,' she added, with reference to her husband's 'anything interesting' remark. She decided not to tell him she'd been asked to interview Graham Parks again.

'Where are the children?' Changing the subject seemed like a good idea.

'They're on the sofa, staring at *The Simpsons*.' Alex had taken a bottle of white wine from the fridge and was now examining the glasses, which, from the look of consternation on his face, appeared to be smeared. 'Might need some more rinse aid in the dishwasher.'

'I'll go and say hello and watch it with them

before their bath, then.' Helen decided to ignore Alex's preoccupation with the less than gleaming glasses and began to exit the kitchen and head in the direction of sofa and *Simpsons*.

'Wait a sec,' Alex called after her. 'Don't you want to take your drink with you?'

Helen stopped and waited while Alex polished her glass with a dishcloth. She was tired now and wanted to say hello to the children and sit down. He seemed to be taking longer than was necessary — if it was necessary to polish the glasses at all — forcing her to hover in the doorway.

At last he appeared to judge the glass sufficiently shiny and turned to pick up the bottle, which he'd placed on the work surface adjacent to the cooker.

'By the way,' his back was to her as he began pouring, 'I spoke to Peter today.'

'Really?' Helen was surprised. Since Alex had left Peter's agency for the higher-profile-creating one that Nikki worked for, they'd not had any contact as far as she was aware. 'What did he want?'

'He said he saw you going on the London Eye today.' Alex turned round, glass of wine poured and ready. He looked straight at her as he said this, handing her the glass with a raised eyebrow, as if he did not think this a likely scenario but wondered what her version of it might be.

'Is that what he called to say?' was the best Helen managed to come up with. She took a large sip of wine, actually more of a gulp, and tried to think quickly.

Should she tell Alex that Peter must have been mistaken? That she was nowhere near the London Eye and it must have simply been someone who looked vaguely like her? But what if Peter had actually seen her close up? He knew well enough what she looked like. If he said he'd seen her there, then he'd seen her. She could tell Alex that she'd simply been passing the Eye on her way back from the exhibition at County Hall, which in essence was true. She had been passing, when she'd bumped into Graham and he'd urged her on to it.

Had Peter seen her with Graham? If so, had they simply been talking? Unless Peter had been on the London Eye in one of the adjoining capsules, then he would not have seen her holding the hand of someone who was definitely not Alex, though he may well have seen her coming through the barriers off the Eye.

If he had then she could have had her reasons for going on the London Eye. It was only Alex, knowing her fear of heights and knowing how she had hated the ride when they went as a family, who would have found any of the reasons she desperate struggled to come up with unlikely.

Fortunately for her, Alex did not seem as preoccupied with the fact that she might have been on the London Eye as he was with the smears he now appeared to have discovered on the second glass.

'No, he phoned to say that a casting director had called him, wanting me to audition for a part in a film with Hugh Grant.' Alex finished polishing and poured himself some wine. 'Apparently they didn't realise I wasn't with him any more.'

'Was that awkward?' Helen asked. 'Talking to Peter about the fact that you left him?'

'Not really. Cheers.' Alex chinked her glass to his. 'I think he knows that we'd outgrown each other. We had a good relationship while it lasted, but it was time for me to move on.'

It occurred to Helen that if someone had been hiding in the cupboard under the stairs and heard Alex's last sentence taken out of context, they might have presumed he was talking about their marriage. She suddenly wondered why he'd closed his laptop so quickly when she came home, almost jumping up and accusing her of being early as if he had been guiltily emailing someone he shouldn't.

Or was she the one feeling guilty for whatever it was that she had done today?

'So what's the film?' she asked. 'And doesn't the call need to go through Nikki now?'

'Ultimately, yes, but Peter knows the casting director, an old school friend or something, so he said he's happy to put me up for it and then if I get it let Nikki deal with it.'

'That's very good of him.' Helen couldn't imagine herself being so helpfully magnanimous in that situation.

'I suppose so.' Alex didn't seem to appreciate that the agent he had rather unceremoniously dumped was graciously acting in his best interests to secure him a major film role. 'Apparently it's some sort of romantic comedy, set in north London. Anyway, it's only a possible casting. We'll see what happens.'

'Interesting.' Helen wasn't sure if Alex had forgotten that this line of conversation had begun by his telling her that Peter had seen her earlier in the day. He hadn't.

'I told him it couldn't have been you he saw,' he said, as the theme tune that signalled the end of *The Simpsons* began playing through the adjoining wall to the living room. 'I told him we'd been on it once and you hated it and swore never to go on it again.'

'I wonder why he thought it was me?' Helen wondered if Alex might shed some light on exactly what Peter had seen.

'You know Peter,' he said. 'He was always a bit vague when it came to faces.'

Helen nodded. That was another thing that had prompted Alex to leave him. Peter often found himself in rooms with movers and shakers but failed to recognise them and ingratiate himself.

'Better go and say hello to Emma and Joe, now that they might actually acknowledge you.' Alex nodded in the direction of the music. 'Then will you give them a bath?'

'Actually, I still need to make a quick call to the office,' Helen told him. 'Can you run their bath and I'll come up and take over when I've finished?'

'Okay, but don't be long.' Alex went into the living room and switched the television over to the Channel Four news. 'Mum's back.'

'Hello,' said Helen, gratefully receiving the

hugs they jumped up from the sofa to give her.

'Mummy, we've been teaching Bugsy to do tricks,' Emma was all excitement. 'Can we let him out again so I can show you?'

'Mmmmm.' Helen didn't give her full attention to what Emma was saying as over the top of their heads she saw that Jon Snow was conducting an interview from the studio on the situation in Afghanistan. Sitting in the chair on the other side of the news desk was Jim Keeble. Alex was watching it too.

'Isn't that . . . ?' he asked.

'Yes,' said Helen.

'Who's that?' asked Joe.

'Mummy's old boyfriend,' said Alex, without taking his eyes off the screen. 'He's still in the country, then?'

'He doesn't look very old,' said Joe.

'No, he's not,' said Helen to Joe, adding, 'Yes, he is' to Alex.

'Bathtime, then,' said Alex, offering no further insight into what he thought about Jim Keeble still being on the scene, and started up the stairs to the bathroom.

They had a sort of unwritten rule that whoever had done the bulk of the childcare during the day got to dodge the bath and bedtime routine, the witching hour in which both Emma and Joe were tired but keen to expend every last drop of energy in the run-up to going to sleep. They both seemed to operate on the rechargeable battery principle — i.e., they recharged better and more fully if they were completely spent before they began — and only seemed able to benefit from the restorative effects of sleep if they had expended every last smidgen of energy climbing up the banisters, aiming their clothes from a distance into the laundry basket, treating the bath as if it were flume time at the local swimming pool and arguing and physically fighting with each other.

Supervising this witching hour managed to drain all the remaining energy from whichever parent was on duty, and by virtue of Alex having picked them up from school and fed and entertained them, tonight it was Helen's turn.

'Mum, we're doing the Tudors and I need an orange to make a pompadour.' Emma plonked herself on her mother's lap. 'And clothes, too.'

'Really? What sort of clothes?' Helen thought that a pompadour was an eighteenth-century hairstyle and not one that required oranges, and wondered if her daughter had the right word.

'Not clothes that you wear.' Emma was now winding Helen's hair round and round her index finger. It hurt slightly but she didn't want to be seen to be pushing her daughter away, having only just appeared in her day. 'They are like little bits of twig things and you stick them in the orange to make the room smell nice.'

'Oh, a pomander!' Helen now realised what she was talking about. 'And you mean cloves!'

'Yes, that's what I said,' Emma went on. 'They had to have them because Tudors were really smelly.'

'That's not very nice.' Joe joined them and tried to edge Emma out of the way by climbing on to Helen's lap from the other side.

'Jo-Jo, don't push!' Emma shoved him.

'You said Tudors were really smelly and that's rude.' Joe seemed to think this justified any pushing there might have been.

'They were smelly because they only washed once a year.' Emma had obviously learned something today.

'Well you'll be smelly too, unless you have a bath,' Helen told them. 'Dad's just running it for you. I need to phone the office and then I'll be up.'

'But you've just been at your office,' Joe protested.

'I know, I won't be long. Go on.' Helen manhandled them both to the foot of the stairs. When they'd gone protesting to the top, where Alex was waiting, bath ready, she went back into the kitchen and closed the door.

She dialled Justin's number and he answered.

'Hi, Helen. Can't stay away from work?'

'Well I'm at home but I've just remembered I've got a hospital appointment tomorrow morning, which is when I'd arranged to interview Graham Parks.' She didn't think Justin would argue with a hospital appointment or dare ask if it was anything serious. 'Is there any chance someone else could do it, instead of me?' She had arranged to go to Graham's flat to speak to him again, and suddenly doing so seemed utterly risky.

'I don't know. It's a bit late in the day to start rearranging. Couldn't you make it later or something?' Justin sounded frustrated. He probably wanted to go home himself, and she had just presented him with something else to be dealt with.

'I can't really change the appointment,' she lied.

'I mean, can't you just go and interview him later? Or see if he can come into the office or something?' Justin obviously thought it was her problem to sort out.

'Okay, I'll do my best,' Helen told him, thinking that perhaps getting Graham Parks to come to the offices of the *Sunday Review* would be the best solution. It was like a goldfish bowl in there. Even the private interview rooms could be seen into by the whole of the Sports section, and Travel too. It would be safer to talk to him there, but of course, she'd have to call him again to try to rearrange.

34

'There's someone here to see you.' The fourteenth-floor receptionist had called Helen to alert her of the arrival at the office of Graham Parks.

'Okay, I'll come and meet him.' Helen put the phone down and took a deep breath.

'I've booked the interview room,' she said to Justin, who had his head down, furiously typing. A double-page-spread deadline was looming.

'Great, thanks. We only need eight hundred words. See if you can just get him to talk a bit about stress levels in the army, his own personal experiences, any friends or colleagues who crashed under pressure, and then can you bash it out by four?'

'I'll do my best,' Helen replied. She had time. She'd spent the morning at home instead of at her pretend hospital appointment and had managed to finish the exhibition review, so the interview with Graham Parks was all she had to do today. But she had numerous misgivings about meeting him and writing the piece, not least the fact that she knew, but he didn't know that she knew, that he had had a breakdown.

Her mobile rang on her desk as she got up to go. It was Katie.

'Hi, I'm just about to do an interview,' Helen told her. 'Can I call you back later?'

'I just wondered if Emma could come back

with us after school,' Katie said. 'Hannah says they need to practise a dance or something. Is that okay?'

'Fine, if you don't mind,' Helen told her. 'Alex was going to pick them up from school today. I'll call him when I've finished this interview.'

'I'll call him,' Katie answered. 'You sound busy. Do you want to pick her up on your way home from work?'

'Are you sure that's not going to be too late?' Helen felt guilty that Katie always seemed to be looking after Emma and she rarely returned the favour. 'I could get Alex to pick her up earlier.'

'No, they need a lot of time, apparently,' Katie joked. 'I'll give them dinner. See you later, then?'

'Yes. See you later.' Helen hung up and left the office.

She popped into the ladies' toilet on the way to reception, making sure she was presentable in a way she had not bothered to do on their first meeting. She looked slightly flushed — that was nerves — but she'd washed her hair this morning and put on a green top that suited her. Although she'd never match up to Venetia Taylor standards, she thought she looked okay.

Graham was sitting on one of the swivel chairs that circled the reception desk. Each floor of the tower block that housed the *Sunday Review* had its own round reception area, enclosed on all sides by offices that could be viewed through the glass panels. Visitors to the fourteenth floor could opt to wait facing inwards, towards the desk and a table with a pile of newspapers and magazines, or turn their chairs around and watch

246

the journalists going about their business. The Review section was on the outer reaches of the building, so Helen and her colleagues were not subject to the scrutiny of visiting strangers, which she imagined must be very off-putting. Anyone sitting opposite the reception desk looked straight into the newsroom. They were usually too busy or pretending to be too busy being preoccupied with what was going on in the outside world to notice anyone within, but it wasn't unusual to pass through reception and find a cabinet minister or some other senior-ranking official staring intently as the drones in the newsroom went about their work.

He had his back to her when she came in and appeared to be surveying the same scene she'd caught the Prime Minister watching a few weeks ago. But when she approached his chair from the side, she saw that he had his eyes closed.

'Graham Parks,' she said, using his surname partly to appear more professional in front of the receptionist and partly because, curiously, she usually thought of him by his full name anyway.

She had first met and been introduced to him as Graham Parks. As an author he always carried both his names. No one would ever say to her, 'Did you interview Graham?' or 'Have you read Graham's book?' — he was always referred to in duplicate, and she found that she liked the weight of both names. If she thought of him as Graham Parks, it somehow created the impression of a safe distance between them.

'Helen Collins,' he replied, opening his eyes and smiling one of his disarming smiles. His tone was too fond, too familiar. She liked the way he said her name, as if it were a treasured possession, as if he took pleasure in simply uttering the words, but in the office she wished he'd been brusquer, not said her name at all, merely affirmed that he was who she had said he was.

She wondered if the receptionist had detected the note of familiarity in his tone, but she appeared intent on filing her nails.

'Thank you for coming in,' Helen said briskly. 'I'm sorry about the last-minute change of plan.'

Graham stood up and took his coat from the back of the chair. Helen had been worried he might kiss her, but he seemed to appreciate that here she needed to keep things formal.

She'd spoken to him only briefly the night before. She'd hoped he would not answer his phone but he had, and she'd told him in a hushed voice that she was at home and had remembered that she had another appointment the following morning that meant she would not be able to go to his house, as previously arranged.

He'd asked if she could come earlier or later but she'd refused, wary now, having been spotted on the London Eye, of putting herself in a situation that might lead to something she couldn't control.

She had told him there was a tight deadline for the piece and if he couldn't make it into the office then they'd arrange for another reporter to come to his house at the prearranged time.

He'd agreed then to come in to the *Sunday*

Review, saying he would happily talk to her but not anyone he didn't know.

Helen made small talk as they wove their way between the desks of her colleagues to the relative privacy of the interview room.

'There's a big report out about stress in the armed forces and the lack of support for soldiers who've suffered some form of trauma,' she said as they passed Justin, who was sifting through the pages of the report, trying to reduce its contents to a limited word count and make it readable in the process.

Helen paused by the water cooler.

'Do you want a drink?' she asked. 'I can get someone to bring us tea or something from the coffee bar. Or we have water!' She gestured towards the upturned five-litre bottle of Scottish spring water with its accompanying stash of plastic cups.

'The *Sunday Review* hasn't gone green yet and made its staff drink tap water?' Graham said.

'Not since the last outbreak of legionnaires' disease,' Helen answered. There had been an incident in the building a couple of years ago and a man in his sixties who worked in the canteen had nearly died of the pneumonia strain. Since then, they'd all been told not to drink water from the central system.

'In that case I'll have clear, still Scottish spring water in a heavily processed plastic cup.'

Helen smiled and poured two cups before pushing the door of the interview room with her shoulder.

'Here, let me.' Graham opened the door and held it while she walked in front of him, slopping a bit of water as she passed.

'Sorry,' she said. 'I think I splashed your shoes.'

'I don't think that's going to give me trench foot, do you?' Graham appeared to be keeping up the theme of water-borne military-associated diseases.

Helen placed the cups on either side of the large table, indicating that he should sit opposite her, a safe ninety centimetres between them.

'This isn't easy for me, you know,' Graham said, sitting down and looking at her steadily, focusing on her face with a look that seemed to say to Helen, 'We can try and be businesslike, but I can't ignore what there is between us.'

'It's not easy for me, either.' Helen tried to acknowledge the implicit look. 'I'd rather they'd sent someone else to talk to you, but as I'd already met you, I was the logical choice.'

'No, I mean, it's not easy for me to talk about stress in the army,' he said.

His look, she realised, was direct but almost pleading, asking her not to probe too far, to be easy with him.

'You didn't have to do it,' she said, and was surprised by the harshness of her tone. She saw him recoil slightly and move his hand, which had been resting on the table alongside the glass of water, back slightly into his own space.

'Sorry.' She spoke more softly. 'I mean you could have said no. You didn't have to agree just because I asked you. It was the easy option for

Justin, getting me to talk to you, but he could have found someone else if you hadn't wanted to do it.'

'I nearly told you about stress in the army when you first came to interview me.' Graham now had both his hands on the table, palms upwards in a gesture of openness. 'I knew that once the book was out, people would start asking questions about my past, try to fill in the missing gaps. I'd worked out a way of avoiding those questions, but there was something about you. I felt as if I could open up, tell you stuff that I haven't really told anyone.'

'I have that quality; that's why I'm a good journalist.' Helen laughed and then wished she hadn't. He was trying to be honest, trying to broach the subject of something painful, but why? Because she needed help to fill a hole in the paper, or because he wanted to?

'Sorry,' she said again. 'But I'm finding this difficult, this trying to be a professional and ask all the right questions when you are sitting there appealing to me as someone else.'

She saw Graham looking at her.

'Someone I can probably never be,' she added.

'Do either of you want a tea or coffee?' asked someone, from the doorway.

Helen stiffened. She hadn't noticed the door open or Justin come in. How long had he been there? Had he heard what she'd just said?

'Hi, I'm Justin May.' He had extended a hand to Graham, who was standing up and shaking it. 'I'm just wading through a fifty-two-page report on mental health in the armed services. It's all

251

rather turgid. We were hoping you could bring it to life a bit with your own side of things.'

'I'll try to help.' Graham was sitting down again. 'And no to the tea or coffee, but thank you for asking.'

Justin raised his eyebrows at Helen. She wasn't sure if he was annoyed at his curt dismissal by Graham, or if he was querying whether she wanted a drink.

'I'm okay, thanks,' she replied, which seemed an apposite reply to both scenarios.

35

Helen could hear music as she turned into Katie's street. She presumed it was teenagers pumping up the volume of an iPod dock in a bedroom somewhere. It was only when she drew close that she realised the noise was coming from Katie's sitting room.

The window was slightly open and she could hear Emma and Hannah singing along to Rihanna's 'Umbrella'.

Helen rang the doorbell, unsure whether anyone would be able to hear it over the din. The curtains were drawn, but through them she could make out the forms of her daughter and her friend dancing around the room.

When no one answered the door, Helen wondered whether to climb into the flower bed and call to Emma and Hannah through the open window. She decided to ring the bell again first, pressing it harder and for longer this time.

'Coming!' she heard Katie call, and then the trip-trap of shoes on the floorboards in the hallway.

'Sorry,' said Katie, flinging open the door. 'Did you ring before? I thought I might have heard the bell, but I wasn't quite sure. Come in.'

Katie looked lovely, as always. She was wearing a silky floral tunic top. Helen usually just wore jeans and a T-shirt on the days she was at home with the children. Anything nicer would only get dirty. She wondered whether, if she didn't have to go to work, she would ever wear anything other than jeans and T-shirts.

'You look nice,' she said to Katie. 'Is that top new?'

'Yes.' Katie smoothed the fabric over her hips. 'I bought it earlier this week.'

'It looks great,' Helen said, following Katie back into the house. Perhaps, she thought to herself, if I were with the children all the time, I would dress up at home a bit more often.

Right on cue, Emma and Hannah came dancing out of the sitting room. They had been dressing up themselves. Both girls appeared to be wearing dresses, which were actually tops of Katie's, tied around the waist with scarves and offset with a lot of plastic jewellery.

'Hi, Mum.' Emma sounded happy. 'We're making up a dance for *Britain's Got Talent*.'

'It's not ready yet, though,' Hannah chipped in. 'We need to practise more.'

'Well, I'm afraid I need to take Emma home now,' Helen replied.

'Not yet, Mum. Five more minutes,' Emma pleaded. She always wanted five more minutes. 'Can't you have a cup of tea or something?' she insisted.

'Okay. But only five minutes,' Helen told her as she followed Katie into her kitchen.

'It's a bit quieter in here,' Katie said, closing the door behind them.

'You haven't been dancing round the dinner table, then?' Helen joked as she surveyed the plates with the remains of what looked like fish and chips stacked up beside the sink.

'Katie's been dancing on the table,' said an Irish voice, and Helen noticed that Cary was sitting in a chair beside the fridge, holding a large glass of wine.

'Oh, hello,' said Helen. 'I didn't notice you there.'

'You remember Helen, don't you?' Katie said to him

'Of course,' Cary said, standing up. 'How could I forget?'

He moved across the kitchen and kissed her on both cheeks, full of Irish charm, thought Helen.

'How are you, Helen?' he asked. 'Have you had a good day?'

'Well, thank you,' Helen replied, looking around to see if Leonard and Connor, Cary's son, were in the room too. 'And my day was okay,' she added. 'Are the boys here too?'

'Leonard's gone to bed,' Katie said, opening the door of the fridge. 'And Connor fell asleep on the sofa, so we've put him in Hannah's bed for the time being.'

'I expect he'll wake soon.' Cary looked up at the ceiling, as though he might be able to see through it to his sleeping son.

'Is Philip home?' Helen asked.

'No, he's at a conference in Oxford,' Katie said, as she took a bottle of wine out of the fridge. 'He's staying overnight. Do you want a drink, Helen?'

'No thanks.' Helen was tempted, but thought she should get going. 'I told Emma she only had

255

five minutes, and I expect you've had enough of her.'

'Are you sure?' Katie hovered by the fridge.

'No, I ought to get back.' Helen was resolute. 'You seem to have had Emma a lot recently. Would Hannah like to come and play at our house one day next week?'

'I'm sure she would.' Katie put the wine back in the fridge. 'And actually, I did want to ask you a favour.'

'Sure.' Helen waited for her friend to ask.

'I wondered if you might be able to pick Leonard up from nursery on one of your days off and have him until we need to pick the girls up from school?'

'Of course,' Helen replied. 'Have you got something nice on?'

'Well, there's an old friend from college I want to meet up with.' Katie sounded a little vague. 'And it would be nice if I could do it without having Leonard in tow.'

'I'd love to have him,' Helen said. 'I seem to be going to Spain on a press trip next weekend and I'll probably have to leave on Friday, but any other time.'

'Cary,' Katie said, 'could you have a look at the calendar and tell me if there's anything on it on Thursday or Friday the week after next.'

The calendar was pinned to the wall near where Cary was sitting. Helen could see from where she was that it looked fairly empty, but Cary studied it, obligingly.

'Thursday fortnight is entirely free,' he said, looking from Katie to Helen, as if he was somehow brokering this childcare arrangement.

'Are you sure?' Katie said, looking at Cary, who nodded. 'Could you have Leonard then?' she asked Helen.

'I don't see why not,' Helen replied. 'I'll check my diary when I get home, but it should be fine. Now, I must round up my daughter.'

She thought when she said this that Cary might take her cue and think about leaving too, but he showed no signs of intending to go anywhere.

'I'll come with you,' Katie said, following Helen into the sitting room, where Emma and Hannah were still dancing.

'Emma, you need to get changed now,' Helen said to her daughter. 'It's time to go.'

'What does ravishing mean?' Emma asked, beginning to remove the scarf from around her waist.

'Very beautiful,' Helen told her. 'Why? Did someone tell you you looked ravishing in this outfit?'

'No,' Emma said, putting her arms up so that Helen could pull the top over her head. 'Connor's dad said Hannah's mum looked ravishing.'

36

Alex had strewn the Sunday papers around the living room in an uncharacteristically chaotic fashion. He'd almost jumped out of bed when Emma had crept into their bedroom in an over-dramatically quiet manner, tiptoeing with large bouncy movements that ensured the floorboards actually creaked rather than the carpet simply absorbing the impact of her small feet, and asked if she could watch television.

This Sunday morning ritual of creeping in and asking to watch TV usually led to one of two things: either Alex and Helen would go back to sleep for another half-hour, or they'd make the most of the fact that they were unlikely to be interrupted unless the cartoons were taken off air.

This morning Helen had been in the mood for the latter option, and was a bit put out when she heard the shower running before Alex came back to the bedroom fully clothed and announced that he was going out to get the papers.

Admittedly he had recently become slightly obsessed with possible highlights in the listings sections and had taken to buying vast mountains of weekend papers, through which he would rummage as if immersed in a game of pass the parcel, discarding travel, property and news until the music stopped and he hit upon the prized TV guide.

Flipping this open, he would often discover that the game was not yet over: *Muddy Water* had not been singled out as the 'one to watch' the imaginary music would start again and he would resume passing news reviews and sports supplements to imaginary friends before once again finding something with potential to unwrap.

Of course there was usually a method to this madness, with Alex ordering the discarded supplements into separate tidy piles, one with sections he thought he or Helen might want to read and the other destined to go straight into the recycling.

This morning, however, this methodology appeared to have been abandoned and a system more suited to a toddler's party adopted. Alex was flicking through tabloids with the frenzied manner of someone who was close to reaching the prize.

Helen surveyed him from the doorway of the living room. She was still in her dressing gown, on her way to fetch herself a cup of tea in the absence of any indication from her husband that he would get her one. Emma and Joe were glued to the television screen, the volume turned up high to obliterate the crescendoing sound of rattling newspaper pages.

Helen felt a slight knot of anxiety as she watched. She wondered what he would say when he saw the piece with Graham Parks, and if he'd ask her why she hadn't mentioned that she'd interviewed him again. That would mean she had met up with him at least three times, as far as

Alex was concerned, surely enough for him to think that she must be getting to know him rather well.

She took a deep breath, trying to calm her nerves. Perhaps they hadn't given her a byline. After all, the spread belonged to Justin. They might have credited him with all the work and included Graham Parks' personal experience of stress in the armed forces in a box on the edge of the page, without identifying who he had divulged his innermost feelings to.

* * *

'Fucking brilliant copy,' Justin had texted her as she made her way home on Friday evening. 'You really got him to open up.'

Helen had smiled at the compliment, hoping the minor triumph might protect her against the looming job cuts, and reflected again on what Graham had told her in the interview room during the afternoon.

'Ed, the character in the book, he's not that dissimilar to me,' he had begun. 'I made him a teacher, and a seriously flawed one at that, but ultimately he's someone whose job got too much for him and there were repercussions for the rest of his life.'

'Is that what happened to you?' Helen didn't want to say too much. She was in interviewer mode, allowing her subject to answer questions, though she felt she was probably also in pseudo-psychotherapist mode, waiting for her patient to open up, prompting him only by remaining relatively silent.

'I thought it would be a game of soldiers at first. Despite the way I look now, I was very fit and sporty at school.' Graham was fixing on a point in the distance, no longer looking directly at her. 'A lot of people hated boarding school, but I loved it. I was popular because I was captain of the football team; I had respect from teachers and peers that I never had from my parents. I thought the army would be like a continuation of this idyll. Lots of sport in the form of training, camaraderie, the satisfaction of making my way up through the ranks. And at first it was. But I never really expected to see active service.'

Helen briefly recalled the few facts she'd been able to find by Googling him: Germany, Iraq during the first Gulf War, and then Bosnia, before he left.

'And I never expected to find myself facing a prison sentence for GBH at the end of it all.'

She looked up, but made no comment.

'It's a cliché, but people have no idea what it's like. The first Gulf War was okay. The lads used to joke about going to Iraq to get a good tan. Some of them have got Gulf War syndrome now, but I came out of it fairly unscathed. After that I did a stint in Northern Ireland, which was scary. We were hated out there. I wanted out at that point, but then I was sent to Bosnia, which was a fucking mess.'

Graham took a sip from his glass of water.

'I couldn't sleep when I came home on leave, couldn't get the images of coked-up, gun-toting teenage Serbs out of my head, or the desperation on the faces of the Bosnians trying to get on to my helicopter. That was one of the last things I did in the army, tried to evacuate some of the refugees. But it was chaotic. No one had decided who should go first, and I had to choose some over others, with no apparent reason. I can still hear the cries of one particular man when I go to sleep at night. His wife and two children were on the helicopter, but he'd been left behind. I'd never really heard a man cry like that before. It sounded as if every emotion he'd ever felt was wrapped up in this loud, manic wail. He obviously thought he'd never see them again. I don't know if he ever did. If I'd wanted to split up families, I could have been a divorce lawyer.'

Graham smiled at his joke, as if he thought it was time to lighten the mood.

'But you probably saved their lives,' Helen told him. 'You gave his wife and children a chance — the hope of a future.'

'I took away that man's hope of a future.' Graham was twisting his hands round each other. He was visibly distressed now, and what Helen wanted more than anything was to take his hand in hers and tell him . . . tell him . . . what, exactly?

She could offer platitudes along the lines of him having done his best, that he had no choice, that right now she wanted to leave the office and go to bed with him, for what it was worth.

She shifted her position in her seat and sat on her hands.

'Go on,' she said, hearing the pseudo-psychotherapist rear her head again.

'I couldn't get that scene out of my head when I came home on leave. I was in a pub one evening with some of the others, and there was a bit of a rush on at the bar. This group of lads was jostling to get there, and when the barman served someone else, one of them shouted that he was first and pushed in front of this guy who'd been waiting. I couldn't see what was actually happening; I could only see the man who'd been about to get on board the helicopter to be with his wife and kids, and I went for the guy who'd queue-jumped.'

Graham stopped. He looked at her now and she had to look back; it wasn't fair not to.

'I didn't know I was capable of such violence. I'm ashamed to tell you this. I don't want you to know what I was like, what I suppose I am like. I started beating the living daylights out of this poor lad, whose only crime was to be a bit mouthy. I couldn't stop. Everyone was trying to pull me off him. When they did, all I could hear was this chorus of people saying. 'He's a fucking nutcase.'

'I guess they were right. That's what the military psychiatrist told the court anyway. It got me out of prison, being a fucking nutcase, and my time in the army was nearly up anyway. I was allowed to leave early, on medical grounds. I actually started writing as part of my treatment programme.'

He was still now, calm again, much as he had been when Helen had first met him, almost as if he felt he could relax now that he'd told her some of what she already knew.

He laid his hands on the table again. They were within easy reach of hers. She began to ease her hands out from under her thighs as the door opened. She wanted to put them over his as he had done to her on the London Eye.

'How are you doing?' asked Justin. Honestly, he had no sense of timing, or manners come to that, barging in in the middle of her interview.

'Fine.' Helen glowered at him.

'Great.' Justin stood there, looking at them both. 'Will you be able to file the copy by four, then?' he asked.

★ ★ ★

'Shit.' Alex had paused in his page-turning, and from where Helen was standing, she could see him tense his shoulders as he bent towards the page that had caught his attention. Was it a bad review, another programme nominated the 'one to watch', or was it her piece with Graham Parks that had caught his attention? He still appeared unaware that she was there, so she cleared her throat.

'Fuck!' Alex jumped and snapped round. 'How long have you been standing there?'

'Daddy said fuck.' Joe's attention had been momentarily diverted from the mesmerising antics of Sportacus, who was saving a cat trapped on the roof of a building by bouncing from a trampoline on to a ledge, then swinging from a handily positioned rope on to the rooftop. For no apparent reason the phrase 'hearts and minds' came into Helen's brain.

'Fucking Daddy's picture's in the paper.' Emma was also distracted by the unfolding drama in the living room.

'Don't use that word,' Alex told them both, closing the paper hurriedly.

'You did.' Emma was not about to be told off by a hypocrite. 'He's been saying fuck all morning.' She beamed at her mother, who couldn't help laughing.

'What's the picture you seem so anxious about, then?' Helen asked Alex. 'Did someone get a shot that made your hair look grey?'

'No, Daddy looks handsome.' Emma had opened the paper again. 'And this girl is very pretty.'

Helen looked over her daughter's shoulder and saw that beneath the headline 'MUDDY WAITERS', Alex did indeed look handsome. Candlelight was flattering, and the flashbulb of the photographer appeared not to have disturbed him as he sat in a restaurant, presumably somewhere in Manchester, looking across the table at a radiant Venetia Taylor.

'I can explain,' said Alex, as Helen left the room in desperate need now of a cup of tea, if not something stronger.

Helen felt angry. Angry that her husband had been having dinner alone in a restaurant with Venetia Taylor and had not told her about it. If there was an explanation, as he was now

265

protesting there was, why hadn't he been upfront about it in the first place? Whatever the reason or the excuse, she was furious that he'd been stupid enough to get snapped gazing across the table at Venetia Taylor. Now there was smoke, whether or not there was fire.

She was smouldering herself, stoking up grievances for an argument they would finally have that evening, after the children had gone to bed.

She was angry, but also curiously relieved. Seeing this picture made her feel less guilty about having agreed to have dinner with Graham Parks again, when he'd asked her as she'd escorted him back to the lifts of the *Sunday Review*.

37

'You make the most of this opportunity, young lady,' Helen said, carefully wrapping the baby's head so as not to cover her mouth and nose. She felt uneasy about parcelling the baby up this way, winding bubble wrap around her limbs before slipping her into a super-large padded envelope, but she was headed for Belarus, and surface mail seemed the best way of getting her there.

Helen had persuaded Emma and Joe to sort through their toys by promising them the proceeds of anything they could sell on eBay. Emma's Baby Annabell, a lifelike doll that shed actual tears (as long as you had managed to activate her electronic sucking mechanism and got her to drink a full bottle of water first), had reached quite a good price. Helen was surprised at first how high the bidding had gone, thinking that you could buy new dolls for not much more. Then she noticed that the two highest bidders were from eastern Europe, where lifelike baby dolls were obviously harder to come by.

The irony was not lost on her: women from former Soviet states bidding for toy babies that they received through the post, while Western women travelled by no-frills airlines to various parts of the Eastern bloc in order to collect real live babies from orphanages and bring them home to surround with dolls.

Helen unwrapped the baby again. She'd taken

the batteries out when Emma stuck Baby Annabell on the top of a pile of books, clothes and a selection of toys that came free with McDonald's Happy Meals. Now she decided she had better just test that she still had all her mechanical faculties before sending her to her new home. She undid the battery cover on the baby's back and put four new batteries into the space where a real baby's kidneys would have been. Baby Annabell began to gurgle with delight and blinked her eyes at Helen. She was incredibly lifelike. The computer chip with a recording of actual baby noises saw to that.

There had been a time when all the girls in Emma's class took their various models of Baby Annabell to school with them. One evening, as Helen was putting her to bed, Emma had insisted that she had brought the wrong baby home, adamant that, despite being identical in every respect to her own doll, the one Helen was trying to tuck into bed with her did not sound right.

They say mothers can recognise their own baby's cries, but Helen wasn't so sure. When Emma was born, the couple that lived next door had a six-month-old baby whose lungs had twenty-six weeks' worth of growth on Emma's and managed to penetrate the party walls. On numerous occasions during the night Helen would jump out of bed, convinced that the source of the noise was Emma, only to realise that she was sleeping soundly in her Moses basket and she had been woken by the cries of another baby entirely.

When Emma had undressed the 'wrong' Baby Annabell, she had been proved right. The one she'd brought home was not wearing a nappy, whereas Emma made sure she changed her baby every morning and took it to school in a clean one. She had recognised her own baby's cry, apparently possessing a maternal capacity absent in her own mother.

Baby Annabell began to cry now as Helen laid her on the kitchen table in preparation for parcelling her up again. It provoked a strange reaction in her. She felt like crying herself. She didn't want Baby Annabell to go to Belarus; she was going to miss her. She wondered whether she should include a note with the packing slip asking her new owners to let them know that she had arrived safely and how she was getting on.

Of course it was not the doll per se that she would miss, but the younger Emma who had played with her so assiduously and who now considered herself too big for dolls and too big to be kissed when her mother said goodbye to her at school.

Everything appeared to be slipping away from Helen. Her children were slowly but surely growing up, their need for her ebbing with each new half-centimetre pencilled on the section of kitchen wall where Alex recorded their heights. Her job, the one thing that tied her to her pre-children past, appeared to be at risk, and Alex was increasingly wrapped up in his work.

★　★　★

When she'd asked Alex about the picture of him having dinner with Venetia Taylor, he'd somehow managed to make it seem as if she was the one who was in the wrong for asking.

She'd confronted him in the kitchen, trying to keep her voice even so as not to alarm the children, who were in bed but probably not quite asleep.

'So that's why you leapt out of bed and ran to the shops this morning.' She realised she was brandishing a corkscrew accusingly at him as she spoke.

'I didn't leap out of bed.' Alex slowly poured himself a glass of wine, calmly carrying out his evening routine as if nothing was out of the ordinary. 'You're over-reacting.'

'Am I?' Helen sat down. 'I saw the way you flicked through those papers. You were obviously looking for something. What were you going to do, tear the page out before I came down and hope I never found out?'

'Okay.' Alex sat down at the table opposite her. 'I did get up early and buy the papers because I knew there was a possibility of there being a picture in one of them. But I wasn't going to keep it from you; I just wanted to let Venetia know.'

'But until you were papped, you weren't going to bother telling me you'd been out to dinner with Venetia.' Helen was furious, not least because Alex was so calm.

'You're as bad as they are.' Alex was presumably referring to the subs who'd written the headline. 'You make it sound as if it was a date or something.'

'What was it exactly, then?' Helen realised she was being hypocritical, but she couldn't help herself. 'A nice cosy candlelit meal for two doesn't exactly fulfil my idea of a script meeting.'

'We just went for a meal after the recording.' Alex sounded agitated now. She had succeeded in winding him up. 'I had a meal after the show with a fellow cast member. I sometimes go out for meals with Nick or Chris or Chloe and you think nothing of it. I don't stop having to eat just because I'm away.'

'But this time Nick and Chris and Chloe weren't there,' Helen snapped. 'It was just the two of you, and a photographer saw you and obviously thought you looked very cosy, and yet still you didn't think to tell me.'

'Well, you don't tell me everything,' Alex countered.

Helen felt suddenly sick. Did he know more than he'd been letting on? What exactly had Peter told him when he called after seeing her on the London Eye? Had Alex somehow found out that when she'd been to dinner with Graham, his publicist had not been there? Had he read texts on her phone or seen the emails she'd saved on her computer?

'What do you mean?' she asked nervously.

'You didn't tell me that your ex-boyfriend was back in the country,' he said.

'I did.' Helen felt relieved. 'I told you he brought a book into the office. The one by that author I did the piece with. And I told you I'd bumped into him in the lift.'

'But you didn't tell me that you went for a

drink with him,' Alex replied. 'Katie let that slip when we had lunch there.'

'It was just a quick glass of wine after work,' Helen said defensively. 'It didn't seem important.'

'It was important enough for you to tell Katie all about it,' he countered.

'It just came up in conversation,' she said. 'You know how we are. We talk about anything and everything. You're not usually interested in the finer details of my life.'

'I am interested to know that you've been having cosy meetings with your ex, who happens to be splitting up with his wife and who sends you emails saying he wants to meet again,' Alex returned.

'Have you been reading my emails?' Helen was indignant and worried.

'I saw one, which was open on your computer, when I was helping Joe do something. I didn't actively snoop, if that's what you are implying,' Alex countered.

'Well why didn't you say something at the time, if it bothered you?' Helen asked.

'Because I shouldn't have read it,' Alex admitted. 'And I wouldn't if it hadn't been there open on the desktop. And because I trusted you to sort out whatever it is you need to sort out with Jim Keeble.'

'I dont need to sort anything out with Jim Keeble,' Helen reiterated. 'He's in the past. I just happened to run into him at work. It's not important.'

'And neither is Venetia.' Somehow Alex

seemed to have used Jim Keeble to justify himself. 'I'm sorry I didn't tell you we had dinner after the show one night. I'm sorry I didn't tell you exactly what we had to eat or that someone photographed us eating it. It wasn't important, but Venetia was upset about it, so I wanted to warn her.'

'So you are more worried about Venetia's feelings than mine?' Helen was raising her voice now.

'Of course I'm not. I didn't think you'd mind. Someone takes a picture of us having a meal after a recording. So what? It's no skin off my nose, but Venetia has spent large chunks of her life trying to get away from photographers. She was upset when this man suddenly started taking pictures. She didn't want it to be printed, because she thinks it will spark interest in her and she'll have to start spending her life trying to avoid photographers again.'

'She should have thought of that before she agreed to do the photoshoot for the women's mag with you.' Helen took a gulp of wine. 'She can't have it both ways. And she should have thought about it before she decided to join *Muddy Water*. If she didn't want the attention, she shouldn't have sought it out.'

'You can be hard-hearted sometimes.' Alex downed his glass of wine. 'She's a single parent. She needs to work and she's an actress. She didn't have a choice. I'm trying to be friendly towards her, that's all. Let's leave it there, shall we? I'm going to bed.' He put his glass on the side and walked out of the room.

Was he right? Helen asked herself. Was it as straightforward as that? Was she imagining there was more to his relationship with Venetia Taylor than there actually was? Was she making things worse by accusing him of something that didn't exist?

★　★　★

The next day, Helen went to the recycling to get a fresh sheet of paper in which to wrap Baby Annabell and found herself looking at the photograph of Alex and Venetia again. It could be a perfectly innocent picture, but she still felt a stab of jealousy at seeing her husband with another woman. She closed it and picked out the review section of the *Sunday Review*.

'HEARTS AND LOST MINDS'. The headline on the front page gave a taste of what the main story was about. Beneath it there was a picture of a man in camouflage uniform, his head buried in his hands, and the subtitle 'Military breakdown: are the pressures of army life too much?' She looked inside and found Graham Parks gazing directly at her; his calm, grey eyes had a slight pleading quality. It was a good picture. She wondered where they had got it. It was unlike the ones that were taken when she had first interviewed him about his book. He looked more soldierly in this one; he was slimmer, had slightly more hair and a look in his eyes that was different. He looked like a man who needed caring for.

She took the batteries out of the doll again so

that she stopped crying. She rewrapped her in the Motoring section, and then went to her computer to print off a postage label.

Alex was on his way to Manchester. They'd parted on frosty terms. He had still not forgiven her for picking an argument and spoiling his last day at home. She had not forgiven him for whatever it was he was not to be forgiven for, and there had been an undercurrent of tension still tangible that morning.

'I'll see you tomorrow evening, then,' he had said as he watched her weighing Emma's old doll on the kitchen scales.

'Wednesday,' Helen had corrected, noting that the doll weighed under a kilo, so the postage to Belarus would not be too high.

'I'm back early this week,' he had reminded her. 'I've got a vasectomy booked on Wednesday.'

'Of course.' This was in the diary. Helen had asked him if she should take the day off work and go with him, but he hadn't wanted her to. Perhaps this was why he was so grumpy. Here she was mourning the departure of a doll that to her signified an age in which the children had been young and the future endlessly rosy. Perhaps Alex's impeding snip signified the same to him. She softened towards him, leaving the doll on the scales like a newborn having its first weight recording with a midwife.

'I'll see you tomorrow evening then.' She kissed him, and although he kissed her too, it was brusque and formal, no warmth extended.

'See you then.' He'd left, still angry.

* * *

Helen went to her eBay account and navigated her way to Print Postage. She was surprised to find that Belarus was part of Europe and it cost no more to send Baby Annabell to the former Soviet Union than it would to France. She pressed print, then went to the feedback section of her account. Helen loved eBay feedback. She found she got so little of it in the rest of her life that a few words telling her she was a great eBayer made her feel incredibly positive.

Mothering was a thankless task at the best of times, Alex was more appreciative of the talents of Venetia Taylor than her own at the moment, and in the office there was so much back-stabbing and people trying to hold on to their own jobs that no one ever said anything positive about anyone else's work.

So she felt ridiculously pleased when she sold a book on the online marketplace and someone told her that it had arrived quickly. Even though she had no control over the workings of the post office, she took this as a great compliment. Today there was feedback from someone to whom she had sold a very old Teletubbies VHS that Emma and Joe no longer wanted.

'Very well packaged, arrived super fast. A+++ eBayer,' it read.

Helen knew it was ridiculous to feel so elated, but when no one ever told you they appreciated you, you began to feel kindly towards anyone who did. Graham Parks appeared to appreciate some of the qualities she possessed. He had emailed her on Sunday to say how much he'd liked her treatment of what he'd said. He had told her again that he didn't really like to talk about his time in the army, but that she possessed an intangible quality of compassion and warmth that made him want to tell her more than he had told anyone for a long time. That was A+++ positive feedback.

38

'This is very lovely,' said Katie, taking the biscuit tin from Helen's kitchen cupboard.

'What's that?' Helen asked, putting the kettle on to make the coffee she had semi-forced her friend to have after taking the children to school.

'This note from Alex.' Katie waved a piece of paper towards her. 'Sorry, I couldn't help reading it. Haven't you seen it?'

'No.' Helen was confused. 'Where was it?'

'Stuck to the biscuit tin,' Katie told her, handing it over. 'I imagine he thought one of you would find it if he left it there.'

'Normally he'd have been right.' Helen took the note. 'But we've been a bit all over the place for the last couple of days. I never quite got round to eating biscuits.'

In fact, Helen thought to herself, there were several reasons why the biscuit tin had been untouched for over twenty-four hours. Firstly, she'd been working yesterday and the children had been at the childminder's until almost bedtime, and definitely well past biscuit time. Secondly, she had tried a few times to call Alex in the evening to talk but each time had gone straight through to his voicemail. Thirdly, while her anxiety about Alex over the argument they'd had about him and Venetia would normally have sent her straight to something chocolatey, she had checked her natural inclination to comfort herself with sugar because Graham Parks had called her and they'd talked on the phone for nearly an hour.

'Aren't you going to read it?' Katie asked, at the same time shaking her head as Helen proffered a biscuit. 'No thanks.'

'Dear Emma and Joe,' it said. 'I hope you have a lovely couple of days while I am away in Manchester. I will miss you all but am back early this week so will be able to take you both to school on Wednesday. Emma, I hope you have a great music lesson and the naughty boys don't spoil it this week. Jo-Jo, have fun at football, be good and look after Bugsy and Mummy. Lots of love, Dad.'

'That's odd — he doesn't usually leave notes.' Helen wondered what had occasioned this one. Was it a small act of contrition or a portent of something more sinister?

'It shows he cares,' Katie said, sitting down at the kitchen table. 'I wish Philip would take a bit more notice of what goes on in our family.'

'But he does,' Helen said, putting the note down as she went to make the coffee. She'd bumped into Katie at the school gates and invited her back for a quick chat, despite Katie's insistence that she didn't have very long as she had an appointment at home later that morning. 'Philip adores you all.'

'Maybe.' Katie looked at her watch. She was definitely anxious not to be too long. Perhaps they should have gone back to her house, but Helen's was en route and she had desperately wanted someone to offload some of her anxiety about Alex on to.

'Of course he does.' Helen noted the irony that she was the one offering marital reassurance when she had hoped that her friend would be able to do this for her. 'Philip is completely devoted to you and Hannah and Leonard.'

'Well sometimes he has a funny way of showing it,' said Katie, sipping her coffee. 'Or not showing it really. I'm sure he hasn't taken in that Hannah and Emma's music lessons are being spoilt by disruptive boys, even though she has told him. And he would have no idea what else was on the timetable. Alex actually knows that Joe has football on a Monday.'

'Well, you know what Alex is like about football,' Helen said through gritted teeth. 'I'm not sure Joe even really likes it, but Alex goes on about it so much, I think he pretends to enjoy it just to please him. Anyway, just because Philip doesn't bother himself with the finer details of family life doesn't take away from the fact that he is a part of it.'

'In body if not in spirit,' Katie said. 'Sometimes I feel as if he is simply a lodger in our house. He goes through the motions, but at the moment his mind is elsewhere.'

'Alex is the same.' Helen brought the conversation back round to her own insecurities. 'Perhaps they're both having some sort of mid-life crisis.'

'Why, what's up with the housewife's heart-throb?' Katie joked. 'Is he getting a motorbike, or taking up golf?'

'Not yet.' Helen took the lid off the biscuit tin and absent-mindedly began devouring a large chocolate digestive. 'But he seems to be falling for the other classic mid-life stereotype.'

'Which is?' Katie took a biscuit too.

'Oh, you know.' Helen pushed biscuit crumbs around the table with her finger. 'Taking a bit too much interest in a younger woman.'

'What younger woman?' Katie asked.

'Venetia Taylor,' Helen replied, wishing almost as soon as she'd said it that she hadn't. Somehow voicing insecurities made them appear more real. Now that she had Katie's full attention, she wasn't sure she wanted to divulge the details of the argument she'd had with Alex or her fears about what might be going on between him and Venetia. She wasn't even sure what her fears were exactly. Having read Alex's note, she felt reassured that he still loved them all and that everything would be all right when he came back. She was worried that if she opened up to Katie, she would be unleashing something she could not pack back up again.

Fortunately, Katie did not appear to take her seriously or be particularly interested.

'Venetia is hardly a younger woman,' she said through a mouthful of biscuit. 'She's only a few years younger than you and she's got a child. She doesn't fit the stereotype at all.'

'Well she's very beautiful,' Helen insisted. 'And Alex seems to be with her pretty much all the time when he's away.'

'Sorry.' Katie paused, realising that her out-of-hand dismissal might have been tactless.

281

'But you're not seriously worried about her, are you?'

'I guess not.' Helen decided it was best not to have this conversation with Katie, and was about to change the subject.

'Whereas Philip's PhD student is only about twenty-three.' Katie helped herself to another biscuit. 'And he spends far more time with her at the moment than he does with me and the children.'

'I feel like that too sometimes,' Helen concurred, but Katie didn't seem to be listening to her.

'He's been late back several times in the last few weeks and he never calls to let me know,' she said. 'He just arrives home saying he got caught up in a discussion with Maria about her thesis. It's driving me mad.'

It was now Helen's turn to question if Katie really thought there was a threat to her marriage.

'Does it really bother you?' she asked.

'I don't know,' Katie replied. 'I used to think that Philip wasn't capable of having an affair. He's too disorganised, not duplicitous enough. I mean, I couldn't imagine he'd be able to get round to it in between doing his job and getting himself dressed, but maybe his way of having an affair is just to have one without even bothering to cover his tracks.'

'I think you're right that he's not capable of having an affair,' Helen tried to console. 'Not because he's not organised enough — because he is organised at work — but because he loves you too much. He's probably just caught up in this woman's thesis. You know what he's like about sixteenth-century poets. That's what you love about him.'

'Maybe you're right,' Katie replied slowly. 'But I think we're all capable of having affairs, no matter what we think.'

Helen caught herself blushing and got up to put the kettle on again. It took her by surprise, the blush, and she wondered if Katie was talking about her. She was about to ask if she wanted more coffee, but Katie started talking again.

'I mean, some people are obviously conniving bastards and set out to screw everything in sight.' She laughed, and then was serious again. 'Whereas others never set out to deceive anyone but it happens anyway.'

Helen busied herself with refilling mugs and kept quiet.

'Sometimes I think it might be better just to get on with it and get over it. Do you know what I mean?'

'I'm not sure that I do,' Helen answered, wondering if this was a hypothetical question or pertinent to their own situations. 'What *do* you mean?'

'I'm not quite sure myself,' Katie said, looking at her friend as she spoke. 'It's just that when people have affairs, they often say it was just for sex and then they go back to being happily married. And sometimes I think maybe everyone needs to go off and have 'just sex' with someone else, and maybe it doesn't really mean anything.'

'Except someone always gets hurt.' Helen had already thought about this, and she knew the scenario was an attractive but unrealistic one. 'Are you saying you want Philip to shag his student just to get it out of his system?' She was incredulous.

'No,' Katie replied. 'That's not what I mean really.'

39

'Why don't you stay and finish your meal?' Helen asked Graham, as she fished her purse from her bag to pay for what she had ordered.

'No, I'll walk you to the tube,' Graham insisted. 'I didn't come for the food anyway. I came because I wanted to see you.'

'I'm sorry,' Helen said. She'd already apologised several times since she remembered, as they sat down to order, that she had promised to get home early tonight.

'It's okay. You don't have to keep apologising,' Graham said as he beckoned the waiter and asked for the bill.

'Is everything all right?' asked the Australian, whose name tag identified him as Gerard.

'Yes. Fine. Lovely,' Helen said. 'It's just something came up and we need to get home.'

She said 'we' because it seemed easier to let the waiter believe that they were together and they both needed to go.

'Kids?' asked Gerard, stressing the i so that it sounded like 'keedz'.

'Something like that,' Helen replied, taking out enough money to pay for the drinks she and Graham had had and the food they'd ordered.

'They haven't started cooking the mains yet,' Gerard told them. 'So you only need to pay for the starters.'

'Thank you,' Graham said. 'We'll try and

come back for the mains another time.'

'See you then.' Gerard picked up the pile of notes and coins they'd counted on to the table.

'I really am sorry,' Helen said again as they walked back down the street towards the tube. She turned to her left, where Graham had been walking but he was no longer there.

'It's okay honestly,' his voice said from behind, as he popped up on her right.

'Where did you go?' she joked to lighten the atmosphere.

'Men are supposed to walk on the side nearest the road,' he said, falling into step with her again.

'That's very chivalrous,' Helen said, liking the way that Graham was always considerate towards her.

Alex belonged to the 'isn't it insulting to feminists?' school of thought and never let a woman pass through a door first, gave up his seat on a bus or helped mothers with buggies down stairs. Helen wondered if she was partly to blame for his attitude. In the early days of their relationship she had been at pains to prove that she was perfectly capable of doing things every time Alex tried to do something for her. In the end he had given up.

But, she pondered, in middle age she was no longer defiantly independent, and she appreciated the old-fashioned gentlemanliness of some of Graham Parks' gestures.

'Is that so I don't get my gown splashed by a hackney carriage or something?' she asked.

'No,' he replied. 'It's so you don't get hit by a

car or mugged by a cyclist!'

'Oh.' Helen considered his response and wondered if it was his military training that made him think of these things. She knew London well enough to feel fairly safe when she walked around at night, but she felt safer for being with Graham Parks. She imagined that if they were accosted by a paranoid schizophrenic or sat next to someone with an improvised bomb on the tube, Graham would know what to do.

It was ironic, thought Helen, that she felt safe with someone who posed such a risk to her happy little world.

As if in response to her thoughts, a young man ran past as they began walking up King's Cross Road, shouting obscenities over his shoulder to a gang of other youths pursuing him towards Farringdon.

'I wish we could get away somewhere,' Graham said.

Helen was not quite sure whether he meant away from the late-night aggro of London or for the two of them to go somewhere together.

'I'm going to Santander for work next weekend,' she volunteered, wondering as she said it if there was any way that Graham might come with her.

'And I'm reading at a festival in Yorkshire.' Graham quashed that idea. 'Is work sending you anywhere else in the near future?'

'Eastbourne, in a couple of weeks' time,' she told him, thinking that it would be nice if he could go there with her. It was only a day trip, but at least by the sea, she wouldn't be worrying about anyone she knew spotting them. 'I'm going to an exhibition at the art gallery there,' she told him. 'Do you want to come? Then we could always have Eastbourne!'

She wished as soon as she'd said this that she hadn't. Not because she wouldn't like him to come to Eastbourne with her but because she'd used a line that she thought of as Alex's. Admittedly it really belonged to Humphrey Bogart in *Casablanca*, but Alex used it every time they'd been somewhere new and had a good time.

The previous September, they'd been to Sweden without the children. Alex had a day's filming for an outdoor clothing commercial, which had been shot just outside Stockholm, and Helen had joined him for a few days after he'd finished. They had had a wonderful weekend.

'Now we'll always have Stockholm,' he'd said on the plane home, taking her hand, and she'd laughed, thinking that there were an awful lot of places they would always have.

'Have you been to Eastbourne?' she added, hoping to obliterate 'we could always have Eastbourne' by talking some more.

'I went there to meet my birth mother,' Graham said as they reached the entrance to the tube station. 'She was in a home.'

'I didn't know you were adopted,' Helen said, wishing they were still in the restaurant and she had more time to have this conversation with him.

'I didn't know until a few years ago either,' Graham told her. 'Although I always felt there was something missing.'

This wasn't the sort of statement to which you could reply 'I really have to go now'. So Helen stopped at the top of the steps leading down to the underground.

'I've heard people say that before,' she said, hoping Graham would explain what it was he felt had been lacking.

'My parents, my adoptive parents,' he went on, 'couldn't have children when they adopted me, but not long after, Mum got pregnant with my younger brother.'

'That seems to happen a lot,' Helen observed.

'They were wonderful parents,' Graham said, 'and I think they tried their best to treat us both the same, but I always sensed that Chris was the preferred child. I used to think it was because he was the youngest and he was blond and curly-haired and bright. They just seemed to adore him.'

'I'm sure they loved you.' Helen had meant to say this reassuringly, but it emerged sounding like a question.

'Yes,' Graham replied, looking at her and holding her gaze. 'They loved me. But not enough.'

At that moment Helen had absolutely no desire to break off their conversation and go home to Alex. What she really wanted to do was succumb to all the feelings she had for Graham Parks and take him into her arms, there and then on the pavement in the gathering dusk.

He looked away and carried on speaking. 'That seems to be the story of my life.'

40

The leaflet Alex had brought back from the doctor when he first went to enquire about having a vasectomy warned that one of the side effects of the operation was irritability. Helen had prepared herself for this, promised to ignore any untoward comments, and decided to make an effort to keep the house tidy so that slight chaos would not contribute to his bad mood.

She should also have remembered that he was actually having the operation and not arranged to meet Graham Parks for dinner after work.

Having done so rather belatedly, she opened the front door to her home with some trepidation. Alex was obviously a textbook patient. He appeared more angry than irritable.

'Where've you been?' His tone was accusing.

'I'm sorry.' Helen curbed her natural instinct to be defensive and went for humility in its place. 'I got caught up with work'.

'What was so important that you couldn't get home on time today?'

'I had to interview a woman whose mother wants her to take her to Switzerland for an assisted suicide. I'm really sorry I didn't get back earlier. It was pretty heavy stuff, not the kind of interview you can say, 'sorry, have to go now' when you've done listening.'

Helen was surprised once you started lying how easy it was to sound convincing. She used to have more of a conscience. Her scruples used to jump up and demand assuaging at the prospect of the tiniest white lie. But these days she could often come up with them at the merest suggestion of an awkward encounter and convince all around her that she was telling the truth.

A few weeks previously, for example, she'd been at a play centre with Emma and Joe and, unwilling to pay astronomical prices for food they would probably barely touch, she'd decided to economise by taking her own sandwiches.

The play park had welcoming signs all around saying 'NO FOOD OR DRINK THAT IS NOT BOUGHT HERE CAN BE CONSUMED ON THE PREMISES. ANYONE SEEN DOING SO WILL BE ASKED TO LEAVE.' She decided that the just-out-of-college-aged staff were probably not so enthused by their jobs that they would bother to pursue anyone flouting these rules.

She presumed wrong, and found herself being berated by a twenty-something jobsworth who began his dressing-down by asking her if she could read.

'I'm really sorry,' Helen had replied. 'I should have mentioned it when I came in, but I have asked about it when I've been here before and it's always been okay. My son has a very severe nut allergy and I daren't risk buying food. He had to be rushed to hospital once, after someone in a café buttered a sandwich with a knife that had been used for peanut butter. Of course if the rules are inflexible, I understand and we'll have to stop coming here.'

The jobsworth had retreated, unable to come up with a response to such a well-thought-out and plausible excuse. The friends that Helen was with had also found it so convincing that they had asked her how long Joe had this non-existent, made-up-on-the-spur-of-the-moment allergy.

Now, without having previously thought much about it, she found herself telling her husband, who had today undergone an operation he hadn't wanted to have, that there was a genuine and good reason why she had not come home to see how he was.

'When's it going to run then, this piece?' Alex at first was not entirely convinced.

'Not until the mother dies,' Helen told him. 'I have to keep it a complete secret until she's been to Switzerland and taken the drugs that will kill her. If her daughter is complicit in assisting her then she could be charged. So for now we have to say nothing.'

'You could have called me.' Alex appeared to believe her big fat white lie. 'I've been sat here wondering where you were.'

'Sorry.' Helen was contrite again. 'I just wanted to get home as soon as possible and see how you were. How did the operation go?'

'Cancelled.' So Alex's irritability was not down to the operation itself.

'What do you mean, it was cancelled?'

'I mean one of the surgeons who spends his days rendering middle-aged men infertile had flu and so they had to cancel all his operations.' Alex's answer was loaded with resentment.

'So will they reschedule, will you have to go to the bottom of the waiting list again?'

'They said they should be able to do it in the next three or four weeks, but I might not get much notice. I'll try to let you know, though, so you can get home from work on time.' Alex sounded sarcastic.

The two of them were still standing in the hallway. Helen put her bag down and hung her coat on the hooks.

'Perhaps I can come with you next time?' she asked, trying to be conciliatory, but Alex turned away.

'Have you had anything to eat?' he asked, heading towards the kitchen.

'I'm not sure.' For the second time this evening, Helen felt completely uncertain about what she wanted from her life.

A few hours earlier, she'd been sitting in the corner of a quiet restaurant, opening up to Graham Parks, as they waited for their starters to arrive. She had told him about the possible job cuts at the *Sunday Review*, about Alex's preoccupation with work and in particular with Venetia.

'Sometimes I feel as if I'm not good enough for anyone any more,' she'd said, looking at him watching her steadily from the other side of the table.

'I can't believe that's true,' he had replied, reaching his hand across the table and covering hers.

She hadn't taken it away, enjoying the moment but not sure where it might lead.

When she looked up, Graham had held her gaze.

'You are a beautiful, intelligent, sane, loving woman,' he'd said softly. 'I — '

'Don't,' Helen had interrupted, remembering suddenly that it was today that Alex had had the snip. 'Don't spoil things. I have to go.'

Alex was definitely riled now. 'You must know if you've eaten or not,' he said.

Now that she thought about it, she realised she was not sure whether having ordered a meal, toyed with the starter and left halfway through eating it counted as having had something to eat. She wasn't particularly hungry, but it would lend more weight to her made-up excuse for being late if she said she needed something now.

'No, I haven't eaten. Not since lunch.' She followed Alex into the kitchen and poured herself a glass of wine. Alex already had one, sitting on the table.

He walked over to get it, and found that Helen was crying.

'What's the matter?' She appeared to be forgiven now. He put his arms around her and she buried her head in his chest and sobbed.

Helen hadn't anticipated this. She'd thought she could handle the minor deceptions, her feelings towards another man, her telling herself she wasn't actually doing anything wrong. But back home with Alex, the man she had loved for the past twenty years, she found herself wishing she'd never encountered Graham Parks.

'Come here, sit down.' Alex was shepherding her towards a chair. He pulled another alongside and put his arm around her. 'I don't understand what's going on here, Helen. You're all over the place at the moment.'

'I know,' Helen sobbed. 'It's just that everything seems to be slipping away.'

'What do you mean?' Alex took a sip of wine and pushed her glass towards her, in the hope that alcohol would calm her, not knowing she'd already had a glass or two with another man.

'I don't know really.' Helen had been good at coming up with an excuse for not getting home earlier, but she couldn't find a way to tell Alex why she was crying. 'It's just . . . I don't know. The children are getting bigger and we won't be having any more, and there are cuts at work and I'm worried that I might lose my job, and . . . '

'And what?' Alex was stroking the back of her neck, gently soothing her. With hindsight, Helen wished that at this point she'd stopped talking, stopped crying, kissed her husband and had something to eat with him.

'And you seem to be spending more and more time with Venetia. It's as if we're all going our separate ways, and I want to get back to how it was.'

She realised as soon as the words were out that it was never a good idea to accuse your husband of something if there were no real grounds for it.

'Don't be ridiculous.' Alex's arm shot away from her shoulder and banged the table with such force their respective glasses moved a few inches across its surface. 'I spend time with Venetia because I work with her. That's all there is to it.'

'But you're always talking about her and having dinner with her after work and doing extra photoshoots with her.' Helen hated the whining sound in her voice and the fact that she was saying these things out loud, but she couldn't help herself.

'That's because it's my job.' Alex was back at the cupboards now, angrily removing packets of pasta from the shelf, putting saucepans on the hob with more force than was necessary. 'That's like me saying you're spending too much time with that author you interviewed and then had dinner with. It's your job. I don't question what you do and who you are with when you're not here. Why are you doing it to me?'

'I don't know.' Helen was surprised that Alex had brought up Graham Parks. Perhaps their second meeting had bothered him in the way his working with Venetia bothered her. 'Things just don't seem right.'

'Well if they don't seem right, it's in your head, not because of anything I've done,' Alex said. 'We've never lived in each other's pockets. I never stop you going out and seeing friends or having drinks with old boyfriends, because I trust you, and I don't understand why you don't seem to trust me any more.'

Helen didn't reply, because the answer that came to mind was that maybe it was because she didn't trust herself any more.

Alex didn't like arguing. Neither did Helen. When they did argue, neither of them seemed to have the capacity to bring the row to a swift conclusion. Instead they said things that opened up a can of worms and then left them hanging in the air, or crawling around the kitchen, unresolved and festering.

'Pasta with bacon and olives.' Alex signalled that for him this discussion was over. 'Is that okay for you?'

'Yes, thank you.' Helen knew that they might have finished talking for the evening but that the argument was unresolved. 'I'll just go and check on the children.'

41

If you weren't supposed to sleep on an argument, then flying off to Spain for a long weekend on an unresolved marital spat probably wasn't a good idea either. Helen had been looking forward to a few days in Santander courtesy of the *Sunday Review*, but now that she was actually standing in the queue to go through security, she was dreading it.

She always found it difficult leaving the children for any length of time. Today they had conspired not to make it easy by inventing coughs and stomach pains that might prevent them from going to school, and telling her how much they were going to miss her. In the same breath they had asked Alex if they could have Coke with marshmallows in it for breakfast, because they were sad that Mummy was leaving.

'Mum's not going for ever,' Alex said, to Helen's relief, because thirty-six hours after she'd accused him of paying more attention to Venetia than he should, he was still not really talking to her. She felt that if she left without some sort of reconciliation, then what had been said would remain unresolved.

'No, you can't have Coke and marshmallows for breakfast,' Helen told Emma, who was already opening the door of the fridge in anticipation of at least one parent capitulating to her demands.

'Just Coke, then?' Joe asked. 'Because I feel as if I am going to cry, and Coke helps me stop crying.'

'Well I'll be back on Sunday and you will have a lovely weekend with Daddy, so there's no need to feel sad. If I let you have Coke for breakfast, your teacher won't let you go to school, so no.'

'Meanie.' Joe seemed to have forgotten how much he was going to miss her. 'When are you going anyway?'

'As soon as I've said goodbye to you all.' Helen's bag was ready and waiting in the hall. She was taking the underground to Heathrow, and was allowing herself at least an hour to get to the airport three hours before take-off. 'Goodbye, handsome.' She tried to kiss Joe, who ducked his head, nearly immersing his face in his bowl of cornflakes.

'Bye, meanie,' Joe replied, bringing his head up suddenly so that he headbutted her hovering face.

Helen's eyes immediately began smarting from the impact of his tightly packed skull on the bridge of her nose.

'Goodbye, Mummy, don't cry,' Emma said, throwing her arms around her waist and endeavouring to make her stay put.

'I'm not crying,' Helen said. 'There are just tears coming out of my eyes because Jo-Jo headbutted me.'

'Bye then,' said Alex. No endearments, no 'have a good trip' no 'we will miss you' or even 'I will miss you'.

Helen tried to put her arms around him, but it

was awkward. Alex had his back to her and was busying himself with the toaster.

'Can you come to the door with me?' she asked, wanting a proper goodbye away from the children.

Alex put two slices of bread in the toaster and pushed down the on button before following his wife to the front door.

'I don't like leaving like this,' Helen told him, reluctant now to go.

'Look, there's nothing more to be said.' Alex was already turning back to the kids in the kitchen.

'Wait,' Helen pleaded. 'Aren't you at least going to say goodbye?'

'I did say goodbye.' Alex knew that she wanted something a little less cursory but wasn't prepared to give it. 'Have a good trip.'

He kissed her briefly on the lips, but there was no tenderness in it.

'I'll see you when I get back, then?' Helen had made it sound like a question.

'Of course,' Alex was moving away from her. 'The toast has popped,' he added, by way of explanation, as if the buttering of toast was something that had to be attended to without further delay.

★   ★   ★

Helen texted Alex from the airport. 'Waiting to go through security. Will miss you. Love you. Hx'

'Everything's a bit of mess, isn't it?' she glanced up to see who was describing her life right now so accurately and looked straight into the face of a security officer.

He indicated the see-through plastic bag that contained toothpaste, shampoo and a small bottle of moisturiser. She noticed that the top of the moisturiser was not closed and the inside of the bag was saturated with white cream.

'I can't really see what's going on in there,' the officer said.

'Oh God, sorry,' Helen muttered. 'Do you need me to open it up or anything?'

She glanced round at the queue behind her; everyone was impatient to get through and didn't want to be held up any more than was necessary.

'Take it to the table over there and get another bag,' ordered the security man.

Helen did as she was told, showing the soiled bag to the female officer at the table, who handed over another transparent bag and a handful of tissues with a weary expression that suggested that women presenting spilt toiletries was a regular occurrence.

Her phone began to ring as she was wiping anti-ageing day cream from the neck of her toothpaste tube. She answered it without checking who the caller was, hoping that Alex had relented and was calling to wish her a safe journey.

'Helen?' said the voice at the other end.

'Graham,' she replied.

'Are you okay? You sound a bit muffled.'

'I'm just trying to get through security at Heathrow,' she told him. 'Can I call you back?'

'Okay. Yes, can you? I was worried about you.'
He hung up.

Helen returned various liquids and pastes to the pristine transparent bag and rejoined the queue.

The same security officer waved her through and she found herself in the departure lounge with two hours before her flight was scheduled to leave. Plenty of time to return Graham's call.

42

By the following day, Helen felt calmer, warmed by the sun and a brief call from Alex.

She'd been sitting on a beach when he'd rung, making a few notes for her piece and watching Spaniards parading near the water's edge in tiny bikinis. From behind the security of her sunglasses she'd been intrigued by two couples now standing as a foursome a few feet away.

They had approached each other from opposite ends of the beach. Both couples had walked with their arms around each other, synchronising their steps and looking into each other's faces. When they encountered their mirror images approaching, they disengaged and greeted each other with numerous kisses and, Helen noted, caresses. Skimpily clad though they were, their hands ran the lengths of each other's bodies, as if they were not casual acquaintances, friends even, but lovers desperate to get at each other, even though they were in a public place.

Helen was intrigued by this southern European greeting, so different to the stiff British handshake. Perhaps, she thought, this difference in approach to members of the opposite sex accounted for the British divorce rate soaring. If you wanted to get your hands on someone else's body, you had to have an affair with them, and inevitably recriminations and punishments followed. Whereas here it seemed you could show that you appreciated someone else's body right in front of their partner, without anyone doing anything other than taking it as a compliment.

The vibration from her mobile phone roused her from her musing. She cursed the intrusion, but was pleased to see it was Alex.

'Hi,' he said. Could she detect a note of contrition in his voice? 'How are you doing?'

'Fine, good,' she answered. 'It's lovely here. I've spent the morning seeing all the must-see things, and now I'm just sorting out my notes.'

'I thought you'd be relaxing on a beach by now.' Alex's tone was teasing; the anger of the last few days appeared to have receded.

'Well, I am sorting though my notes on a sunlounger on a beach,' she admitted.

'I knew it.' He was laughing now, and Helen felt relief at the sound. 'Anyway,' he added, 'the children wanted to have a word with you. I'll put them on.'

'Okay.' Helen heard him handing the phone to Emma.

'Mummy, we bought two coconuts from the market this morning and some ribbon. I'm going to make a secret house for the rabbit in the garden.'

'That's nice.' Helen wondered what form the rabbit dwelling might take. 'Don't make it too secret or you won't be able to find him to put back in his hutch, and the fox might get him.'

Helen's warning was not without reason. One of the neighbours had called round to tell her a few days previously that she'd seen a fox in her garden at nine in the morning.

'I'm just going to put ribbons all over the bush he likes lying under, I think he'll like that.' It sounded to Helen as if Emma was already halfway into the garden, ready to get on with the task. 'Jo-Jo wants to talk to you now.'

The line went quiet, and Helen wondered if Emma had forgotten to pass the phone on to Jo-Jo and left it somewhere while she went into the garden. After a few moments she could hear Alex in the background urging Joe to talk to her.

'Come on, Joe, just say hello to Mum,' he was saying. 'Then you can have the coconut.'

'I don't want to talk to Mum, I'm busy,' Joe replied, but he appeared to have the phone thrust into his hand anyway. She could suddenly hear him breathing up close.

'Hello, Jo-Jo.' She smiled as she spoke to him. 'I didn't know you liked coconuts.'

'Yes I do.' Joe sounded cross, as if she was accusing him of something bad. 'I've always liked them.'

Helen knew this was not true. Every now and then, when a coconut presented itself, Emma urged her to buy one, but Joe had refused to even try to eat its flesh, dismissing it after one nibble as 'like soap'.

'So were you about to eat some when you called?' she asked.

She liked the conversations she had with the children when she wasn't with them, and the ones she overheard them having with Alex when he was away. The importance of having them — 'Can we phone Daddy now, can we phone him now? Please . . . ' — always seemed in direct disproportion to their content once they happened.

She smiled now in the knowledge that she would carry this phone call with her for the rest of the day. From it she had gleaned that Alex appeared to have mellowed towards her and that the children had made him buy coconuts and were decorating the garden for the sake of the rabbit, which cared more about eating the garden and less about what it looked like.

'I'm not going to eat any.' Joe sounded disgusted by the very suggestion.

'I thought you said you liked them.' Helen was used to her conversations with Joe being nonsensical.

'I do.' Joe was contradicting himself without appearing to know it. 'I like throwing them against the steps in the yard so they smash up. Emma's going to pick up the bits and wash them when I've finished.'

Helen laughed, and whether it was his perception that she was laughing at him or simply because he had something better to do, Joe appeared to cut her off.

She tried calling back, but it went straight to voicemail. She left a message.

'Hi, it's me. I'm still on the beach. The kids disappeared off the line, but I hoped I might talk to you. I guess you're busy smashing coconuts. Love you.'

The Spanish foursome were approaching the area where she sat. One of the men began talking to the boy who sold tickets for the sunloungers. He gestured towards a row of plastic recliners alongside Helen and they came to take up residence next to her. The women were now walking with their arms around each other. The men began a display of male authority by rearranging the loungers to no great effect, flexing the reclining backs a bit before wedging them firmly in the seated position, then checking that they wouldn't be going anywhere by pushing their legs more firmly into the sand. Nothing was really any better than before they began this operation, not as far as the chairs were concerned anyway, but the men obviously felt better for asserting themselves over the territory. The women waited patiently while they sorted everything out, only sitting when they received the gesture to do so.

Helen secretly admired the machismo of Spanish men. It reminded her of the maleness in Joe, who liked coconuts because you could smash them rather than eat them and would never in a million years think to decorate a bush with ribbons because it would be nice for the rabbit.

She wondered if these men talked through their marital spats or simply whisked their wives off to the bedroom. She suspected the latter, and decided to forgive Alex for being a man and not wanting to talk at length about problems that were intangible, or perhaps, she admitted to her sunnier self, imaginary.

She put her notebook away and felt content for the first time in the last few days. The sun was warm on her face, her feelings were warming towards her husband, and she wished she hadn't agreed to meet Graham Parks at the airport on her way home.

43

Even in the vast cavernous halls of Heathrow airport, Helen could not relax entirely, worried that somebody she knew — or worse still, someone Alex knew — would be going on holiday and would see her being met by Graham Parks. Or perhaps some baggage-handling fiasco was unfolding without her knowledge and photographers from the world's press would descend on the terminal building, ready to snap frustrated travellers sprawled across benches.

Helen had been out of touch with world events for the past three days as she'd raced round Santander, preoccupied with fitting in the palace and the ocean centre as well as the numerous tapas bars that required a mention in her travel feature.

Two days previously, when she'd been leaving the UK, she'd welcomed Graham's call, having been getting the cold treatment from Alex, and eagerly agreed to his suggestion that he meet her at the airport on her return. He lived a few tube stops from Heathrow, and, knowing that she was worried about being seen with him in public, suggested that a coffee bar there was as anonymous a meeting place as any.

Perhaps if anyone saw them she would say that he was waiting for a flight. If Alex saw a photograph of her having lunch with him while angry travellers sat next to an empty carousel, she would tell him he just happened to have been at the airport, on his way to . . . where exactly?

She'd discuss this with Graham. She could see him now, as she made her way though the nothing-to-declare aisle, waiting with the ranks of taxi drivers sporting signs that said things like 'Kowoski' and 'Dharliwal' and 'Delegates from Japan's frozen food corporation'.

Because she was paranoid that one of the delegates from the frozen food corporation would be someone Alex knew from his spell as a foreign language teacher in Tokyo, or that Mr Dharliwal was a distant relative of his sister's husband, she was less than effusive in her greeting of Graham, merely nodding and smiling as she walked around the line of drivers scanning faces to see if they matched the names on their placards.

'You didn't bring a sign,' she said, holding her hand luggage and the plastic bag from the news stand in Spain defensively in front of her. She'd stopped there to buy water, and Spanish tat for the children. The bag now made it impossible for Graham to embrace her. Instead he was forced to accept only the briefest of air kisses.

'I'll bring one next time you go somewhere,' he answered, trying but failing to make slightly more physical contact than Helen had allowed, stretching his arm out to rest it on her shoulder but finding himself rebuffed by the bulk of her rucksack. 'If you'll let me, I'll drive you back to my place for lunch. Can I take one of your bags?'

'It's okay,' Helen replied, looking around her

for familiar faces or signs of world press activity. 'Is anyone on strike or have the computer systems here crashed or anything?' she asked.

'No,' said Graham. 'Not that I know of. But it doesn't matter anyway. You're back. Are you hungry?'

Not really, thought Helen. She was never hungry when she saw Graham — too many butterflies — but they always seemed to be eating together.

'Starving,' she lied out loud, wanting to go and sit somewhere where it might look as if she'd bumped into him and was simply having a quick bite to eat before she made her way back to Alex and the children.

She reached instinctively for her phone to switch it on again, then decided not to. There would probably be a message from Alex wondering if her flight had arrived on time and when she would be home. It had been and she could have been back in time to have supper with him and the children, but she would tell him there were queues for passport control and she'd had to wait for a train. Or that she had bumped into Graham Parks at the airport, killing time before his flight to somewhere, and had stopped briefly to talk to him. She wanted to be as honest as she could be with Alex. She'd like him to know that she'd met Graham at the airport — not that it was a prearranged meeting because she wanted to spend half an hour in his company, but the fact of their meeting.

He wouldn't mind her having a quick cup of coffee with Graham, still safe in the knowledge that he was fat and bald and therefore unlikely to hold any great attraction for her. But he might be fed up with being in sole charge of the children for three days, and at the point where he would go mad unless she walked through the door and allowed all the responsibility to fall back on her.

'We could go to Wagamama or Yo Sushi, if you prefer,' Graham was saying, walking at her side as they headed in no particular direction. He looked peculiarly naked with nothing to carry, while everyone around them sported holdalls or dragged wheelie bags or emptied the contents of plastic bags into backpacks so they only had one item of hand luggage.

'Whichever is quickest.' Helen realised as soon as she'd said it that it sounded rude. He had come to the airport to meet her. She had wanted to see him. He wasn't asking her to do anything more than have a bite to eat, and it wasn't his fault that she felt guilty that she was delaying her return home.

'Well, it's an airport. They're all quick.' He didn't sound cross, just slightly disappointed. This was not the meeting either of them had imagined, but then their meetings never were. Caught between wanting to be his friend and wanting to be free to be more, Helen was invariably on edge, never quite as relaxed as the first time they'd met.

He shouldn't expect anything of me, she thought, wondering why, having been looking forward to seeing him all the time she was in Santander, she now wanted to get away.

Perhaps it was the head space she'd enjoyed

while she was there, the freedom to go where she pleased, when she pleased, even though she had to fit a lot into her itinerary. There was no one saying they were bored and wanted to go, or hungry and needed something to eat, or busy and needed her to take over. When she had been packing on Thursday evening, she hadn't wanted to go. She'd looked in on the children sleeping. Jo-Jo had turned over in bed, muttering 'I love you, Mum', always aware of her, even when he was asleep. Emma had been curled up around a stuffed dog, her mane of hair spread across her face so she couldn't see her, still defiantly independent.

She'd begun to miss them even while she was still lying next to Emma cuddling her while she slept, but as soon as she was on the tube to the airport, they had started to recede from the forefront of her mind. Once she was airborne, she had her habitual fret about the plane crashing and them being left motherless, but in Santander, sitting in a bar with a strikingly handsome man from the local tourist office, she had more or less forgotten that she'd ever had them.

Now, she was looking forward to giving Emma the plastic flamenco dancing doll and Jo-Jo his bull-fighting T-shirt, anticipating the love and laughter they would surround her with when she walked through the door.

'We can just have a quick cup of tea here, if you like?' Graham was saying, anxiously, as they walked parallel to a branch of McDonald's.

'No,' said Helen. 'I'm sorry. Let's go to

313

Garfunkel's.' she suggested this as it was right next to them.

She was always apologising to him when they met or emailed, making excuses for having to rush off somewhere else, always feeling she was letting him down by returning to her own complete life, leaving him with the fragmented pieces of his own.

They squeezed themselves into a corner. The tables and chairs were too close together, maximising the number of travellers the restaurant could process in the time between check-in and boarding. Graham seemed slimmer amid the plethora of families tearing through plates of chips lest their flight was delayed and they didn't get to eat again that day. But the space between his chair and the table was still a tight squeeze. Helen's allotted territory was even smaller, but it suited her. She had her back to the wall and a full view of the restaurant, where she still feared someone she knew might appear. She had hardly any leg or elbow room, and every now and then she would make physical contact with Graham without meaning to.

'It's good to see you,' she said, looking at him properly for the first time since she'd emerged from airside. 'How are you?'

'I've been a bit distracted,' he told her. 'I've been trying to start on another book, set in Croatia. I can't get going, though. I find that even when I write fairly innocuous words like Split or Dubrovnik, I start getting flashbacks.'

A waitress who sounded as if she might be from Croatia herself had squeezed through the ranks of parked diners and was standing with a pen that said 'I love LA' hovering above her notepad. Helen wondered if she had ever been to LA, if someone had bought it for her, or if one of the diners had left it lying on a table and the staff had added it to the pen pot on the counter next to the till.

Graham asked for a chicken Caesar wrap and Helen said she'd have the same. She was too tired to think about what she wanted. She'd enjoyed the recommendations of the man from the Spanish tourist authority over the past few days. 'Gambas is a typical dish you get only in this region,' he would intone, pointing to a section of the menu, or 'This cheese is particularly good at this time of year', and she'd been extremely grateful to be able to say, 'I'll have that then' without having to wonder if she would have been better off with the lamb or the cake.

If Alex had been with her now, he'd have asked if she was sure. He thought it a waste of going out if they both had the same thing. He liked them to maximise the experience by covering as much of the menu as possible, and was frustrated by what he saw as Helen's lack of spirit of adventure. Graham appeared to find it entirely reasonable that she liked set menus because they meant she only had to choose between meat and fish. He agreed there was no point in ruining a meal out by agonising over whether your dining companions had made better choices than you, and made no comment when she chose the same as him.

'How are you? Really?' Graham was looking at her.

'Fine.' Two days ago she had been ready to pour out to him her suspicions about Alex and Venetia. Now that she had slept on her paranoia for a couple of days, it all seemed slightly ridiculous, and any sharing of her concerns with Graham would make it seem as if she was allowing him the hope of some sort of relationship with her.

'A bit tired,' she amended. 'I had quite a full itinerary and woke up at five this morning, worried that I would oversleep and miss the flight. But I had a good weekend. Santander is lovely and the weather was great. Apparently it had been raining for five days before I arrived, so I was lucky.'

'I've never been to northern Spain.' Graham looked up at her. 'I wish we could have gone together.'

44

Helen had found it hard to tread the line between trying to persuade Graham not to accompany her to the tube and being rude. She had already felt she was erring on the side of rudeness, bolting down her lunch while giving the briefest, most functional responses to his questions, at times wishing she had not agreed to meet him at the airport and was already on her way home, at others wishing she could relax and enjoy this brief opportunity to spend some time with him, almost away from it all.

There was no reason really why he should not come on the tube with her. He would get off a couple of stops down the line. No one would see them. But she felt as if she was having to make too many transitions in one day. First thing this morning she had been a single free agent, checking out of a hotel, having coffee in a café overlooking the beach, wandering around a Spanish city with the need to be at the airport a couple of hours before take-off the only demand on her time.

She had walked off the plane no longer a single free agent, still childless, but straight into a meeting with a man with whom her relationship was yet to be defined. As soon as she stepped on to the tube and began slowly edging though the tunnels closer to home, she knew she had to begin to readjust to being a wife and mother.

She needed space. She wanted Graham out of it.

But he was coming with her.

She had the sensation that they were going home after a holiday together as he guided her towards the tube, taking the lead in negotiating the eastbound underground maze, not because it was foreign to her but because it was more familiar to him. Their carriage was almost empty.

'What is it you live in anyway?' Helen asked, suddenly curious as to where he lived, and how.

'A thick layer of chaos.' Graham smiled.

'Really?' She hadn't yet tried to picture him at home. She'd thought of him in lots of other ways. In the army, as a schoolboy with Chloe's brother, with friends, in the succession of jobs he'd had after leaving the army, with his publisher, but not closing the door on the outside, alone in a world that was of his own making. This would probably tell her more about him than imagining him in all the other circumstances.

It appealed to her, the idea that his home was chaotic, the opposite of her own ordered house, its tidiness dictated by Alex's obsessive streak and causing her anxiety every time she wondered if she'd left her towel on the bathroom floor. She imagined living in a world where other things were more important than order. It seemed a more vital, energised place.

'Is it a chaotic house or flat or caravan?' she wondered out loud.

'Flat,' Graham answered. 'Spacious, though, since it's located at the far reaches of the Piccadilly line. Plenty of space to breathe if the

318

chaos is not too out of control.'

'I'd like to see that.' Helen laughed, conjuring up a mental picture of chaos as a rather large shaggy dog, which sometimes lay prone across the living room floor, getting in everyone's way but not causing too much trouble, but at other times became restless, pacing around the house and turning in circles, unable to find anywhere satisfactory to rest.

'I'd like you to see it too,' Graham replied. His tone was serious and she saw he was looking at her, maintaining eye contact, making her flustered. 'Will you come?'

'I can't.' Helen looked away from him, up at the tube map, wondering if they were nearing his stop. 'I have to get home. I've already delayed my journey long enough.'

'I don't mean now,' Graham told her, briefly touching her hand so that she looked back at him. 'But sometime. I'd like you to come and see me at home one day. Have lunch or something. Will you?'

'I don't know,' Helen told him, knowing it would have been better just to say no, because going to his flat would involve overstepping the boundaries she had created for herself in her relationship with him. She wanted to get to know him better; she wanted his attention and the reassurances he gave her that she was a person worth knowing, but she wanted to couch all of this in terms of friendship, and she wanted to keep this friendship out in the open as much as possible. Yes, there were emails and texts and even meetings that she kept to herself, but she still hadn't done anything she shouldn't.

'My stop,' said Graham. 'Think about it.'

He leant over the arm rail towards her, encircling her in a hug, and kissed her.

It was a brief kiss on the lips. Anyone watching would have thought nothing of it. It was a kiss from someone saying goodbye to a friend on the tube. But when he planted his kiss, his lips lingered very slightly. It was an indiscernible amount of time, but just long enough to make Helen wish it had lasted longer.

'Goodbye,' he said, half turning as he walked towards the sliding doors. They opened, then closed behind him, and he waved from the platform as the train departed.

Helen wondered, not for the first time, what it would be like to kiss Graham Parks.

She couldn't remember the last time she had kissed Alex, not properly. There were numerous perfunctory hello and goodbye kisses, some slightly more passionate foreplay-style ones, but they hadn't had a long, passionate snog for years. Married people didn't seem to kiss any more. It seemed to be another one of those things that there was never quite enough time for, like foreplay and conversation. Everyone these days knew that you needed some sort of sex life to keep a relationship going, but often they were in such a rush to get on with the rest of their lives that they simply cut to the chase and left out all the pleasurable bits that could lead up to it.

The stops between Graham's station and home seemed innumerable. She wanted to get back now, quickly. She'd wasted too much time at the airport. She wanted to see the children and Alex. She wanted to walk through the front door and feel the security of being home, in a place she knew, with people with whom she felt safe. She wanted the children to surround her with love and laughter, as she knew they would, and for Alex to have missed her and be relieved she was home. And when Emma and Joe had gone to bed, she wanted to pour herself and Alex a glass of wine and tell him she was glad to be home and that she had missed him and that she loved him. Then she wanted to lean against the work surface in the kitchen and put her arms around him and snog him.

45

The house seemed different when Helen opened the door. Her instant reaction was that something must be wrong, because there were muddy boots strewn across the hallway. If Alex and the kids had been to the park, they'd have been home at least a couple of hours ago. Under normal circumstances Alex would have taken the boots straight round to the back yard, hosed the mud off and put them away. She found she was slightly annoyed that he hadn't. His verging on the edge of obsessive tidiness might be irritating, but it had its benefits.

She tried to suppress the feeling that something was not quite right and to concentrate hard on the thought that maybe they had just been having too much fun to worry. The sounds coming from the kitchen seemed to bear this more sympathetic theory out. There was much laughter, interspersed with squeals from Emma and cries of 'me, me, me' from Joe.

'Hello!' Helen called out, and was gratified by the kitchen door bursting open and Emma and Joe emerging wearing aprons covered in flour and faces covered in smiles and what looked like chocolate. Could they have been baking? Alex usually shied away from cooking with the children. Too much mess, too many of the raw ingredients eaten before reaching the oven and too much arguing about who got to use the mixer or the really sharp knife.

'Mum, you're back!' Joe wrapped his mucky arms around her and buried his sticky face in her leg.

'High five!' greeted Emma, brandishing a wooden spoon for the purpose and buttering Helen's hand as she returned the greeting. 'We're making a cake for you to have when you get back. It's not ready yet, though.'

'A cake, how lovely.' Helen wondered if this was a peace offering from Alex. It was a nice thought and she knew it would have been an effort for him to allow the chaos that cake-making entailed.

She slowly raised herself from her children's embrace and looked towards the kitchen, expecting to see Alex standing there, shrugging his shoulders to acknowledge the unusualness of it all. Instead she saw her mother standing tentatively by the door, not wishing to intrude on the welcome her daughter was getting from her children.

'Mum?' Helen was confused. 'What are you doing here?'

'Alex had to go up to Manchester a day early,' her mother answered. 'He asked if I could help out until you got back.'

'He never mentioned it to me.' Helen could not help feeling that this made Alex's absence somehow suspicious. 'He's known for a while about this trip and he said he was going to be here to look after Emma and Joe.'

There was an accusatory tone to her voice that did not go undetected by her mother, who jumped to Alex's defence.

'He was here for most of the time,' she pointed out. 'He left early this morning. How was your trip?'

'Fine.' In those few moments Helen had almost forgotten about the trip, so preoccupied had she become as to why Alex had left early without telling her.

'I spoke to him yesterday,' she said, although no one appeared to be listening. 'He never mentioned it.'

'I don't think he wanted to spoil your weekend,' her mother replied, in the tone she used when she felt that Helen was not adhering to some preferred rule or moral code. It was the 'Is that a new dress?' tone of voice, which implied that the dress was either too short for someone her age or had cost too much for someone who should be spending her money on things that would benefit her children. 'He wanted you to enjoy yourself and not have to worry about things here. He's very considerate like that.' She stressed the 'considerate'. 'Now then, our cake should be nearly ready. Why don't you come and have a cup of tea and tell us all about Spain?'

Helen did as she was told. Her mother still held that power over her. She didn't like to argue or complain or do anything that might make Bridget look at her as if she was a spoilt little girl, even if she was now too old for her mother to come out and say it.

'Okay.' The oven timer was ringing now. The cake was ready to come out. It smelt good, warm and chocolatey and comforting. Perhaps her mother was right. Perhaps all she needed was a piece of cake and a cup of tea to quell the disquiet she felt about Alex not being there.

'Can I get it out, can I?' Joe was ready to pull the oven door open.

'I'm doing it.' Emma was agitating, hopping up and down next to Joe, hoping her presence would be enough to make him back off without requiring an extra shove. 'It's too hot for six-year-olds. I need to get it out.'

'I'll do it.' Granny was in control. 'Emma, you can turn it out of the tin, and Joe, you can cut us all a slice. Oh . . . '

The cake did not appear to have risen. The spongy chocolate had just about foamed around the edges of the tin, but in the centre there was a deep well of sog. The children were not happy with the outcome.

Her mother was saying something about it tasting just as nice, no matter what it looked like.

Helen could not help feeling that the cake was mirroring her return. She'd imagined getting home to the predictable order of her life, a warm welcome and being suffused with love. Instead there was mild chaos, no Alex and chocolate cake that was sunken and soggy.

It did taste nice, though, her mother was right about that.

'So, was your flight delayed?' Bridget asked. 'Alex said he thought you'd be back an hour or two earlier, but I said you'd probably be held up.'

'The flight was okay, but I had to wait a long

time for my bag to be unloaded.' Now she realised she was lying to her mother too. She hoped she would not notice that she only had one bag, which was small enough to be carried as hand luggage.

'And you had a good trip?' Her mother was obviously hoping for a bit more out of her.

'Yes.' Helen was truthful now. 'It was a lovely place and it was nice to be away, even though I missed everyone, obviously.'

'Will you play a game with us now?' Emma had finished her cake and wanted to reclaim her mother, putting her firmly back where she belonged by tying her into a long round of Monopoly or Trivial Pursuit — a contract that bore no get-out clause.

'In a minute,' Helen told her. 'You two go and get a game ready and I'll come in when I've helped Granny tidy up the kitchen.'

It was strange the way she called her own mother Granny these days. She hated it when Alex called her Mum, as if now that she was a mother she had somehow stopped being Helen to him. She wondered if her mother minded being called Granny, as if all the love and care she had lavished upon Helen throughout her lifetime was forgotten now that she'd been reincarnated as a grandmother.

But her mother was still her mother.

'Are you okay?' she asked Helen. 'You seem a bit distracted.'

Helen wondered if Bridget, who seemed to possess the power of omniscience, knew that she had delayed her journey home to have lunch with Graham Parks.

'I'm just a bit put out that Alex isn't here,' she told her. 'I was looking forward to seeing him.'

'Well, he'll be back in a few days.' Her mother was ever the pragmatist.

'I know, but I won't have seen him for almost a week by the time he gets back.' Helen wasn't sure if this was a good or a bad thing. Would a week reduce the argument they had had before she left to water under the bridge? Or would it give time for the tension between them to simmer and boil over into something bigger?

She needed to talk to someone, and her mother was there, offering her more tea.

'To be honest, we haven't been getting on that well lately,' she confessed, wondering how her mother would react.

'It'll pass.' Bridget was businesslike. 'More cake?'

'No thanks.' The remark made her determined to discuss her marriage further. She was genuinely worried about the state of relations with her husband, and it irked her that her mother's reaction was to ask if she wanted more cake.

'I'm serious, Mum. Alex is away more and more these days, and he seems increasingly preoccupied with work and less worried about us.'

'He's doing very well at the moment,' her mother said, a reply that did not really seem to follow on from what Helen had just said.

'I know, but we still need him too.'

'He's doing it for you, Helen. It must be hard

for him being away from home, but it's his job and he does it and he lets you get on with your job too and go off gallivanting for the weekend.'

'It was work,' Helen protested. 'I went to Spain for my job. It wasn't just fun.'

'Well, Alex's work probably isn't all fun either.'

Helen wished she had never said anything to her mother. She should have anticipated that she would side with Alex. She'd always liked him, from the moment Helen first took him for lunch at her parents' house a few months after they'd first met. Alex had been charming, funny and helpful. He had also managed to programme the new video recorder her parents had bought a few weeks previously but been unable to work out how to use. This feat endeared him to them more than any of his personal charms or the fact that he made their daughter happy.

After that first meeting, her mother had phoned to say how wonderful they had both thought Alex was, letting slip 'It was lucky he didn't have a girlfriend when you had your accident. I imagine he is quite a catch.'

She'd managed to imply in that sentence both that Helen should consider herself extremely fortunate to have ended up with Alex (which she did) and that she, rather than Alex, was responsible for the accident. Helen, she seemed to think, ought to make a big effort to ensure that Alex stayed with her. If she ever mentioned that she found his obsessive-compulsiveness slightly annoying, her mother would respond with, 'You must not drive him away with your untidiness.' If she joked that he drove her mad

328

when he took to his bed for a week with a cold while she muddled through, she was told, 'You never did have much patience.'

It was the wrong way round. Parents were supposed to think that no man was good enough for their daughter. Hers seemed to think that their daughter was not good enough for anyone.

'Alex is not always that easy,' she said, daring Bridget to defend him further. She wondered whether, if she told her he beat her up and interfered with the children, her mother would find a way of making such behaviour seem acceptable.

'No one's that easy, Helen,' Bridget said. 'And marriage isn't all plain sailing.'

She was obviously not comfortable talking to her daughter like this, and began tidying away tea things and busying herself with washing up. Helen poured herself some more tea and prepared to join the children for a lengthy board game.

'I'm sure you're right,' she said, more to signal that she was ending the conversation than because she believed that to be the case.

'You marry the man you love,' her mother said, scrubbing the cake tin vigorously, as if by doing so she would deflect attention away from what she was saying, 'but you have to keep loving the man you marry, too.'

46

Spain already seemed like a distant memory, and yet only eight hours ago, Helen had been having quince jelly for breakfast. It had been warm on the terrace of the hotel overlooking the bay, and she had felt well, relaxed and ready to go home. Now that she was back with the penetrating cold of London making her shiver, with her mother dismissing her anxieties about her marriage and with the children being hyperactive, she felt firmly rooted in her real life. The plastic souvenirs she'd grabbed at the airport for Emma and Joe were the only real evidence that she had actually been away.

Meeting Graham Parks at the airport also seemed like a distant memory. Although Helen could conjure up a physical picture of him, the warmth she felt when she was with him was as hard to recreate in her mind as the feeling of a sun that made you want to retreat into the shade. She tried to recall the way his brief kiss had seemed to linger and made her want to kiss him more. Then she tried to forget and bring her thoughts back round to the relationship she really did have, with her husband.

She turned the central heating up a degree to compensate for the shock of the temperature change, remembering as she did so how chilly the atmosphere had been before she left.

Emma and Joe were finally asleep. The

excitement of her homecoming and the reproaching her for having been away had kept them up a couple of hours past their customary bedtimes, but she'd finally managed to settle them and pour herself a large glass of wine. She took this into the empty living room.

Alex's absence was most noticeable here. He would usually have been beside her on the sofa on a Sunday evening, enjoying a drink with her, putting the weekend to rest while anticipating the week ahead. And if he had been, the room would have been tidy. She couldn't quite summon the energy to clear away the legacy of the day's Lego construction or sort the Sylvanians from the Scrabble. She realised when Alex was away that while she found his need for order irritating, she missed the harmony he created when he was there.

She missed him, too. She took a large gulp of wine, hoping its effect would be medicinal and quell the anxiety she felt about his absence.

On principle she didn't want her mother to be right, but she hoped that she was, and that Alex had left early without telling her solely out of consideration for her. She tried to brush aside fears that he was not there because he was avoiding her or had taken the opportunity of her being away to get back to Manchester, and Venetia.

She was being silly, he had told her as much. She was the one with something to hide, projecting on to Alex her guilt at having had several meetings with another man, making him

331

appear to be in the wrong when in reality it was her.

Much as she would have preferred to ignore her mother's advice, she couldn't help thinking about her counsel to marry the person you loved and love the person you married. To newly-weds this sounded easy. Of course you would love the person you married. That was why you'd married them, after all. But a few years down the line it was easy to lose sight of that, to find that the love was shared amongst children, friends, new people and people who flattered you by seeing something in you that those others didn't.

She thought back to her conversation with Katie, about how before she had children she used to think that there was a finite amount of love allotted to each individual and a finite capacity to love. She recalled how she was terrified when she was pregnant with Emma that she would not be able to love her, or that if she did, it would stop her loving Alex as much. Then she discovered that she loved Emma more than anything and she loved Alex all the more because of it.

But just as she had found enough love for Alex, then Emma and Joe and even the rabbit, she could see now that she could also love Graham Parks, if she allowed herself to.

Who was she fooling? She'd already begun to love him. Just because she didn't do anything about it didn't make the fact that she had feelings for him any less true.

But she didn't want to love him, as much to protect Graham as to protect herself and Alex and the family. There would only be heartache in it for him. And she wasn't prepared to sacrifice Alex and the children for whatever he might offer her.

People frequently had affairs and told their new lovers they were in a loveless marriage, but often they were lying. They still loved their partners, and once the affair had run its course, they went back. Even those who left for good might still love their ex because they were the mother or father of their children, or just because they had a long history together. This caused their new partners jealousy and heartache because they weren't the sole focus of their world, just one person who was loved along with all the others.

Helen's friend Caitlin was in this position. She'd met Henry at work. She was in her late thirties; he was in his early fifties with a wife and two children. She began having an affair with him knowing he was officially unavailable, and when his wife found out, she threw him out. This was the outcome Caitlin had secretly hoped for, but now that they were together and had a young child of their own she wasn't sure it was the outcome Henry had wanted. He'd certainly not wanted another child, and she'd had to get pregnant 'accidentally'. Henry missed the birth as he was at a concert his eldest daughter was playing in. They had very little money and she had had to go back to work full time almost as soon as their daughter was born. She never said it, but she sometimes wondered if they would all have been better off if Henry had stayed with his first wife. He still loved her — 'She is the mother of my children,' he would say when Caitlin quizzed him on this. Having taken him away from those children, Caitlin felt she could not argue with him.

Helen did love Alex, of course she did, and now that the glass of wine she appeared to have drunk without realising was coursing through her bloodstream, she felt it all the more keenly. She would call him and tell him, having forgotten the anxiety and irritation she'd felt that he'd not been there when she came home. She would ask him about his work instead of getting at him for doing it. She'd tell him about her weekend and thank him for not diminishing her enjoyment of it by troubling her with domestic arrangements.

She dialled his number, wondering if he would know it was her when his phone began to ring. Their home number was not programmed into his mobile phone. Whenever Alex was away he always called her on her mobile. She'd asked him why once, and after some prevarication about how she might be out and he wanted to maximise his chances of actually speaking to her, he admitted he did not know what their home phone number was.

This was the age of the mobile, after all. Alex had his phone and she had hers. As he was the one who was away the most, she tended to call him on his, and he reciprocated. It didn't matter, but secretly she resented the fact that he did not know or use their home phone number. It was as if by not doing so, he had opted out of an aspect of their life that should have been shared.

Helen waited, looking forward to hearing the soft timbre of Alex's voice. It was one of the things she had liked about him when they first met. He spoke clearly. As an actor, he needed to. There was no harshness in his voice, no overt projection. He could make himself heard without that. It was a kind voice. She had liked listening to him, regardless of what he was saying. Now she liked waking up in the mornings and hearing him ask if she wanted a cup of tea. People didn't often cite a nice voice in their list of desired attributes in a partner, but she imagined that waking up next to someone whose voice grated or whined would put an unbearable strain on a relationship.

It wasn't the voice she was expecting that answered the phone.

'Hello, Alex's phone,' said a female voice. Helen was momentarily tongue-tied. Who was this? 'Hello! Is there anyone there?' The voice was slightly slurred, as if the person speaking had been drinking.

It was Venetia. Helen was ninety-nine per cent certain. Why was she answering Alex's phone? The logical answer was that they were rehearsing together. Venetia was on a break, and so answered it for him while he was going through his lines.

Helen knew she should say something. Ask Venetia to tell Alex she had called and that he should call her back when he was free. But she had paused too long. She could hear Venetia saying, 'There doesn't seem to be anyone there. Someone must have sat on their phone and dialled the number . . . '

She'd put the phone down and knew she should call back, but then she'd have to explain why she had said nothing on the previous call. She'd wait. Next time she'd say something. Or perhaps Alex would look at the missed call, recognise the number as their home phone for once and call her back.

There was nothing unusual in someone answering another person's phone, she told herself. But the fact that someone had answered Alex's phone and that someone had been Venetia unsettled her again. She needed another glass of wine, though perhaps a cup of tea would be better, more comforting.

She got up to go to the kitchen, then nearly tripped over a Sylvanian picnic as she ran back to the living room to answer the phone before it flipped to the answering machine. She wanted to reach it before the voice — which was hers but didn't sound like her — kicked in. She wanted Alex to be on the other end, sounding familiar, coming up with a convincing explanation as to why Venetia had answered his phone.

'Hello?' Even though the distance from kitchen to living room was no more than eight yards, the sprint had left her breathless.

'Hi, Helen, you sound a little out of breath.' It was a woman, not Alex. Helen didn't immediately recognise the voice.

'It's Chloe,' the caller identified herself.

'Hi, Chloe!' Had it been Chloe who had

336

answered Alex's phone? *Muddy Water's* production assistant probably sat surrounded by cast members' mobile phones while they rehearsed, fielding calls in case any of them were important. Helen felt ridiculously relieved.

'Is Alex rehearsing? I tried to call him a few minutes ago.' If Chloe asked why she hadn't said anything, she'd use mobile idiosyncrasies as her excuse and claim that she hadn't been able to hear her voice so had hung up. It happened.

'Alex? No, I thought he'd be at home.' Chloe sounded confused.

'He's not here.' Helen fought to try to keep her voice normal. If Alex was in Manchester rehearsing, then Chloe would be there too. 'I've just got back from Spain and he was apparently called to a script rehearsal or something. I've been trying to get hold of him.'

'I don't know anything about a script rehearsal. I'm sorry.' Chloe did sound apologetic, as if she was somehow to blame for Alex being somewhere other than where he should have been, as if she knew where he might be but would rather not let on.

'Perhaps I've got it wrong.' Where the hell was he then? 'My mother was looking after the kids when I got home, and she doesn't always take in all the details. He's probably got a meeting with his agent or something.' She was trying to sound unperturbed but wasn't sure that she was carrying it off. 'Anyway, if it was Alex you wanted to speak to, do you want to try him on his mobile? You might have more luck than I did.'

47

'Can I come and see you at your flat?'

'Of course, you know I'd love that. When do you want to come?' Graham sounded pleased. Not smug, I-knew-you'd-capitulate-in-the-end pleased, but pleased that she wanted to see his home, spend some time with him there, allow him more than a few moments snatched between those when she was supposed to be somewhere else with other people, people who weren't him.

Nevertheless, she was still snatching time. How did women like her manage to have affairs? she wondered. She could see how people like Alex could manage. He was away so much, he had plenty of opportunities — numerous nights in Manchester, countless legitimate and above-board hotel rooms to which he could invite women, if he wanted.

It was harder for her. Her time was never her own but was divided between home, work, Alex, Emma and Joe, Shana, Vincent and Justin. There were odd moments into which she could fit friends, carved out of a hectic schedule. Sleep was sacrificed for catching up with the latest gossip or heartache, and now, invented delayed flights, fictitious late-night meetings and fabricated working lunches gave her excuses to see her newest 'friend', Graham Parks.

'Can I come for lunch on Wednesday?' she asked him now. 'As I was away at the weekend, the office owes me a bit of time in lieu. I could come then.'

'Are you okay?' asked Graham, sensing that her change in attitude towards visiting him at home was caused by something other than an irrepressible desire to see him.

'I'm not sure,' she told him truthfully. 'I'll talk to you then.'

'Okay, I'll look forward to it.' Graham's voice sounded distant on the other end of the telephone line. Helen wished she could see him sooner. Wednesday lunchtime was the first possible chance she had to walk away from her commitments and spend a couple of hours with her escape clause.

She had to be at work first thing in the morning, needed to spend the next evening with the children, having been away all weekend, and had promised to look after Hannah and Leonard for Katie the following afternoon.

Having agreed to go to Graham's flat for lunch gave her something new to worry about, something to take her mind off driving herself mad wondering why Alex had gone up to Manchester early and what he was doing there with Venetia.

She could still recall the knot of anxiety she had felt when Chloe had told her it was her she had called to speak to. She'd sat down on the sofa suddenly anticipating the worst, but it hadn't materialised.

Chloe hadn't rung to tell her that her misgivings about the time Alex appeared to be spending with Venetia were well founded. She had rung to invite Helen and Alex to a party.

'I know I'll be seeing Alex at work tomorrow, but if he's anything like Tom, he'll lose the invitation, fail to put the date in his diary and forget to tell you!' Chloe laughed. 'And I'd really like you both to come. So I wanted to make sure you knew too.'

Tom was Chloe's boyfriend. Helen had never met him. Alex had told her he worked for a charity and seemed 'very nice'. That had been the extent of her knowledge of him. Now she also knew that he wasn't very reliable as far as passing on information was concerned. What man was?

Chloe had been right in assuming that Alex was like Tom. He regularly told friends that they'd love to come to dinner and that he'd check with Helen first but to assume that they were free. Then he'd fail to check with her, forget all about it and only remember when the host called, an hour after the time at which they'd been invited, asking if they were still coming.

Chloe was wise to go straight to the organ-grinder.

'Is it a special occasion?' Helen asked her.

'My thirtieth, actually.' Chloe was still young. 'But I don't want any presents. I just want everyone to be there. Can you come?'

Normally Helen would not have hesitated in replying. It was in a few weeks' time. There was nothing in the diary. Although she'd only met her a couple of times, she liked Chloe, and she usually liked being with Alex when he was with his colleagues.

'We're free as far as I know.' She did not want to commit fully. 'But then Alex seems to keep getting called for unplanned script meetings a lot, so I'd best check with him first.'

'Sure,' said Chloe, apparently unfazed by the casual mention of unplanned script meetings. Did she mean 'sure' as in 'That's a good idea, check with Alex and get back to me' or 'Sure, he has a lot of unplanned script meetings, and even if I'm not at this one right now, they do exist.'

'Will it be a big do, then?' What Helen wanted to say was 'Who else is coming? Is Venetia Taylor on your guest list?' but she resisted the temptation and instead hoped she could get Chloe to give her the answer to this question without actually asking it.

'Not that big,' Chloe answered. 'Actually, that was another reason I called this number, rather than asking Alex at work. I'm not exactly keeping it hush-hush but I am trying to give the impression it's low key. There will be a few people from work but not the whole bloody lot of them!'

Chloe laughed, so Helen laughed too. Still no clue as to whether Venetia Taylor would be on the guest list.

'Well it will be nice for me, if we can come, to see whoever is there,' Helen said. 'I always feel as if Alex has a totally separate life when he's up in Manchester. It will be interesting to see some of the people he spends his other life with, if not all.'

'Not much of a life,' Chloe chuckled. 'And he spends most of it talking about you and the kids.'

'Does he? How boring for you!' Helen wondered if this was true. She'd imagined that once he left for Manchester, he simply forgot about home, immersed himself in work and all that it entailed, and only began to think about her and the children when he was on the train heading south to London, as he prepared himself to become a husband and father once again.

'Not at all.' The tone of Chloe's voice was warm and friendly, suggesting that she was smiling. 'Anyway, I won't keep you. I hope to see you then.'

'I hope so too. Thanks for the invite. I'll let you know for sure as soon as I've spoken to Alex.'

She did manage to speak to Alex later that evening, but didn't tell him she'd spoken to Chloe. She wanted him to volunteer information about why he was in Manchester, but he didn't. He simply asked whether she'd had a good time in Spain, reiterated what her mother had already passed on about a last-minute script meeting and then said that he was tired and needed to go to bed, as they had an early start in the morning.

While Chloe hadn't delivered the devastating blow she'd feared, Alex hadn't given her the reassurance she craved either. So she'd called Graham, recalling the brief kiss he'd given her on the tube, wanting him to make her feel better than she did. It was only lunch, she told herself, and she was allowed to have lunch with her friends.

48

'Thanks for looking after these two,' said Philip, nodding in the direction of Hannah and Joe, who were lying on their stomachs by the fridge, attempting to extract a miniature skateboard from underneath it.

Helen wondered if he realised that the jeans-clad bottom sticking up in the air did not in fact belong to his own child but hers. Philip was notoriously vague. He had once come with Katie to pick Hannah and Leonard up from Helen's house and greeted Joe with a distracted 'Hello, Leonard' as he accepted a glass of wine from Helen.

'That's Joe, not Leonard,' Katie had pointed out, in slight but not utter disbelief.

'He's two years older than Leonard.' Helen had underlined the most obvious difference. The boys did both have blond hair, but Joe was a good deal bigger.

'That's not the point,' Katie had said. 'He could be exactly the same age but he's not our child.'

'Oh well, I've had a hard day.' Philip seemed to think this mitigated his failing to immediately recognise that Joe was not his own child.

Today Helen decided not to point out his mistake and instead poured him a drink and told him it was no trouble.

'It's good for Katie to get out.' Philip raised

343

his glass. 'Cheers, Helen.'

'Cheers.' She clinked his glass.

'Why do you do that?' asked Joe, standing up, miniature skateboard in hand, and revealing his true identity.

'It's to make sure there's no poison in the glass,' Philip told him, unperturbed by the fact that the now fully extended child was not the one he had thought it to be while prone.

'Is it?' Helen had not heard this theory before. 'Why's that, then?'

'I think you're supposed to clink with a bit more gusto than we did,' Philip told her, 'so that some of the drink slops into the other person's glass. Then, if it was poisoned, he or she would have to drink some of it.'

'Well I never knew that,' Helen said, thinking how Philip was always a mine of interesting information. 'Cheers again!'

She raised her glass and hit it more forcefully against Philip's. Some wine sloshed on to the table, but she didn't think she'd managed to get any of it into his glass.

'Where's Katie, anyway?' she asked.

'Gone to the cinema with some parents from Leonard's nursery.' Philip dipped his finger into the wine that had spilled on the table and licked it. 'Safe to drink. I thought she would have told you.'

'I haven't actually spoken to her for a while,' Helen said, smiling and dipping her own finger in the spilled wine. 'She texted to ask if I could have Hannah and Leonard this afternoon. I didn't know what she was planning.'

'She seems to have met up with a few new people through his nursery,' Philip said. 'I'm glad, I think she gets bored being stuck at home, and I've been very tied up with work lately.'

'With your PhD student?' Helen asked, wondering as she did whether she should.

'Students and departmental stuff,' Philip said. 'Nothing in particular, but work always seems to mount up.'

'Katie said you had one student in particular who was demanding of your time.' Helen realised she was stirring slightly, but Philip didn't appear to mind.

'That's probably Maria,' he told her without apparent fluster. 'She's Italian, doing a dissertation on lyric poetry in sixteenth-century Naples. She's very bright, but she does need a bit of hand-holding.'

'Not literally?' asked Helen, unable to resist.

'No,' Philip laughed, 'not literally. I keep trying to persuade Katie to do a PhD. She's got such a brilliant mind, it's a shame she's not really using it at the moment.'

'She's a brilliant mother, too.' Helen felt that this needed pointing out. 'It's pretty time-consuming looking after young children.'

'I know, I do appreciate that,' said Philip, although judging by the way he was attempting to bat away Leonard, who had wandered into the kitchen and was trying to climb on to his knee, she was not sure that he did. 'I just think Katie gets bored and needs something to keep her going. That's why it's good that she's been going out a bit more lately.'

345

'Yes,' Helen agreed, although it was news to her that Katie had been going out more lately. She hadn't told her about any nursery parents' trips to the cinema, and certainly hadn't mentioned this one when she'd asked if Helen could look after the children.

Helen didn't mind, but she did think it was slightly odd. Perhaps Katie thought she would feel left out if she wasn't invited too. But Helen didn't know many of the parents at Leonard's nursery, and found it hard to squeeze cinema trips in between everything else anyway.

'Do you know what they've gone to see?' she asked Philip, out of curiosity.

'I've no idea. She may have told me, but I'm not sure,' he answered, characteristically vague about the finer details of his wife's evening out. 'Anyway, how are you both?'

'We're fine, I think,' Helen told him. 'Alex is in Manchester at the moment, and I was away at the weekend, so I haven't seen him for a few days.'

'Oh yes, come to think of it, I think I saw him at the underground station on Sunday,' Philip said. 'I suppose he was heading off to Manchester then.'

'I suppose so,' Helen concurred. 'Did you speak to him?'

'No, he was on his phone,' Philip said. 'Anyway, I ought to be getting these two home, and you'll be wanting to get Emma and Joe to bed too, I imagine?'

Helen glanced at the kitchen clock. It was half past six. In an ideal world she would have Joe bathed and in bed by half past seven, and Emma half an hour later. She rarely managed this, especially when Alex was away.

'They don't look very ready for bed, do they?' she said, as the four children ran though the living room making Red Indian noises and beating each other with cushions from the sofa.

'No, they don't,' Philip agreed. 'Still, time to get going. Come on, you two. Mum will be home soon and she'll want to see you before you go to bed.'

'I'll get their bags and coats,' said Helen, heading for the hall.

'Working tomorrow?' Philip asked.

'No.' Helen tried to sound casual as she thought about the fact that she would be going to Graham Parks' flat. 'I've got a bit of time off. I might try to fit in a film or something myself.'

'Good idea.' Philip bent down to help Leonard put his coat on. 'You should ask Katie if whatever she saw was any good.'

49

Helen's surroundings seemed to be at pains to warn her that what she was about to do was foolhardy. 'World Officially More Dangerous' read the billboard outside the newsstand at the tube station. 'Dangerous, dangerous' hummed the underground train as its wheels ran over the tracks. Even when it stopped to let passengers on and off, there was no escape from its admonitions. A young man sat opposite her and fished in his rucksack for a copy of *Dangerous Liaisons*, which he proceeded to read. Leaving the train and passing through the chambers of South Ealing station, Helen was greeted by a large yellow sign reading 'Danger, Men at Work'.

'I know, I know,' she muttered audibly although to herself. 'I know what I'm doing.'

Actually, as she took out her copy of the London A–Z and looked up Graham's address, she wondered if she did know what she was doing. She was on his patch now, crossing into uncharted territory, unsure of the rules that would apply once she got there.

She found the street easily, but paused at the end. She hadn't reached the point of no return. It wasn't too late to turn back and go home, but then again, having got this far, she might as well have lunch.

It hadn't been easy getting this far. Emma and Joe were on a go-slow in the morning. Helen hadn't helped by spending longer than usual deciding what to wear. She wasn't sure what was riding on this meeting with Graham Parks, but she did want to look reasonable, whatever the outcome. As she dithered about in front of the bedroom mirror, the children decided to go into the garden and let the rabbit have a run around. Normally this would have been fine. Today, as Helen only arrived downstairs when they actually needed to leave the house, the fact that the rabbit was out and hopping around the garden was going to make them late.

'We need to go now,' she shouted to a silent house. 'Emma, Joe!'

'We're in the garden,' Emma shouted back, oblivious to time. 'We're playing with Bugsy.'

'You need to put him away now.' Helen tried not to sound impatient. This had the effect of making everyone drag their feet more slowly. She looked out of the kitchen window and saw Joe haring round the garden after Bugsy, who was showing no signs of wanting to be caught. The rabbit was leaping high into the air, jumping over or dodging toys that littered his path, completing several figures of eight around the tiny patch of back lawn before Joe dived and rugby-tackled him, pinning him to the ground. The dive had two effects: the rabbit was caught and could now be put back in his hutch, and Joe was now more or less covered head to toe in mud. He no longer looked as if he was ready for school.

Helen decided to ignore the mud, telling herself it would dry off as they walked.

'Let's go,' she said, locking the back door and

distributing school bags at the same time.

She wanted shot of the children now, to know they were safe at school and that she was free to make the transition from wife and mother to whatever she was when she was with Graham Parks.

Joe began wheezing on the way to school, his asthma triggered by early-morning contact with rabbit fluff. Helen didn't have his inhaler, but hoped it would settle once they stopped rushing and he was sitting in his classroom.

She'd half expected her phone to beep as soon as she stepped off the tube, with a message from the school saying that Joe was having trouble breathing and could she come and collect him, but there was nothing. He had obviously calmed down, and his breathing with it, once the early-morning rush was over.

Nevertheless she felt guilty that she hadn't waited around to make sure he was okay, or gone home and brought his inhaler to school in case he needed it during the day. She'd noticed that the attendance records of children whose parents both worked were much better than those with at least one stay-at-home parent. This, she suspected, was not because they were less ill than their counterparts but because unless they were at death's door, their parents needed them to be at school so they could get on with their jobs.

She'd done this many times herself, leaving one child or other with a slight cold that turned out to be flu, a sick feeling that developed into full-blown vomiting and, on one occasion, a cough that revealed itself to be pneumonia.

She had told Joe's teacher that he was wheezing a bit as they'd been rushing and that Alex rather than her would be picking them up, as he was coming home early. She was forgoing her opportunity to get home early too, by going to Graham's flat.

Graham opened the door to her, looking slightly damp and smelling of aftershave, as if he was not long out of the shower and into a newly ironed white shirt.

'Come in,' he said, ushering her into the hallway and offering to take her coat. Once he'd hung it on a peg on the back of the door, he'd turned and greeted her again.

'Hello,' he said, putting his arms around her and encircling her in a hug that was more familiar than any contact they'd had to date. As he held her to him, Helen realised that things were different. They were no longer in public. Graham's greeting could be less restrained. She had asked to come to his flat and now she was here. There was therefore a presumption that the rules had changed.

But Helen wasn't quite ready to start playing a different game. She extracted herself from his hold as graciously as she could, muttering something about getting out of the hallway.

She looked around the living room, which was somewhere in between the total chaos that Graham had described to her previously and the total order of her own home. A vacuum cleaner still standing by a bookcase suggested that he had spent some time trying to reduce the level of chaos before her arrival.

'You look lovely,' he said, watching her take in her new surroundings. 'Can I get you a drink? Wine? Beer? Gin? Vodka? Whisky? Brandy?'

He had a fully stocked drinks cupboard, then.

What Helen really felt she needed was a large brandy to steady her nerves or a glass of wine to help her relax, but she decided it was too early in the day.

'Could I have a cup of tea, please?' she asked, relaxing as she said it, as if the normality of asking for tea would make things okay.

'Tea, then.' Graham smiled and began putting the kettle on. 'Have a seat.'

Helen sat on a smallish brown leather sofa behind a coffee table. Graham approached with two cups of tea and sat next to her.

'It's a nice flat.' She reverted to small talk.

'It has had a bit of a makeover this morning,' he told her. 'I tidied up — or rather, launched a major clean-up operation.'

'I hope you didn't embark on a war on squalor on my behalf.' Helen took up the military manoeuvring theme.

'I did,' Graham answered. 'It's not every day a beautiful woman comes to lunch. I do have to clean up sometimes, and that seemed like a good reason.'

'Don't say that.' Helen could feel him looking at her; his eyes, which always took her in in a way that made her feel as if she was the entire centre of his attention, were burning into her. She felt flattered but uncomfortable.

'What? That you are a beautiful woman? You

know I think you are. Take it as a compliment.'

'Thank you.' Helen did as she was instructed and bit back her impulse to tell him he didn't look so bad himself. 'I don't get many compliments these days.'

'I'm sure that's not true.' Graham had put his tea on the table and seemed unsure what do with his hands. Helen wondered if he was going to touch her. She wanted him to but feared what any physical contact might lead to.

'Well, I do actually.' She tried to hold him back with a joke. 'But only from Joe, and they don't really count.'

'What does Joe tell you?'

'He says I am the most beautiful woman in the world, that he loves my brown slippery hair and he likes my bumpy bits!'

'Bumpy bits?' Graham intoned.

'I am sure you can guess,' Helen laughed, sexual tension momentarily dispersed. 'Something smells good. Is that lunch?'

'There is something in the oven that will be your lunch,' Graham answered. 'It won't be ready for a while, though. Are you sure you wouldn't like a glass of wine beforehand?'

'Go on then.' Helen did feel as if she would be better able to deal with the situation if she'd had something to drink.

Graham went to the kitchen and came back with two glasses, a corkscrew and a bottle of Chablis.

'What made you change your mind?' he asked as he began peeling the foil away from around the cork.

'I succumb to offers of alcohol easily,' she answered.

'No, I mean what made you decide to come here? You were adamant you couldn't the other day.' Graham looked hopeful as he said this, hopeful that after weeks of Helen telling him she couldn't be more than a friend, something might have changed.

She waited for him to finish pouring them both a drink, then took a sip of hers and a deep breath.

'I wanted to spend some time with you,' she told him, truthfully. 'I wanted to not always be rushing somewhere else, never quite getting beyond a few scraps of conversation and . . . '

She paused and took another sip of wine.

'And what?' Graham was waiting.

'And I think Alex is having an affair.' As soon as the words were out the enormity of what she was saying hit Helen. Up till now, she had been nursing secret, private thoughts about what her husband got up to when he was away. When she said it out loud, the reality of what his having an affair would mean struck home.

If he was having an affair, that meant he had been having sex with another woman, lying to her, and putting their whole family at risk. The sudden recognition of this made her want to cry. Graham putting his arm around her and pulling her to him made her do just that.

'What makes you think he is having an affair?' he asked, stroking her, soothing her like a child.

'I don't know really.' Did she want to say what

she thought? Did she want to list to Graham all the little things that made her suspicious?

She took a deep breath, wiped her eyes and decided to say no more about it until she had spoken to Alex.

'Maybe I'm wrong,' she told Graham. 'I'm sorry. Can I go and wash my face or something? I must look a state.'

'Don't be sorry,' said Graham. He still had his arm around her, and he let his hand slide from her shoulder down the length of her arm until it was resting over her hand, holding it, comforting her but keeping her where she was. 'And you still look beautiful.'

He was looking at her, and when she looked at him she knew he was going to kiss her and she was going to kiss him back.

In the back of her mind, she remembered her conversation with Katie, and told herself that maybe this way she could get Graham Parks out of her system; maybe the unaddressed sexual tension between them could be dispelled if she finally did something about it, and afterwards she would be able to shrug it off and go back to how things had been before she met him.

In the forefront of her mind she wasn't thinking much at all; she was just kissing Graham Parks. He was holding her closer and closer, tugging at her clothes, untucking her shirt from the top of her trousers, running his hand underneath it, and she was powerless to stop him.

'I love you, Helen,' Graham said. 'There's no point in pretending otherwise.'

355

50

'You're back early.' Alex opened the front door when he heard Helen fumbling with her keys on the other side. He was smiling, welcoming her home with the big embrace she'd longed for and been deprived of when she came back from Spain.

She felt safe being held by Alex, his bulk and smell blotting out the thought of what might have happened if he'd not called her when he did. She wanted to stay like this with the front door open behind them, but she also wanted to get inside and find out what the crisis was that Alex had mentioned in his message.

She'd been kissing Graham Parks, and there was an inevitability to the whole situation. The covert flirtation and pretending to be friends were over. Her phone had rung like an alarm bell, warning her to stop then, before it was too late. To Graham it was simply a slight annoyance that caused him to pause as his hand slid up the back of her shirt towards her bra strap.

'Ignore it,' he'd said, as he felt her tense.

'It might be important.' She'd stopped kissing him as the phone had stopped ringing. Then a bleep sounded indicating that the caller had left a message.

'I'd better just check,' she had said, extracting herself from his hold and reaching for her bag on the floor by her feet. 'Joe was wheezing a lot

356

when I left him this morning. It could be school trying to get hold of me.'

'Mobile phones ... ' Graham muttered, reminding Helen of her dad, who was convinced that anything invented post-1950 was responsible for all the evils of this world. She wondered what he'd think if he knew that it was the ringing of a mobile phone that had distracted his daughter from potential adultery.

The message was from Alex. He sounded unsettled. He said he was home and there was 'a bit of a crisis' there and asked her to call him.

'It was Alex,' Helen told Graham. 'Something's up. I have to go.'

Already she was tucking her shirt back in, brushing her clothes with her hands as if trying to shift crumbs, although there were none. It was the fact that Graham Parks had been touching them that she was trying to shift.

'Do you have to?' Graham's tone was pleading. 'Can't you phone and find out what's happened?'

'Then he'd ask where I am and I'd have to make up somewhere I might be in case he's already phoned me at work.' She paused to look at him as she scooped her bag off the floor.

'I'm sorry,' she continued. 'I have to go. I should never have come. I can't do this. I'm sorry, but I can't.'

'Will you call me later?' he had asked.

'I'll try.' Helen was promising nothing and headed for the door. She didn't stop to say goodbye. She had to get out. She had to get home. She had to be where she belonged.

'I didn't go in today,' she told Alex. 'Shana let me have the time off in lieu for spending the weekend in Spain. I went into town to do a bit of shopping. What's happened? Is it Jo-Jo? Where is he?'

She didn't want to spend time explaining her whereabouts and her reasons for being home now. She needed to know what the crisis was. She feared that Joe might have had an asthma attack and needed to be brought home by Alex and, completely selfishly, half hoped that he had, because it would put her back at the centre of things. She would be needed to sit by Joe's bed, to administer his inhaler and stay with him until his breathing eased, or take him to hospital if it got worse.

'Joe's still at school. He's fine, as far as I know.' Alex was still holding her, no longer in greeting but in reassurance as he heard the agitation in her voice and registered the look of fear as she asked about Joe.

'He was wheezing a lot this morning,' Helen gabbled. 'I thought he'd settle down once he was at school. I should have stayed with him.'

'It's not Joe.' Alex's voice rose slightly. He needed her to calm down and stop talking. 'It's okay. There's nothing to worry about. I'm sorry if my message alarmed you.'

He was stroking her head and her back as he held her, calming her, kissing her as though she was a child who was upset about something that could be put right with kisses and cuddles.

'It's the rabbit,' he said. 'The door of the hutch was open when I came home, and he's

358

gone. It looks as if a fox has got him.'

'Bugsy?' Helen was confused. She had told Emma and Joe to put him away before they left. But she hadn't checked that they'd locked the hutch properly. She knew Joe found the catch difficult to manipulate. She should have made sure he'd managed. 'Are you sure he hasn't just got out? Is he anywhere in the garden?'

'I've looked everywhere.' Alex sounded apologetic, as if it was his fault, when Helen knew it was hers. 'And there's a trail of fur, as if he was involved in a scuffle. I was going to get rid of it before the children came home.'

Helen looked out of the kitchen window towards the garden, where earlier in the morning Bugsy had been hopping with Joe in hot pursuit. She'd been too rushed to savour the scene, which had been one of pure childhood happiness. Now, because she'd been in a hurry to leave so she could meet Graham Parks, that scene would never again be replayed, not with Bugsy, anyway.

They went into the garden. There was a two-metre-long trail of grey-brown fur leading to the garden wall. Helen looked over it, dreading what she might see on the other side, but apart from a few more patches of fur dotted around the neighbour's garden, there was no sign of their family pet.

'I'll sweep this up before Emma and Joe get home.' Alex was looking in the shed for something to clear the fur with. When he turned around, he saw that Helen was sitting on an overturned flowerpot, part of the obstacle course Joe had created for Bugsy earlier in the day. Her head was in her hands and she was shaking as she sobbed.

'I know,' said Alex, squatting next to her and holding her. 'Poor Bugsy. He was a lovely rabbit.'

'What will we tell the children?' Helen gasped, in between sobs.

'We'll say he ran away,' Alex said, pulling her closer to him so that her tear-stained face was buried in his chest. 'To join some wild rabbits in the park or something.'

Helen managed a small laugh, but as it was halfway out it morphed into another sob.

'It's okay.' Alex was still soothing. 'It's not your fault. I know you loved that rabbit. You're bound to be upset.'

Helen allowed herself to be comforted, although she felt like a fraud. She *had* loved the rabbit. She would miss him and all the joyful scenarios he had helped create with Emma and Joe, but she was crying not for the loss of the rabbit; rather for everything she might have lost if he hadn't got out of his hutch and disappeared. She was crying for fear of what she might have done if Alex hadn't called her when he did.

'He was part of the family,' she said, looking at Alex there beside her, so familiar, so solid, so reliable.

'I know.' Alex kissed her again.

'I don't know what I'd do if I ever lost you,' Helen turned and studied him. He was so handsome when she looked at him properly, with fresh eyes, rather than the eyes that were used to seeing him around the place and getting slightly annoyed with him for some mundane reason.

'You're not going to lose me.' Alex held her closer. 'Not if I have anything to do with it.'

51

'Can we make a sign? Can we? Please, please?' Emma and Joe were less bothered by the disappearance of Bugsy and more excited by the prospect of papering the neighbourhood with notices asking if anyone had seen him.

'If you want.' Helen was relieved that they did not seem unduly upset by the loss of their only pet, but also a bit worried that they might be in some way emotionally stunted and unable to grieve for the rabbit, which had to all intents and purposes been a substitute baby brother.

The sign they came up with did little to reassure her on this count.

'HAS ANYONE SEEN THIS RABBIT?' Emma had written in bold Times New Roman, beneath which they had inserted a jpeg of Bugsy and beneath that the date and time they had last seen him.

Helen and Alex had omitted to fill them in on the details of the fur-strewn garden, but had warned them that their signs might not yield any direct sightings.

As Emma typed a final line to the near-completed poster, Helen realised they were quite desensitised to death, and that she and Alex might just as well have served up all the gory details with the news of the rabbit's disappearance.

'If anyone has seen him please call 8319

0089,' Emma had written, before adding 'or any signs of him (such as blood or fur or bones).'

'Mum was more upset than you are,' Alex had admonished her.

'I just want to know what happened,' Emma said, matter-of-fact in her response. 'Can you help us put them up now?'

'Okay.' Alex had tousled Emma's hair as she gathered a sizeable armful of missing-rabbit posters from the printer. 'Shall we all go?'

This latter comment was addressed to Helen, but she could not quite face pinning Bugsy's furry wet-nosed face to trees and lampposts.

She also needed a few moments alone to compose herself and make a call.

'I think I'll stay here,' she said quietly, and Alex had kissed her as he left with the children, a lingering kiss like the one Graham Parks had given her on the tube a few days ago.

'See you in a bit,' he'd said as the small family group made for the door. He turned as they went out. 'Will you be okay?'

She'd nodded, mouthing 'I think so', and gone into the kitchen to call Graham.

He'd texted her several times since she'd left his flat that morning.

'Let me know if everything is okay' had been the first, followed by 'Are you okay? Call me when you get the chance', and finally 'I need to speak to you.'

'Hello, it's Helen,' she'd said when he answered.

'Helen, I've been worrying about you.' He'd sounded relieved that she had called. 'Is everything alright? Is your son okay?'

'Yes, he's fine, but a bit upset. The rabbit seems to have been eaten by a fox.' She heard Graham laughing at the other end of the line.

'Thank God for that,' he said. 'I thought from the way you rushed off and the fact that you didn't call that something awful had happened.'

'It is awful,' Helen insisted. 'He was a part of the family.'

'Of course.' Graham sounded as if he was trying to be sympathetic but was not utterly convincing. 'Were the children very upset?'

'Yes.' This didn't seem to be an entirely accurate summary of their feelings. 'And so was I. I loved the rabbit. Alex has gone to help them put up missing-rabbit posters, but there was a lot of fur in the garden, so I don't suppose we'll ever see him again.'

'When will I see *you* again?' Graham had dismissed the rabbit from the conversation faster than Helen felt was appropriate. Hadn't he seen *Fatal Attraction*? Didn't he know the impact the death of a rabbit could have on a family or a film genre?

'Today's lunch got burnt. Can you come again, later in the week? Or for dinner?'

'I don't think so.' As soon as she said it, Helen realised she should have been more definite.

'Next week, then, or one evening after work?' Graham's tone was not exactly pleading, but it was persuasive.

'I can't come back,' Helen told him. 'I'm sorry, but it's not what I want. I should never have come today.'

'I'm glad you did.' Graham was coaxing her now. 'I just wish you could have stayed for longer. Please, Helen — '

'I don't know what I was doing today,' Helen interrupted. 'I wasn't thinking straight. I haven't really been thinking straight since I met you. I don't think I can risk seeing you again. I'm sorry.'

'But what about the last couple of months?' Graham persisted. 'Every time we met, every email you sent. There is something between us, Helen. You mean a lot to me. I thought I might mean something to you, too.'

'You did . . . you do.' Helen faltered, not sure what she was trying to say. 'I like you, Graham. You don't need me to spell things out. I'd like to see you again, but it's because I have feelings for you that I can't. I *have* to stop this now. I'm sorry if I led you to believe in any way that there could be something between us, but I now know there can't be.'

There was silence at the other end of the line. Helen wondered if Graham had listened to her speech, which had taken some effort to deliver, or if it was lost in the tumbleweed of Orange mobile network failure.

'Are you still there?' she asked.

'I love you, Helen,' Graham said. 'I know you are married and have a family, but there is something between us and I can't ignore that.'

'Maybe there is.' Helen was cautious. She didn't want to hurt his feelings by dismissing them as romantic and unrealistic, but neither did she want to give him any hope that things might

365

continue along the lines they had been going. 'But I have to ignore it. I don't want to hurt you, but I don't want to do anything that would damage my family either. I'm sorry. Really I am.'

There was more tumbleweed, and as Helen had nothing left to say, she added, 'I have to go now. They'll be back home soon.'

'Can I at least see you one last time?' Graham broke his silence. 'There's something I was going to tell you today that I'd rather tell you face to face. How about dinner again? So that I can say goodbye.'

'Lunch.' Helen thought she at least owed him that. 'Friday looks possible for me.'

'That suits me. What time?'

Helen could hear the key turning in the lock. Alex and the kids would be upon her in seconds.

'Twelve thirty,' she said, hanging up before they were within earshot.

52

'We need to talk,' said Alex, pouring himself a large glass of wine. They both needed a drink after the drama of the day. Helen suspected she needed one more than Alex. She definitely needed one if he wanted to talk. Did he suspect something? Had he heard her on the phone to Graham? Or was he about to tell her something about himself that she didn't want to hear?

'What do you want?' he asked her, having already taken a sip of his own glass of red. Maybe he needed one more than she did. Maybe whatever he had to tell her was worse than what she didn't have to tell him.

'I'll try some of that!' she joked, using a line her grandmother had always employed when asked if she'd like something everyday and ordinary. She never just said 'Yes please' but always implied that the cup of tea or slice of bread and butter being offered to her was a new delicacy that she had yet to sample, and that by tasting it she might be doing you a favour.

'I'll try some' seemed to imply that you were doing market research on whatever it was that was being offered, rather than giving her something you knew full well she liked.

'Here you go.' Alex handed her a glass. 'See what you think of that.'

Helen took a sip, pretending to register

surprise. 'Mmm, could do with a bit more sugar, perhaps.'

'It's an acquired taste.' Alex put on a mock serious face, then let it slip into a real serious face. He needed to talk. He'd said as much. 'Shall we go into the living room?'

'Okay.' Helen followed him reluctantly. She'd enjoyed the moment of levity over the wine, putting off the talk she'd been anticipating would come sometime soon.

What did Alex have to tell her? What was she going to tell him? Anything? What was there to tell? For a relatively short time she'd been having secret meetings with another man who she had been very attracted to. Earlier in the day she'd been to his flat and if her phone hadn't rung might well have ended up sleeping with him. Would she have slept with him? It had seemed inevitable at the time. All that saying that she was just friends with Graham Parks but keeping her meetings with him from Alex suggested she was always at risk of committing adultery with him. Yet now, as she sat on the sofa next to her husband, she couldn't imagine it. Couldn't imagine it at all.

The way he'd laughed when she'd told him the rabbit had died had surprised her. She'd expected more understanding, and it made her realise he had little understanding of the mundane ordinariness of family life. To him the details must have seemed just that, mundane and unimportant, but to Helen they were *her* life. Alex knew the rabbit was a poor substitute for the third child she wasn't going to have (come to think of it, his rescheduled vasectomy was in two days' time — which was bad timing). Happiness was in those details.

She found herself gripping the edge of the sofa cushion, hoping that her hold on its spongy interior would soften the blow of whatever it was Alex had to say.

'I'm sorry I wasn't here when you got back from Spain.' He put his hand on her arm briefly as he said this, reminding Helen of how much she had been wanting to kiss him when he came home. She still wanted to. Maybe it was him she'd wanted to kiss all along. Graham Parks, because he was different and new, had just made her feel it more. But now she realised she hadn't wanted him really, only to rekindle some of the passion of her early relationship with Alex.

'It's okay,' she replied. 'You had a script meeting. I guess it was unavoidable.' Her tone was conciliatory. She didn't want to accuse him of anything, remembering how he'd bristled when she'd mentioned his absences before. 'I'm sorry for being hard on you before I left.' By apologising for her earlier suspicions, she could bring up the subject of his whereabouts without pointing the finger of accusation at him.

'I wanted to be here.' Alex was holding her hand now. Was this good? Or was he trying to cushion the blow he was about to deal? 'The house seemed empty without you. I know you spend a lot of time here without me, but it felt all wrong you not being here.'

Perhaps it was good.

'And,' he went on, 'I didn't actually have a

369

script meeting to go to . . . '

No, it was bad.

'Where were you, then?' Helen couldn't help the note of accusation creeping into her voice. She was a hypocrite. She knew that much.

'I was with Venetia.' Alex's tone was even, explanatory, not even tinged with regret. How could he sit there so calmly holding her hand and tell her that he'd been with another woman?

'What do you mean?' she stuttered, pulling her hand away from his, thinking she knew full well what he meant.

'Oh no, I don't mean *with* with.' Alex laughed nervously and made a grab for her hand again.

Helen snatched it away. It was a childish impulse: 'It's my hand.' 'No, it's my hand.'

'What *do* you mean, then?' she asked.

'It's been building up for a while,' Alex said.

'What has?'

'The situation with Venetia.'

'What situation with Venetia?' Helen could imagine what the situation was. Why couldn't he just come straight out with it, tell her what was going on instead of making her draw the details out of him as if she was probing a reluctant interviewee?

'I couldn't tell you before.' Alex had taken her hand again. This time Helen left it there, but she wasn't responding to his hold.

'Why not?' She thought she knew the answer. Because he was a coward, because he couldn't face telling her, because he didn't want to tell her what was going on until he was absolutely sure of his feelings for Venetia.

370

'Because you're a journalist,' he replied.

That took her by surprise.

'What has that got to do with it?' She moved away, further along the sofa, taking her hand with her. Did he really think she would pass the details of her own husband's affair with Venetia Taylor on to the press? She didn't want those details to come out any more than either of them did.

'We all promised the producer that we would be discreet, that we wouldn't say anything to anyone at all as it would only make things worse,' Alex told her. 'I've been wanting to talk to you about it for a while, and I think you suspected something, but we were all trying to protect Venetia. It will probably come out in the end, though.'

'What will come out?' Helen thought she knew, but she was going to make him say it. He couldn't sit on the sofa in their living room and confess adultery in code, not actually confessing it at all.

'Venetia has a drink problem,' Alex told her. 'She's an alcoholic, I suppose, although she can cover it up pretty well, but nevertheless it's a problem.'

'How serious?' Helen had been expecting to ask this in relation to Alex's feelings for Venetia, not in relation to a drink problem she had never imagined Venetia to have.

'Serious enough for her to be dropped from the programme. She was quite good at disguising it at first. Telling us all the fluffed lines were because she was nervous, but it soon became pretty obvious that it was more than that.'

Helen was stunned and shocked. The last thing she had expected to hear was that Venetia Taylor was an alcoholic. Moments ago she had felt nothing but anger and mistrust towards her; now these feelings were turning into sympathy and concern.

'But surely dropping her from the programme is the worst thing they can do?' she said. 'Couldn't they just have given her a bit of time off?'

'The producer has been suggesting that.' Alex paused to take a sip of his wine, then as if realising the inappropriateness of drinking more, put his glass down again. 'But she refused to admit she had a problem, and in the end they decided the only thing to do was let her go.'

Helen still wondered how this involved Alex. Why did Venetia having a drink problem mean that he had to spend the weekend with her when he should have been at home looking after his children?

'That's why I had to go up last weekend.' He seemed to know what she was thinking. 'The producer asked to meet with her, but he was worried how she would react. He thought she needed someone she trusted to be with her, and . . . '

'He asked you.' Helen finished the sentence for him. 'But why didn't you tell me that was where you were? Just because I'm a journalist? I wouldn't have told anyone if you had trusted me.'

'I know that.' Alex was apologetic. 'I didn't

372

think I needed to. I'd been asked not to, and it didn't seem important that I tell you, though I think I may have been wrong.'

Helen sensed that Alex was asking her to tell him what she had thought about his absence, but she felt she was no longer in a position to accuse him of anything when there might be a perfectly rational explanation.

'I'm sorry I didn't tell you,' he went on. 'But I thought that if I did, you'd cancel the trip to Spain and I knew you wanted to go, so I asked your Mum if she could help out.'

'Did Mum know what was going on, then?' Helen couldn't believe he would have told her mother the details and not her.

'No, I wouldn't risk telling her; it would have been all over the south of England before we knew it.' He laughed. 'I just said that I had to be at work that weekend and I didn't want you to have to cancel your trip.'

'It wasn't that important,' Helen told him, knowing that what he said was true. If she'd thought he wouldn't be at home, she would have cancelled the trip rather than ask her mother to look after the children.

'I thought it was,' Alex said. 'You were worried about job cuts and you've seemed a bit distracted lately. I thought you probably needed some time to yourself.'

Helen wondered how distracted she must have appeared to him and what exactly his interpretation of her mood had been, but she said nothing.

'Obviously in a few weeks' time people will know that Venetia's no longer in the show,' Alex continued. 'Hopefully by then she'll have done something about the drinking.'

'Poor Venetia.' Suddenly she was no longer the impossibly glamorous, beautiful wife abandoned by her football-playing husband yet still irresistible to all other men, but a rather sad, scared single mother unable to face her life without alcohol.

'That's why there were so many extra rehearsals, too,' Alex continued. 'I'm sorry I didn't explain those to you properly either. I didn't like having secrets from you, but somehow it felt disloyal telling anyone that Venetia had a problem. She needed to sort herself out but she didn't need people talking about her.'

'No.' Helen was mulling over Alex's words. It made sense now. Alex had never been one to gossip. He was someone people took into their confidence for this reason, someone people trusted. If Venetia had a problem, Helen could see that Alex would have been the logical person for the producer to ask for help. He would have tried to get Alex to talk to her. He would have wanted him on hand to look after her and persuade her to get help when she was told she'd be leaving the programme. If you knew what was going on, it all fitted perfectly. If you were suspicious, you might interpret the facts differently.

'I thought you might have been having an affair with her,' Helen confessed.

53

'Who's that at this time of the morning?' Alex asked, irritated by the interruption of the persistent ringing of the doorbell.

'They'll probably go away if we ignore it,' Helen said, looking at her watch. 'Anyway, it's eleven thirty, which is a perfectly respectable time to ring the doorbell.'

They were in bed on a weekday morning, having found themselves both at home, alone. Helen had taken the children to school, while Alex phoned various children's farms to find out if any had baby rabbits for sale. They had intended to spend the rest of the day going out to buy one, or maybe even two, but when she came back after dropping Emma and Joe off, Alex had told her there was only one place that had baby rabbits, but they were still too young to be separated from their mother.

'Fortunately our babies are not too young to be separated from you,' he had said, putting his arms around her from behind and sliding his hand down the front of her shirt. Then he'd started unbuttoning it until it was open, and begun unzipping her jeans, and moments later there was a trail of clothes leading up the stairs and they were desperately grabbing each other, kissing whatever parts of their bodies their mouths came into contact with.

The night before, there'd been less urgency

and more compassion to their lovemaking.

When Helen had told him she'd thought he might have been having an affair with Venetia Taylor, his initial reaction had been anger and defensiveness, but then he'd been open and frank and they'd talked until late before eventually heading upstairs for a much-needed reconciliation.

'I won't pretend I didn't find her hugely attractive when she first joined the cast,' he had admitted. 'And she seemed to like me too, which I found very flattering.'

'Why wouldn't she?' Helen had replied. 'But she knew you were married.'

'Of course,' Alex reassured. 'And I thought that the fact that I was married, I mean I am married, gave me leeway to flirt with her, because I thought she knew that it would never go anywhere.'

'And did she?' Helen asked, reasoning that now they were actually talking properly, she could ask whatever she wanted.

'No, I think she thought I was genuinely interested in her.' Alex paused and looked at Helen when he said this, deliberately making eye contact to show that he was being honest with her. 'There was one evening when we were going out after work,' he continued. 'She suggested having a meal at some new restaurant, but I wanted to go through my lines for the next day first, so I told her I'd meet her there. I thought that there would be a few of us going, but when I got there it was only Venetia, and it was all very cosy and candlelit.'

'That was when the photographer snapped you,' Helen surmised.

'Yes.' Alex nodded. 'I realised as soon as I got there that I'd obviously been giving her the wrong impression, and I was explaining this when the photographer popped up out of nowhere.'

'Go on,' Helen said.

'Well, if I'm honest, I was telling her that I thought she was great and of course I fancied her — who wouldn't? The irony was that thinking she fancied me too just made me want you more. So I was just telling her that I did like her but that I was happily married when the photographer came over to our table and flashed his camera in our faces.' Alex paused and took a sip of wine. 'Venetia was really upset and angry and she stormed out of the restaurant.'

'What was she upset about, you or the photographer?' Helen asked.

'Both, I think,' he answered. 'I stayed to pay the bill, and when I got back to the hotel she was in her room but she wouldn't open the door. She just told me to leave her alone.'

'That was probably just as well,' said Helen, wondering what might have happened if she *had* opened the door.

'Look, I know I was stupid,' said Alex. 'Incredibly stupid and naïve to think I could be flattered by her attentions and get away with it. I'm being totally honest with you, Helen. I did flirt with her a lot, and none too covertly, but I thought it was just harmless flirtation and I never even for a moment considered cheating on you.'

'Not even for a moment?' Helen asked, and before Alex could deny this, she went on, 'Because that would only make you human. You don't have to say you never think about sleeping with anyone else, because everyone does. I do.'

Now that she had said this, she expected Alex to ask her more, but he didn't.

'I know,' he said. 'You've been a bit distant recently, and I thought it might be because Jim Keeble was around again.'

'It's not Jim Keeble,' Helen said, and tried to think how she might explain Graham Parks to him. She thought she owed it to him to be honest, but as she tried to formulate in her mind exactly what it was that had been going on and what there was to say about it, Alex started talking again.

'I knew you knew something was going on and it was making you anxious,' he said. 'And initially I was embarrassed that I'd been so stupid and let things get out of hand. I'd allowed myself to be flattered by her attentions, but, like I said, I thought you were having some sort of thing with Jim and so I thought it didn't really matter. Then Venetia started drinking a lot and the producer had a talk with the cast and told us not to say anything, and I thought I was doing the right thing by keeping quiet. I'm sorry.'

'I'm the one who should be sorry,' Helen told him. And she meant it.

How could she have doubted his loyalty both to her and to his colleagues? He was a good, trustworthy man, and she hadn't trusted him. Worse still, she'd nearly betrayed him. 'Jim's gone to Chad, but anyway — '

'You don't have to explain,' Alex cut in. 'We've both been a bit distracted recently. I don't need to know why. I trust you, Helen, whatever might happen. I trust you to be faithful to me and to stay with me. I know that sometimes we all lose sight of what's important, but I don't think either of us will ever lose complete sight of it, will we?'

He put down his glass of wine and began kissing her, and Helen knew that she loved him more than she could ever love anyone else.

Twelve hours later they lay exhausted but together, and the doorbell was being rung with increasing intensity.

'Okay, I'm coming,' Helen muttered to herself as she pulled on her jeans and a shirt and ran down the stairs to see who was ringing their bell with such urgency. She tucked her shirt in and pushed her hair behind her ears, hoping that whoever it was would not guess that the reason for her being slow to answer was that she'd just finished having sex.

'You look awful.' Helen would have expected whoever was on the other side of the door to have said as much to her, given her general state of dishevelment, but instead she found herself saying it to someone whose usual state was looking fantastic.

'Can I come in?' asked Katie. It was raining outside and she wasn't wearing a coat and was soaked and shivering.

'Of course.' Helen opened the door wider. 'Did you get caught out?'

'What do you mean?' Katie stopped halfway across the threshold, looking as if Helen had asked if she'd been found injecting heroin in the playground.

'In the rain.' Helen nodded in the direction of the downpour. 'You're not wearing a coat and you're soaked. That's all I meant. Are you okay?'

'No,' Katie answered. 'I'm not. I'm a mess.'

'I can see that,' Helen said, as kindly as she could. 'Come into the kitchen. I'll make you some tea.'

Katie followed her to the back of the house, where Helen put the kettle on and handed her friend a towel that had been drying over the back of a chair.

'Do you want to borrow some dry clothes?' she asked.

'I might have to,' Katie said. 'I had to get out of the house. I haven't even got my keys or my bag. I wasn't thinking about anything except that I had to get out. Philip won't talk to me and I had to talk to someone.'

'What? Why?' Helen couldn't work out what was going on. 'Why is Philip not talking to you? Did you have a major row or something?'

'He caught us,' Katie said. She was still not making sense as far as Helen was concerned. 'I thought he was at college all day today, but he came home early. His meeting was cancelled and he was feeling a bit under the weather so he thought he'd take the rest of the day off.'

'What do you mean, he caught you?' From her friend's demeanour, she imagined that some-thing serious had happened, but she didn't know what. 'What were you doing?'

'Oh God, Helen.' Katie buried her face in the towel. 'I can hardly bring myself to say it out loud. What have I done?'

'Tell me,' Helen said gently.

'I thought you knew.' Katie looked up at her; her mascara was now well and truly smudged, and she looked like a very sad panda. 'I was sure you would have guessed.'

'Guessed what?' Helen asked.

'I've been having an affair,' Katie said. As soon as the words were out, she began sobbing hysterically.

Helen felt as if she had been kicked in the stomach. For the past few months she had been so wrapped up in her own emotions that although she had suspected that her husband was having an affair, she hadn't noticed that her best friend actually was. She moved closer to Katie and held her while she cried. She could feel Katie's whole body heaving with the emotion of it all. She felt she had to hold her tight to stop her physically breaking up.

After a while, Katie seemed a little calmer.

'Do you want a drink?' Helen asked. 'Tea, coffee? Or do you want something stronger?' She felt as if she needed a drink herself. There had been far too much emotion packed into the last twenty-four hours. It seemed there was going to be a lot more.

'Tea will be great.' Katie smiled at her thankfully and wiped her face again as Helen carried two mugs of steaming liquid back to the table and sat down. She didn't really want to find out more, because it would make it all too real, but she knew she was going to have to.

'Who have you been having an affair with?' she asked.

Katie took a deep breath and let it out. Then she took a sip of tea and started crying again.

'With Cary,' she said. 'I've been having an affair with him for the last three months. I can't believe you hadn't guessed.'

'No.' But now that Katie had told her, she wasn't really surprised. 'I didn't guess. I thought you were just friends. I haven't really been much good to you lately. I've had other things on my mind.'

'We were just friends to start with,' Katie began explaining.

Helen was on the verge of asking how their early friendship had mutated into an affair, but she didn't really need to. She knew how things progressed, how if you weren't careful, feelings you thought you had under control could emerge and wreak havoc in your life.

'I never meant it to happen,' Katie told her. 'I really didn't. I liked being in his company and we started spending quite a lot of time together. At first it was always with Leonard and Connor. We'd go to the park or take them swimming or sometimes have lunch, and then we started meeting up when they were at nursery.'

'What did you do then?' Helen asked.

'We had coffee. We went for walks. We went to the cinema a couple of times,' Katie told her. 'It was all fairly innocent stuff, but there was always this slight undercurrent of sexual tension, and then there was this one day when we'd been sitting in the café in the park and a pigeon shat on my head.'

'Is that relevant?' Helen had to suppress a small laugh at the image.

'My hair was filthy,' Katie said sheepishly. 'Cary suggested we went back to his house and I could have a shower there before we went to pick the kids up again.'

Helen waited, thinking she already knew what was coming next.

'I don't know why it happened then, but it did. I thought maybe if we just slept together once we'd somehow get whatever it was out of our systems, but it just made me want more.'

'What did you plan to do?' Helen asked.

'I didn't really think about it,' Katie said. 'Philip has been so busy at work recently. He hasn't been around much and it was easy just to carry on. But now he knows and I don't know if he'll ever be able to forgive me.'

'Do you want him to?' Helen had to ask. Perhaps Katie did not feel the same way about Philip as she felt about Alex. Perhaps she wanted Cary more than she wanted Philip and would end up leaving her husband for her lover.

'Oh God, yes,' Katie said. 'When he walked in on us this morning, I thought I was going to die. It wasn't just the fact he'd caught us, it was the look on his face. I've never seen it before. He looked utterly broken, and I did that to him.'

Both women looked up quickly as the kitchen door opened and Alex wandered in wearing only a towel wrapped round his waist.

'I wondered where you'd got to,' he said to Helen, before taking in the fact that she was not alone.

'Oh, Katie, hello.' He was mildly embarrassed about his semi-naked state. 'Was that you at the door? I thought it was probably just someone come to read the meter and they'd have gone by now.'

'No, it was Katie.' Helen gave him a look with which she tried to imply 'and she's very upset and we're having a heart-to-heart and you're not really welcome'.

Alex appeared to understand what her frowning and nodding was intended to convey.

'I was just about to take a shower anyway,' he said, retreating back towards the hallway. 'See you later, Katie.'

'Did he have a late night?' Katie asked, obviously thinking it a bit late in the day to be having a shower. Then she looked more closely at Helen and noticed that she wasn't altogether entirely dressed herself. 'Or have you two been . . . ? Oh my God, I'm sorry. I knew you were in, because the lights were on, but I thought you were just working or something . . . Sorry. I thought I was the only one having sex in the middle of the morning.' She laughed a laugh that was close to tears.

'That's the first time we've done it in the middle of the day for a long time,' Helen told her, feeling embarrassed not just that her friend now realised she'd been ringing the doorbell while they were having sex, but also that she was back on track with Alex while Katie and Philip's own marriage seemed to be well and truly off the rails.

'You know what the worst thing is?' Katie said.

Helen couldn't imagine anything much worse than being caught by your husband in your own bed with someone else.

'I think Philip is more angry with me for taking advantage of Cary than for actually having an affair,' Katie said. 'He said Cary was vulnerable because his wife had died and hadn't I stopped to think how it would affect him.'

'It takes two,' Helen said, consciously considering that two was not terribly many for it to take. If she had had more time and been a bit less fearful, or if Alex had been a little less loyal and more enamoured of Venetia Taylor, would she be the one sitting here, sobbing into the teapot?

'What will you do?' she asked.

'I don't know.' Katie shook her head in despair. 'I've well and truly screwed things up, haven't I?'

54

'I can't stay long,' Helen said, walking slightly in front of Graham as the waiter led them to a table in a quiet corner of the restaurant.

He tucked them in and handed them menus, half bowing and giving Helen an appreciative smile. Only the Italians could really get away with those looks. The ones that said, 'I think you are an attractive woman and this pleases me, and here you are with someone of the opposite sex all set for a meal that will probably lead to one thing only, and this pleases me also.'

His cursory glance at them as they came through the door together obviously told him that they were a couple; their body language must have indicated that they were not completely comfortable with each other and therefore must be positioned somewhere around the fringes of the room, away from the families and work groups and the couples who were so definitely couples that there was no point in tucking them away — they'd probably only argue about domestic issues. The edges were for intrigue.

Helen wondered whether, had the waiter known that in fact she wasn't here on a secret romantic tryst, he would have seated them elsewhere. She was glad he hadn't. She'd wanted to go out in public, but not too public. They needed the restaurant setting to keep this meeting within boundaries, but they also needed enough privacy to talk.

'Do you have to get back to work?' Graham asked.

'No,' she said, waiting for the waiter to disappear. 'I have to take Alex to hospital.'

'Is he okay?' Graham asked, looking concerned.

'Yes, he's fine,' Helen said, a feeling of warmth rising inside her as she thought of him. 'He's having the snip this afternoon. I promised to take him.'

'We could have met up another day.' Graham looked slightly annoyed that she was squeezing him in between work and her family, but Helen reflected that that was the way it was.

'No.' She looked at him. 'It's better to get it over with now.'

'Is that what we're doing?' Graham asked, absent-mindedly bending the menu in his hands as he spoke. 'Getting over something?'

'Yes,' Helen said quietly. 'I'd like things to be different, but they're not. I can't see you again, Graham, not after the other day. I think you know how I feel about you, and in other circumstances perhaps things could have been different, but they're not.'

'Did you tell Alex where you were last week, when he called?' He didn't add 'when you were with me at my flat, kissing me on my sofa'. He didn't need to.

'No,' Helen answered quietly. She had told Alex a bit about Graham Parks, but not that. 'I wanted to tell him,' she went on. 'But I've been

387

getting so many things wrong over the last few months and I didn't want to get that wrong as well. I didn't know how to explain how I ended up at your flat. It seems so ridiculous now.'

'It seemed wonderful at the time.' Graham reached a hand out across the table to touch hers, but she pulled it back, sending a piece of cutlery clattering to the floor as she did.

Diners at nearby tables looked across momentarily. Helen bent to pick up the offending fork, but the waiter beat her to it, whisking it away and replacing it with a clean one and asking at the same time if they would like something to drink.

He was a welcome distraction. By the time he'd disappeared to fetch them a bottle of mineral water, the other diners had lost interest in Helen's momentary clumsiness. Nevertheless, she lowered her voice.

'Look, Graham, I'm sorry,' she said. 'I know it's harder for you than it is for me. I have a husband and a family. They are my life. I tried to be clear from the start, but I liked you a lot and I got muddled and stopped thinking straight.'

'I know where you are heading with this speech,' Graham interrupted. 'I've heard it before, some of it from you, some of it from other women, and no doubt I'll keep hearing it again until I finally find someone who feels about me as I do about them. Can we go back a bit first?'

'What do you mean?'

'The last time we spoke, properly, you thought Alex was having an affair. You were upset. I hated seeing you upset. I thought I could make you happy. I thought that if Alex was stupid enough to have an affair, then he deserved to risk losing you.'

'He wasn't having an affair.' Helen glanced at the waiter, who was advancing towards them carrying glasses and a bottle of water. She could wait for him to go though the rigmarole of opening the bottle and pouring it or carry on anyway and pretend he wasn't listening. 'He hasn't been having an affair, I got it all wrong.'

She told Graham what Alex had told her about Venetia, about her drink problem, about the extra recordings scheduled to accommodate her. She told him about the times Alex had had to take her home because she'd been too drunk to get there on her own, and how he'd been in Manchester last weekend to hold her hand when she lost her job and to try to persuade her that she needed help.

'And do you believe him?' Graham looked sceptical.

'Why wouldn't I?'

'Well, she's a very attractive woman and he's a bloke,' he said, half laughing and half shrugging.

'Yes, and he told me that at first he was attracted to her and she seemed to like him,' Helen said. 'He was flattered by her attentions. There was a lot of flirting, but it never went beyond that, though I think Venetia really did want something to happen.'

'But Alex never did?' Graham asked.

'I'm sure he did sometimes,' Helen said truthfully. 'I'm sure he thought about it. There must have been times when he wondered if he could get away with going up to her hotel room, and times when he went back to his own room and imagined that he had.'

'But you believe him when he says he never did?' Graham asked.

Helen nodded.

'Why?'

'Because I trust him, because I *have* to trust him. Because we neither of us can know what the other is doing every minute of every day, and the only thing we can do is trust each other.'

'Does he trust you?'

'Yes, he does.' Helen took a sip of water. 'I told him I was meeting you the very first time we had dinner together, the time you came up with some excuse about me working on your website.'

'You obviously saw through that.' Graham smiled.

'But I kept quiet about all the other meetings, the phone calls, the texts and the emails. They were my secret, but I think he knew that there was something going on.'

'What makes you say that?'

'I didn't realise at the time, but when we were talking the other day, it was obvious that he must have known that something in me had changed, and he seemed to guess that it was because I was getting attention from another man.'

She didn't tell him that Alex had thought the other man was Jim Keeble. She was pretty sure Alex had suspected there was someone else, but he hadn't asked her if there was. All he wanted to know, when they talked, was that the two of them were sound again, back focusing on each other, free from the distractions of the past few months.

'But if he suspected something, why didn't he say anything?' Graham asked.

'It's hard to explain,' Helen said, thinking that there was so much in a marriage that was inexplicable to anyone not in the relationship. 'Alex has always given me space. It's as if he accepts that in the course of a marriage it will be threatened by outsiders and that's just something you have to deal with.'

'I still don't understand why he would just let it go,' Graham persisted. 'If he really loved you, surely he would fight to keep you?'

'It's not like that,' Helen told him. 'He does really love me, I am sure of that, but he doesn't possess me. He loves me enough to let me have whatever relationships I need to have with friends and colleagues and even ex-boyfriends without worrying that I might be going to have an affair with one of them. He trusted that our relationship was strong enough that I could flirt not-so-innocently with another man without damaging it. I trusted myself too, when I first met you — it was only when I started to suspect Alex and Venetia that I began worrying what I might do.'

'And don't you worry what he might have done if Venetia hadn't had a drink problem? If she had been the drop-dead-gorgeous, uncomplicated, available co-star she first appeared to be?'

'I was, wasn't I?'

'What?'

'Worrying what he might be up to. But I had less reason to worry than he did.' Even now, Helen felt alarmed by how close she had come to completely betraying Alex's trust.

'And do you love him?'

'Of course I do. I always have. Right from the moment when he knocked me over. Sometimes I love him more than at others. Sometimes I hate him. But I always love him too.'

'And do you, did you ever feel anything for me?' Graham looked dejected.

'Yes, I did. I do.' Helen reached across the table now and held his hand. 'When we met, I felt immediately connected to you. If I hadn't already been married, I would have wanted a relationship with you. But I was, I mean I am. I shouldn't have allowed myself to have any feelings for you, but I did. That's why I can't see you any more.'

'I love you, Helen,' Graham said. 'Does that not mean anything?'

'Yes,' Helen said. 'I could have loved you too. I think that's true. If I was free to. But I'm not, and I love Alex more than I think I could ever love anyone else. I lost sight of that for a while, but it's true. I'm so sorry.'

Graham put his knife and fork down and looked at her directly, making her the sole focus of his attention. 'I was going to tell you this the other day.' He cleared his throat as if he was about to make some big declaration, and Helen held her breath, willing him not to. She gave a big sigh of relief when he went on, 'I've been offered a job in Alaska. Flying helicopters again, ferrying oil workers to platforms. I wasn't sure whether to take it or not. They want me to start next week.'

'So soon?'

'If you had given me any reason to hope that I might have some chance with you, then I would have turned it down.' He paused, waiting for her to say something, but she remained silent.

The silence was broken by an intruder.

'Hi, Helen!'

Helen looked up and recognised Fiona Haste, a former colleague on a local newspaper whom she had not seen for several years.

'I thought it was you!' Fiona had no qualms about interrupting. 'I've been having lunch with some colleagues. We've finished and they're just leaving . . . ' She broke off to wave to a couple of women making their way towards the door. 'But I thought I saw you skulking in the corner.'

Her words were loaded, and Helen wondered how she could explain away Graham's presence and make it seem natural. She needn't have worried.

'Hi,' said Fiona, introducing herself. 'I used to work with Helen on the *Clapham Courier*. I'm still there, for my sins. Aren't you Graham Parks?'

'Yes.' Graham looked confused. One book was not enough to get recognised on.

'I read Helen's piece about you in the *Sunday Review*,' Fiona said. 'I only bothered to read it because Helen had written it, but it was interesting, so I bought the book and thought it was great.'

'I'm glad you liked it.' Graham's tone was dismissive, but Fiona didn't notice.

'We were just leaving,' Helen said, hoping Fiona might go. 'You should give me your email address.'

'Oh, I thought you might be interviewing Graham Parks again and I might be interrupting, but if you're just leaving, I'll head out with you. Which way are you going?'

'To the tube,' Graham said, at the same time as Helen muttered something about getting a taxi.

'Oh well, I'm going to the tube myself. Mind if I walk with you?' Fiona seemed oblivious to the atmosphere. 'I haven't seen Helen for ages. Is there another book in the pipeline?'

'I don't think so.' Graham raised his shoulders in a gesture that suggested Helen was responsible and should do something to get rid of her garrulous former colleague.

Helen shrugged back. Perhaps it was better this way.

There was a taxi waiting outside the restaurant.

'Is this your cab, Helen?' Fiona asked.

'I didn't order one.' Helen asked the driver if he was waiting for someone.

'No, just stopped to have a pizza with my brother-in-law,' he told her. 'He's the chef here. I'm working again now, though — where do you want to go?'

Helen gave him her address, hoping he would say he never went that far south on a Wednesday, so that she could walk to the tube with Graham and lose Fiona in the process. This was to be her chance to say goodbye to him.

'Hop in, then,' said the cab driver.

'Nice to see you again, Helen.' Fiona planted an air kiss in the vicinity of her cheek.

Graham opened the door for her.

'Goodbye, Helen,' he said, leaning towards her and kissing her on the lips. It wasn't the parting shot Helen had imagined when she set out earlier in the day. She had thought that as this was to be their final encounter, she would allow herself at least a proper kiss goodbye.

Fiona raised her eyebrows in a vaguely questioning manner as Helen got into the taxi and the driver began to pull out. She turned to see Graham watching and waving to her. Fiona was saying something to him. He was still watching as the taxi rounded a corner, forcing him out of her line of vision.

'Cheer up,' said the driver, looking at her in his rear-view mirror. 'It might never happen.'

'No.' Helen smiled, obediently. 'It never did.'

Acknowledgements

Thanks to Nick and Linda, for getting me started, my writers' group, especially Josie, Caroline and Marian, for keeping me going and Helen Skelton for her support and laughing a lot (albeit she was laughing at my spelling and typing errors). And thank you Peter Straus for making it possible for me to thank you, in print, in the back of an actual book and Imogen Taylor for making it all such a pleasure.

JAMRACH'S MENAGERIE

Carol Birch

1857. Jaffy Brown is running along a street in London's East End when he comes face to face with an escaped circus animal. Plucked from the jaws of death by Mr Jamrach — explorer, entrepreneur and collector of the world's strangest creatures — the two strike up a friendship. Before he knows it, Jaffy finds himself on board a ship bound for the Dutch East Indies, on an unusual commission for Mr Jamrach. His journey — if he survives it — will push faith, love and friendship to their utmost limits.

THE GOOD MUSLIM

Tahmima Anam

In the dying days of a brutal civil war, Sohail Haque stumbles upon an abandoned building. Inside, he finds a young woman whose story will haunt him for a lifetime to come . . . Almost a decade later, Sohail's sister Maya returns home after a long absence to find her beloved brother transformed. While Maya has stuck to her revolutionary ideals, Sohail has shunned his old life to become a charismatic religious leader. And when Sohail decides to send his son to madrasa, the conflict between them comes to a devastating climax. Set in Bangladesh at a time when religious fundamentalism is on the rise, *The Good Muslim* is an epic story about faith, family and the long shadow of war.

TIME'S LEGACY

Barbara Erskine

Abi Rutherford has walked out of her job, disturbed by the erratic behaviour of her boss. Kieran Scott's behaviour seems even stranger because he is rector of St John's, a Cambridgeshire parish. Something going on there has disturbed him deeply. Centuries ago, a stranger came to the fenlands of western England with a story that would bring hope to the downtrodden. But following him were oppressive forces determined that no gentle-eyed healer should undermine the unity of Roman rule. The stranger says he's come to save people. But he may be the one in need of rescuing . . . What connection is there between these events and Abi and Kieran? Are these ancient echoes to be feared, or could they provide the answer to a long-silenced secret?

Thirkell